HARLYN TREMAYNE

An Historical Romance

JANE JACKSON

WILLIAM KIMBER · LONDON

First published in 1984 by
WILLIAM KIMBER & CO. LIMITED
100 Jermyn Street, London SW1Y 6EE

Typeset by Scarborough Typesetting Services
and printed in Great Britain by
Biddles Limited, Guildford and King's Lynn

This book is dedicated to
my husband, Peter,
who gave me the idea and was with me
every step of the way.

Author's Note

I have made every effort to present an accurate picture of life in the Cornish towns of Falmouth and Truro in the 1860's and in so doing have used names prominent in the county at that time. However, all the characters and events portrayed in this book are fictitious, with one exception.

Caroline and Anna Maria Fox did indeed live at Grove Hill, and were co-founders with their father Robert Were Fox, of the Polytechnic Society, where the first British experiments with nitro-glycerine took place in 1865.

Acknowledgements

I wish to extend my sincere thanks for their invaluable assistance to Professor N. J. G. Pounds, Mr Philip Fox, Mr Derek Toyne of Falmouth School of Art, the Curator and staff of Truro Museum, the staff of Falmouth Library, Mr Peter Davies, and to Mrs Eileen Hance, who typed and corrected the manuscript under extremely difficult conditions.

I would also like to acknowledge and thank G. C. Fox & Co., for information concerning ship construction and costs, conditions of service, shipping movements and cargoes of the period.

While I was researching this book, Oliver Price in his capacity of Secretary then President of the Royal Cornwall Polytechnic Society, gave generously of both his time and knowledge. Oliver died last year, but is remembered with gratitude and affection.

1

Rain hurled itself with the force of lead-shot onto the deck above her head as Harlyn Tremayne, hands shaking, pulled a rumpled grey blanket from the bunk and clutched it around her soaked and shivering body.

Her ebony hair was a wet and tangled mass and the thin cotton of her dress clung to her petticoats and dripped against her ankles. Collapsing onto the bunk, Harlyn drew in several shuddering breaths, trying to slow her thudding heart and still the panic that fluttered dark wings in her aching head.

The lump in her throat threatened to choke her and she shut her eyes tightly to hold back stinging tears. To give in to tears would be a weakness, and she could not afford to be weak. Crying would solve nothing. She had to be strong, try to think clearly. There must be some alternative.

Outside thunder rumbled and growled and rain continued to splatter and hiss on the deck and bulkheads. The schooner fretted and tugged at her mooring lines as though anxious to be free. The movement rocked Harlyn gently in the wooden bunk while night closed about the town.

Save for the creaking timbers the ship was silent. She was alone, and free, perhaps for the last time. Once the contract was signed she would be a prisoner, and like a prisoner she would be constantly watched. Escape, even in her thoughts, would be impossible. She shivered violently.

Pulling the heavy ropes of wet hair away from her neck, Harlyn burrowed deeper into the grubby blanket. Her nose wrinkled at its smell of stale tobacco smoke and seawater. But, though rough, scratchy and none too clean, it gave her comfort.

For the moment she was safe. No one would think of looking for her here. Unbidden, her mind slipped back to the early afternoon when her secure and carefree world had suddenly and irrevocably shattered about her.

* * *

Harlyn's cheeks burned but her chin remained defiantly tilted as she held her father's gaze. Disapproval twisted his features, and just for an instant Harlyn thought she glimpsed fear beneath the obvious exasperation.

Her mother shook her head helplessly, shredding the lace handkerchief clutched in her nervous fingers.

'I don't understand you, Harlyn. Such an honour, such an opportunity.'

'I won't do it, Father, I won't. You can't expect it of me.' Though her voice was determined, there was pleading in Harlyn's wide green eyes. Her hair tumbled in ebony ripples over her shoulders reaching almost to her waist. Small fragments of leaf and twig were caught in the heavy tresses. Only minutes earlier she had been in the orchard helping Nathan, their gardener, groom and general handyman. She had not seen the messenger arrive bearing the fateful letter. William Tremayne clasped the heavy cream paper with its distinctive seal like a talisman.

Harlyn's gaze shifted from her father to the letter and she wished she was back outside in the autumn sunshine among the apple trees from which the house had taken its name, Chyvallon.

Balanced lightly on the wooden ladder she had breathed in their sharp fragrance whilst her slim hands had turned the newly formed apples on the overburdened boughs, selecting with expert and critical eye those to remain, and with a quick twist of a supple wrist removing those which failed to meet her standard.

Nathan had grudgingly allowed that her eye was almost as good as his own, and praise from that taciturn man was praise indeed. The memory warmed and pleased Harlyn, lifting the corners of her full-lipped mouth.

'Harlyn,' William Tremayne's voice was stern, reflecting the displeasure which darkened his face and deepened the frown lines which lately, she recalled, had become almost permanent, 'this is no laughing matter.'

'Indeed, Father, I am neither amused nor flattered by a proposal of marriage from a man three times my age, whom I have met only once, and that occasion a mere three weeks ago.' Harlyn shuddered as she recalled that meeting.

The Ball at the Assembly Rooms in High Cross had been a glittering event. Every window and alcove in the ballroom and refreshment rooms was banked with flowers, their scent blending with the headier perfumes of the ladies, whose jewels blazed and sparkled, reflecting fragmented rainbows under the chandeliers.

Trilling laughter and the lilting strains of music floated on the warm night air as the cream of Truro society danced, supped and exchanged news and gossip, preparing the ground for new ventures of business and pleasure, and laying the ghosts of old ones.

Harlyn, her midnight hair studded with tiny yellow rosebuds and piled high in a chignon of glossy curls which emphasised her fine profile and slender neck, wore a dress of rich cream satin embroidered with seed pearls. It had a scalloped neckline and tiny puffed sleeves, but it was the skirt which attracted the attention of the fashion-conscious women present. Instead of the voluminous crinoline of whalebone or horse-hair supporting yards of material which almost every other woman wore, the skirt of Harlyn's dress fell almost straight in the front and was gathered into softly flowing folds at the back.

Her mother had fretted over the gown, declaring its simpler shape strange, and the whole dress incomplete and lacking decoration when Hetty Knowles, the dressmaker, had brought it for the final fitting. But Harlyn had persuaded her mother to give in to the pleas of her two younger sisters to have the extra braid, lace and fringes added to their gowns instead, instinctively preferred subtle simplicity for herself. Thus Harlyn stood out like a cool, elegant lily among a riot of tropical blooms.

Anticipation of the evening had lent a sparkle to her emerald eyes and a glow to her peach complexion as she flirted lightly with the inevitable cluster of would-be suitors gathered about her and her two sisters. Yet beneath the gaiety and banter Harlyn was surprised to feel herself oddly sad, almost impatient with the superficiality of the chatter and the immaturity of the young men surrounding her. She found herself yearning for she knew not what, only that it was not to be found amid this brilliant, brittle throng.

Social grace assisted her natural good manners in disguising her conflicting emotions, and as she deftly parried the advances of the bolder young men, she was the object of much attention and not a little envy, particularly from mothers with daughters of similar age.

But the closest scrutiny came from a short, plump, impeccably tailored man of some sixty years, who when approached with flattering deference by several of the most influential men present, brushed them casually aside like so many flies, with a chubby white hand, his gaze never wavering from Harlyn.

In his youth Sir Henry Trevellyan had had the delicately sculptured face of a poet. Indeed he considered himself an artist. But the arts he practised were those of darkness, and now, beneath the thin grey strands of once golden hair, pale puffy flesh bloated and distorted his features, evidence of the indulgence he afforded his appetites.

Only his eyes remain unchanged, small and colourless. Chips of ice, blank and opaque, revealing nothing of the man behind them.

Several times during the evening Harlyn had sensed eyes upon her. Intuition told her they were not female eyes, nor were they the usual male glances of appraisal and admiration she had become used to but nonetheless, if she were honest, enjoyed and welcomed.

This was different, somehow disturbing. There was an intensity about this scrutiny which unnerved her, more so as she had no idea from whence it came.

When the sensation grew so strong that her skin began to crawl, she looked around, her conversation faltering, smile fading as she searched the crowd trying to discover the person responsible.

Henry Trevellyan with eyes unblinking, like those of a snake, watched Harlyn, watched her reactions, likening the sudden lift of her head, the widening of her eyes, the tension in her stance to those of a startled faun. The proud carriage, firm chin and aura of radiant health which Harlyn exuded, labelled her an aristocrat. Quite unconsciously she conveyed a nobility which owed nothing to birth, money, or class, but rather to nature's ultimate triumph, blossoming womanhood.

Henry Trevellyan's tongue darted out to moisten lips already slack and wet in anticipation of taming this proud wild creature, of bending her to his will, subjecting her virginal young body to the most subtle cruelties his depraved mind could conjure. He knew this would be no easy conquest. At last he had found a woman of spirit, an adversary worthy of his talents.

Not like his first wife, a milk-sop, who had retreated into madness instead of giving him the battle of body, mind and spirit which he craved. Six months ago she had died, and since then he had been searching for a more suitable partner.

It had been easy enough to find women willing to submit to his whims provided he paid them well. But they were coarse and for the most part, ugly; whores who gave him no challenge, no thrill. Even the younger, prettier ones failed to satisfy. They were all too easily reduced to pleading for mercy or cowering in abject terror. And lately, after the unfortunate incident when a slight miscalculation with the blade had resulted in the death of a raw-boned trollop named Jessie, word had spread among the sisters of the night, and he found that the only women willing to risk the terrible results of his desires were too old or raddled, or disease-ridden for his fastidious taste.

A second marriage was the only solution. A wife was a chattel, owned body and soul by her husband. Sir Henry acknowledged cynically that the mantle of respectability, so worshipped by the English middle class, muffled many an anguished scream.

He could wait no longer and decided to embark at once upon the campaign whose strategy he had been planning for two months, since he had first glimpsed Harlyn at the Whitsun Fair.

He snapped his fingers and without shifting his gaze murmured a few words to the man who appeared beside him. Moments later this same man escorted William Tremayne forward and presented him to Sir Henry. Envious eyes watched as introductions were effected, then the man quickly withdrew leaving Sir Henry and William Tremayne facing one another.

His moonlike face set in a smile which never reached his eyes, Sir Henry spoke several clipped sentences in a voice which reached Tremayne's ears alone. William Tremayne staggered as if under a blow. An astute observer might have wondered at his sudden flush followed by a deathly pallor, but would have dismissed as ludicrous any hazarded guess at shock or fear. After all, Sir Henry was displaying a rare charm and geniality, as Tremayne, a dazed expression on his face, guided the baronet towards the chair occupied by his wife beside which stood his daughters. As the two men approached the retinue of young gallants melted away like snow in sunshine.

After replying coolly to Harriet Tremayne's gushing en-
quiries concerning his health, and commenting as etiquette
demanded on the charming appearance of Rosella and Veryan,
who blushed prettily and took immediate refuge behind their
fans, Sir Henry Trevellyan turned to Harlyn and took her hand,
clasping it in his damp pudgy fingers.

The instant her eyes met his Harlyn knew that this was the
man responsible for her unease. She tried to suppress the shudder that ran through her at his touch.

As his gaze flickered over Harlyn, Sir Henry took in every
detail, from her high cheek-bones, delicately chiselled nose and
full soft lips, down the warm column of her neck where a tiny
pulse beat rapidly, to the soft swell of her breasts only half
hidden by the pearl-strewn satin. His eyes lingered on the flare
of her hips then travelled to her satin-slippered feet, returning
to meet her eyes, their fringe of sooty lashes owing neither
colour nor thickness to artifice.

For the first time Sir Henry's iron control deserted him and
though his face retained its mask of politeness and charm,
lust swelled, hot and naked in his small eyes. His voice was
soft and high-pitched as he raised her hand to his loose wet
lips.

'You are a vision of loveliness, Miss Tremayne. Such beauty is
an honour to behold and must be the envy of every woman
here.'

Harlyn found herself unable to tear her eyes away from his.
She was mesmerised like a rabbit petrified by a snake poised to
strike. Behind the lust in his eyes was an evil which in her
innocence Harlyn did not understand, but which frightened
and repelled her. With an effort she kept her expression calm,
revealing nothing of the revulsion and fear that seethed within
her.

Harriet Tremayne made a fluttering motion with her fan.
The movement caught Harlyn's eye and broke the spell. Quickly
she lowered her gaze, thankful to escape the hot stare that
seemed to strip the clothes from her body, ruthlessly probing its
intimate secrets.

'Thank you, Sir Henry. Though I fear you exaggerate, it is
most kind of you to say so,' Harlyn replied in a level tone, gently
but firmly withdrawing her fingers from their clammy prison.

Her mouth was dry and she could feel her heart thumping. She had an overwhelming urge to wipe her hand down the side of her dress, or to scrub it with her handkerchief. Only a supreme effort of will kept her polite and outwardly serene. Her natural good manners were reinforced by the awareness that Sir Henry's social and financial influence in the town were vast. Her family's standing could be seriously damaged were any member of it to incur his displeasure.

Inwardly she longed to rush from the crowded ballroom to the peace and privacy of Chyvallon, where she might tear off the satin gown, order Amy to fill the tub, and immerse her whole body in warm scented water to rid herself of the sensation of having been defiled by his salacious eyes and soft damp fingers.

'Are you listening to me, girl?' Her father's voice brought Harlyn abruptly back to the present.

'Yes, Father,' she replied quietly, 'but I don't understand. Why marriage to him, of all people?'

'For heaven's sake, Harlyn,' her mother said with some asperity, 'Sir Henry Trevellyan is a very wealthy man.' Harriet Tremayne's voice warmed. 'Just look at the gifts he has showered upon you already. Flowers every day since the Ball and always some trinket hidden among them.' Harriet's eyes sparkled. 'He is a man of great influence, Harlyn. Such a marriage could be of great benefit.'

'To whom? Certainly not to me.' The words burst from Harlyn's lips before she could stop them.

'What do you mean?' William Tremayne's voice was sharp. Looking at both her parents in turn, Harlyn chose her words carefully.

'I have heard stories of a most disturbing nature concerning Sir Henry.'

Harriet looked at the wisp of torn fabric in her hands. For an instant her body seemed to sag. Then her back stiffened and she raised expressionless eyes to those of her eldest daughter.

'Ridiculous lies,' she pronounced, 'born of jealousy and put about by those lacking Sir Henry's wealth and social connections.'

Realising that her mother had deliberately closed her eyes

and ears to anything but the advantage of the proposed marriage, Harlyn turned in silent pleading to her father.

'Where did you hear such rumours, eh?' he said gruffly. With a wave of his hand he dismissed the possibility of the stories being true. 'You should know better than to listen to servants' gossip, Harlyn. You spend too much time with them and neglect your responsibilities to us, your family.' Hurt mingled with anger and bewilderment in Harlyn's eyes.

'But Nathan and Amy are like family,' she protested. 'I've known them all my life. It is thanks to Amy that I can cook, that I know anything of herbal medicines or preserving the fruit that Nathan grows in the kitchen garden. You adored the crystallised fruits I made for you last Christmas, Mama, the honey bon-bons. . . .' Harriet waved the words aside.

'A child's past time, Harlyn, something to while away the odd hour.'

'The horses, then. What about the horses? I can ride horses many men would fear to approach,' Harlyn claimed proudly.

'It's true, girl, they've taught you much,' William conceded. Harriet could contain her impatience no longer.

'Lord above, William, if Harlyn were to marry Sir Henry, she would have an army of servants to cook and sew and look after her house, and coaches to take her everywhere. Such accomplishments as those would hardly be necessary or even fitting for a lady of such high position.'

'Your mother is right, Harlyn. Nathan and Amy know their place, it is time you remembered yours.'

'But, Father, you still have not told me,' Harlyn persisted, 'why is it so important that I marry right at this moment?' Exasperation creased her father's face, but Harlyn continued. 'You have not encouraged suitors, in fact you refused Thomas Grenville when he asked for my hand.'

'You were but seventeen,' William replied brusquely. 'Besides, your mother was convinced that young Grenville was not the man for you.'

'No, he had a good family name but no money,' Harlyn murmured sadly. She had been very fond of Tom Grenville, a slender youth, with unruly, carroty hair and freckles, a lively sense of fun and an unfortunate knack of saying the wrong thing at the wrong time. Yet there had been a sensitivity in him which had struck an answering chord in Harlyn. When he no longer called, she missed him.

William gave no sign of hearing and Harlyn's hopes, which had momentarily risen, were dashed again.

'Besides, Grenville was two years ago,' her father said. He did not mention the other young men, some tentative, some bold, none taken seriously.

'You are now nineteen, Harlyn, and there are your sisters to consider.'

Harlyn's dark brow's flew upward in surprise.

'Rosella and Veryan? What have they to do with it?' Harriet raised her eyes to the ceiling in a show of impatience.

'They wish to marry even if you don't. It is most selfish of you to deny them their chance of happiness.' Harlyn turned quickly to her mother.

'Mother, I would deny them nothing. I love my sisters and would love to see them happy. If they desire marriage, then let them marry.'

'Oh, Harlyn,' Harriet snapped, 'how can they marry before you? You are the eldest.'

Harlyn smiled gently. 'That is a foolish convention, Mother. It is of no consequence to me if they marry first.'

Harriet's anger boiled over.

'Your selfishness amazes me, Harlyn. It may be of no consequence to you, but it matters greatly to the rest of us. What will our friends think? How are we to hold up our heads in society? Your father holds a position of some prominence in the town, are we to become a laughing stock because of your stubbornness?' Harriet stood up glaring at her eldest daughter. Harlyn took a step backwards, the colour high in her cheeks at this attack from her mother.

'You have been offered this wonderful opportunity,' Harriet continued furiously, 'all the things a mother could wish for her daughter, wealth, social prominence, seasons in London, winters abroad, countless servants.' She ran out of breath and finished in a strangled voice, 'How dare you toss all this aside so carelessly?'

'Harriet, my dear, will you leave us for a moment?' There was a tremor in her father's voice, a depth of weariness that caused Harlyn to glance quickly at him. She was shocked to notice how suddenly old he looked, old and desperately tired. The lines on his face were perceptibly deeper and his shoulders bowed as though burdened by a weight almost impossible to bear. Her mother appeared not to have noticed.

'My patience is exhausted, William. I always said you allowed Harlyn more latitude than was seemly for a girl, and this is the result; arrogance, defiance. What will become of her? What will become of us? Oh dear, now I have a headache coming on.'

'Mother, shall I get you some chamomile—' Harlyn began, but Harriet shook her head abruptly as if even her daughter's voice was painful to her, and swept out of the room. Faintly they heard her calling for Amy to bring the spirits of camphor.

Harlyn stood in the centre of the room, the sleeves of her russet cotton dress pushed up to her elbows, her hands clasped in front of her. Her arms glowed golden against her white apron.

William Tremayne sank into a leather armchair beside the hearth. The empty fire place was hidden by an embroidered firescreen and vases of dried flowers. He looked up at his daughter. A lock of her thick hair had fallen forward over her shoulder and the warm lustre of her complexion reminded him of a ripe peach. He met her eyes, so brilliantly green, and read concern in them.

'Harlyn,' he murmured with a tired smile, 'you look like a gypsy.' She gave a rueful pout, pulled off the apron and tossed it aside then perching on the arm of his chair she laid a hand on his shoulder.

'What is it, Pa?' she asked softly, calling him by the pet-name only she used.

William passed a hand across his brow and Harlyn saw that it trembled. She was unaccountably filled with apprehension. It began as a knot in the pit of her stomach, then tentacles of anxiety reached out to all parts of her body and tightened their grip. She moistened suddenly dry lips with the tip of her tongue.

'What is it, Pa? Tell me what is wrong, are you ill?' He hesitated for a moment.

'No, girl, not ill, that would be easier.' Unable to bear his burden alone any longer, he began to speak. For Harlyn, every word was a hammer blow shattering the security she had never questioned, never doubted. She felt as though the very earth had parted beneath her feet and she hung poised over an abyss. One false move would send her plunging into its black depths. Her father finished speaking. There was silence.

'Does mother know?' Harlyn asked quietly. William shook his head.

'I've managed to keep it from her so far. Her mind has been much occupied with you and your sisters lately — as you know, they want to stay on at Aunt Emily's for another week — then of course the proposal of marriage from Sir Henry. . . .' Harlyn's hand tightened on her father's shoulder.

'There will be no marriage, Pa. How could I leave you now?'

'Have you not understood me, girl?' William rasped. 'I'm on the verge of bankruptcy. There's no money left, no credit. We are ruined.' Shame dulled his eyes, and his face was haggard as he looked up at his daughter.

'No, oh no.'

At Harlyn's horrified whisper, William reached up with a trembling hand. 'Forgive me, girl,' he murmured brokenly. She clasped his hand between her own and kissed it, tears spilling over her dark lashes, tracing forlorn paths over cheeks pale beneath their golden glow.

'Pa, there must be something we can do, the Bank. . . .'

William shook his head wearily.

'I've already spoken to Mr Willyams and Mr Buller, but with the prices of copper and tin falling, and mines closing down all over Cornwall, money is already scarce. Besides, I've no security to offer.'

'But you've got shares in Botallack mine and Clifford Amalgamated. They are both still sound. Can't you borrow against them?' Harlyn's forehead was furrowed in thought. William shook his head again.

'Those shares were sold months ago to pay for repairs to *Mary Rose* after Hodges nailed a writ to the mast.'

'Then what about the ships?' Harlyn demanded. 'Can we not raise money with them as security?'

Through his despair William felt a surge of pride. He could not have sired a son finer than this, his eldest daughter. She was proud, wilful and stubborn, but had a fierce loyalty to all she cared for, and a compassion that had sometimes caused him to re-examine his own seemingly generous actions.

When she was only ten years old Harlyn had given her best pair of shoes to a barefooted street urchin who had come begging at the door. The child had seized them but before running off had spat at Harlyn for her charity. When William, torn between berating her for giving away the shoes and comforting her in her distress, had called the child an ungrateful wretch, Harlyn had cried even harder.

The shoes had been cream-coloured kid, he remembered, with a tiny heel and satin ribbons. They were dainty, soft to wear and pretty to look at. With perception beyond her years Harlyn had sobbed that she knew the ragged girl had loved the shoes but she would never wear them. Even if the splayed toes and calloused soles could be crammed into them, how long would the fine leather last in the befouled back streets where pigs roamed freely, rooting in piles of rotting rubbish. The shoes would be sold or bartered for food and when that had gone, what would the girl do, with winter approaching, an empty belly and still nothing on her feet?

At sixteen, Harlyn had sat by the range in the big kitchen rocking a grief-stricken Amy in her arms while Nathan got silently and deliberately drunk in the corner, after the news came that Jed, the only surviving child of the four Amy had borne Nathan, had died of typhus in Bodmin gaol. Jed was one year younger than Harlyn.

He had been sentenced to three months' imprisonment with hard labour for breaking into the Mansion House. Jed had been a big, clumsy, rather slow-witted youth. Everyone knew he could never had dreamed up the scheme alone, and when questioned, he hadn't even known why he was there. The others, being more nimble and more experienced, had evaded capture and furnished themselves with alibis. Jed had been the scapegoat. The magistrate had decided to make him an example of the new tougher punishments. A policy which coincidentally preceded by a few weeks this magistrate's bid for re-election.

Jed had been packed off to Bodmin gaol, tears running down his grubby, bewildered face, clutching the bars of the horse-drawn van as it jolted over the granite sets outside the Town Hall. In the van with him, faces set and sullen, were three older men. One accused of murder and bound for trial at the Assizes, and two convicted of persistent drunkenness and assault.

Whitefaced with fury at this exhibition of so-called justice, Harlyn had threatened to approach the Magistrate and demand another hearing. She had been dissuaded only with great difficulty by a fatalistic Amy who was convinced that such a move, by angering the Magistrate, would only make things worse for Jed, not only from the Court, but the other prisoners as well.

The driver of the prison van, a rough but kindly man, brought the tragic news one night three weeks before Jed was due to be released. Amy had been busy planning a bit of 'sommat special fer supper the day 'e do come 'ome,' when a tap on the back door had interrupted her.

Her scream of anguish had brought Harlyn flying in from the stable where she had been watching Nathan poultice an ugly swelling on the foreleg of her father's hunter.

She had remained with Amy until daybreak, when exhaustion had finally closed the grieving woman's swollen eyelids.

This was Harlyn, his first-born, and though he tried not to show it, his favourite. He roused himself.

'The two brigs trading around the coast, *Mary Rose* and *Tamsin*, are already mortgaged. Repayments are due again in three weeks and I'm three months behind. Both ships will be impounded.'

'How, Pa? How did it happen?' A bewildered frown drew Harlyn's dark brows together. William pulled himself to his feet and walked stiffly across to the huge mahogany sideboard. Opening the left-hand door he took out a tumbler and a decanter half full of amber liquid. As he poured a generous measure into the glass, Harlyn caught the acrid aroma of whisky. Her frown was tempered with concern as she watched her father raise the glass to his lips with a hand that shook uncontrollably. He swallowed deeply, shuddering as the spirit burned its way down. Then he topped up the glass, but instead of returning the decanter to the sideboard, he carried it with him back to the leather armchair.

'*Mary Rose* was carrying a cargo of materials, fine stuff, silk, lace and the like, for Andrews the draper in St Nicholas Street,' William began to explain. 'I was trying to get a contract from the Truro Mercantile Shipping Company. It would have meant regular work and a steady income, and we desperately needed both.

I underbid the others and got the job on a trial basis. But with the bid so low I couldn't afford to insure the cargo. Well, in any case it didn't seem necessary, it was summer time and we'd had a run of fair weather.' His tone became querulous and Harlyn could see he was still trying to justify his decision, though more to himself than to her.

'The squall hit without any warning. It was one of those freak things. *Mary Rose* is old and she's tired. Her forrard planking couldn't take the beating, she sprung and water got into the cargo before the pumps could take hold.'

'The captain,' Harlyn began heatedly, 'what was he—?'

'John Ferris is a good seaman,' William interrupted. 'He was following my orders. I'd told him to push her hard, and I'd told him it was important to get that cargo back here in the fastest possible time. He was only following my orders,' William repeated. 'Anyway,' he paused, rubbing a hand across his eyes, 'I had to pay for the cargo and I didn't get the contract.' He took another drink, then shrugged, but it did not disguise his desolation at the double blow. Sympathy welled up in Harlyn. She pressed his hand.

'What about *Karis*?' she asked tentatively, picturing the sleek lines of the black-painted schooner. 'The fruit trade begins in a couple of months, doesn't it? Surely that will bring in some money?'

William swallowed some more whisky. '*Karis* lost her registration two years ago. I could not afford to have her overhauled and refitted. She's been tramp-trading, anything we could get in home waters. I'll lose her too.' He could not hide his anguish any longer. 'I can't compete any more. I've had to charge full freight rates just to cover the insurance. The crew's been paid but there's nothing left for repairs or revictualling. It's hopeless, completely hopeless.' William sank deeper into the cushions and closed his eyes in utter despair. Harlyn clung to a faint hope.

'*Karis* isn't mortgaged then?' Her father shook his head.

'She's going for auction. The agent said I'd get a fair price. She'll have to be sold to pay off some of the other debts, though I doubt whatever she fetches will cover them all. I still owe Penrose's for the new mainsail for *Tamsin* and the fore and main headsails for *Karis*. I haven't finished paying William Hodges for the repairs to *Mary Rose* and he's threatening legal action. There are household bills, tradesmen . . .' his voice broke.

'What about the Tremaynes at Peneglas?' Harlyn asked as the thought occurred to her. 'Aren't we distantly related? I'm sure—'

Her father shook his head tiredly. 'Josiah Tremayne holds the mortgages on *Mary Rose* and *Tamsin*, and because of our family connection he has already extended the repayment period twice.'

'But surely—' Harlyn protested.

'This is business, girl, and it seems I have no head for it. Besides, I've been informed that Sir Henry Trevellyan is negotiating to buy the mortgages from Josiah.'

Harlyn stiffened at the mention of the hated name.

'But that means Sir Henry will have a monopoly on coastal trading. Surely that would not be good for the Mercantile Company, would it? If he could set the rates and no one could undercut his prices, then many of the small shipping businesses would be ruined. Surely Josiah won't sell?'

William sighed deeply. 'Why not? His interests are not in shipping. The boats are only a liability to him, and I am only an embarrassment.' William swallowed his bitterness with another mouthful of whisky. 'I'd probably do the same in his position. Sir Henry will give him a good price and never miss the money.' He paused. 'I think he wants *Karis* too,' he said miserably, 'though he already has four schooners and two of them are carrying fruit from the Mediterranean.'

Harlyn trembled with rage and indignation; so this is how he tightens the noose about our necks. Not content with taking over most of the local and foreign trade, he has to grind any competitor, no matter how small, into the ground. 'Surely he's not the only possible buyer?' she said while her thoughts raced. How could her father even have considered marrying her to such a man, the man more responsible than any other for his ruin.

'I don't know, how should I know?' William retorted, his voice thin and peevish. 'What I do know is that he is not suffering any economic pressure.' He tipped his head back, swallowing the last of the whisky.

Harlyn reached out her hand. 'Shall I put it down for you, Pa?'

William held the glass to his chest and did not reply. Then he poured himself another drink. The neck of the decanter clattered against the glass and some of the golden liquid slopped over the side and ran down the side of the armchair. Harlyn had never before seen her father in this state.

'What will I tell your mother?' William murmured not looking at Harlyn. 'She has always been so conscious of our position in the town.' Harlyn made no reply. William drank again. 'I'm losing everything, Harlyn', he said softly, 'the business my grandfather founded, the ships, everything. Everything.'

Harlyn looked at him, love and pity tinged with dismay at his recourse to the whisky. Then she saw recollection dawn in the moist eyes he raised to hers.

'There's only one hope, Harlyn, only one.' She stared at him, unwilling to believe that he could ask, unable to accept such a demand.

'No, Father, you can't mean it, you can't,' she pleaded.

'It's the only way, there's no hope except—'

'Except me and a marriage of convenience; your convenience,' Harlyn finished, her voice hollow. 'Is this simply another business transaction, Father? Am I to be sold, like the ships, to pay your debts?' Tears glistened on her black lashes.

Self-loathing was vivid on her father's face. His voice was cracked and harsh. 'Do you think I wanted it this way? Do you think if there was any other way I would not take it? Do you think I feel no shame?' His voice broke in a sob. 'Harlyn, I've indulged you all your life. You have always been my favourite, though in fairness, I have tried to hide it. Having no sons, I suppose I saw more of myself in you than in your two sisters. You were special, my first-born.'

He stared into the glass still clutched in both hands as memories of Harlyn as a baby, as a dainty girl-child growing through puberty and adolescence to the lovely creature she had now become, tumbled through his mind. He roused himself with an effort, his words hesitant.

'This marriage, this alliance would provide you with a secure future. Sir Henry assured me he would not be ungenerous with the settlement. It would enable Rosella and Veryan to remain in society and make good matches themselves.' His voice steadied and grew stronger. 'It would bring such comfort to your mother to see you all safely settled. That is her heart's desire, Harlyn. She's not strong, her health is not what it was, and when she worries. . . . It would mean so much to her.' He stopped speaking, silently pleading for his daughter's acquiescence, all his fear, hope and need concentrated in the gaze he directed at her. When she made no reply, hurt and disbelief like wounds on her pale face, William dropped his gaze and stared at the glass as though he had never seen it before.

'Harlyn, Sir Henry is not a young man. It is unlikely he would live many years, whereas you—'

'Stop it, Pa, stop it,' Harlyn cried desperately. She controlled herself with a visible effort. 'I want to marry, Pa, of course I do. I've thought about marriage since I was a child. Among my friends there is little talk of anything else.' Harlyn rose to her feet, crossed to the window and stared out into the sunwashed garden. She clasped her arms across her body.

'I've dreamed of the way it would be, meeting someone and falling in love. I've tried to imagine how he would look, what sort of a man he would be, how it would feel to have his arms around me—'

'Harlyn,' William was shocked, 'such talk is not seemly—'

'Not seemly? But marriage is the most important event in any girl's life, Pa.'

'That may be so, Harlyn, but one does not speak one's thoughts on such matters.' Harlyn spun round to face her father. The dark curtain of her hair swirled about her shoulders as she moved with feline grace across the polished wood floor covered with fringed, patterned rugs to confront her father.

'I speak of love, Pa, and you call it unseemly. You say I'm your favourite, yet you would sell me to this monster. You are denying me all hope of love. Moreover you must know that you are also denying me the joy of bearing children.' William's mouth fell open.

'I . . .? What . . .?' he spluttered, utterly taken aback by his daughter's statement.

'You cannot pretend you have not heard the rumours, Father. It is said that Sir Henry Trevellyan, the man you would have me wed, is unable—' The flush that crept up the slender column of Harlyn's neck stained her cheeks crimson, but her eyes never wavered from those of her father, 'is not as other men, and cannot fulfil the normal functions of husband and father.'

'But Sir Henry was married for twenty years,' William blustered.

'The marriage was childless, father, and fifteen of those years Lydia Trevellyan spent in the Lunatic Asylum at Bodmin,' Harlyn shot back.

'You don't know all the facts, Harlyn. Lydia was never strong. Besides, her family never said one word against Sir Henry,' William replied, desperation lending strength to his words. 'Harlyn, I repeat, Sir Henry is not a young man, his energies are declining.

Harlyn recalled Sir Henry's small pale eyes, hot with lust as they roamed over her body, and she shivered.

'His demands would be few,' her father stuttered on, 'it would not be long—' he trailed off at his daughter's expression.

In the ensuing silence they faced one another, then William Tremayne's face crumpled and as tears of shame dribbled down his face he reached down for the whisky decanter and with a trembling hand emptied it into his glass.

'No, Pa, don't,' Harlyn begged. He did not raise his head.

'What else is left?' he muttered.

Suddenly the room seemed too small for the enormity of the decision facing Harlyn. She was faced with a loveless, childless marriage, a business transaction in which she figured only as a piece of merchandise purchased to satisfy the depraved whims of a man about whom dark things were known, and even darker things rumoured, or destitution for the whole family. Her happiness alone weighed against catastrophic consequences for her mother, father and two sisters, not to mention Nathan and Amy, none of whom, save the wretched man slumped in the leather armchair, was aware that they hovered on the brink of ruin.

'I've got to have time to think, Pa. You must give me time.' The agonised cry burst from Harlyn's lips as she turned, wrenched open the door and fled from the room and out of the house.

2

Wednesday was market day in the borough of Truro, and on that warm, September afternoon of 1865, the streets were thronged with people and the air was thick with noise.

Bellowing cattle jostled in their pens as farmers bought and sold through the special language of the auction on Castle Hill. The clop of horses' hooves, the jingle of harness and the rumble of carriage wheels mingled with the grunt and squeal of pigs rooting in the mounds of garbage piled in the street. Gulls wheeling overhead screamed mournfully.

Stallholders competed for customers in the crowded streets, extolling with extravagant claims the quality of their wares. One would break off to snarl abuse at the ragged urchins who darted about the stalls, reaching up stealthily with grubby fingers for anything they could grab, then resume the wheedling patter without even a pause for breath.

Women gossiped noisily or quietly exchanged confidences, depending on their social position and the person under discussion. Children raced about, playing hide-and-seek amongst the stalls, causing many a mother and nursemaid to catch her breath in horror as her charge avoided by a hair's breadth the flying hooves and thundering wheels of the carriages and vans which hurtled through the streets with total disregard for life and limb.

Behind the stalls and the packed pavements were the narrow-fronted shops with their small window-panes.

The rich aroma of fresh coffee, roasted and ground on the premises issued from the doorway of Sylvanus and Hamilton James's grocery store. Inside, boxes of tea and sugar, tubs of butter and lard, sacks of flour, rice and lentils and huge cheeses were displayed on shelves and along the wooden counter. Customers asked for as much or as little as they wanted, and watched as it was weighed on the highly polished brass scales before being wrapped in twists of paper.

Several women were crowded around the window of Clinton Andrews's drapery shop, where a large notice proclaimed the arrival that very day of a wonderful selection at specially reduced prices, of broadcloths in varying colours, doe-skins, buckskins, silks, prints, shawls, ribbons and the soft woollen cloth known as saxony.

From Chegwin's bakehouse wafted the mouthwatering smell of freshly baked bread and cakes. Trays of figgy duff, heavy cake and saffron buns lay beside baskets of crusty loaves. Savoury pasties filled with beef and potato, turnip and bacon, leek and hogs pudding cooled alongside others filled with apple or jam.

Two doors down, waitresses in Phoebe Parsons' tearooms were rushing to and fro with pots of tea and hot chocolate, trays of dainty china and dishes of feather-light pastries and cakes to the dozen small tables each spread with a spotless Irish linen cloth and crisply folded napkins. Treading carefully through the clutter of packages and parcels, the baskets and bags which intruded into the narrow aisles between the tables, the waitresses, resembling magpies in their black dresses and starched white aprons and caps, had also to avoid the voluminous crinolined skirts of their well-to-do customers.

A little further along the street, Hetty Knowles the dressmaker had her workrooms behind Alice Curnow's millinery shop. This arrangement proved advantageous to both women, as ladies coming for fittings with Hetty had to pass through Alice's emporium, and as they passed their eyes were caught by the confections of straw, felt or velvet trimmed with lace or feathers, ribbons or ornaments at which Alice excelled. As Hetty informed Alice of the style, colour and material of the dresses she was currently making, the milliner was able to display, as if by chance, the hat to complement perfectly some fashion-conscious lady's ensemble. For this service Hetty received a small commission from Alice for every hat sold. As the popularity of both women rose, they were able to employ extra hands to do the tedious routine sewing of hems and seams in the poky rooms leading off the rabbit-warren of passages in the dark old house, allowing them to concentrate on scouring the newest fashion magazines, English and foreign, for the very latest styles, adding with great flair the finishing touches to their creations.

Down the backlets and opes just off the main streets, fifty different crafts were pursued in makeshift premises adapted from basements and backrooms, stables and sheds, almost everything done by hand. What little machinery was used was powered by turning a handle or pumping a treadle. The chemist worked with mortar and pestle to produce his own medicines, the decorator mixed his own colours and paints, goldsmith and silversmith worked with fine tools hunched over their benches, and the cobbler, with speed born of long practice, astounded his apprentices with his speed and accuracy in joining sole to welt, using a slim hammer and tacks held ready between his lips.

The sounds and smells of the iron foundry, tinsmelting works, the tannery and the candle factory added their weight to air already heavy with the afternoon heat, the stench of open drains and the rotting heaps of household refuse and stable manure.

Scavengers were busy toiling in the gutters with brushes and shovels, attempting to keep the water courses at the sides of the main streets clear so that the putrefying filth would be carried away to the river. Where they had cleaned, water gurgled along the granite courses, seemingly pure and sparkling in the afternoon sunshine. There was no visible sign that this same water contained the sweepings from the kennels of the Four Burrow Hunt, which housed thirty to forty hounds, nor that woolcombers had washed their fleeces in it and fellmongers cleaned their skins; numerous privies had emptied into it, all before it rippled through the streets of the town to where, at the back of the butcher's shop, tripe-dressers washed offal in this same water before displaying it for sale.

Above the general hubbub could be heard the baying of dogs and the jeers and catcalls of the crowd watching the bull-baiting at High Cross.

But Harlyn, as she passed through the bustling streets, was deaf and blind to it all. She was bumped and jostled. Well-fed, well dressed people of the upper levels of society rubbed shoulders with the dregs of the town. Unkempt youths thin and pale, lounging in groups on the corners and pavements, whistled and made lewd remarks as she passed. Drunken men with dirt-encrusted clothing and bloodshot eyes, staggering outside the public houses, pawed at her, leering and drooling.

As she passed one public house, a brawl erupted out of the doorway onto the pavement in front of her. The two protagonists grunted and mouthed obscenities as they gouged and kicked at one another, fists swinging wildly. The connecting blows landed with a dull thud, bringing roars of encouragement from the knot of equally drunken men surrounding the fighters.

Harlyn pushed past them, hardly noticing the uproar. The skirt of her dress caught on one of the stall trestles and tore. The hem was now wet and dirty from the water running down the gutters and the filth and rubbish strewn about the streets.

As the freshening breeze whipped her long hair about her face, without thought or pause, Harlyn automatically twisted the heavy tresses into a careless knot low on her neck. Her head felt ready to burst with the thoughts that raced and tumbled through it. Only one word made sense, one word that grew louder and louder. Escape.

Harlyn was jerked to her senses by a shrill-voiced fishwife loudly cursing a flock of gulls which had descended on her unattended basket and were fighting noisily over the few pilchards left in the bottom. The woman's shriek and waving hands sent the gulls wheeling and flapping in screaming protest.

Dazedly, Harlyn looked around. She was on Back Quay outside the market house, only a few yards from the Town Hall. Two ships were moored to the quay, floating high on the refuse-laden water. The nearest was a barque. The grain that lay scattered on her deck and along the quay was evidence of her cargo, now unloaded. The second, a sloop, belonged to the Truro Mercantile Shipping Company, Harlyn deduced, recognising Albert Mitchell, the wharfinger, and Sam Tonkin, the storekeeper, holding a heated discussion amid piles of crates, boxes and sacks.

Further down the quay was a small brig, and looking past the punts and dinghies to the opposite side of the river, Harlyn could see three Norwegian schooners moored in front of the patent woodworks.

Clouds had been building up in the western sky and now they began creeping across the face of the lowering sun. The wind had taken on a keen edge, and in the few minutes that Harlyn had been standing there, the day had abandoned its mask of summer and bared its teeth in warning of the changing season.

Harlyn shivered, her thin cotton dress offering no protection from the knifing wind. For the first time she looked straight across the narrow stretch of water to Lemon Quay, and her heart thumped painfully. There, moving slightly on the filthy water as if to escape the restriction of her mooring ropes, lay *Karis*.

There was an air of desolation about her. Her sails were carefully furled, but the ropes were frayed. Her paintwork was scraped and dirty. Yet nothing could disguise the beauty of her lines. From her curved, raking stem to her slim quarters and narrow stern she was every inch a thoroughbred.

Harlyn felt a lump in her throat. *Karis* was to be sold, just like her, and it seemed to the same evil master. Harlyn had visited the ship regularly since her childhood, taken by her father in the gig to Garras wharf or Sunny Corner and rowed out to the schooner. Then they had sailed up the river to Lemon Quay.

The crew had smiled at her obvious delight and indulged her when she begged for stories of the voyage. The scent of the oranges had conjured visions of hot sun, sparkling blue water, white buildings and swarthy, black-haired people with flashing eyes and gleaming white teeth, who wore black, tight-fitting trousers and shirts with white lace ruffles under short jackets, who carried slim daggers with jewelled handles in a red sash at the waist. Visions based on stories from the crew, and the visit to her father by Don Luis D'Alvarez, the owner of the orange groves, whose fruit *Karis* carried from its sundrenched native land to the colder, wetter shores of England.

Even if Karis were bought by Sir Henry, and even if, Harlyn swallowed hard, forcing herself to acknowledge the possibility, she went through with the marriage, her feeling for *Karis* would not remain unchanged. The beautiful schooner would be like her, a prisoner, a slave, subjected to the whims of a brutal master, contaminated by his ownership.

He owned neither of them yet, and if she could find another way of saving her father from bankruptcy and the family from disgrace, he never would. She would not accept that the situation was hopeless, she could not, for that way lay utter despair.

A large raindrop splashed on to her cheek and trickled down her face. She raised her hand to wipe it away and another landed on her bare arm. Harlyn looked up quickly and felt a twinge of unease. The heavy grey clouds seemed to be bearing down on her like warships under full sail. Even as she watched, a jagged flash of lightning split the grey billows, and thunder growled menacingly.

She would shelter on *Karis*, spend one last hour on the ship that had given her so many happy hours. Picking up her skirts, Harlyn ran up the quay to the bridge, crossed it holding her breath against the stench of accumulated sewage on the other side of the sluice gates waiting to be released on the ebb tide, and ran down the other side on to Lemon Quay.

The raindrops were falling faster, soaking her hair, running down her face and neck into her thin dress, spashing her feet and legs as she ran.

As she reached the schooner, Harlyn hesitated only a moment, then sped along the gang-plank and jumped lightly down onto the deck. The rain lanced down like arrows, stinging her flesh, saturating her clothes. Lightning flashed once more. Without even a glance round the deck, she rushed aft to the companionway and tugged open the hatch door. Pulling it closed behind her she stumbled down the twisting steps.

At the bottom Harlyn paused, leaning against the bulkhead, and struggled to get her breath back. She listened. There was no sound save the creaking of the ship's timbers, the soft gurgle of water against her sides and the muffled pounding of the rain upon the deck.

Harlyn wondered what had happened to the crew. Then she realised. The ship was to be sold. The crew would have gone home. They would all be with their families.

She felt a moment's intense longing. If only she could go back home and find that none of today had happened, that it had all been just a dreadful nightmare.

Then as her teeth started chattering and shivers racked her, even that seemed less important than finding a rug or blanket to pull around her wet and shaking body. She pushed open the door in front of her and looked into the mess room. It was around the scarred wooden table bolted to the floor that the crew ate, attended by the cook, an ordinary seaman who, if he showed any interest or aptitude for cooking, was relieved of deck duties in return for preparing and serving the food. Having heard tales of huge seas almost washing overboard the small galley shack with its coal stove which stood on deck, Harlyn did not envy him the job.

She backed out, pulling the door closed. Turning round she was faced with two doors. Pushing open the nearest, in the dim light from the skylight which occupied most of the deckhead space, Harlyn could see she was in the Captain's Day Room. She stepped inside the triangular compartment which was built into the stern of the schooner. Narrow, upholstered benches ran along two sides of the triangle. Behind these, wooden panels rose three feet above the deck. Above the panels, a shelf loaded with sea-junk and rimmed with a low rail, ran right round the compartment. Above the shelf were panelled lockers sloping back to the deckhead, where a huge oil lamp, decorated with complex brasswork patterns swung.

At the apex of the triangle, between the bench seats was a small triangular table with a mirror set into the panelling above it. Above the mirror was fixed a telltale compass, enabling the Captain to check the ship's course and heading without having to go up on deck. The table's broad end was supported by a single leg. This, Harlyn knew, could be folded down to allow access to the coal stove built into the forward bulkhead.

Moving further into the cabin, she left the door slightly ajar. A packed kitbag on one of the bench seats told her that someone would be coming back.

Harlyn knocked carefully on the narrow door beside the stove. There was no reply. She knocked again, wanting to be certain she was truly alone before opening the door.

The sleeping cabin was small and austere. It smelled of stale tobacco smoke, sea-water, damp wool and unwashed clothes. Harlyn's nose wrinkled. She stepped inside and looked about her. She had never been in here before. The single bunk was surprisingly large and well supplied with pillows and blankets which, while not particularly clean, felt thick and warm to Harlyn's questioning touch. With shaking fingers she pulled a blanket from the bunk and wrapped it around her soaked and shivering body. The rough coarseness of the blanket suddenly reminded Harlyn of the precariousness of her position and she collapsed on to the bunk, overwhelmed by misery and the shattering events of the day.

After a while the deepening gloom roused her from her thoughts. The outlines of the small cabin had become blurred and indistinct. Realising it must be getting late, Harlyn looked around for a light of some sort but could see none. Then she remembered the oil lamp on the table in the day cabin. She struggled to her feet, clutching the blanket around her. A wave of dizziness washed over her and she leaned against the bunk for support, shaking her head to clear it. She moved to the doorway and about to step into the day room to fetch the lamp, when she froze in mid-stride.

The drumming of the rain on the deck above her head had eased without her noticing. The rhythmic thump she could now hear was the sound of footsteps. The footsteps stopped suddenly at the top of the companionway. The mutter of voices filtered through to her. Scarcely breathing, she strained her ears for the rough burr of Joe Trudgeon, but the voices were too soft to be identified.

Even as the thought went through her mind she knew it was too late to announce her presence. Besides, until she knew who the strangers were, it would not be a wise move. She was alone and unprotected, and with a dirty blanket flung over her wet clothes, hardly dressed in a manner befitting the daughter of the ship's owner. She whirled round and dived back into the sleeping cabin, her heart pounding against her ribs.

As two pairs of footsteps clumped down the wooden stairs, Harlyn had time to push the door almost shut. As they entered, the one in front, taller than the other, was speaking.

'. . . hatch not locked and this door not even closed,' he sounded annoyed.

Harlyn remained motionless, hardly daring to breathe, her legs trembling and one eye close against the crack in the door.

The shorter of the two men moved about the cabin with an ease which spoke of familarity. He lit the lamp on the table with matches pulled from his pocket.

'I don't understand it, sir. I left this door shut, I'm sure I did.' Harlyn noticed he didn't mention locking the companionway hatch. Lifting another lamp down from behind a pile of books on the shelf he shook it to see how much oil it contained, then lit that.

'Do'e want the big 'un lit too, sir?' he asked the taller man, indicating the brass lamp above their heads. The tall man made a brief negative gesture.

'It's sure to need prolonged attention, assuming it isn't empty,' he replied derisively.

With both lamps lit Harlyn was able to recognise the shorter man. It was George Laity, the Mate. She remembered him from her childhood trips on the schooner and most recently from his visit to her home when he called one day many months before to see her father. Her father had spoken highly of him. She also remembered later that same evening hearing the sound of breaking glass, and seeing Nathan helping her father to his bedroom, while her mother, tight-lipped, followed behind. Worried, she had asked her mother what had happened.

'Your father slipped and knocked over a glass vase,' was the taut reply. 'He is a little shaken and is retiring early tonight,' with that her mother had swept past to her own room, giving neither Nathan nor his shuffling, mumbling burden a second glance.

The tall man had been standing with his back to her, but now he moved forward and folded his length on to the bench nearest the door behind which in an agony of tension, Harlyn watched and waited. He sprawled his long legs out in front of him. From his casually arrogant manner, and the deference shown by George Laity, who remained standing until motioned to sit, Harlyn realised the taller man was used to command. It was obvious that he wore authority as unconsciously and with as much ease as he wore his fashionably cut clothes, a fact which immediately aroused the rebel in Harlyn. How dare he lounge so comfortably on her father's boat? Who was he to walk on board and give orders to her father's employees. At his next words Harlyn's indignation swelled almost to bursting point.

'Will you come and work for me then? My offer's a fair one.'

He was trying to steal her father's crew. Only a great effort prevented her from flinging open the door and denouncing him for the backguard he was. She looked at George Laity, waiting to hear his answer.

'There's no doubt your offer's more than fair, sir. 'Tis just, well, I've worked these many years for Mr Tremayne, 'e bin good as owners go, not like some.' Laity was hesitant.

Harlyn was hot with indignation. I should think so, she fumed.

'Tremayne may once have been a good man,' the tall man replied, with heavy emphasis on the past tense, 'but he's had his day. I tell you in confidence, the rumours are not without foundation.'

Harlyn felt her heart contract. So others knew of her father's difficulties. That meant she had little time left to make her decision. Her mind shied away from the thought.

Contempt in his voice, the tall man continued, 'There are other shipowners in Truro who will find themselves in the same position very soon, and they will have no one to blame but themselves. This port is as good as dead.' Harlyn could hardly believe her ears.

'What do you mean, sir?' Laity sounded genuinely puzzled.

'Use your eyes, man. Look at the state of the river. You've got mines like Wheal Jane pouring thousands of tons of mud and slime into the river each year. Calenick Creek is choking up and there's a bar forming in the main channel. The merchants in this town are cluttering up the river frontage with more and more wharves, quays and timber pounds simply to avoid paying tolls, thus constricting the river even more. You've seen for yourself, those structures run from St Clement street right down to Sunny Corner. It's almost a continuous line.' He leaned forward, resting his arms on the table, pointing a finger at George Laity to add weight to his words.

'Add to that the fact that the river is this town's dumping ground for all its rubbish and sewage, and ask yourself, how much longer can the river remain navigable?' He leaned back in his seat once more, totally relaxed and at ease.

'Heavily laden ships of deep draught are already unloading at Malpas. They simply can't get up the river except on the highest Spring tides. Who can afford to wait for those? And how much extra is added to the charges for unloading and reloading on to barges to bring cargoes up to the quays?'

In the silence that followed, Harlyn, though furious at the stranger's criticism of her home town, realised suddenly the truth of his words. She looked more closely at him, consciously studying him for the first time.

His hair was thick and curly, the colour of liquid honey in the lamplight. His face, as hard as if it had been hewn from rock, had jutting cheek bones, a straight nose and a strong, square jaw.

Deep lines were scored on either side of his mouth, giving him a slightly cruel expression. But when she looked at his mouth, it surprised her. Instead of the thin, forbidding gash she expected, it was wide-lipped and sensual. Among the planes and angles of his stony countenance only his mouth gave any hint of gentleness and humour.

Her gaze moved down his body, clad in a suit of fine brown cloth. His shirt looked creamy in the soft light, and his green cravat below the stiff collar was secured by a plain gold pin. His long legs ended in highly polished leather shoes.

He raised an arm and ran a careless hand through his hair. It was not an act of vanity, more a gesture of impatience. He had large hands, but despite their long fingers they were practical rather than artistic. Hands that would do anything their owner demanded Harlyn mused. Her eyes strayed back to his mouth. What would it feel like to be kissed by those lips?

As the enormity of the thought struck her, Harlyn felt a blush burn her face and neck. Unreasonably she blamed her discomfort, her embarrassment, in fact her whole wretched condition on the man lounging in the seat about five feet away from her.

She was wet and shivering, standing in damp shoes with aching legs in a cramped and smelly cabin, listening to one man she didn't know and another she knew only slightly discussing the inevitable decline of the port in which she had been born and brought up, and dismissing her father's business problems with virtually a careless snap of the fingers. And this tall, arrogant stranger could not care less about any of it.

'Why edn' anything done 'bout the river?' Laity asked. 'There was talk. . . .'

'Talk, that's all they'll ever do,' the other man exploded. 'Talk costs nothing, and while they talk and go through the pretence of considering ideas, the river goes on silting up. Have you heard of anything actually being done?' He shot the question at George Laity, who flinched at its suddenness, then shook his head.

'No, of course you haven't. Back in 1827, a naval friend of my father's, Captain Julyan, put forward a plan to lay wood faggots down the eastern bank from just below the town quay to Downe's Point at Malpas, making a towpath along the embankment.

He proposed straightening the main channel and leading subsidiary channels from it to quays on the western bank.'

'But surely that would have cost a lot of money,' Laity protested.

'Estimated capital outlay was £3,000,' the other retorted, 'to be recovered by a levy of fourpence a ton on incoming ships and threepence a ton on outgoing. A second plan was to build two locks, one somewhere between Downe's Point and Woodbury, the other at the town quay. They would have enclosed enough water to allow ships to come up at all stages of the tide. The cost would have been about £5,000. Both of these plans were perfectly feasible, and others were put forward. Somebody mentioned the possibility of dredging the main channel and straightening it. Oh yes, they were all talked about—' disgust was strong in his voice '—but none was ever implemented. Now this port is dying, choking to death in its own filth, and men like Tremayne will go out of business, and whose fault is it?'

Harlyn, though still indignant, realised she had been shown only a part of the picture by her father. He had been so deeply immersed in his own problems that he had not realised, or had refused to see the wider view. She experienced a momentary stab of annoyance, then recalling the tired, grey figure in the armchair, she felt ashamed of her disloyalty. Love and sympathy welled up inside her, drowning the doubts.

'Well, I'd best be on my way, sir,' Laity said, standing up and easing his way out from behind the table.

'And your answer?' The stranger's voice held hardly any inflection, yet somehow Harlyn sensed that he wanted George Laity. Laity looked uncomfortable.

'Sir, tedn' that I aren't grateful for the offer, but—' Laity didn't seem able to find the right words.

'Well?'

'Well, sir, would we 'ave to move down Falmouth way? Only 'tis the wife, see,' his face mirrored his anxiety. 'All 'er family's 'ere. She edn' well, see, and with me away at sea so much I do worry. . . .'

'What ails her, Mr Laity? Has she seen a doctor?' Though the tone was polite, it held little sympathy, Harlyn thought. But Laity did not take offence. He stared at the floor, then at the lamps and finally at the tall man opposite.

'She lost a baby. Our second it would 'ave bin, she edn' . . . 'erself,' he shrugged helplessly.

'You wouldn't have to move, Mr Laity,' the other replied. 'I allow my Captains to live where they choose. As long as they do their jobs to the best of their ability and earn what I pay them, which is not ungenerous, their private lives are their own business. I extend the same conditions to you.'

'Then, sir, I'll be glad to work for 'e.' The tall man stood up and silently extended his hand. Laity shook it, and the stranger resumed his seat. Laity picked up the kitbag from the bench.

'I'll drop this in to Captain Trudgeon. I do pass 'is place on my way 'ome. Can I call 'e a cab, sir?'

At his words Harlyn felt weak with relief. She dared not move. Her legs had lost all sensation. Her wet clothes were sticking uncomfortably to her body and shivers still shook her from time to time. She longed to be home, in a tub full of hot scented water before a blazing fire, with Amy brushing the tangles out of her hair and warming soft towels to wrap her in. The stranger's reply hit her like a slap.

'No, I shall stay on board a while longer. I want to have a closer look at the accommodation. Leave me the keys. I shall want you and two seamen back on board for the midnight tide.'

'Crew's bin paid off, sir. But I can find 'e a couple of men just fer the trip to Falmouth, ef'n you aren't fussy about their state, sir.'

'Mr Laity, I don't give a damn which public house you drag them out of. Just make sure they can stand up and handle canvas by 11.45 tonight.'

Laity grinned. 'Aye, Cap'n.'

The tall man examined the keys Laity had handed him.

'Right, Mr Laity, you are now in my employ and you'll draw pay from today. But as this ship will be laid up for at least two weeks, you needn't remain in Falmouth. I've no berth for you until the repairs are complete. So as soon as we've docked, you will return to Truro. Spend the time with your wife.' The stranger was brusque, as though afraid that his generosity might be interpreted as weakness. 'I'll send for you when I want you.'

Harlyn's heart gave a great thud. She clapsed both hands across her stomach which suddenly felt weak and hollow. What did he mean, the ship would be laid up in Falmouth? Why should *Karis* be going to Falmouth? The auction was to take place in Truro. What was happening? Harlyn's head felt strangely light, as though it were about to float away from her body. She screwed her eyes tightly shut then opened them again. That was a little better.

Laity's face split in a huge grin. 'That's some 'andsome of 'e, sir. 'Tis much appreciated. Do 'e want t'other lamp, Cap'n?' During their conversation one of the lamps on the table had guttered and died. The tall man dismissed him with a careless wave.

'I shan't need it. I just want to look around quickly to refresh my memory. By the way, is she well ballasted? If this cursed wind doesn't drop we'll need the weight.'

'Aye, Cap'n. She's carrying slag from Trethellen smelting works down along.'

'That's all then. Goodnight, Mr Laity.' Then to the complete surprise of both Harlyn and the Mate, he added softly, 'Let her grieve awhile, she'll heal better for it.'

'Aye, sir, thankee, sir.' There was a warmer note to the respect in George Laity's voice, and Harlyn knew that the few kind words had won for the stranger the Mate's complete and unswerving loyalty.

What a strange man he is, she thought. So arrogant and contemptuous one minute, then revealing a compassion totally at odds with his hawk-like bearing the next. He sounded as though he really cared, she thought in bemusement, then berated herself for a sentimental fool. It was only politics. He knew how to get what he wanted from men. And from women too, no doubt. She blushed at her unruly thoughts but had no time to dwell on them as George Laity's feet clattered up the stairs and he was gone.

Moving her weight from one foot to the other in an effort to get her blood circulating again, Harlyn looked carefully through the crack in the door. Her heart missed a beat and she froze. He was holding the lamp high and staring right at her.

He turned and scooped the keys off the table and took a step towards the door behind which Harlyn stood dry-mouthed and petrified. But just as she was sure he would reach out and push it open, he veered away and went through the door to the companionway instead. Straining her ears Harlyn heard him unlock the door of the Mate's cabin.

The relief was so great Harlyn began to tremble. Catching her bottom lip between her teeth to stop them chattering she glanced quickly at the bunk. There was no time to tidy it now. She put her eye to the door once more. The lamp light had gone and she could neither see nor hear the stranger. He must be in the Mate's cabin. She dared wait no longer. It would be only seconds before he finished his inspection in there and she would be discovered.

Holding her breath and praying that the cabin door would not creak and betray her, Harlyn eased it open. Her heart was thudding so loudly she was sure he would hear it. She stepped silently through the doorway into the gloomy darkness of the main cabin. She took another step forward, intent on avoiding the iron stove.

As she reached out to find the end of the table, her right arm was seized in a vice-like grip, and the lamp suddenly swung in front of her only inches from her eyes. Harlyn screamed in pain and fright.

'Well, what have we here?' His voice was soft but had a steely quality in it that sent a shiver of fear like icy water down Harlyn's spine.

Why had she not shown herself before and revealed her identity? Would he believe her when she told him? Why had she come on board at all? Once again her impetuosity had landed her in trouble.

He set the lamp down on the table and with his free hand pulled the blanket from her shoulders and flung it aside. The unexpected movement made Harlyn gasp.

'You are hurting my arm,' she said through clenched teeth, trying to keep her voice level.

'Indeed?' He raised one eyebrow in mock surprise. 'Should I treat a thief gently, then?'

'I am no thief, sir,' Harlyn retorted angrily.

'My apologies,' Harlyn winced at the cool sarcasm. 'In that case you must be either a beggar or a whore. Which is it?'

The question was asked with such icy politeness that for a moment Harlyn was too taken aback to speak. Hot rage coursed through her veins, flooding her pale face with colour. Her eyes flashed green fire and she tilted her chin proudly as she drew herself to her full height.

'How dare you speak to me so? Who do you think you are?'

His eyebrow lifted again and the corners of his mouth lost their stern downward curve. To Harlyn's amazement and fury the tall man began to laugh. It was a deep, full-throated sound of sheer enjoyment.

'Young woman,' he leaned down towards her, 'I know who I am.' For the first time she met his eyes squarely and felt shock tingle through her, for he had the eyes of a tiger. They were amber-yellow in the lamplight, and had a feral gleam that frightened and yet intrigued her. She swallowed the dryness in her throat, tilting her chin a little higher.

'Then introduce yourself, sir, that I may know who treats a lady so appallingly.'

'A lady?' The scarcasm was biting. 'Forgive me, of course I should have guessed from your gown,' he flicked the damp sleeve of her torn and dirty dress, 'and your coiffure.' His eyes, as they rested on the tangled mass of wet hair coiled roughly on her neck, were disparaging.

Harlyn flushed again. She had completely forgotten her bedraggled appearance. At his words she instinctively raised her free hand to her hair, but caught herself and forced her arm back to her side without completing the movement. He noticed her action and recognised the pride that forestalled it. A momentary gleam of admiration softened his steely gaze.

'I am Jared Carlyon, shipowner, of Falmouth,' he said, sketching a mocking bow and releasing her arm. But he remained close enough to seize it again should she show any sign of flight.

'Oh, a Falmouth man.' Harlyn invested the words with all the contempt she could muster, making it clear by the expression on her face and in her voice that she should have deduced his origins from his behaviour.

She glanced down. Her arm was red and bruised and beginning to swell. The marks of his fingers were livid against her golden skin. As the blood resumed its circulation, the pain in her arm and hand was considerable, but she bit the inside of her lip rather than betray the fact.

'And you, Madam? Who are you?'

Harlyn hesitated. How to answer? If she lied and claimed false identity she had nothing to back up her claim. Yet if she told him the truth, would he believe her in the circumstances? She made her decision.

'Do you intend to bid for this schooner at the auction?' she asked.

His eyebrows came together in a frown. 'I fail to see why that should concern you,' he replied coldly.

'It concerns me greatly, Mr Carlyon,' she retorted, 'I am Harlyn Tremayne, the owner's eldest daughter.'

'Captain,' Jared murmured absently, setting the lamp on the table and folding his long length on to the bench, obviously satisfied that Harlyn's revelation of her identity precluded any further attempt to escape. He did not invite her to sit.

'I − I beg your pardon?' Harlyn was confused.

'I said Captain, Miss Tremayne. I am Captain Carlyon.'

'My mistake, Captain,' Harlyn returned tartly, stressing the title.'I mistook you for a gentleman, how foolish of me.' The moment she had uttered the words Harlyn could have bitten off her tongue. His face set in anger and under the thick brows his tawny eyes glinted dangerously.

Harlyn swallowed. Why couldn't she control her impulsiveness? She needed this man's help if she was to save her father and her family. She could hardly expect his assistance if she continually hurled insults at him. Even if he did deserve them, she thought rebelliously.

She lowered her head and folded her hands in front of her, assuming what she hoped was an air of abject apology.

'I'm sorry,' she whispered. 'I should not have spoken so.'

She did not see the quirk of amusement at the corner of his mouth and the light of challenge in his eyes. His voice was soft, but again held a hint of steel.

'Don't try my patience too far, Miss Tremayne. Now, why were you hiding aboard my − this ship?' Harlyn did not notice the correction. Biting back the flood of words that rose to her lips, she took a deep breath to collect her thoughts and steady her voice. Instinctively knowing that Jared Carlyon would recognise one false word, white lie or prevarication, she chose her words carefully.

'I sought refuge, Captain Carlyon. Refuge from the rain, and from personal problems which seem,' her voice wavered, 'insurmountable.'

He ignored her distress. 'Why this ship?'

'Because she's my father's and because I know her well. I have sailed on her occasionally since I was a child. Only in the river it's true, but it was a real adventure for me.' Harlyn heard the note of defiance creeping into her voice and fought to control it. Her head felt hot and her legs were heavy. She longed to sit down, but her stubborn pride would not let her ask his permission.

'Also because I wanted to say my own farewell to her,' Harlyn went on. 'Although she belongs to my father now, she won't for much longer.'

'You presume too much, Miss Tremayne.' He studied her, watching her reaction to his words. 'I might choose not to make an offer.'

'You think you are the only person interested? Then it's you who presume too much,' Harlyn replied tartly. Jared's eyes narrowed, but he went on smoothly.

'I should be surprised if there was much interest in her. My surveyor says she requires a great deal of work. She should be resheathed, her forrard planks are spongy with rot. Her caulking needs replacing and much of the rigging. I wouldn't be surprised if she's nail-sick in places. She needs completely repainting and we haven't yet mentioned the sails.'

Harlyn's heart sank as he listed the defects. She was beginning to feel slightly dizzy. 'So Father won't get much money for her,' she murmured dispiritedly. The dizziness was coming over her in waves but she fought it, determined not to reveal any sign of weakness in front of this hard, arrogant man.

'Then I wonder, sir, that you are interested in her at all. Sir Henry Trevellyan obviously has more belief in her soundness than you do.'

He did not move, nor did his face alter its expression, but Harlyn sensed the interest her remark had kindled. Though he sprawled casually on the bench, there was an alertness, a tension about him that reminded her yet again of a tiger. He turned his piercing amber gaze on her.

'Why tell me this?'

Harlyn's heart was pounding and she felt curiously lightheaded. The room seemed to be moving around her. She tried to concentrate.

'He mustn't get her. You must stop him,' she blurted,

desperation in her voice. She must concentrate, speak the right words if she was to persuade and convince him that Sir Henry Trevellyan should not become the new owner of the schooner. But would he listen? Why should he? Why should he help? In her weakened state, confusion and doubts undermined her. How could she convince him? What inducement could she offer? He broke into her whirling thoughts.

'You are too late, Miss Tremayne. The auction took place this afternoon. The schooner is sold.'

The room spun faster. Something was terribly wrong. 'But . . . then who. . . .?'

But even as she spoke her legs began to give way. As the colour drained from her face and her eyelids fluttered, Harlyn reached out with both hands in a curiously appealing gesture, a last effort to fend off the threatening darkness. But it overwhelmed her, and with a small sigh she toppled forward on to the wooden floor.

3

Jared Carlyon did not move. He stared contemptuously at the prostrate girl. It was a measure of his knowledge of the devious ways of women that he assumed her faint to be a pretence. But after several seconds had passed and she had made no movement or sound, suspicion gave way to concern, and with a quick step he was beside her on one knee.

Gripping her shoulders to turn her over, he was shocked to feel the coldness of her body through the damp cotton dress.

'Little fool,' he muttered through set lips as he eased her onto her back. The movement of his arm loosened the heavy hair from its rough knot, and it tumbled in an ebony mass across her face and shoulders. He smoothed it back, suddenly aware of its weight and texture and the subtle perfume, faint as a breath, that rose to his nostrils. It hinted of jasmine and musk and sunshine, but the harder he tried to capture its essence, the more it eluded him.

Harlyn had still given no sign of returning to consciousness. He could not let her remain on the bare wooden floor any longer. Scooping her up in his arms as if she were weightless, he strode across the main cabin, kicked open the door of the sleeping cabin and laid her gently on the bunk. Then he fetched the lamp and set it down beside the bunk whilst seating himself on the edge.

There was almost no colour in her creamy skin. Her thick lashes rested like small fans on her cheeks, and her face in its unconscious state, was childlike and vulnerable. Her midnight hair tumbled over the grubby pillow like crumbled satin. She seemed to be hardly breathing.

Jared bent towards her and holding his own breath could just feel the faint warmth of hers on his cheek. Again he caught the tantalising perfume of her hair.

Against his will, for he had no time for any problems or entanglements outside his own sphere of interest, this stubborn, bedraggled creature intrigued him. He lifted his hand and with a gentle finger, thoughtfully traced the outline of her oval face. His expression was unfathomable.

The moment was shattered as a shiver rippled through Harlyn and her teeth began to chatter. Jared's face at once assumed its characteristic half-sardonic, half-contemptuous mask. What was he to do with her? If she remained in those wet clothes any longer she would develop lung fever. He could hardly just sit there and let that happen, nor could he take her home unconscious.

With a slight sigh he began to unbutton the front of her dress. His fingers were quite steady and deliberately impersonal as he eased the damp cotton from her arms and shoulders. Systematically he removed all the wet and mud-splashed garments until she was clad only in her shift. Then he pulled two more blankets from the chest at the bottom of the bunk and tucked them closely around her.

Straightening up, Jared went out into the main cabin. Selecting another key from the bunch, he unlocked one of the lockers and brought out a bottle of brandy and a glass. Captain Trudgeon had been an eminently sensible man when it came to keeping out the cold. Returning to the sleeping cabin, he poured a generous measure then reseating himself on the bunk, he slid an arm under Harlyn's shoulders and propped her up, putting the glass to her lips.

She caught her breath and twisted her head away as the fumes caught in her throat. But Jared forced the spirit into her mouth, and though she spluttered, she swallowed most of it.

As the brandy began to revive her, a rosy flush warmed her cheeks. Gradually the shivering ceased. Jared put the glass down and gently pulled his arm from under her, laying her back on the pillow.

He stared at her for a few moments then stood up abruptly, unaccountably disturbed by her fragile, glowing beauty framed in the grubby pillows and rough dark blankets. He seized the brandy and disdaining the glass, took a long swallow straight from the bottle, grimacing as the fiery spirit burned its way down. An unreasoning anger shook him. What was he doing here, playing nursemaid to some hare-brained slip of a girl? The St Aubyns would be waiting for him at the Red Lion. There would be a delicious meal with fine wines, a roaring fire, and Camilla.

Camilla, with skin like milk and silky blonde hair, always immaculate, twisted and waved and curled into the latest fashionable styles, wearing exquisite gowns of the finest materials. Camilla, with a clear, high voice that tinkled like bells when she laughed. Camilla, pretty, witty, the darling of County society.

Jared raised the brandy bottle once more and felt the spirit course through his veins. It was time the girl woke up, her swoon had lasted long enough. He put the bottle on the floor, leaned over, and patted her face.

Outside the wind howled and keened in the rigging. Inside the small, cramped cabin, the lamp light hinted at a gentler, more intimate atmosphere.

As she drifted back from the darkness of unconsciousness, Harlyn could feel something tapping her face. She was warm and comfortable, floating in a peaceful half-world, free from problems and fears. She didn't want to wake up.

The tapping persisted. Harlyn tried to raise her hand to fend off whatever it was, but her arm wouldn't move. Suddenly she felt trapped. Faces loomed in front of her, distorted and hideous.

Her mother's, closed and angry, her father's harassed and desperate, Sir Henry's, wet-lipped and avid, and the tilted brow and piercing amber gaze of Jared Carlyon, mocking her.

Harlyn began to struggle, trying to free her arms, panic rising like a dark tide within her. She gasped for breath and a piteous cry broke from her lips as she turned her head from side to side to escape the visions.

She felt hands on her shoulders, shaking her, and a voice. But it was far away and she couldn't hear the words. The faces swam in front of her, moving faster, until they mingled and blurred.

Jared looked down at the moaning threshing figure. Through the thin shift her skin was hot under his hands and he was surprised at the strength in her slender limbs.

All traces of mockery had been wiped from his features by the concern and puzzlement which drew his brows together. He released Harlyn's shoulder, drew back his hand and slapped her; a stinging blow which jerked her head sideways. Her eyes flew open, tears of shock and pain spilling over her lashes.

'Forgive me,' Jared said gravely. 'I could not rouse you, and you seemed sorely troubled.'

Harlyn stared blankly at him, still in a state of confusion. Drawn by her total defencelessness, her vulnerability, a strange new emotion gripped Jared. He wanted to protect this waif. Without realising he moved, he leaned towards her. Harlyn gasped. The tiny sound broke the spell. Jared released her shoulders and stood up abruptly. Harlyn struggled to sit up.

'What happened?' she asked dazedly. Then she noticed her dress and petticoats plus other items of a more intimate nature on the floor beside the bunk. As she sat up and the blankets fell away she looked quickly down at herself. The soft light of the lamp revealed the outline of her body, veiled only by the fine lawn shift. Harlyn looked up at the man standing beside the bunk, her eyes wide and fearful, vivid colour staining her cheeks.

'Oh,' she gasped. 'What . . .? Did you . . .?' Jared inclined his head.

'There was no one else on hand to save you from a severe chill,' came the bland reply. As he spoke Harlyn smelt the brandy on his breath. Her nostrils flared.

'You've been drinking,' she blurted, and clutched the blankets protectively to her bosom.

The gesture was not lost on Jared. And you wanted to protect her, an inner voice mocked him. He raised a sardonic eyebrow.

'Fear not, Miss Tremayne,' he said with exaggerated courtesy, 'your honour, such as it is, remains unsullied. It is not my habit to force my attentions upon young women, least of all those who appear to be unconscious.'

As his words registered on her confused and weary brain, Harlyn felt anger sear through her like white-hot flame. She trembled once more, but this time from rage.

'How dare you,' she whispered, almost speechless in her fury. Totally forgetting her state of undress, she scrambled off the bunk and stood facing him. She drew herself up to her full height, but even then the top of her head only reached his chin. She looked up at him, her mouth quivering, her eyes blazing green fire.

'How dare you,' she choked out the words a second time, unable in her fury to find others with which to flay him. Her arm flew upward.

Jared saw the movement and guessed her intention. His hand shot out in an instinctive reflex motion, his fingers closing about her wrist before her blow could connect.

'Hardly the action of a lady, Miss Tremayne,' he said coolly. Though seemingly unmoved by her outburst, he was in fact taken aback by her rage. Jared wondered for an instant if his words had been unjust. There was as much hurt and indignation as anger in her reaction.

'And yours has hardly been the behaviour of a gentleman,' she spat back.

As he looked down into the stormy green pools of her eyes, once again he felt strangely drawn to her. She was a puzzle, an enigma, a challenge. She looked like a trollop in her torn and dirty dress, her hair loose and tangled. Yet she smelled fresh and clean, and good breeding showed in her speech and her manner. He still held her wrist and knew that his grip must hurt her, yet she did not flinch or wince. She had courage, in fact it bordered on arrogance, an attribute not becoming to a well brought-up young lady.

He watched the anger suddenly die in her. Not of its own accord, he felt sure, but pushed aside by something else, something more desperate. She had a hunted look about her. What could it be that had driven her from home and family to seek refuge on this ship? She had said something about personal problems. But what problems could a girl of her background possibly have? Yet she didn't look the type to flounce out in a huff because she could only have two new dresses instead of three, but, appearances could be deceptive.

He was about to speak, to ask her what troubled her so deeply, but it was as though she read his thoughts. She deliberately lowered her eyes, withdrawing from any contact, rejecting him. The atmosphere between them immediately changed, became distant.

Jared released her wrist, seeing the marks of his fingers like four scarlet bands on the golden skin. Harlyn clasped her hands in front of her to still their trembling. Keeping her eyes lowered, she licked her dry lips, then forced the words out.

'I thought . . . I thought I heard you say the schooner was sold. Is that correct?'

'It is,' Jared replied.

'Who . . . who?' Harlyn could go no further.

'She belongs to me.'

'Then I am guilty of trespass. I beg your pardon.' She swallowed and her voice wavered. 'Please wait outside.'

Jared picked up the brandy bottle, made a mocking bow and withdrew without a word, closing the door softly behind him. The vision of her body, high-breasted and slender, veiled only by the cloudy shift, burned in his brain. Shame was an emotion Jared Carlyon had never experienced, so he did not recognise it. All he knew was that she aroused all his male instincts, but at the same time made him feel oddly uncomfortable.

Yet he had done nothing, he hadn't even said much. Dammit, a man was entitled to draw conclusions when a bedraggled female is found hiding on his ship and when he asks her a few simple questions, promptly faints. The whole situation was ridiculous.

He raised the bottle to his lips, then recalled her eyes, wide with anxiety and fear when she had smelt the spirit on his breath. He slammed the bottle down on the table. God damn it, couldn't a man even take a drink? Suddenly he began to laugh.

As the door closed behind him, Harlyn sank down on the edge of the bunk. She was utterly exhausted. Her shoulders drooped and her back curved like the stem of a wilted flower. Her wrist ached cruelly and she rubbed it. She felt utterly bereft. What was she to do? She had sought refuge on *Karis* only to find the schooner no longer belonged to her father but instead to the tall stranger with face and manner as cold and hard as granite, who treated her like some tavern wench. But she could not go home, so where was she to go? Round and round the question spun.

A sudden sound and a burst of laughter from the other side of the door made her jump. She stood up and began to struggle into her still damp clothes, blushing furiously at the realisation that the man in the outer cabin had removed her garments one by one while she was unconscious. The knowledge and the resulting embarrassment made her fingers all thumbs. When she had with much fumbling, fastened all the buttons and attempted to shake out the worst of the creases, Harlyn ran unsteady fingers through her tangled mane of hair. Dividing it roughly, she plaited it into a loose braid which hung like a thick rope over one shoulder, the ends curling gently against her breast. While her hands were occupied with tidying herself, her brain was working feverishly.

She had to get out of Truro, away from Sir Henry. Jared Carlyon had told George Laity that he was taking the boat back to Falmouth that night. Her mother's sister Rebecca lived in Falmouth. The family had not seen her for years as Harlyn's mother regarded Aunt Becky as rather common. She had married a miner and moved first out to Twelveheads, then down to Falmouth where her husband worked at Great Retallack, mining for zinc, while they saved for passage on the Diamond Steam Navigation Company's steamer to Natal. Tin mines all over Cornwall were closing down as costs soared and cheaper ore could be imported from abroad. Becky and Arthur were going to Africa, to the gold mines, just as soon as they got the fare.

Then a letter from Aunt Becky informed them that Uncle Arthur had been involved in an accident in the mine, and they had had to spend their savings on medical treatment. Harriet Tremayne had interpreted this as a plea for money and had from that moment washed her hands of her sister. A short note some weeks later had informed the family that Arthur had lost his leg and that Becky had found employment in an hotel. There were no further letters.

Harlyn had almost forgotten Aunt Becky, but now the memory of a short, buxom woman returned strongly. Aunt Becky would understand, of course she would, for hadn't she left home against her family's wishes? Surely she would give Harlyn refuge while they worked out what to do. The problem was, how to get to Falmouth?

She had no money so there was no chance of getting on any of the coaches which travelled the ten miles each day. Even to sit on top cost three shillings. That left only one possibility. She would have to find some means of staying on board the ship.

Having made her decision Harlyn folded the blankets neatly and placed them on the bunk. Then as new determination strengthened her, she drew herself up, brushed her hands down her skirt, and taking a deep breath walked out into the main cabin, picking up the lamp as she went.

Jared had just replaced the bottle and glass in the locker and was closing the door. He turned, a smile playing at the corners of his mouth.

Harlyn hated him in that moment. She clasped her hands tightly in front of her. He was laughing at her. This was nothing more than an amusing incident to him, a story to tell his friends over dinner or a glass of wine. Her life lay in fragments and he laughed. What a fool he must think her. She could expect no help from him, that was certain. She would have to rely on her own wits and whatever courage she could muster to solve the problems that faced her.

'Miss Tremayne,' Jared inclined his head, 'I trust you are now recovered? I will call a cab and see you home.'

'Do not trouble yourself, Captain Carlyon,' Harlyn replied coolly, 'I know the town and can find my own way home.'

'I must insist,' Jared was implacable. 'As you know the town, you must also know of the drunks and vagabonds abroad at night, even in such weather as this. I cannot allow you to be exposed to such dangers.' He took an ornate silver watch from his waistcoat pocket. 'I have an appointment at the Red Lion for which I am already late, but I shall accompany you home first.' He paused, as if awaiting some reaction from Harlyn.

When there was none he went on, 'No doubt your parents will be greatly concerned by your absence.'

At the mention of her parents, Harlyn felt a great lump in her throat and hot tears pricked her eyelids. Would they really be worried for her, or would their concern be for themselves. She pushed the thought from her, biting the inside of her lip to keep her mouth steady. She would not reveal her misery for his amusement, nor satisfy his idle curiosity.

'As you wish.' Her reply was calm, but her mind was in a fever. How was she to get away from him? He picked up the lamp she had brought out from the sleeping cabin, turned down the wick and blew it out, replacing it on the table, then picking up the other lamp and the keys he turned to her.

'If you are ready . . .?' Harlyn nodded and head high she walked past him and up the stairs.

It was still raining, a dull persistent rain which fell with a gentle hiss into the filthy water and made the yellow pine deck slick and shiny. The wind whined in the rigging, its low moan rising with the gusts to a thin scream.

A plan was forming in Harlyn's mind. Even though the idea of what might lie ahead terrified her, she would not, could not go home. She blessed the rain. Turning to Jared who was close behind her, Harlyn twisted her lips into a smile.

'Captain Carlyon,' she began, her voice soft and apologetic, 'I fear I have caused you much trouble.'

Jared looked swiftly down at the girl standing beside him in the cramped space at the top of the companionway. Her sudden change of attitude came as a complete surprise, but a very pleasant one. She was being sensible at last. His reminder about her parents had obviously touched her conscience, and she must have realised that home was the best place to be. Yet the abrupt reversal of her former attitude aroused his suspicions.

'Indeed you have, Miss Tremayne. But I will allow that the circumstances of our meeting showed neither of us to advantage.'

'How generous of you to say so,' Harlyn murmured, her face aching with the effort of keeping the contrite smile in place. 'There is, however, one last favour I would beg.'

'Oh?' Jared raised one eyebrow, suddenly wary. He had been right to be suspicious. This young woman was not to be trusted.

'What might that be? I hope you are not going to insist again on going home alone, I could not permit it.'

'No, indeed, Captain Carlyon,' Harlyn replied through clenched teeth, the muscles in her cheeks beginning to tremble from the strain, 'you have made that quite clear.' He looked at her sharply. 'And I thank you for your concern,' she added hastily. 'No, the favour I ask is simply the loan of a blanket to protect me from the rain and cold wind.'

Harlyn allowed herself to shiver as another gust of wind blew rain across the open hatchway. She had been holding herself under such rigid control that as soon as she let go, her whole body shook and trembled.

Jared studied her. Her face was pale and pinched, and her teeth chattered audibly. Though still dubious he found he could not ignore the appeal in her luminous green eyes.

'Of course,' he said curtly, 'I'll get one for you.' He turned to go down the stairs again. Harlyn held him with a hand on his sleeve.

'I have kept you long enough from your appointment, Captain. If you would be good enough to find a cab, I will fetch the blanket myself. It will save time.' Tentatively she reached for the lamp. Please make him go, she prayed, please don't let him be suspicious. Jared hesitated a moment, the doubt clear on his face, then allowed her to take the lamp.

'Don't worry, Captain,' she smiled tremulously, 'I shall not hide myself in your cabin again.'

Her words and smiles did not allay his doubts, but time was pressing and the St Aubyns were not people to be kept waiting. After all, she couldn't go far. He nodded, and raising his collar against the rain strode down the gangplank and along the quayside.

Harlyn watched until he was halfway along the quay, his tall figure leaning into the wind, then she flew down the stairs, through the day cabin into the sleeping quarters. Seizing the two folded blankets off the bunk she tucked them under her arm and rushed out into the day room. Grabbing the other lamp off the table she shook it. The hollow splash confirmed what its lightness suggested, the oil was low. She looked feverishly around for matches. There must be some somewhere, but she couldn't see them.

Harlyn rushed about the cabin almost tripping over in her

haste. Where were the matches? He would be back in a moment and it would be too late. She raised the lighted lamp high above her head and its glow reflected from a small metal container on the shelf. Of course, they would be in a metal case to keep out the damp. She had been looking for a wooden one.

Setting the lamps on the table, she lit the second one, trimming the wick carefully. Then she replaced the matches on the shelf. He would not call her thief again. Anger flared as she recalled his accusations.

Picking up both lamps and securing the blankets more firmly under her arm Harlyn climbed the stairs to the deck. Peering round the hatchway, she looked along the quayside. There was no sign of him. Quickly she put down both lamps and closed the companionway hatch.

Faintly she could hear the clipclop of horses' hooves, soft then loud on the gusting wind. She stood for an instant, eyes straining in the darkness. Under the pale glow of the gaslight at the corner where the quay met the street she saw a horse and cab turn on to the quay. Harlyn snatched up the lamps, placed one on top of the hatch, and holding the other one low, crouching almost double she scuttled to the far side of the hatch then forward along the deck until she reached the fo'c'sle hatch.

The hooves were louder now, the jingle of harness clear above the roaring wind and splattering rain. Almost dropping them in her haste, Harlyn set the lamp and blankets down and pulled at the wooden door. It would not move. Her heart thumped painfully. It was locked. It couldn't be, it just couldn't. Not daring to bring the lamp forward in case it was seen, Harlyn tugged at the door again. This time it moved slightly.

The horse stopped, its iron-shod hooves slipping and clattering on the quayside cobbles. Panic surged in Harlyn. In a moment it would be too late. Jamming her fingers into the crack round the doors, Harlyn heaved frantically. She felt her nails tear as the warped wood squeaked in protest. She froze, almost sobbing. Had he heard?

She saw the door of the cab open. He leaned out looking back along the deck towards the lamp on the companionway.

'Miss Tremayne,' he called. He couldn't have seen her. Desperate to get out of sight, but terrified in case any movement or sound caught his eye, Harlyn moved as swiftly and carefully as she could. Easing the fo'c'sle hatch open as quickly as she dared, ignoring the stench that erupted from the black hole, she tossed the blankets down into the darkness below. Climbing over the lip surrounding the opening she felt for the iron rungs of the ladder. Then with most of her body concealed below deck level she leaned forward and quickly grabbed the lamp and drew it down beside her. Pulling the doors almost closed, she watched through the crack.

The moment she lifted the lamp a wave of tingling horror washed over her as she realised that in her haste she had left the full one on the companionway hatch. The lamp she held was less than quarter full. It was too late to go back.

Harlyn looked up in time to see him climb out of the cab and stride up the gangplank. He went straight to the hatch and lifted the lamp high.

'Miss Tremayne,' his voice was sharp, imperious, 'Miss Tremayne, the cab is waiting.'

Harlyn eased herself down the iron ladder, the lamp held down by her side, so that no light showed. She had to see him leave before she would feel safe. Safe! There was nothing safe about what she planned. A bubble of hysterical laughter rose in her throat and Harlyn bit her bottom lip hard in an effort to regain control of herself.

Jared unlatched the doors and flung them back. His voice thundered down the stairs, echoing through the cabins.

'Miss Tremayne, I am in no mood for games. My patience is exhausted. Come out this instant.' He listened intently and when no reply was forthcoming, he snatched up the lamp and ran down the stairs. He was back within seconds. As he held the lamp high above his head, looking quickly about him, Harlyn felt her heart contract at the anger on his face. If he should discover her. . . .

He lowered the lamp, slammed the doors shut and locked them then blew out the lamp and set it in a niche by the hatch. He strode across the deck looking neither left nor right, and down the gangplank. Every muscle of his lean body was taut with fury.

The lying little hussy had made a fool of him. He had been taken in by those limpid green eyes and the pleading smile. He who had always prided himself on his judgement, who had never yet been bested by man or woman, had fallen prey to the wiles of a simple girl.

'The Red Lion,' he ordered the driver curtly as he flung himself back against the leather seat.

No, he told himself harshly, this was no simple girl, this one had all the cunning of a vixen. He was well rid of her. God knew he had enough problems without looking for more. She had been a minor inconvenience, now she had gone from his life as suddenly as she had entered it. Everything was back to normal.

It had been a long day. He was tired and hungry. A delicious meal in good company awaited him. A blazing fire and fine wine to warm and comfort him, well out of this confounded wind and rain. He tried to find the enthusiasm which normally accompanied such thoughts, but tonight was strangely absent.

Where was she? Why had she run away again? If she was who she claimed to be then what could have driven her to such desperate lengths?

Fleeting glimpses of Harlyn chased across his mind; her white face as she had crumpled into the swoon; the fear and anguish in her cries as she had lain semi-conscious on the bunk; the scent of her hair and the warmth of her skin under his hands, and the flooding crimson blush as she realised she was almost naked.

Jared felt a stirring within him, and was surprised by both its occurrence and its strength. He had had his share of women, taking them when he felt the need. Despite the stringent moral tone of the day it was not difficult. But he had steered clear of serious involvements. His ambition to build a shipping fleet of his own absorbed most of his time and energy. Besides he had little patience with the convoluted conversations and endless small talk etiquette demanded, and mild flirtations merely bored him. His lean good looks and unusual eyes caused many a flutter in a maidenly bosom, and provided a challenge for ladies of experience, but the sardonic tilt of his brow and the twist of mockery lurking about his mouth warned of deeper, more dangerous currents.

The cab clattered to a halt. Looking out and seeing the black-beamed Tudor façade, Jared realised with a start that he had reached his destination. He climbed out and paid the driver, then resolving to put Harlyn out of his mind he walked purposefully into the bright welcoming warmth of the inn.

Harlyn watched the cab drive away. Then clinging to the ladder with the hand that held the lamp, with her free hand she pulled the doors tightly closed and slowly, carefully climbed down the ladder.

The sounds of the gusting wind and hissing rain were deadened. Harlyn shivered. She reached the bottom of the ladder and put her foot out, seeking the reassuring firmness of wooden planks. Instead her foot landed on something soft. Unable to shift her weight quickly, hampered as she was by the lamp, she felt the thing give way, then burst with a soft squelch. A musty sweet odour invaded her nostrils and she almost screamed out loud.

Stumbling backwards she let go of the ladder, holding the lamp high and at the same time dreading what the light might reveal. She felt her knees sag with relief. It was not some nameless horror, she told herself firmly, feeling the shaky breaths of reaction catch as sobs in her throat. It was only an apple, a rotten, mildewed apple, left behind by one of the crew.

Harlyn held the lamp up once more, her eyes becoming accustomed to the thick darkness. Beyond the pale globe of light cast by the flickering lamp, she caught sight of two dark mounds. Already overwrought, her nerves stretched like wires, she held her breath, expecting them to move, to spring at her. After a few seconds she realised they were the two blankets she had brought from the Captain's cabin. She let her breath out in a soft, tremulous explosion.

Harlyn held up the lamp and looked about her. The compartment was not very big, considering four or five men usually lived and slept in it. The bulkheads, floor and deckhead were stained and greasy with soot and smoke from the bogey stove. This straight stove with a funnel fixed on top to the deck was the only source of heat, but could not be used for cooking. Harlyn reached out her hand, but the iron was as cold as stone. She shivered and opened the small doors. Nothing but ash. There was no kindling, no coal, nothing with which she could start a fire. In any case, she chided herself, there would be too great a risk of discovery.

Harlyn set the lamp down on one of the two small forms which appeared to be the only furniture the cabin held, apart from a stinking bucket with a rough wooden lid, whose purpose was obvious. Her body racked by uncontrollable bouts of shivering, Harlyn picked up one of the blankets, shook it out and wrapped herself in it. Its coarse roughness was an immediate comfort. Clutching it about her, Harlyn pulled the other form closer, pushing both against the bulkhead. Now she had a make-shift bunk. She was about to lie down when she noticed a steady drip of water falling on to the form from the deckhead above.

The deck planks were strained and the caulking needed replacement. Wearily she pushed the forms further forward, away from the drips, then putting the lamp on the floor beside her she lay down on her hard bed and pulled the other blanket over her. Immediately she felt a little warmer. Her eyes were gritty with tiredness and her eyelids so heavy that they ached. Harlyn turned on her side, drawing her knees up and curling herself into a ball. She pulled the blankets tight about her ears. No one would find her here. She must try to sleep, to gather her strength, for she would surely need every bit of it in the days ahead.

In a few hours she would be in Falmouth, the rapidly expand-ing, busy port at the mouth of the harbour. Rumour said it was a wicked place, full of vice, that the streets were full of foreign seamen and bad women enticing them even in broad daylight. Harlyn's stomach churned, an uneasy mixture of fear and excitement. Would Aunt Becky remember her? More import-ant, would she help?

Harlyn realised that once she reached Falmouth she would have to let her parents know she was safe. Would they forgive her? Would she be able to make them understand? And what about Sir Henry Trevellyan, what would he do? Maybe if she were not there, he would leave her parents alone, maybe he would find someone else to marry. But even if he did, it would not save her father from ruin.

At that very moment Sir Henry stood in the hall at Chyvallon listening to the stumbling explanations of William and Harriet Tremayne as to why their eldest daughter was not present to receive him.

After many minutes dissembling, pleading on Harlyn's behalf a headache and other minor feminine indispositions, which Sir Henry brushed aside with growing impatience, William Tre-mayne, in an agony of guilt and not entirely sober, blurted out the truth. In a disjointed rush of words he told of Harlyn's reaction to Sir Henry's proposal, and her headlong flight after learning of the desperate state of her father's business affairs.

Sir Henry's only visible reaction was to grow paler. His glacial eyes became diamond hard, and the forefinger of his right hand rubbed unceasingly against his thumb, producing a dry rasping sound which tore at Harriet's shattered nerves until she wanted to scream.

'I'll find her,' Sir Henry said softly, 'I'll find her.' Harriet practically fell upon him, babbling her thanks, begging him not to mind Harlyn's foolishness, it was nothing more than nerves, the fears of an innocent girl.

Trevellyan let her prattle on. She and the drunken sot behind her were the key to the girl's return. Once she was back he would dispose of them with as little emotion as he would expend on swatting a fly.

So Harlyn had run away sooner than wed him, despite the pressure on her father. That proved at least that she had the kind of spirit he sought. His rage began to subside. Sooner or later he always got what he wanted. And he wanted her, now more than ever. In fact, now he thought about it, this little episode had added piquancy to the situation.

He would find her. He had a wide network of contacts, people who worked for him, people who owed him for past favours, puppets whose strings he could pull.

He would find her and he would wed her. Then slowly, with infinite patience and total enjoyment he would bend that wayward spirit until it broke.

Only one thing could mar the delightful picture he had conjoured, only one totally unacceptable thought. He felt the corrosive acid of rage burn within him. What if, when she were found, she were no longer virgin? She was an innocent abroad in a dangerous situation, anything could happen to her. His body jerked in an uncontrollable spasm. If that happened, he would destroy the man responsible, and anyone else, important or not, who had helped her.

He brushed Harriet's hand from his arm, his face an expressionless mask.

'Say nothing of this to anyone. She will be found and she will be returned and everything will go ahead as planned. Remember, Harlyn has a mild indisposition and is confined to her room. For your sakes and hers . . .' He left the sentence unfinished, but the threat hung in the air between them, unmistakable. Then the plump, dapper little man turned and without another word, walked out of the house.

Harlyn's breathing slowed and deepened as she drifted into exhausted sleep. Beside her the lamp flickered and dimmed. The yellow flame became tinged with blue as the wick sucked up the last remaining oil. Harlyn did not see it. But in the corners of the fo'c'sle brown, furry bodies watched, whiskers twitching, eyes gleaming like tiny beads. The soft scraping of their scampering paws and the muffled squeaks were drowned by the creaking timbers as the boat moved restlessly, tugging at the restraining ropes, anxious to be free and moving out into the open sea where the wind was already whipping the tops from the steepening waves as the Atlantic cauldron spewed forth another storm.

4

The dining room with its famed cedar panelling was huge, more than seventy feet long. In the vast fireplace two large tree trunks were being consumed by hungry flames. Serving maids in neat uniforms darted about with plates and trays of food, their faces flushed from their exertions and the heat of the kitchens. But despite the size of the room, Camilla St Aubyn's clear high voice rang out like a bell above the rumble of conversation and the clatter of cutlery.

'Jared, you really are the most frightful bore this evening.' There was a momentary pause, then everyone continued eating and talking as before.

'Camilla!' Her mother's tone was both reproachful and indulgent. Camilla leaned forward, pouting. The lace ruffles on her pale blue brocade dinner gown tightened over her full bosom and the milk white flesh, with its dusting of fragrant powder, quivered invitingly, a sight which usually intrigued Jared, but which tonight he scarcely noticed.

'Jared, what is the matter with you, are you ill?'

'Leave the man alone, Camilla.' Richard St Aubyn's voice was also indulgent, but held a note of command which his daughter heeded. She settled back in her chair and stared ostentatiously at the ornate ceiling.

'I beg your pardon, Camilla, Lord and Lady St Aubyn,' Jared said hastily, annoyed with himself. 'I must apologise for my bad manners. No, I am not ill, Camilla, though I am touched by your concern.' Jared's words, delivered as they were in a gently mocking tone, brought a hint of a smile to St Aubyn's lips, and elicited an exasperated sniff from his daughter.

'I must confess, my thoughts were on the weather,' Jared apologised.

'The weather?' Camilla repeated incredulously, her vanity dented. 'Hardly a matter of immediate importance I should have thought.'

'On the contrary,' Jared returned patiently, 'to a seaman, the weather is always of paramount importance.'

'You're not at sea,' Camilla said crossly. Lady St Aubyn was finishing the last morsel of the confection of meringue, pureed fruit and whipped cream she had chosen for her dessert and so missed the exchange. A woman of hearty appetite and correspondingly large proportions, she allowed nothing to disturb her enjoyment of mealtimes. By simply ignoring everything but the blandest platitudes she created a little oasis of contentment and concentration around her which set her apart from the rest of the company. She replaced her spoon on the dish and touched her lips with her napkin, leaving it crumpled on the table beside her plate. A small sigh of satisfaction escaped her and she looked round the table, smiling happily.

St Aubyn smiled back at his wife, enjoying her enjoyment. Watching the unspoken communication, Jared felt a momentary pang of envy. He shifted his gaze to Camilla. Even sulking she was pretty. Though in time her voluptuous curves would expand into plumpness, she would still be pretty. Her silky hair, the colour of ripe wheat, was styled *à la sévigne*, drawn into a bun at the back of her head, with clusters of ringlets falling forward over each ear. Tiny rosettes of blue lace, each centred with a blue rosebud formed a band across her head and were woven among the bunched curls. The material of her dress and the rosebuds perfectly matched her eyes. Eyes which were directed upon him now, above a pert turned-up nose and a small, full-lipped mouth, itself reminiscent of a rosebud.

Jared smiled at her, a rueful smile, another though silent apology. He knew he was not good company and he knew Camilla was disappointed. Other than the perfunctory remarks demanded by etiquette, he had had almost nothing to say to her. As she watched her now he could see twin furrows mar the smoothness of her forehead, and a quizzical watchful look appeared in her eyes.

That Camilla had a brain he was well aware, it was simply that much of the time she chose not to employ it on anything more demanding than the design of her next ballgown and the colour of her accessories. But when she so wished, she could be remarkably astute, and it looked to Jared as though she had decided to expand some mental energy upon him.

With considerable relief he heard Lady St Aubyn suggesting to her daughter that they withdraw to the lounge. Jared knew Camilla did not wish to go, but he also knew she would not flout convention and demand to stay.

Though on the few times they had dined together since being introduced by a mutual merchant banker friend, Jared had enjoyed St Aubyn's company, tonight he would gladly have foregone the port and cigar ritual. He was restless and un-settled. Like all seamen he had an instinctive weathersense, and he was not happy about the force of the wind which hurled rain like handfuls of pebbles against the curtained windows. It had backed round to the north-west and that meant that tide and wind would be against each other.

'Jared?' Incisive and impatient, Camilla's tone pierced his thoughts as she and her mother pushed back their chairs. He got up quickly and assisted Camilla to her feet, placing her lacy stole about her shoulders. As his fingers brushed the milk-white skin, he was reminded vividly of other skin, golden and hot to the touch beneath a simple lawn shift. Framed not by lace but by a rough and dirty blanket.

His face remained immobile but Camilla, her woman's intuition signalling trouble, laid her soft hand on his sleeve, and with the instant change of mood which was so appealing a part of her character, she whispered:

'I think we must talk soon, Jared.'

When the ladies had disappeared in a rustle of crinolines, the men seated themselves in the smoking room. With a glass of port before them and cigars lit and drawing evenly, St Aubyn studied Jared for a few moments.

'All that stuff about the weather didn't fool me,' he began without preamble, 'Your mind hasn't been present for at least half the meal.' Jared looked up quickly, but St Aubyn continued, 'Have you got business problems, my boy?'

Jared liked the austere-looking man who sat opposite him. The aquiline features and thin build belied a dry sense of humour and a generous nature, whose warmth was concentrated on the wife he adored and his beloved only daughter. The eyes that met Jared's were friendly and concerned.

'No more than usual, sir.' He shook his head. 'Shipping is fraught with problems. Cargoes to be found, delivery dates to be met, repairs to the ships, crews to be employed or dismissed, the list is endless. But,' he shrugged and smiled, 'they are an inherent part of the business and one accepts them. My thoughts really were on the weather, though that is a poor excuse for my bad manners. I have to take a ship back to Falmouth tonight.'

St Aubyn leaned back comfortably in his chair and drew on his cigar.

'How many ships do you have at the moment?'

'Since this afternoon, four,' Jared answered promptly and with a certain pride. 'I picked up a bargain at the auction, not new, but basically sound.'

'The other ships,' St Aubyn said. 'Where are they and what are they doing?' Though the words were peremptory the tone was not, and Jared sensed that St Aubyn was not asking out of idle curiosity. Curious to know what lay behind the older man's interest, Jared answered without hesitation.

'My best clipper schooner, *Seawind*, is a fruit trader. She carries pineapples from the West Indies, melons from Spain and Portugal, oranges and lemons from the Azores and the western Mediterranean.'

St Aubyn looked thoughtful. 'To be a fruit trader a vessel has to be classified A1 at Lloyds, doesn't she?'

Jared masked a smile. St Aubyn had obviously been doing some homework.

'That's right. Only the very best are used in the fruit trade.'

'Don't the fruit traders have some sort of special protection?'

Jared was nonplussed for a moment, then it dawned.

'Not just fruit traders, all southern water ships are protected by a felt and yellow metal sheath. If they are built specifically for fruit though, they are usually sheathed at or just after launching.'

'Does this sheath cover the whole body of the ship?'

'No, only the hull from the load waterline down to the keel.'
St Aubyn swallowed half his port.

'Explain to me how it's done,' he ordered.

Jared sipped his own port and drew on his cigar. 'After caulking, the hull is tarred heavily and wide strips of felt soaked in tar are moulded onto it. Then light gauge yellow metal sheets are pressed on top of the tarred felt and secured with copper nails.' Jared shrugged. 'That's it, except that I had the metal painted over with green copper anti-fouling as well.'

St Aubyn looked dubious. 'I must say on top of the capital outlay for the ship, it sounds rather expensive. Is it really necessary?'

Jared laughed and tapped the ash from his cigar. 'If it wasn't done, the hull would be drilled through and the ship ruined within one month.'

St Aubyn's eyebrows rose in surprise and he looked puzzled.

'Marine animals, jiggers, worms, barnacles and the like,' Jared explained. The Med is full of them and they have hearty appetites for unprotected wooden hulls.'

'So if a ship is protected by this sheath, she can go anywhere in the world, but if not, she's restricted to home waters?'

'That's right,' Jared nodded. 'I have two more topsail schooners. They were originally fruit traders too, but they lost their classification through old age,' Jared grinned, 'so I had them reclassified and they are now on salt-fish. Exporting dried cod from Newfoundland,' he explained.

'Where do they take this fish?' St Aubyn was absorbed.

'One goes to Portugal, Spain, Italy or Greece, the other to Brazil or the British West Indies.'

'Once the ships have unloaded the fish, what do they do then?'

'My brokers try to have cargoes waiting for transport to England.'

'What sort of cargoes?'

'*Seaspray* brings back general cargo from the Med. It could be marble from Leghorn, or wine from Spain, even currants from Portugal. *Seabird* carries hides from the Rio Grande.'

'I notice all your schooners have a 'sea' prefix to their names,' St Aubyn observed with a hint of amusement.

'It's good business, sir,' Jared replied evenly. 'I'm building up a fleet of deep water traders. I've invested everything I've got in them. They are all good sound ships, registered and classified.

But I'm in competition with other owners with bigger fleets and greater capital, and perhaps more contacts among merchants with cargoes to sell.' He shrugged almost off-handedly. 'I want my ships to be remembered.'

St Aubyn wasn't misled by the apparent casualness of his guest. Ambition burned brightly in Jared Carlyon.

'Why use schooners on the Atlantic trades, surely bigger ships would be more profitable?'

Jared shook his head.

'Not necessarily. Of course it depends on the destination of the cargo, also its point of origin. For example, if we are talking about fish from Labrador, that will have been brought down to the large ports of Harbour Grace or St John's only partially processed. Now, if its destination is the hot South American ports, it will be packed in salt-bulk in drums. Then the merchants use brokers to hire ships of anything up to 1,000 tons to carry that particular cargo. But the fish going to the Mediterranean countries is simply carried as loose cargo. Big ships can't get into the little ports, harbours and inlets along the Newfoundland coast, where each settlement catches and processes its own fish, so this is where the smaller schooners have the great advantage.'

He smiled and leaned forward to tap more ash from his cigar. 'In fact the schooner's arrival at the settlement to collect the fish is the event of the year, and an excuse for a terrific party.'

'Mmmmmmm.' The social life of Newfoundland villagers was obviously not of interest to St Aubyn, who appeared deep in thought.

'Tell me, Carlyon, what rate of cargo is lost through spoilage, on the small ships, I mean.'

'Virtually none, sir. Unless the ship is actually lost, which, thank God, is rare. Only highly classed vessels are used in this trade. It's so exacting the ships need to be in really good condition. Merchants simply won't risk using lower grade ships. It's the same in the fruit trade. As far as the fish is concerned, given a sound ship, the condition of the cargo on arrival depends on the dunnaging.'

'The er . . .?' St Aubyn's eyebrows rose once more.

'The way in which it is packed in the hold.'

St Aubyn, finishing his port and pouring himself another glass, gestured Jared to continue. He offered the decanter but Jared shook his head.

'First, lengths of small trees, known as longering or longhirst, are laid on the floors of the hold, then spruce brushwood is laid on top of that to a depth of six inches or nine inches in the bilges. Lastly strips of bark called ranes or rinds are placed on the brushwood and the fish lies on top of that, dry and well-aired.' St Aubyn nodded.

'How many trips do your fish schooners make in a year?'

'Only one, sir.'

'Indeed?' St Aubyn registered surprise. 'Would not a bigger ship be able to make more? If you concentrated on the South American route, you would surely double your profits. Seems sound economics to me.'

Jared's smile did not waver at the implied criticism, but his eyes narrowed, the soft amber becoming topaz-hard.

'With respect, sir, you are making a common mistake in assuming that bigger is automatically more lucrative. This does not apply in shipping. I make no apology for being a schooner man,' he said softly. 'In my opinion there has never been a better all-round trading vessel devised than the topsail schooner. Nothing can touch one for economy, speed, power or handling. They are as good in restricted or sheltered waters as they are deep sea, which makes them ideal trading vessels either in home or foreign waters.' Jared warmed to his theme, his voice becoming more resonant.

'They can sail off the wind as well as any square-rigger of similar size, yet can give the square-rigger a point or more in sailing on the wind—'

'Enough,' St Aubyn laughed, raising his hands in mock surrender, 'you grow too technical for me.' His smile faded and a purposeful expression replaced it. 'I stand corrected. Obviously you know the shipping business far better than I do. In fact, I know very little about it.' He leaned back in his chair surveying Jared. 'Which brings me to the reason for these questions. You have already realised that they were not simply idle curiosity, and you have shown great forebearance with what might have appeared to a less astute man mere passing interest or even impertinence.'

Jared inclined his head, accepting the compliment as his due. He had indeed realised that something lay behind the aristocrat's interest, but had not defined what it was.

'As you are no doubt aware, I am a wealthy man,' St Aubyn

said quietly. 'I have property all over Cornwall, and my invest-
ments in the county's tin and copper mines have paid handsome
dividends.' There was no trace of pride or boastfulness in these
statements, St Aubyn was simply setting out facts.

'But foreign competition is closing the Cornish mines, and I
do not feel inclined either to buy shares in some foreign enter-
prise, or to prop up some last ditch stand by mine owners who
refuse to face economic facts. Which means,' he smiled disarm-
ingly, 'I have a large amount of money to invest, and I have
decided to invest in shipping.'

There was a moment's silence. St Aubyn, still smiling awaited
Jared's reaction. Jared, meanwhile, was well aware that St
Aubyn was no empty-headed aristocrat, relying on Agents and
Advisors, or gambling with his money, but a hard-headed
businessman with a keen nose for profit. There were other shipowners in Truro and in Falmouth with bigger fleets and greater
experience. So why was St Aubyn interested in his small venture?

Though Jared was proud of his ships and the business he was
building, he was realist enough to know that it was still in its
infancy. There were others far better established, Sir Henry
Trevellyan for one. Why was St Aubyn interested in him rather
than Trevellyan, or Carne of Falmouth, Stephens at Point, or
Ferris? Like an iceberg nine-tenths of St Aubyn's plan was still
below the surface. He would commit himself to nothing until
more was revealed. Jared showed nothing but polite interest.

'May I congratulate you on your foresight, sir,' he said with
sincerity. 'There is no doubt that with the rising demand for
foreign goods, new trade agreements and the increasing opportunities to sell our own products abroad, shipping is a very wise
investment. Might I ask how active a part you intend to take in
the business, sir and which aspect interests you most?'

This was not the reaction Richard St Aubyn had expected.
Taken aback by Jared's attitude of total non-commitment and
also by the questions, he was for once lost for words.

'Which aspect? Ah, well . . . I . . . er.'

Jared grinned inwardly at the other's confusion. Though he
liked and respected St Aubyn as a man, he resented patronage,
and it pleased him to see the aristocrat disconcerted.

'Yes, sir, which aspect? For example, do you intend to buy
vessels and find your own masters to sail them? You would of

course require surveys to be done and classifications to be registered, depending on where you wished to trade. Would you employ Agents to deal with the merchants and find cargoes for your ships, and charter out your ships for the cargoes available, or would you prefer to brave the Exchange yourself? Again bidding for cargoes would depend on the classification of the ships you bought, also on the qualifications of the master. Certificates of servitude are acceptable for older masters with command experience but the Merchant Shipping Acts, which are coming into force, require masters to have different qualifications to command different sizes of ship.'

St Aubyn's characteristically bland expression began to change. Jared went on relentlessly:

'Of course there are expedients to deal with this situation, but they do become complicated. Or perhaps you wish to invest in a yard and be involved with actual ship-building or repair and maintenance. Naturally, the most successful of those are family concerns, where fathers and sons have specialised and handed down their skills for generations. As a matter of fact, repair and maintenance are breaking away from ship-bulding and becoming a separate, specialist industry. Again for either one, unless you intend to install a manager, and it certainly isn't easy to find a reliable, fully experienced man, you would need to aquaint yourself with the techniques of survey and classification, plus the business side of yard management, also brokerage. . . .'

'That will do.' St Aubyn's face was thunderous and his voice was icy. 'Do not presume to patronise me, young man.'

'You misunderstand me, sir,' Jared replied calmly. 'My intention was simply to aquaint you with the many different facets of the shipping business.'

'Your intentions,' St Aubyn returned with irony, 'whatever else they may be are certainly not simple. However, you may rest assured that you have given me a more comprehensive picture of shipping than I previously possessed, and I'm obliged to you for the instruction.' He sniffed.

'My pleasure entirely,' Jared murmured, maintaining a straight face with some difficulty. St Aubyn's next words disorientated him once more.

'Camilla is my only child,' St Aubyn said softly. There was a note of sadness in his voice. The remark was followed by a pause, and Jared wondered if a response from him was expected. But St Aubyn went on, speaking almost to himself.

'I should have liked a son. Matter of pride perhaps, carrying on the family name and all that. Still, it would have been. . . .' He caught himself and continued briskly, 'But Camilla is a fine girl, a bit headstrong, spoilt, there's no doubt about it. But she has a brain, make no mistake, Carlyon. She doesn't bother to use it very often, but it's there. She has a fine pedigree.'

Jared was struck once more by the aristocracy's penchant for discussing the lineage of their wives and offspring as if they were bloodstock. The thought amused him. Perhaps in effect, that is exactly what they are. But he was totally at a loss as to where St Aubyn was leading him. What was he up to? Did he intend to try and interest Camilla in the shipping business? Jared knew Camilla was intelligent and her brain could be remarkably astute when it suited her, but Camilla in shipping? He had a vivid picture of sails trimmed with lace, ribbons round the mast and flowers on the windlass. He shook his head. No the idea just didn't hold water. God, what a pun. His tiredness was beginning to show.

He wondered what the weather was like now. Had the storm worsened? He desperately wanted to look at his watch, but to do so before St Aubyn had finished his exposition would invite further sarcastic comment, and Jared had no wish to offend, nor to be reprimanded for his bad manners a second time that evening.

St Aubyn was still speaking, and Jared pulled himself together in time to hear the word 'wife'.

'I beg your pardon, sir, I didn't catch that.'

'Really?' St Aubyn said drily, well aware that Jared's attention had wandered, as indeed he intended that it should. He wanted an honest reaction from the young man who very early in his business career had obviously learned not to reveal his thoughts or emotions.

'I said, for the man able to handle her, she'll make a very good wife.'

Jared's mind was playing tricks on him. He had another sudden mental vision. But it was not of Camilla, her plump, pretty face dimpled in a smile beneath a stylish coiffure and her elegant crinolined dress, with its lace-edged decolletage, shimmering in the firelight. His vision was of a tumbling confusion of midnight hair, twisted into an untidy knot; a wet, torn russet brown dress, flashing green eyes and a disdainfully curled lip uttering scornfully, 'Oh, a Falmouth man.' He banished the vision. A man would have to be a complete lunatic to even consider marrying that, and he considered himself the sanest man he knew.

'Not me,' he said with utter conviction.

'I beg your pardon, sir?' St Aubyn's voice was shocked and icy. Jared cursed himself for a careless, thoughtless fool.

'Please forgive me, sir. I meant no disrespect.' Jared felt sweat trickle down his sides. The devil take that damned girl. Why did she keep coming back to haunt him? She was nothing, a nobody. She meant trouble, and trouble was something he could do without. He had enough problems in his life already.

'Camilla is a fine young woman,' Jared said in all sincerity. 'She has beauty, wit, style and grace.' St Aubyn looked slightly mollified. 'She also has a fortune, which is something I do not. My business is young, I am just starting. A man in my position has nothing to offer a young woman like Camilla.' Had he covered his gaffe? St Aubyn gave him a penetrating stare.

'You catalogue her virtues readily enough.'

'Sir, I have seen them all for myself in our short acquaintance.'

'And her vices?'

Jared smiled. 'Too strong a term for the indulgences afforded a beautiful, adored, only child.'

St Aubyn inclined his head.

'Had you your own fortune, and were able to approach my daughter on level financial terms, would you consider yourself equal to her?'

'Sir, in those circumstances, I should consider myself her superior,' Jared said evenly. St Aubyn's brows lifted but he remained silent. There was a slight pause then Jared spoke lightly but firmly.

'But as I seek no fortune save that I make for myself, I have never presumed to consider myself a contender for Camilla's hand in marriage.'

'Do you fence?' St Aubyn asked suddenly.

Jared was surprised. 'No.'

'You should,' St Aubyn returned drily, then continued, 'you have established, with great tact, I may add, that you are not after my daughter's money.' St Aubyn smiled, a genuine smile of real warmth. 'If I had entertained the slightest suspicion that you were, then this conversation would never have taken place.'

'It has been most interesting, sir, and I appreciate your frankness,' Jared said and yielded to the temptation to look at his watch. 'Perhaps we should rejoin the ladies. I fear my preoccupation with business matters this evening has already caused your daughter some annoyance, and I must take my leave soon.' He leaned forward, about to rise from his chair but St Aubyn put out a hand to stay him.

'No doubt she'll survive, and I have one more thing to say.' He sat very straight, holding Jared's gaze, pursuing his mouth as he searched for the words he wanted.

'You are an honest man, Carlyon, and a proud one. You want to make your own way in the world and owe thanks to no one. I admire that. But why make life more difficult than it need be? Camilla wants you, she has made that quite clear, without saying as much. I am fed up with fighting my way through the rich chinless wonders and the penniless fortune hunters who buzz around my daughter like wasps around jam.' He rubbed his hands together and looked at them for a moment, then returned his gaze to Jared's face. 'I'll speak plainly and ask you to forgive my bluntness. Marry my daughter and make her happy, Carlyon, and I'll invest £50,000 in your fleet, for you to use as you think best.'

Jared felt the colour drain from his face then flood back. Now it all made sense. The sounding out, the questions, the seemingly unconnected leaps in the conversation. Why had he not realised? He must be more tired than he knew. How could he not have read the signs?

'Sir, I . . . I don't know what to say,' he stammered, 'except,' he added hastily, 'you do me a great honour, a very great honour. I am hardly—'

'Oh spare me any claptrap about not being worthy,' St Aubyn broke in, raising both hands. 'If I didn't think you worthy, I should not have put the idea to you.'

Jared's mind was racing. What an opportunity, what an alliance. He had the beginnings of a very profitable business. With that kind of capital investment he could open his own yard, build his own ships. The names of craftsmen, sawyers, shipwrights sprang into his mind. Money breeds money, and with aristocratic connections as well, there was no limit to what he could achieve. He was fond of Camilla, she amused him. She would make an excellent wife, would give him healthy children, and provided her social life was not unduly curtailed by domesticity she would cause him not a moment's concern.

From every angle it was an excellent proposition. St Aubyn, like himself, was a man of his word and no contract could be more binding than his hand on the matter.

'Well?' St Aubyn smiled, amusement at the younger man's obvious shock curving his lips. But as he realised that Jared was not immediately going to accept his offer, the smile faded and a certain quizzical expression took its place.

'Sir, I'm overwhelmed,' Jared murmured. Why was he not seizing the gift offered him? What held him back from grasping St Aubyn's hand and putting the seal on a secure and successful future? St Aubyn seemed to sense something of the struggle taking place in the younger man. He knew full well that most men of his acquaintance would have seized the opportunity without a second thought, would have said yes before the words were out of his mouth. That Jared Carlyon had not increased the respect St Aubyn felt for him.

'As a proud father, I fail to understand your hesitation.' Jared made as if to speak, but St Aubyn forestalled him, 'Equally, from a business point of view there would appear to be reason for your reluctance, but I accept that you might require a little time to consider the matter.' His tone implied that while he accepted it he certainly didn't understand it.

'You are most gracious, sir, and your forebearance is more than I deserve.' Jared rose to his feet and St Aubyn followed suit. 'I am bound for Falmouth on the midnight tide. I have to get the newest member of my fleet down to Carne's yard by the morning,' Jared said.

'And we leave for London first thing in the morning. There is a bill going through the House on which I must speak. We return in a week. Perhaps you will have reached a decision by then?' St Aubyn was every inch the aristocrat. No hint of his thoughts or wishes disturbed the calm urbanity of his expression. Jared knew he could learn much from this man, also that he would prove an invaluable ally in the cut-throat world of business.

'Perhaps you would do me the honour of dining with me in

Falmouth on your return, sir. I promise you an answer by that time.'

St Aubyn nodded, then paused. 'No, wait, I've a better idea.' There was a glint in his eye. 'I'm to attend the Beating the Bounds ceremonies here in Truro to mark the limits of the town's territorial waters. A special ceremony has been arranged to celebrate the visit to Cornwall of the Prince and Princess of Wales. There is to be a boat trip along the boundary with Falmouth's waters, returning to Truro in the evening with dinner at Tregothnan Boat House. I am attending at the express invitation of the Mayor and Burgesses of Truro. They too are aware that I have capital to invest,' he smiled ironically, 'and are keen to advance the interest of Truro, and keep that upstart port of Falmouth in its place. You will be my guest.' There was more command than invitation in the request.

'*Touché*,' murmured Jared, perfectly aware that his appearance at the function would be on a par with Daniel inviting the lions to dinner. He was also aware that this was St Aubyn's way of extracting payment for being kept waiting for his answer.

'It will be an honour and a pleasure, sir,' Jared replied calmly.

They made their way from the smoking room along the passage to one of the withdrawing rooms, where Lady St Aubyn nibbled sweetmeats while her daughter created a small hurricane, such was the speed and force with which she minipulated her fan. As the two men entered she jumped to her feet.

'What on earth have you been doing? We've been sitting here for simply ages. It's been so boring,' she pouted, looking like a beautiful child.

'We've been discussing business, and had you stayed you would have been even more bored.' St Aubyn patted his daughter's cheek. 'Now I fear Captain Carlyon must leave us, he has much to attend to.'

Camilla's face fell, and her rosebud mouth trembled. She looked from her father to Jared and back again. Then not seeing what she sought, she stamped one satin-slippered foot in exasperation and whirled around.

'I am going to retire,' she announced, and she was gone. Lady St Aubyn beamed up at Jared.

'Such a high-spirited girl,' she sighed, 'but marriage will calm her. I remember when I was her age—'

'Yes, my dear.' St Aubyn placed an arm around her shoulders, cutting off her reminiscences with gentle tact, 'I also remember when you were her age.' His voice was tender, and as she looked up at her husband, a shine in her eyes and the warmth of a blush on her cheek, Jared saw for an instant the girl St Aubyn had married, and the love they still shared.

He felt again a quick, sharp pang of envy, then derided himself for a sentimental fool.

'Sir, Ma'am, your hospitality has been most generous, but I fear my behaviour this evening has left much to be desired.' Jared smiled apologetically, and taking Lady St Aubyn's hand bowed over it, 'My sincere apologies, Ma'am.'

'Oh, you silly boy,' she beamed. 'I expect you've got a lot on your mind. Pay no heed to Camilla, she's just cross because you spent time talking to my husband instead of her. It will do her no harm.'

'Sir,' Jared shook hands with St Aubyn. 'A safe journey and a safe return.'

'I shall see you on the twentieth. Meet me here at six.' In St Aubyn's anticipatory smile Jared saw that, regardless of his decision, St Aubyn was looking forward with relish to the hornets' nest their appearance together would stir up.

A liveried footman touched his cap. 'Cab, sir?' Jared looked up as the wind snatched his hair.

'No. No thank you.'

He drew in a lung-full of the cool night air. The squall had passed, and though drops of rain still fell intermittently, splattering on to the shiny wet cobbles, and plopping into the granite courses at the roadside, now flowing fast, swollen with rain-water and debris, Jared knew he would have time to walk to the dock before the next squall arrived.

He needed the physical exertion of a swift walk. He needed to rid himself of the tightness behind his eyes, of the tension knotting the muscles of his shoulders and neck.

He crossed Boscawen Street and prudently avoided the narrow alley between the Town Hall and Thomas Daniell's Mansion House. Though providing a short cut to the quays, it was at night the haunt of thieves and drunks, and was used by prostitutes with nowhere else to entertain their clients.

Jared strode down lower Lemon Street towards the bridge. The hissing glow of the lone gas lamp fell upon his tall figure and as he passed the shadowed doorways whores beckoned, coaxing or pleading in hoarse whispers, offering love for the price of a tumbler of gin. Their crude invitations barely masked the urgent desperation to embrace the oblivion provided by the juniper flavoured spirit.

As Jared walked on giving no sign of having heard them, which indeed he scarcely had, so involved was he in his own thoughts, the pleas and whispers became catcalls and curses, which in their turn died away to hopeless silence.

Jared reached Lemon Bridge, and holding his breath against the putrid, gut-wrenching stench which rose from the accumulated sewage behind the sluice gate, he hurried across and turned on to Lemon Quay. The wind had broken up the clouds and was hurling them angrily across the sky. Through a gap Jared glimpsed a pale three-quarter moon.

The schooner floated high on the filth-laden water, tugging restlessly at her warps. Jared felt a tingle of pleasure as he looked at her. She might be old and she was badly in need of repair, but her lines were those of a thoroughbred. For the same price he could have bought a half-completed hull from John Stephens, but something about this boat had caught his attention, fired his imagination, and despite his surveyor's report he had followed his instinct and bought her. A few weeks in Charlie Carne's yard at Falmouth Bar and she would be ready to join *Seaspray* running salt-fish to the Mediterranean countries. She would be reclassified and reregistered in her new name, a name proclaiming the spell she had cast over him, *Seawitch*.

5

The wind's keen edge cut through Jared's elegant coat and he shivered. He was tired. His normally well-ordered mind disrupted and confused by the day's events, he considered postponing moving the schooner until the morning and indulging himself in a good night's sleep in a soft bed in one of the good hotels. The thought was truly tempting.

But, he reminded himself, if he gave in to it, the eight hours' sleep he gained would cost him two days' work on the schooner which would still have to be paid for. He sighed and stepped on to the gangplank.

From the top of the quay he heard his name hailed. Turning, by the light of the gas lamp he saw George Laity coming down the quay. His heavy jacket and thick trousers tucked into leather boots a far more suitable outfit for the night's journey than the beautifully tailored suit Jared wore. Laity had a small bundle under his arm which he thrust towards Jared.

''Tis a 'ot pasty, sir. The wife sent ut to 'e. She be some glad I got work seein' as 'ow so many abn. She was so feared we'd 'ave to move from 'ome. And, well . . .' he kicked some stones off the quay into the water, 'I told 'er what you said, 'bout the grievin'. She cried. 'Tis the first time I seen 'er weep since . . . 'tis a good sign, sir,' he finished gruffly, and pushed the parcel, wrapped in ragged but snowy white linen, into Jared's hands. Jared looked at the man before him who was staring in any direction but at his Captain, then he looked at the small parcel in his hands, whose warmth he could feel through the cloth wrapping.

'Thank you,' he said simply.

Laity nodded once, closing the subject.

'I got crew, Cap'n. Both schooner men wanting to git back to Falmouth.' Jared glanced over Laity's shoulder at the two men shambling down the quay. Their shoulders were hunched inside their jackets and hands shoved deep in their pockets. Well, at least they could walk, Jared thought as the smell of drink reached him ahead of the two shuffling figures.

Jared eyed the two men who stopped just behind Laity. Both were dirty and unshaven. Jared raised an eyebrow.

'Their names, Mr Laity?'

'This is Joseph Glasson, of Penryn,' Laity indicated a small wiry man with bowed legs whose heavy jacket looked too large for his thin frame.

'Glasson,' Jared nodded at the man.

'Cap'n,' Glasson muttered, returning the nod. Then without warning he burst into a paroxysm of coughing that threatened to rupture his lungs. When it was over he wiped his mouth with the back of a hand which shook uncontrollably.

Jared said nothing, merely glancing at Laity who shrugged. Then he looked at the other man. Short and thickset with a woollen cap pulled low over his forehead revealing lank, greasy hair curling over his collar, something about him sounded a warning note in Jared's mind. Wherever there was trouble this one would be in the thick of it.

'Your name?' Jared was abrupt.

'Pascoe, James Arthur Pascoe, Cap'n sir.' The words were slurred and the tone hovered between arrogance and contempt.

Jared decided to ignore it. The man obviously had a chip on his shoulder about something. He turned to the Mate.

'We're going to have to warp her over to the weather side of the river, otherwise it will mean a tow and that would take too long, even if we could hire a gig, which in this Godforsaken place is doubtful. I want Glasson to go across to Back Quay while you loose the forward ropes and let her head come round. Pascoe can watch the after ropes and free her stern when you've passed the forrard ones to Glasson. Then he can winch her across on the farthest bollard.'

'Beggin' your pardon, sir,' Laity murmured, glancing round at the two men, 'but would it suit better if I went on the quay and let Glasson 'andle the warps on board?'

Jared's voice was cool. 'No, Mr Laity, it would not. I'm not running a charity. If Glasson is taking my money he'll do whatever he's told to do, otherwise he has no business here.'

'Aye, sir.' Laity gave a half salute, which elicited a snort of derision from Pascoe.

'Did you say something, Pascoe?' Jared's tone was icy.

'No,' the other growled, staring out over the water.

'That's just as well because I will not tolerate trouble among my crew, and while I pay you, you are my crew, and I expect the job to be done well and quickly in accordance with any instructions I, or Mr Laity, may give you. Do I make myself clear?'

'Aye,' came the reluctant grunt.

'I beg your pardon?' Jared's tone froze by a further two degrees.

'Aye, Cap'n.'

'Then get to it.' Jared stepped aside and let Pascoe on to the gangplank. Glasson was already shuffling off along the quay towards the bridge. His eyes still on Pascoe, Jared lowered his voice.

'That's the best you could get?' Laity shrugged.

'They was all I could get, sir. No one wants a short trip. Them as lives 'ere says the cost of getting back wouldn't make it worthwhile. They two is both desperate to git 'ome to Falmouth. Unless I'm mistaken Glasson 'ave got lung fever, and 'twouldn' surprise me if Pascoe be wanted by the law.'

Jared raised his eyes to the heavens but refrained from comment. He started up the gangplank with Laity close behind.

'Sir, I do b'lieve Cap'n Trudgeon left an old reefer in the chest at the end of 'is bunk. You'll need un afore the night's out.'

'Thanks,' Jared nodded and strode aft along the deck to the companionway hatch, unlocked it and went down the stairs. As he entered the day room, just for an instant he thought of Harlyn. But no sooner had the thought formed than he banished it, a frown drawing his brows together and darkening his tawny eyes.

He placed the linen-wrapped pasty on the table, a brief smile softening the angular planes of his face. Then lighting the lamp he collected the jacket, carefully avoiding looking at the bunk, and was out of the sleeping cabin in moments. The reefer, impregnated with the familiar smells of tar, salt water and tobacco smoke wasn't too bad a fit. Jared remounted the stairs, leaving the small lamp lit and secured to the shelf by a hook. He went aft to the wheel.

Pascoe had loosed the stern mooring ropes, and as the schooner's head came round, her bowsprit missing by inches the brig moored to the opposite quay, Jared saw Laity in the bows toss the coiled rope across the few feet of dark water to Glasson who hurried in a half-stumbling run towards the bollard. The rope fell several yards ahead of Glasson and began slipping back off the quay into the water. Jared held his breath. If Glasson didn't reach it in time, the schooner would head downstream then back towards the quay to which her stern was still tied.

Glasson reached the rope as the last few feet were disappearing over the stone quay. The speed with which he looped it around the iron bollard spoke of long experience, but Jared could see his shoulders heaving and hear the racking cough above the gusting wind as Glasson winched the schooner across the narrow stretch of black water.

'Let go the stern rope,' Jared shouted over his shoulder to Pascoe, and felt the schooner's stern begin to swing out into the river.

'Get that rope in quickly, Pascoe. Mr Laity, on to the quay for the stern rope,' Jared shouted.

Laity raised a hand in acknowledgement. There was still a dark strip of water between the bow and the quay when Laity leapt, landing several feet down the quay from Glasson. He ran down the rough stones towards a huge iron ring set in granite.

'Pascoe, heave that stern rope over,' Jared ordered, putting the wheel hard over to use what little way the ship had to bring her stern around. There was no reply, and when he looked round, Pascoe had the soaking wet rope not in coils but in a jumbled heap.

'Get it over, man,' Jared shouted urgently.

Pascoe grunted and heaved the mass of rope over the side. For an instant it looked as though it would miss the quay entirely. But Laity dived forward and snatched the tangled loops dragging them through the iron ring before they could slip free.

As the two men on the quay pulled the schooner into her new position facing down the river, Jared turned to Pascoe, his face as bleak as blasted rock, his voice cold and determined.

'Make no mistake, Pascoe, if there are any more "accidents", you'll go overboard.' To make certain the man understood him, in level tones Jared finished quietly, 'And I'll be the one who pushes you. Now get forrard and take Glasson's place. I want Mr Laity free to make sail.'

As Jared walked forward to the bow of the schooner to check the windlass and anchor, in the dark stuffy compartment beneath his feet, Harlyn stirred, moving uneasily on the hard forms. But her exhaustion was so great that the changing sounds and unfamiliar movement of the ship did not awaken her.

Inspection completed, Jared returned to the stern, checking the positions of his small crew. Glasson was back on board, in the bows, ready to pull inboard the warps as they were freed. Pascoe was on the quay, and Laity by the foremast.

Jared glanced at the sky. The clouds had piled up once more and lay like a thick, heavy blanket above his head, rumpled and angry. A few spots of rain hit his face, trickling down, leaving cold tracks where they had been.

He turned his head and sniffed the wind. It had come round slightly and now blew from the north-west, carrying with it the stench of the town. Jared knew that when the tide turned the sluice gates by Lemon Bridge would be opened and the day's accumulated sewage would be released to be carried down the river to the sea. Except that it rarely got that far. Instead, as the tide receded, the foul mess was stranded on the mud banks and in the narrow channels, polluting the water and beaches and choking the dying river still further.

Jared took out his watch, tilting it so as to see by the light of the gas lamp on the quay.

'I'm not waiting for the turn, Mr Laity. I don't want this cursed stink following us all the way down river. The wind is almost on our beam and strong enough to counter the last few minutes of the up-tide. Set her free.' Jared purposely did not give the Mate instructions for setting the sails, waiting instead to see if the man's eye for wind and water conditions was all he had been led to believe.

'Let go forrard,' Laity shouted to Pascoe, and began sheeting home the lower topsail as Pascoe slipped the rope from the bollard and ran down the quay. Glasson began heaving the rope in over the gunwale, coiling it as it came.

'Let go aft,' yelled Laity, and as the rope snaked across the widening gap Pascoe jumped back on board. As the wind caught and filled the triangular sail, Laity ordered Glasson to hoist the foresail and while he did so Jared spun the wheel and the schooner eased away from the quay and out into the channel.

'Pascoe,' shouted Laity, waving with an outstretched arm as the wind tore the words away, 'get up here.'

Jared rested his hands lightly on the wheel, testing its play and the response of the vessel to his movements. He watched Pascoe slouch past and sidle crabwise along the deck. Unable to hear Laity's instructions, Jared watched Glasson and Pascoe set the inner and outer jib, then the mainsail.

As the wind filled the spread canvas, the schooner seemed to gather herself together. Picking up speed and heeling slightly, she sliced through the dark, rippling water.

They passed the timber pounds and warehouses which sprawled all along the bank of the river. They reached Sunny Corner and Jared saw the black shape of a half-completed vessel on the stocks of William Withell's boatyard. Other boats in various stages of repair lay high on the bank or floated alongside the small quay. All seemed deserted. There were no human sounds to break the silence, only the creak of the spars, the slap of water on the hull as the schooner moved down the river, and the wind keening in the rigging and sighing in the woods above the river bank.

Laity joined Jared at the wheel. 'How do 'ee find 'er Cap'n?' he shouted above the wind.

Jared grinned, his teeth gleaming white in the darkness. 'She handles well. Yes, I'd say she's fair.'

'Go on, Cap'n, 'andsome she is. Know the river, do 'ee?'

Jared shook his head. 'I've studied the chart, but I've not sailed these waters.'

'Well, sir,' Laity put his mouth close to Jared's ear, 'with a nor'wester, Cap'n Trudgeon used to tack at Lambe Creek and again at Malpas Point. Gave us a beam wind then fer Mopus Reach.'

Jared nodded. 'See to it then, Mr Laity.'

'Aye, Cap'n.' Laity moved catfooted down the deck, pushed along by the force of the wind. The manoeuvres were completed without incident, both Glasson and Pascoe responding quickly to the Mate's orders. Laity came aft. Standing alongside Jared he looked up at the taut, full canvas.

'Must be making five or six knots, Cap'n. Us'll be down along Falmouth in no time 't all. Like to get yer 'ead down for a bit, would 'e? You do look buggered, beggin' yer pardon, sir.'

Jared grinned, feeling the strain around his eyes and in the back of his neck. He had been concentrating hard, the river was unfamiliar to him, and transferring the information on a chart to the reality of a winding stretch of water in the darkness, took great mental effort. He let go the wheel, stepping aside.

'She's yours, Mr Laity. Don't hesitate to call me if you feel it necessary.'

'Aye, Cap'n.' Laity moved forward at once, his hands replacing Jared's. He drew himself up proudly.

Jared masked a smile as he made his way to the companionway hatch. He knew full well that nothing short of a typhoon would induce Laity to call him. The Cornishman's pride was such that he would run himself ragged proving the Captain's faith in him was justified.

The mouthwatering aroma of the hot pasty filled the Day room, but Jared was too tired to feel hungry, and was also still satisfied by the meal he had consumed at the Red Lion. He paused for an instant as he heard the mate's voice raised above the wind, then the snap and crack of canvas and the squeal of ropes through the blocks as the mizzen was set. A tiny frown appeared between his brows. That was a fair amount of canvas they were carrying, especially in this wind. He considered questioning Laity's decision, then thought better of it. If he queried every move the Mate made, the man's confidence would soon be undermined and resentment would take its place. Best to leave things as they were. Besides, boats were like people, each having its own idiosyncrasies. Some responded better in heavy weather with more canvas set, others with less. Laity knew the schooner and he knew the river, Jared did not. Anyway, he was simply too tired to climb back up the stairs to the deck. The frown smoothed out and he yawned hugely, stretching his aching shoulders.

He lay down on the bunk without even bothering to remove the reefer, and within moments was deeply asleep. With his head to one side and mouth slightly open, the hard angles and planes of his face were softened and he looked strangely vulnerable.

Above him Laity was revelling in the feel of the schooner. She was like a live creature, responding to his lightest touch on the wheel. Contentment coursed through him. Cap'n Carlyon could rely on him. Yes, sir, he'd show him. Laity knew himself a fortunate man. Some captains were a law unto themselves, dictatorial and harsh. They treated their crew like slaves, keeping them short of proper food, overworking them, docking their pay at the slightest excuse. Secure in the knowledge that without a reference a man would have a hard time getting a berth.

He had been lucky, by God he had. Cap'n Trudgeon had been a hard master. He could remember one time he'd been asked by the crew to tell the Captain that in heavy weather rainwater and even sea water were pouring in through the fo'c'sle deckhead because of strained planks. The Captain's only reaction had been a sarcastic reminder that even a fool should know that a poker heated in the stove and drawn along the seams would melt the pitch and seal the leaks, and he had more important things to think about. But he had never kept them short of food. The frequent appearances of oranges, lemons and fresh vegetables on the mess table had ensured that none of Trudgeon's crew had ever suffered from spongy gums, nosebleeds and haemorrhages beneath the skin which characterised the dreaded and debilitating disease of sailors, scurvy.

Laity raised his eyes to the mastheads as a stronger gust hit the schooner. She answered immediately to his hold on the wheel, her head coming round a point into the wind. Like a woman she was, he mused, needed a gentle touch, and his thoughts went to his wife.

A pert, saucy little thing she'd been when he married her. They had both worked hard to make their tiny three-roomed cottage cosy and comfortable. With help from relatives who had donated unwanted furniture, odd bits of crockery and a few dreadful ornaments, they had transformed it into a home. How they'd scrimped and saved. Mary, as well as working down at the candle factory had taken a cleaning job, and he'd given her every penny of his pay.

He recalled the last few evenings before their wedding when he had polished the old brass bedstead inherited from Mary's gran, until it had shone like gold, the lamplight reflected in its burnished bars and knobs. Mary had put the last few stitches into the huge patchwork quilt stuffed with goose feathers. They had stolen glances at each other behind her mother's back. Hers shy, his burning, both so aware that soon, very soon they would lie together in that bed, between the crisp cotton sheets whose edges Mary had embroidered with an intricate design of leaves and flowers. Some of the cottons she had bought, and others she had begged from her uncle's tiny haberdashery shop.

Their wedding night, and the nights that followed had brought them joy and laughter. Their shyness with each other gradually fell away like discarded clothes, and as their knowledge of each grew, so did their happiness.

Then their first baby came along. Robert they called him. A strong, lusty boy, born quickly and easily. Though it had seemed to him, pacing the floor below, that the birth had taken forever. The midwife and Mary's mother had laughed at him. But Mary had understood the wetness in his eyes as he'd looked down at her and their babe, nuzzling at her swollen breast.

As the baby had grown so their love had deepened, mellowing from the all-consuming peaks of passion to the broader, gentler slopes of family caring and closeness. But when she had become pregnant a second time, things had changed.

Right from the start it had been different. Instead of the radiant glow of good health which had enveloped her during her first pregnancy, Mary had been pale and listless. Instead of her previous boundless energy, every action had seemed an effort. She became unusually quiet. Even the antics of young Robert as he struggled to walk, balancing precariously on chubby legs, failed to bring a smile to her lips.

One night she had lain his arms and he had pleaded with her to tell him what was troubling her. Huge tears had rolled down her pale cheeks as she had confided in a broken whisper that she feared there was something wrong with the baby. He had tried to persuade her that her fears were simply the result of tiredness and the changes in her body.

She seemed to take comfort from his words and for a few days had been almost like her old self. Then her labour had started four weeks too soon. He had been away, taking a load of china clay to Runcorn. When he had returned it was all over. After a long and painful labour, the baby, a girl, had been born dead. She had been perfect but tiny, and according to Mary's mother, had never drawn breath.

The midwife and Mary's mother had dealt with everything. The tiny body had been bundled in a sheet and hurried away, and while Mary lay in an exhausted sleep, the child had been buried, its mother never having seen it, in an unmarked grave without ceremony.

Laity knew this was the custom in such cases where the child had not been baptised. Yet an unreasoning shaft of anger pierced him. How could a newborn baby be guilty of any sin. Yet unless it had been baptised, 'washed clean', there could be no funeral, no blessing. Like most seafaring men, George Laity was superstitious and the anomaly over his dead child worried him deeply.

But his own fears and worries paled when he saw his Mary. She seemed like a stranger to him. Her eyes were dull, like those of a blind person. Though they faced the outside world, they looked only inward. Her firm pink flesh melted away and the skin of her face was stretched taut over cheek and jawbone. Thanks to her mother and the midwife there had been no child-bed fever, because if there had, he knew without doubt Mary would have died, simply lacking the will to live.

She had barely responded to his homecoming, locked in some dark and lonely hell of her own. He was worried. Her mother was worried. They tried hard to lift her out of the well of depression into which she had plummeted. No one mentioned the dead baby. They had not told Mary where it was buried and she had not asked. Best to put it out of mind, her mother advised him. With rest and good food she would soon be fit again and she was young enough to have plenty more.

Laity had wondered for a moment, not mentioning the baby? Pretend it had never happened? But the women were adamant and they knew more about these things than he did. His own sense of loss was blunted by his concern for his wife, and for his son who was too young to understand, yet was aware that something was wrong with his mother. Robert became difficult to handle, alternating bouts of withdrawn silence with tantrums of screaming temper.

After ten days lying-in Mary had got up from the bed and life had returned to normal. Well, it appeared normal on the surface. Robert settled down again and he went back to sea. Mary once again took an interest in her home and her family. But somewhere deep inside her a key had been turned and part of her was now beyond his reach. He had tried, God knows he had tried, but it was almost as if she blamed him, though for what he had no idea.

He had hated it, hated the distance between them, but had not known how to cross the chasm that now divided them. Then that evening, after showing Captain Carlyon over the ship, something Carlyon had said had sown the seed of an idea. At first he had dismissed it angrily. It was too dangerous. It would be like tearing open a wound. But then he reasoned, if a wound was healed over poison, you had to reopen it to draw the poison out. He resolved to do it.

The market stalls were closing as he had hurried back to his cottage. But two posies of flowers remained in the flowerseller's basket and he had chosen the fresher one, newly sprinkled with rain.

When he walked into the cottage Mary's mother was there, bouncing a freshly bathed Robert on her knee, while Mary put pasties in the oven and stoked up the Cornish range.

'Get your coat, Mary, we're going out for a while.' She had looked at him, bewildered yet aware of the tension in his voice, then she had noticed the flowers still clutched in his big fist.

'What? Where?' she had begun, then seeing the determined look on his face, and the nerve which jumped beneath his eye, she had put on her coat without another word and had run upstairs to fetch a shawl for her head.

Mary's mother had looked from one to the other, her stare remaining on her son-in-law.

'I'm telling 'er', he said quietly, 'and what's more I'm showing 'er the place.'

'You shouldn',' she began, but seeing the look on his face she amended it quickly. 'I 'ope you know what you're doin',' she warned, shaking her head.

'So do I, Mother,' he had replied. 'But it can't go on like this.'

"Tis bound to take time, boy,' the older woman had hissed.

'Time won't make no difference, 'tis more than that.' Mary had come back into the room. Leaning down she kissed her son's rosy cheek. Her eyes were very bright.

'Don't you keep un up late now, Ma. We won't be gone long.'

And they had gone out together into the dusk, the wind snatching at their clothes and throwing rain into their faces.

The ground beside the cemetery was overgrown with bracken, and thorny brambles scratched their ankles and dragged at Mary's long skirts. Ripe juicy blackberries hung in heavy clusters and the grass grew tall and lush, but here and there small clearings had been made in the undergrowth. Some were barely visible, weeds and grass having grown back, almost obliterating the signs of disturbance. But behind a bush a small mound of bare earth was blotted with dead leaves, and it was beside this that Laity stopped.

Suddenly he found it hard to speak. The lump in his throat threatened to choke him. Turning to his wife he gently placed the flowers in her hands. She gazed up at him, a fine trembling shaking her body, her eyes huge in the lowering darkness. The rain made patterns on her skin.

'See,' he said, his voice cracking, "tis all right. The little one, she be safe.'

Mary tore her eyes from his and stared at the mound. A low animal moan came from her throat and she sank to her knees beside the tiny grave. Rocking to and fro as though in pain too great to bear, she placed the flowers on the dark wet earth, patting it and smoothing it as if to reach her dead baby underneath.

Laity watched her for a moment, then bending down, gently raised her to her feet. Her tear-stained eyes met his and read the worry and concern in them. His hand rested on her shoulder and she covered it with her own, gripping his fingers.

'I never seen 'er,' she whispered. 'They wouldn't speak of 'er. They meant well, but—' She turned her head and looked down at the small hillock, streaked with rain, and the flowers, bedraggled, mud-tinged, a lighter blur in the deepening darkness. She turned back to him, tried to speak. Instead her face crumpled and huge tears rolled from under her tightly shut eyelids.

Laity pulled his wife close to him and held her as the dam burst and the tide of grief, so long held back, overwhelmed her, shaking her body with tearing, racking sobs. He had lifted his face to the cold rain, letting it wash away his own tears. Then they had returned home, not speaking, their hands clasped tightly.

Robert had been put to bed, protesting sleepily, and they had had supper, Mary's mother staying for the meal. Her sharp eyes probed, shifting from one to the other. After the table had been cleared and the dishes washed, Mary had sat down by the range and picked up her sewing. But after a few minutes Laity had noticed her fingers were still, and from her bent head tears were dropping and trickling over her hands. Mary's mother shot a savage look at her son-in-law.

'What is it, my 'andsome?' she crooned, about to get up and go to her daughter.

'Leave 'er,' Laity ordered in a voice which surprised even himself with its sharpness.

'Well, really,' Mary's mother bridled, then turned to her daughter. ''Tis all 'is fault you're upset, my 'andsome. I said no good would come of it. I knew 't wadn right nor proper.' She glared at Laity. 'Now see what you done.'

Mary raised her head. Her eyes were swollen and wet and tears glistened on her cheeks, but her face as she looked at the stocky figure of her husband brimmed with love and gratitude.

'No, Ma,' she said thickly, 'you be wrong. 'Twas a good thing 'e done.'

Later when he had tucked her into their bed pulling the goose-feather quilt close around her before leaving for the dock, she had asked him what had prompted him to do it.

''Twas sommat Cap'n Carlyon said when I told un you'd lost the child. 'E said to let 'ee grieve. But when I thought on it, you'd adn 'ad no chance. 'Twas all stuck inside 'e, making 'e bad. Tears can't bring the little mite back, I do know that, but pretendin' she never 'appened, that don't make no sense neither.' He touched her face gently with a calloused hand. 'Be all right, will 'ee?'

Mary nodded, her lips compressed to still their tremble. She tried to laugh, but it emerged as a strangled sob.

'I do feel some silly. Now I started I can't stop.'

'Don't 'ee fret 'bout that, my bird,' Laity smoothed back her hair. 'You cry all you want. 'Tis better out than in.' He bent and kissed her.

'George,' she sobbed, 'take a pasty fer the Cap'n, 'tis a cold night.' He smiled and nodded and went quietly out of the room, leaving her sobbing softly into the pillow.

Downstairs Mary's mother was ready to leave. He would walk with her to her own cottage before going on to the dock. She had wanted to stay, in case Mary had needed her, but Laity had firmly declined her offer. She still had a disapproving frown on her face as she picked up her basket and pressed her hat angrily into place.

'I never 'eard the like of it,' she muttered, 'upsettin' the girl like that. Tedn right nor proper.'

'Now mind you leave 'er be, Mother,' Laity warned, 'else I'll 'ave sommat to say.' The old woman subsided in a welter of sniffs and mutters.

Another gust hit the schooner and she heeled again. Laity brought her up another point. The wind was now directly on their beam and the sails were full and taut as the vessel creamed through the water past Tregothan Estate.

Laity felt an odd vibration shudder through the boat. She was driving too hard, beginning to feel top-heavy. Gusting as it was, the wind was unpredictable, and this was further aggravated by numerous little creeks and inlets along the river trapping the wind and funnelling it back, causing whirlpools and eddies in the air, adding new strains to the already stressed and laden masts.

'Pascoe, Glasson,' Laity shouted, and the two seamen shuffled from the lee side of the deck where they had been sheltering from the weather.

'Lower the mainsail.'

''Bout bloody time,' muttered Glasson, choking back a cough, ''e'll 'ave the masts off 'er afore we git there.'

'What about the foresail?' Pascoe shouted back.

'Leave it be, jest do what I said,' Laity roared.

'Them forestays don' look sound, frayin' they are,' Pascoe returned. Laity hesitated but the contemptuous tone in Pascoe's voice so infuriated him that he pushed the momentary doubt to the back of his mind.

'Don't you question my orders,' Laity snarled. 'Leave it be I said, jest git that mainsail down.' Pascoe shrugged and the two men turned away along the deck to do the Mate's bidding.

'And, Pascoe,' something in the Mate's voice halted him, 'when that sail is secure, you git down in the chain locker and check the forrard planking.'

Pascoe froze then spun round, his mouth open to protest. The chain locker was a small, dank, foul-smelling compartment in front of and below the fo'c'sle where the anchor ropes and chains, covered in weed and slime and mud from the river bottoms were stored. The cramped space was always cold and thick with the stench of decay. It also acted as a lock-up for seamen guilty of repeated drunkenness or violence, a spell in that stinking hole being sufficient to sober even the wildest spirit. Work in the chain locker was the most hated job among seamen.

'Not a word, Pascoe,' Laity grated. 'The Surveyor warned about they forrard planks. Now you git down there and check 'em. Take a bully light from the fo'c'sle.'

Hatred glittered in the seaman's eyes but he held his tongue. Leaving Glasson to finish securing the sheets and rigging of the lowered mainsail, Pascoe, seething with rage stumped off towards the bow. He had a long memory especially for what he considered injuries done him. Some day his chance would come for revenge and when it did, he'd grab it with both hands, sure as hell burned he would.

6

As she turned restlessly on the narrow forms, Harlyn's fitful and exhausted sleep was disturbed by dreams. Haunting images which frightened her, slipping away before she could recognise them, only to be replaced by others even more disturbing. There was movement and noise, footsteps, they seemed to be bound up in her dream, and yet— Her eyes snapped open. For an instant she didn't know where she was, then memory flooded back. The vibration and angle of the hull and the muted sound of rushing water told her the schooner was moving. She was on her way to Falmouth and safety.

Suddenly Harlyn's senses screamed a warning. Fully awake, her heart thumping furiously and every nerve straining, she sat up. She didn't make a sound, scarcely daring to breathe. There was someone else in the dark, stuffy cabin.

A match flared and Harlyn gasped in fright, clapping her hand to her mouth in a vain effort to stifle the sound.

'Wassat? Who's there?' The man was as surprised and shaken as she. Holding the spitting match high he spun round. Harlyn, dazzled and half-blinded by the unexpected light, huddled back into the corner, clutching the blankets.

She could see nothing of the man's features, only a stocky, black shape behind the tiny halo of light.

'Mr Laity?' Harlyn's voice was tremulous. 'Is that you?' Pascoe did not reply. The longer she thought he was Laity, the better for him. The match spluttered and died. The darkness seemed thicker than ever. A muffled string of curses poured from Pascoe's spittle-flecked lips as with shaking fingers he fumbled for another one.

'Mr Laity?' Harlyn's voice now held terror.

The bitch would start screaming in a minute. At last he managed to strike another match. In its flaring, yellow light he advanced towards Harlyn, his mouth open in a leering travesty of a smile, revealing broken, blackened stumps of teeth. Savage joy welled in Pascoe's chest. He could hardly contain the laughter that bubbled inside him as he gazed in the flickering light at the petrified girl before him.

So, the Mate had a nice juicy little whore tucked away for his own comfort. The devil certainly looked after his own, exulted Pascoe. He had not expected the chance for revenge to come so soon, nor in so sweet a form. When he'd finished with this little chicken, that jumped-up bastard Mate could have the leavings.

'You're not Mr Laity,' the small voice croaked, dry-throated with sudden, overwhelming fear. Pascoe chuckled. The sound made Harlyn's blood run cold.

Pascoe groaned at the throbbing in his loins as a wave of lust surged through him, leaving him breathless and shaking in its wake. It had been a long time since he'd had a woman, too long. Saliva drooled from one corner of his mouth.

Harlyn scrambled backwards, feeling the rough planks hard against her shoulders. Her eyes darted from side to side, desperately seeking some means of escape, but the hunched figure of the man shuffling towards her blocked her way and her vision.

"Tis all right, girlie. Don't fret 'bout Laity,' Pascoe crooned, 'I got something 'ere'll 'elp you fergit 'e,' and he chuckled again.

The realisation that she was in mortal danger shocked Harlyn into action. Filling her lungs with the foul air, she opened her mouth to scream. But Pascoe anticipated her and flung himself forward, tossing the match aside and clamping a filthy hand over her mouth before she could utter a sound. The weight of his body knocked her off the benches and they fell in a tangle of arms, legs and blankets on to the filthy floor.

The sensation of the girl's soft, squirming body beneath his own nearly drove Pascoe insane with desire. With an arm across her throat to hold her down he began tearing at the neck of her dress, grunting with frustration as the material resisted his efforts.

Blind terror lent Harlyn strength and she fought like a tigress, twisting and heaving. Her hands found his cap and tore it off. Locking her fingers in his lank, greasy hair, she pulled with all her might, dragging his head backwards. He gave a yelp and pressed down harder with the arm across her throat.

Harlyn could scarcely breathe. There was a tearing sound and she felt cold air on her bare skin. Then his hot, foetid breath enveloped her as his mouth, wet-lipped and drooling clamped on to the tender flesh of her breast, biting and sucking.

Panic, horror and revulsion flooded through Harlyn. She was beginning to feel light-headed from lack of air. Pascoe, now groaning in a frenzy, his face buried in her shoulder and breast, was scrabbling at her skirts. The blanket twisted around her legs hampered his movements and frustration was making him wild.

In an attempt to free the blanket, he lifted his weight off her for an instant. Harlyn seized her chance. Gasping in lungfuls of thick, stinking air, she jack-knifed her knees up to her chest and kicked out with all her strength.

Pascoe gave a strangled grunt as one foot caught him in the pit of the stomach. He fell sideways, snatching his arm off her throat to save himself.

Harlyn sucked in deep, sobbing breaths. Her head felt as though it would burst. Pascoe lunged at her again and she began to scream. Shriek after shriek filled the cramped space with ear-splitting sound.

He grabbed her shoulders and she lashed out with both feet. Her hands hooked like talons, she clawed at the sweating, slobbering face above her, felt the flesh tear and gouged even deeper, driven by some atavistic urge to blind, maim and destroy the male creature attempting to violate her.

The fo'c'sle hatch crashed open and Glasson stumbled down the ladder holding a lamp.

'Jesus,' he choked as the light fell upon the writhing, struggling figures. Harlyn's strength was almost exhausted and her screams had weakened to ragged sobs. Pascoe, panting and slavering, was wild-eyed and sweating as he turned his head to the light.

'Get out, get out,' he gasped hoarsely.

Glasson seemed mesmerised. 'Mr Laity says you bin too long, you're to come and 'elp git the upper topsail down. Wind's gustin' 'arder. There's a squall comin'.'

His eyes never moved from Harlyn's sprawled, trembling body, her torn dress disarranged, her face dirty and streaked where sweat and tears mingled, and twisted in anguish and terror. Her eyes as they turned to Glasson were wild with fear, like those of a trapped animal.

'Help me, help me,' she panted, her voice husky and strained, her throat bruised and sore.

'Bugger, Laity,' Pascoe spat. 'I got unfinished business with 'is whore. You tell un that. Tell un anything you like, but get out, unless you want the leavings.'

The brief respite had renewed his strength as it had sapped Harlyn's and with a slow, deliberate movement he lowered his head to her breast, chuckling evilly as his teeth closed on the soft flesh.

Harlyn began to struggle once more, but her movements were erratic and lacked any real strength. Tears of rage and pain rolled down her face and into her tangled hair. Hopeless sobs racked her as with a last desperate effort she cried to Glasson.

'The Captain, in God's name, tell the Captain.'

'Want 'im to watch, do 'ee?' Pascoe laughed, then growled at Glasson. 'Get out.' His body was arched like a bow and trembling as he reached for the hem of Harlyn's skirt.

Glasson stumbled up the ladder, feeling the tightness in his lungs and the fever coursing through his body. He breathed shallowly, trying not to trigger the reflex which would start him coughing again. There had been more blood last time. It had frightened him. Despite the chill of the wind, he felt sweat on his body, making his clothes damp and clammy.

'Where the hell is Pascoe?' Laity roared at him.

Glasson flinched. He felt the spasm in his chest. He shook his head, trying to keep his breathing light. He didn't want to cough. He felt fear tear at his guts with sharp claws. That girl was frightened, more than frightened, she was nearly mad with terror. For a whore used to handling seamen, such fear was out of place. Glasson was not very bright but he sensed something was terribly wrong. He owed Laity nothing, but he was no friend of Pascoe's either. The girl's face flashed before his eyes. He recognised that fear, that mortal terror. Then it occurred to him, what if she wasn't. . . .?

He felt his lungs contract and the pain knifed through him. Sweat started out in huge drops on his forehead.

'Glasson, you snivelling wretch, where is Pascoe? What the hell is he doing?'

Laity snarled, glancing alternately at Glasson and at the top-masts which were bowing and flexing under the strain of the taut canvas. His face was creased with worry, his knuckles white with the force needed to hold the wheel steady.

Glasson clutched at his chest as his lungs contracted and he tried to hold back the coughing. He pointed to the fo'c'sle.

'A girl,' he gasped, 'there's a girl down there, and Pascoe is—' he couldn't finish. With an explosive gargle the coughing began in earnest.

It took Laity a couple of seconds to understand what Glasson had said and all its implications. The Captain, he'd have to wake the Captain. He looked at the hunched man before him, barely hearing the wet, racking coughs as Glasson spat his life-blood into the filthy, red-stained rag held to his mouth.

'Take the helm, hold her steady,' Laity ordered Glasson. 'Come on, man, for God's sake, I've got to git the Captain.'

Laity dragged the weak and shaking man behind the wheel and propped him against it. He was desperate. The topmasts would not hold under the weight of canvas and the force of the wind for much longer. They were fast approaching Pill Creek, a channel off the main river which acted like a funnel in a northerly gale.

With a last look at Glasson who had dragged himself upright and was wrestling with the wheel, Laity flung himself down the companionway and burst through the day cabin into the Captain's sleeping quarters.

Jared was sprawled fully clothed on the bunk, the glow from the lamp on the shelf in the day room highlighted the planes and shadows of his face. At the urgency in Laity's voice he came awake at once, his eyes gritty and his mouth dry, and was on his way up the stairs before Laity had finished talking.

'If Glasson can hold the course, you get those topsails down,' Jared ordered, 'he'll be too slow. I'll deal with Pascoe and his jade.' The wind snatched the words from his lips and he felt spots of rain on his face. Another squall was approaching, and it was coming in fast. Grabbing the lamp from Laity and seizing a boathook as he raced along the deck, Jared swung himself down the fo'c'sle ladder.

The girl's cries were weak, pain-filled and almost drowned by the panting grunts of the seaman sprawled across her, one of his hands twined in her hair holding her still while the other skittered like an ugly crab on the white skin of her thigh. The air was charged and Jared felt the hair on his neck prickle at the fear which emanated from the girl.

Dropping the lamp, Jared lunged at Pascoe with the boathook. The honed barb pierced the thick material of the seaman's jacket as though it were butter. Using all his strength

Jared twisted and pulled, yanking Pascoe off the girl and slamming him against the bulkhead. Pascoe's face came up and hit the planking with a dull thud. There was a wet squelching sound as his nose split. He gave a groan and slumped to the floor unconscious.

Jared heaved the boathook free and tossed it aside, then he turned to the girl. She had pulled herself up into a sitting position. Slowly, painfully, she was trying to rearrange her torn clothing. Her hair hung down over her face and shoulders in a tangled mat. She shook ceaselessly and her breathing was punctuated by shuddering sobs.

'Are you all right?' Jared's voice was harsh and angry. Without waiting for a reply he went on, 'What the hell were you doing here anyway? There's surely enough work for you round the docks and the pubs. You're trespassing on my ship.' An anguished sob, quickly stifled, was the only reply. 'Come on,' Jared's voice was brusque and impatient, though not entirely devoid of kindness, 'we'd better get you out of here.' He leaned down to help her to her feet.

As his hand closed round the top of her arm, she gasped with pain. The torn bodice and sleeve parted to reveal livid bruises, visible even in the dim lamplight. Jared's jaw tightened. In spite of his anger and impatience he felt a twinge of sympathy for the girl who swayed, head bent beside him, just reaching his chin.

Suddenly, a thread of memory tugged in Jared's brain, something indefinable, and shock tingled through him. He spun round and snatched up the lamp. Holding it close to the girl he let go of her arm. Without his support she staggered and almost collapsed. Jared cupped his fingers under her chin and twisted her head towards the light. She tried to resist but his fingers were steel, and the tangled mane fell to one side. There in the lamp's glow was revealed the face which had haunted him all evening.

'Oh my God.' The words were a stunned whisper. 'You.' Harlyn's eyes were closed. The black shadows under them emphasised her pallor beneath the streaked dirt and the blood-stippled scratches. Jared felt blind, unreasoning anger flare in him.

'You stupid, *stupid* girl. What the hell were you doing down there? My God, if I were your father I'd give you the biggest hiding you've ever had, though I don't suppose you've ever been chastised, more's the pity, it might have knocked some sense into you. What possessed you to indulge in such a stupid, dangerous, hare-brained scheme as hiding in the crew's quarters? Didn't you think of the risk? Didn't you have any idea of what might happen?' He stopped abruptly, anger subsiding as he studied the ashen, trembling figure before him. 'Well, no doubt you realise now.'

Harlyn opened her eyes. Huge tears welled from their emerald depths, hung quivering for an instant on her lids then toppled over and spilled down her pinched face, leaving twin tracks through the grime. She could not hold his gaze. Her head dropped forward and her hair swung down like a cloak to protect her in her shame from his probing stare. Her words were a hoarse murmur, speech was obviously an agony.

'I'm sorry.'

Jared felt murderous rage sweep through him. In that instant he would have killed Pascoe. Harlyn swayed again. Fearful that she would fall Jared released her chin and slipped his arm around her shoulders. She flinched from him. His grip tightened involuntarily.

'He didn't. . . .?' She shook her head and he felt a shudder rack her from head to foot. He let out his breath in an explosive sigh, unaware that he had been holding it.

'Come along, I'll take you to my cabin. You can rest there.' Anger and the fear of what might have befallen her were inextricably mixed. This confusion in his emotions caused him to appear cold and disdainful. 'This time you will be quite safe.'

Harlyn nodded dumbly. The shock of her experience was beginning to take hold.

When they reached the deck rain was beginning to fall. Large cold drops lanced into them, building up speed and intensity. They fought their way back along the canting deck, leaning into the wind, the schooner heaving beneath their feet. Through narrowed eyes Jared could see Glasson braced against the wheel, his body jerking as he coughed. Laity was on the other side of the deck frantically tugging on the ropes leading to the upper topsails. Jared paused.

'What's the problem? Why aren't they down yet?' he shouted.

'The ropes are frayed, they're catching,' Laity yelled back. 'She's heeling too far and the tackle won't run.'

'Can't you pay her off?' Jared shouted, looking up anxiously at the overstrained and creaking masts.

'Daren't Cap'n, we're too close to the bank.' Not a man to waste words, Jared did not repeat the necessity of getting the sails down as quickly as possible. Laity knew well enough the danger that threatened. Instead he guided Harlyn quickly aft towards the companionway, casting a quick look at Glasson, who seemed to have stopped coughing and was labouring to hold the wheel steady, his back hunched against the pounding rain, as the schooner drove on under her burden of water-logged canvas.

Jared had just seen Harlyn creep into the bunk he had so recently vacated, huddling into the coarse, unwashed blankets like some small wounded animal, when a prolonged creaking groan followed by a tearing crash sent him flying up the stairs to the deck.

The intense fury of the squall lashed him the moment he left the cover of the hatch. The rain was so heavy it was as if sheets of water were suspended from the black, full-bellied clouds, which hung so low the masts almost pierced them.

Within seconds his jacket was sodden and heavy with water, and his hair was plastered to his scalp. Narrowing his eyes Jared looked up at the foremast. The violent wind and deluge of rain had proved too much for the strained topmast. The sail had split and the mast had snapped like a twig at the cap, where lower and topmasts joined. It now hung down in a tangled web of rigging and torn canvas swaying and smashing against the lower mast.

Laity had taken over the wheel just as the squall had hit, his physical strength alone keeping them on course in the maelstrom of wind and water. Glasson was attempting to grab one of the flailing ropes attached to the broken mast.

'Don't try to secure it,' Jared yelled. 'Get an axe and cut the whole lot free.' His voice was barely audible above the howling wind. Water poured down his face and neck and dripped off his chin. He took the wheel from Laity. 'Get the foresail down first.' Laity nodded and hurried down the deck.

They were out of the river now and into the Carrick Roads. Though there was more room to manoeuvre, it was much rougher. The black mass of water was without form or pattern. Waves formed and broke, white-frothed tops torn off by the shrieking wind. Heaving mounds of water were built up and demolished by conflicting forces of wind and tide, and the rain beat down as if by its weight to flatten the restless sea.

As Laity and Glasson cut the last of the tangled rigging free, Jared brought the schooner's head closer to the wind. She heeled over, allowing the jumble of wood, rope and canvas to fall clear of the boat and flop into the heaving water. The next day or the day after it would be washed ashore and abandoned at the high water mark, rejected by the angry sea. Too paltry a prize compared with the hulks which littered the seabed. Some whole, simply overwhelmed by the mountainous seas, others smashed and broken on shoals and banks and the rocks off Trefusis Point.

Jared remembered his father telling him of the loss of the transport ship *Queen* in 1814 on those very rocks. She had been returning from Spain with women and children, and invalid soldiers who had fought with Wellington's army. Her anchors had failed in the south-easterly gale, a wind especially dangerous for ships in the outer harbour, and she had drifted onto the rocks and broken up with the loss of almost two hundred lives. Jared had seen the commemorative stone in Mylor churchyard.

The rain lost its vicious force and the wind began to ease. Free of her burden the schooner rose more easily. The mate trudged back along the deck and dropped the axe on the hatch cover. Both men looked at the sky. Clouds raced and tumbled, the thick blanket torn and riven by erratic air currents. The rain was now intermittent and as they looked, just for a second stars were revealed, diamond bright in the murky gloom.

Laity sniffed the air. 'Wind'll change soon.'

Jared made no reply. He seemed preoccupied.

'We'll never beat up Penryn river 'gainst un.'

Jared shook his head. 'We're not going up river. The boat is going to Charlie Carne's yard on the Bar. We should make it before the tide drops too far.' His mouth opened in a huge yawn. Now that the danger was past, Jared felt fatigue wash over him once more. But Laity's next remark pierced his lethargy like a fine blade.

'That maid all right, is she?'

'Yes.' Jared's reply was brief and curt. Laity seemed to expect something else, some remark about her presence on board, but at Jared's silence he shrugged and turned away.

'I'll give Glasson a 'and furling that foresail. Will 'ee want the main and mizzen til us git round the point?'

Jared nodded. 'Just a minute, Mr Laity.' The mate turned back and watched Jared fumble for words. 'William Tremayne's family, did you ever meet them?'

'Aye, Sir.' Laity looked puzzled. Now it was Jared's turn to wait for the mate to say more, but Laity didn't know what his Captain wanted to hear.

'What about his eldest daughter?' Jared stared straight ahead, steering the ship with the utmost concentration.

'Miss Harlyn? I've knowed she since she were a bitty child. She've growed into some pretty maid, but she's some 'andful.'

'What do you mean by that?' The question was quick and sharp.

'No disrespect, sir. She idn a bad girl, I don't mean nothing like that. 'Tis just that she be, well, diff'rent from th'other girls. You wouldn't think she come from the same fam'ly as 'er younger sisters. I think meself she was 'er father's favourite. All the same, if the rumours be true, I do feel some sorry for she.'

'What rumours?' Jared could not hide his interest. Laity hesitated. It was not always wise to repeat gossip. Too often, if it was bad news, the carrier was blamed for being the cause.

'Come on, man, you can speak freely. What rumours?'

So that's the way of it, Laity thought to himself, remarking his Captain's undisguised curiosity.

'Well, Sir, 'tis said Sir 'Enry Trevellyan do want she fer wife.'

Jared was thankful for the darkness. The conflicting emotions suddenly exposed by Laity's revelation were, he knew, visible on his face. He had seen Trevellyan for the first time at the auction, their paths never having crossed before. He recalled the puffball appearance of the baronet, his bloated face and body at odds with his delicate almost feminine gestures and the rigid uprightness of his stance, as though by standing tall, he would actually add inches to his height. The overall impression Jared had received during his brief study of the little man was one of disturbing power. His position, wealth and influence ensured that the deference shown him was marked, but his cynical disdain of it was equally so. Though Trevellyan obviously expected and demanded such deference, he openly scorned the men who gave it.

Jared was not given to flights of fancy, but the image he had of the baronet despite his outward chilly calm, was one of a fiercely boiling pot with its lid jammed on, preventing any escape of steam or release of pressure. Far from being a source of amusement, Jared found the image a disturbing one with many connotations.

'I'll see to that sail then, Cap'n,' Laity broke into Jared's thoughts.

Jared nodded. 'And check if Pascoe is still unconscious. If he is,' he added, 'leave him; if he isn't, warn him that if he shows his face on deck before we reach Falmouth, I'll break his neck and throw him to the fish.'

The cold fury in the Captain's words surprised Laity. That was some fuss to make over a dockside whore. She knew the risks, coming on board a ship, though God knows when or how she got on board. She'd 'ave made more money round the pubs, damn fool maid. He thought of his Mary and the trembling smile she had given him through her tears, and as he strode off down the deck, the unfortunate girl in the Captain's cabin was banished from his mind.

For Jared Carlyon the situation was very different. As he guided the schooner toward Falmouth harbour, images of Harlyn crowded his every thought.

Harlyn, wide-eyed and fearful when he had first discovered her in his cabin; standing tall and proud, despite her wet, tangled hair and bedraggled gown as she had told him her name and demanded his; flushed and trembling with anger, clad only in her shift as she had hurled her fury at him. And then another image, gut-twisting, that proud expressive face hollow-eyed with shock and fear, the open, level gaze veiled and shame-filled as she flinched away from him.

Why did it bother him? He did not know her, she was nothing to him. She had been incredibly stupid stowing away like that. One might say she deserved the fate which had so nearly befallen her.

Deep in his heart Jared felt a burning shame. Shame at his thoughts and shame for his sex. She had not invited that horrifying experience. Her foolhardy, brave, vulnerable innocence had been her downfall.

So she was to marry Trevellyan. She would live in a fine house, surrounded by servants, have beautiful clothes, be protected from any worries more serious than seating arrangements for dinner parties. Perhaps responsibility would settle her down.

Fine, you've decided what's best for her, Jared scoffed at

himself. So, faced with such a wonderful future, why did she run away? He vowed he would find out what could make a well-brought-up young lady risk her safety, her reputation and the disgrace to her family. He could not believe it was merely the age difference between herself and Trevellyan. It wasn't that she mattered to him, God knows he had quite enough to keep him busy without added problems, especially a problem with fathomless green eyes and an independent nature.

But damn it, in the last twelve hours every way he'd turned she'd been under his feet. In such circumstances a man might be forgiven for being curious.

7

'Come along, Miss Tremayne, we must leave the ship.' Jared Carlyon's peremptory summons reached Harlyn in her exhausted sleep. Warm and flushed, her hair spread about her like a tangled web, she glowed like a jewel amid the rough, grey blankets.

With eyes still closed she yawned and stretched, flexing her limbs and arching her back with unconscious feline grace.

She did not see the spasm twist Jared's face as the stab of desire caught him unawares. She had no way of knowing that he had stood unmoving for several minutes, watching her as she slept. When the nightmare had caused her to whimper and her face to crumple, his hand had reached out of its own volition to touch her, comfort her, soothe away the hurt, calm the fear. But if the gesture had been instinctive, the withdrawal was deliberate, and Jared had thrust his hands deep in his pockets and rocked back on his heels, his lips twisting in self-mockery, the sardonic tilt of his eyebrow more pronounced than ever.

'Miss Tremayne, kindly rouse yourself, I have business to attend to.'

The cool, laconic and condescending tones of the Captain's voice pierced Harlyn's subconscious and she jerked upright, her sea-green eyes wide, and her grubby, blood-streaked face as vulnerable as a child's.

'I'm sorry,' she whispered, and pushed the heavy mass of black hair back over her shoulders. The movement caused the torn bodice to gape and fall open, revealing livid bruises, black and purple on the creamy skin of her breast and throat.

Jared's jaw tightened at the sight, his face hardening as if to stone. The feral gleam in his amber-yellow eyes frightened Harlyn. Her hands flew upward and she made vain attempts to somehow fasten the torn edges together. Her shoulders drooped and her fingers began to tremble. Why did he stare so?

She drew in a deep, shuddering breath, straightened her back and climbed stiffly to her feet. She ached all over and knew she looked an unsightly mess. Harlyn did not consider herself vain, but knowing her appearance was unbecoming put her at a disadvantage with the cold, taciturn man standing before her.

'Might I trouble you for some water, Captain Carlyon?' Her voice was raw and husky and speaking caused her considerable pain. 'Please, do you have a comb?'

She felt the blush warm her cheeks as she uttered the words. To have to face him in this state was bad enough, but to have to ask him for the means of repairing the ravages of the previous night was mortifying. She waited for him to make some cutting remark, but he said nothing, only nodded briefly, and reaching into the pocket of his jacket took out a wide-toothed comb and handed it to her.

'There's a mirror in the day room. I'll see about some water,' he said curtly and walked out of the sleeping quarters with Harlyn following, clutching her torn bodice with one hand and shaking out her skirts with the other.

As they entered the day room there was a knock on the door and before Jared could answer or Harlyn retreat, Laity had opened the door and walked in. His eyes flew immediately to the girl and though Jared stepped in front of her, it was obvious from his shocked and disbelieving expression that Laity recognised her.

'M — Miss Harlyn,' he stuttered, looking from one to the other. 'Oh God, are you all right, miss?' Harlyn moved from behind Jared.

'Yes, thank you, Mr Laity. Thanks to the Captain I wasn't much hurt.' She could not suppress the brief shudder which ran through her.

'But what the 'ell, begging yer pardon, miss, was you doing on board?'

'That is what I intend to find out, Mr Laity,' Jared broke in smoothly, and the hint of steel underlying the mild tone caused a flutter of nervousness in Harlyn's stomach, 'but at a more convenient time.' The subject was closed. Thrusting a hand into his pocket, Jared withdrew a soft leather bag and opening it shook several coins into his hand and passed them to Laity.

'Pay off Glasson and give him a shilling extra. See that he gets to the Sailor's Home, it's off Hull's Lane, leading from Arwenack Street, almost opposite the Customs House. They'll either get him to his own home, if he has one, or they'll take him into the Seamen's hospital.' His face darkened and the expression on it made Harlyn shiver. 'As for that scum Pascoe, get him off the boat and out of the yard before we come topside, and warn him if I ever lay eyes on him again, he'll regret he was ever born.'

'Aren't 'e going to get the P'lice, then, Cap'n?' Laity looked surprised.

'And expose Miss Tremayne to the public gaze when she has to give evidence?' Jared said impatiently.

'Oh, I never thought—'

'Obviously.' Jared cut in. 'Will you please bring Miss Tremayne some water?'

'I'll do that first, Cap'n,' Laity said and hurried out.

Jared shrugged and turned away. He pulled a canvas bag from one of the lockers and began sorting books and charts from the shelf and packing them into the bag. Laity returned moments later with a wooden bucket and a tin mug.

'Barrels is almost empty, miss. 'Twas all I could find, but 'tis clean.'

'I'm sure Miss Tremayne does not expect the refinements of a boudoir, Mr Laity, though you play the ladies' maid, exceeding well.' Laity coloured briefly, and Jared could have bitten his tongue. The man had not deserved such a jibe.

'Here's your due,' Jared said abruptly. 'Order me a cab and get yourself back to Truro on the mail coach.' He tossed the leather bag at Laity, who caught it deftly. 'I'll send word when I need you.'

Hefting the bag, Laity realised by the weight that he had been generously paid.

'Thank 'ee kindly, sir, and — God bless 'ee.'

Jared raised an eyebrow and glancing at Harlyn who was vainly trying to hold her torn bodice in place, he murmured:

'I rather think I have the Devil's attention right now.' He sighed and returned his attention to the Mate. 'I hope, when you return to Truro, you too will consider Miss Tremayne's reputation, Mr Laity.'

The Mate looked puzzled for an instant, then his face cleared and his voice dropped to a conspiratorial whisper.

'My lips is sealed, Cap'n. I wint say nothin' to no one. Don't 'ee fret now, Miss 'Arlyn.'

'Goodbye, Mr Laity, and thank you.' Harlyn smiled at the Mate.

'Bye, Miss,' Laity nodded to her. 'Bye Cap'n,' he sketched a brief salute to Jared, and stepped out, closing the door behind him. There was a moment's silence. Jared resumed his packing. Harlyn picked up the tin mug, dipped it into the bucket and sipped the cold water. It was slightly brackish, but was nectar to her parched and bruised throat.

'I appreciate your concern, Captain Carlyon,' she murmured hoarsely. She wanted to explain how the whole terrible incident had come about, but was uncertain of where to start or even how to engage the attention of the cold, unbending man who stood with his back to her, so busy with his own affairs.

Her feelings towards him had undergone a subtle change. He had rescued her, saved her, snatched her from the culmination of a degrading and terrifying ordeal. Now, instead of resenting him as an arrogant intruder into her father's affairs, virtually stealing her beloved *Karis*, she felt herself drawn to him, wanting his understanding both of her present plight and of the crisis which had catapulted her into this desperate situation.

He glanced briefly at her over his shoulder, then continued sorting and packing the sea junk from the shelf. He opened and closed the lockers, placing the brandy bottle on the table. He did not look at her as he spoke.

'My concern, Miss Tremayne, is for my own reputation. I have no wish to face a kidnapping charge—'

'Oh, but I—' Harlyn began, horrified realisation dawning.

Jared ignored her interruption. 'Nor do I want it spread abroad that I carry whores for the comfort of myself or my men,' he went on. 'The brokers and merchants upon whom my livelihood depends would not look kindly upon such behaviour;

upright, Church-going pillars of Society that they are,' his lips curled in a cynical smile, 'and my business would suffer accordingly.'

Harlyn's face flamed at his cutting rejoinder. She was simply an embarrassment, an encumbrance, a nuisance to be got rid of as quickly as possible. Right, she would remove herself as fast as she could.

She looked at the bucket then at Jared, whose broad back was bent over the small table which now held numerous odds and ends on which he appeared to be concentrating his whole attention. If she carried the bucket into the sleeping cabin, it would only give him further cause for biting remarks, and Harlyn didn't feel she could cope with any more just at the moment.

Turning her back to Jared, she knelt down and lifting the hem of her dress, tore a wide strip from one of her petticoats. She pushed up her sleeves and bent over the bucket. Harlyn rubbed her hands and arms clean, then scooping up the water she rinsed her face over and over, wincing a little as the cold water bit into the scratches. But as she dried herself on the strip of cotton she felt greatly refreshed and more in command of herself. Picking up the comb she began the difficult job of untangling her ebony tresses. After several minutes' work the knots were loosened and the comb slid freely through the heavy curtain of hair. The familiar rhythm and sweep of her arm comforted Harlyn, restoring her sense of normality. Her eyes lost their focus and her face relaxed into its habitual gentle smile.

Even had she looked up she would not have been able to see Jared watching her in the mirror, the books in his hands forgotten, his own expression one of mingled intrigue and exasperation.

Harlyn dropped the comb and started guiltily from her reverie. Jared busied himself once more as she expertly divided and braided her hair, wrapping the plaits round her head, weaving the ends of the hair into the plaits to secure them. There now remained only the problem of the torn bodice.

No matter how she arranged it, it would not remain in place.

'Shall you be much longer, Miss Tremayne?' Jared enquired coolly, his attention centred on the bulging canvas bag which he was endeavouring to fasten. Harlyn could feel the blush burning her cheeks.

'Captain, I've no wish to detain you, but I don't know what to do about . . . about . . . this.' She clutched the jagged edges of the material together. Jared swung round his face stony, but something in his amber eyes flooded Harlyn's cheeks with crimson.

He walked towards her and examined the tear. Gently pushing her trembling hands aside, he tried to match the jagged edges of cloth together.

Harlyn did not know where to look. He was standing so close. At his nearness all her senses seemed suddenly heightened. She was aware of his breath on her hair. She could feel, across the inches that separated them, the warmth of his body, smell the wool of his jacket.

She glanced up under her lashes. His mouth, the lips smooth and well-defined, did not have its usual half-mocking twist. Harlyn liked it better this way. It was the only gentle feature in his craggy face. Were his lips warm − or cold, she mused. Immediately her flush deepened further and she dropped her eyes. If he knew her thoughts—

'I think I have something which will suffice for the time being.' He turned to the bag and after a few seconds rummaging, pulled out a small tin box which he opened and laid on the table.

'Come here, there's more light,' he ordered, drawing Harlyn towards him. His hand, warm and immensely strong, closed completely around the top of her arm. Though his fingers pressed the bruises she felt no pain, only a quivering awareness of his touch. He released her and took something out of the box.

'You must keep perfectly still,' he warned.

'What is it? What are you going to do?' She could not contain the question. Her voice was still husky though her throat did not hurt quite so much.

'I have some small fishhooks here, though I doubt they've ever seen a fish. I'm going to pin the edges with those.' As he spoke, Jared slipped his fingers inside the shoulder edge of the tear. 'Your pardon, Miss Tremayne,' he murmured, and overlapping the edges of the material he held them in place with his thumb while he selected a fishhook from the tin. With infinite care he pushed the barbed point through the two layers of thin material, threaded it back, then pressed it flat.

'Two more should secure it on this side,' he murmured his

brows drawn together in concentration. Harlyn turned her head aside, eyes lowered. Though she appeared to be studying the floor, in reality her eyes registered nothing. All her senses were concentrated on the part of her shoulder where his fingers gently brushed her skin as he inserted the other two hooks. She could feel her skin tingle and burn at his touch. The sensation was not unpleasant but it was unnerving. What if he should notice?

She felt his hand slide lightly from her shoulder to the top of her breast. She swallowed convulsively. A shudder rippled through her.

'Do keep still, Miss Tremayne, or I'm quite likely to do us both an injury.' His voice was cool and impersonal.

He's like a block of ice, Harlyn thought furiously, he has no feelings at all. The touch of his hand on my skin makes me shiver and burn, I'm in turmoil inside, and he feels nothing. There must be something wrong with him, he can have no emotions at all. Or maybe there's something wrong with me. Maybe it's bad to feel these things. I feel afraid, but it's not like last night. That was horrible, horrible. This is a different kind of fear. It makes me feel hollow inside, soft like jelly. I shouldn't be thinking these terrible thoughts, Father would say it was unseemly.

Harlyn felt the prick of tears on her eyelids, then a bubble of laughter expanded and burst inside her. She was losing control. That must not happen. If Captain Carlyon had any idea of the shameful thoughts tumbling through her head, his lips would curl in that disdainful way and his voice would drip icy scorn as his words cut like blades to her very heart. Harlyn swallowed and closed her eyes.

Jared clenched his teeth in an all-out effort to keep his hands steady. Sweat stood out in tiny beads on his forehead and he could hear the thump of his heartbeat as the slow fever of desire coursed through his body. So, she is nothing to you, his other self mocked, she is a mere problem to be solved and disposed of as quickly as possible. Behold the man of steel, the single-minded businessman, the man totally in command of himself and his emotions. And he had no reply.

The girl stood meekly before him, her slender frame quivering imperceptibly. Was she so frightened of him? Her head with its heavy cap of braided hair was turned away, exposing her small, pink ear and the creamy column of her throat, its perfection marred by the ugly bruises.

He felt an almost overpowering urge to fold his arms about her and crush her slim body against his, to press his lips to the delicate and vulnerable spot between back and shoulder and breathe in the warmth and fragrance of her skin.

And if he did that he would terrify her. It would be cruel, and inhuman, especially after her experience of the previous night. She would assume he really did think her a whore.

He carefully pressed the last hook flat and withdrew his hand, dropping it to his side. Harlyn raised her head and their eyes met.

Emerald and amber. They swayed fractionally towards one another. The powerful emotions in each acting as a magnet to the other.

Harlyn's lips parted and her breath caught in her throat as a tiny sob.

The sound jerked Jared back to reality. Abruptly he turned away from her. He strode into the sleeping cabin returning with a blanket, which he folded in half, corner to corner. Then, contriving not to touch her at all, he placed it around Harlyn's shoulders.

He turned back to the table seizing the brandy bottle. His fingers gripped the top, but instead of opening it, he suddenly jammed the cork in tighter and with controlled violence thrust the bottle into the canvas bag.

Harlyn murmured polite thanks from a throat sore and stiff with tears. For an instant she had thought — but his rejection had been total. There was no doubt. He felt nothing for her.

She was utterly alone. There was no one she could turn to, no one in whom she could confide. What was to become of her?

As Harlyn pulled the blanket tight about her, she gathered also the tattered remnants of her pride and fanned the embers of her spirit.

Not quite alone. There was still Aunt Becky, and Aunt Becky was a relation, not a stranger, and surely blood ties counted in a situation like this.

Then doubt assailed Harlyn. Blood had not counted with her mother when she had disowned her only sister.

But that was not *her* fault, it was nothing to do with her.

Surely Aunt Becky would understand that? The first thing was to find her. Harlyn had her address, at this moment it was her most precious possession. She was not completely alone after all.

Jared picked up the canvas bag and pushed a small cloth-wrapped parcel along the table towards her.

'You must be hungry,' he said gruffly. 'Mr Laity's wife sent a pasty for me last night, but I had already dined.'

Harlyn reached out, picked up the parcel and carefully unwrapped it. Though now cold, the pasty made her mouth water in anticipation. She looked up at him shyly.

'Would you care for half, Captain?'

'Thank you, no.' His reply was definite. 'We shall leave the boat very soon. Please stay here while I speak to the yard owner. I don't wish to have to make unnecessary explanations.' His voice hardened, 'and I mean stay here.' He moved to the door, dropping the bag at the entrance.

Harlyn put out a hand. 'Please, Captain, may I wait on deck? I would welcome some fresh air. I feel so — so enclosed. Please?' She begged, her eyes huge in her pale face.

He studied her for a moment. 'Very well,' he said at last. 'Wait in the stern and speak to no one, and keep your wits about you,' he warned.

Clutching the blanket with one hand and the pasty in the other, Harlyn followed his tall figure up the companionway and on to the deck.

Jared walked briskly down the gangplank and along the jetty to a small brick building. The yard office, Harlyn supposed, as he disappeared inside.

She made her way to the stern of the schooner. The early morning air was cool on her face. A watery sun was creeping up the pearl coloured eastern sky. The gale had moderated and now a fresh breeze blew from the west.

Harlyn breathed in deeply. She was glad to be free of the confines of the cabin and her enforced proximity to Jared Carlyon. Distance between them would help restore her emotional balance.

Deliberately turning her thoughts from him, Harlyn bit into the pasty. It was delicious. It occurred to her that she had eaten nothing since lunch the previous day. Shock and fear had destroyed her appetite until now.

Suddenly she was ravenous. Harlyn chewed and swallowed,

savouring the light, crisp pastry containing seasoned meat, potato, onion and turnip.

As she breakfasted Harlyn turned her back to the schooner and the rising sun, and gazed at the panorama before her. Across the river to her right lay Trefusis Point. The water, still rough and disturbed from the night's gale, edged a fringe of white lace along the rocky headland. Above the rocks cows grazed peacefully on the grassy plateau and above that, gorse-covered hills rose, steep-sided and flat-topped. The gorse gave way to woods as Harlyn's gaze wandered upriver. Nestled in a valley between two hills and backed by a third, lay the village of Flushing.

From her lessons in local history at Miss Apworth's Academy for Young Ladies, where at their mother's insistence Harlyn and her sisters had received their education, she recalled that in the late seventeen hundreds, the packet ships, swift, three-masted clippers, carrying mail to exotic corners of the world, had berthed in the narrow stretch of water between Falmouth and Flushing.

Many distinguished sea-faring men had built themselves elegant houses in classic Queen Anne style along the waterfront of the small village on the opposite shore.

Harlyn sighed as she finished the last crust of her pasty, and having no napkin, licked her fingers guiltily, making sure not one crumb escaped.

It must have been such a romantic time, with social events every night. According to Miss Apworth, who seemed to know an awful lot about it, it was difficult to move about the streets for the gold braid and uniforms of the officers and crews of the packets and the naval frigates stationed there to protect shipping.

But sometime in the early 1820's, she couldn't remember exactly when, the Admiralty had taken over the Packet Service from the Post Office, and at once the service began to decline.

Instead of continuing to run the fast and elegant clippers, the Admiralty had replaced them with ten-gun brigs, despite expert advice that they were totally unsuitable.

Harlyn remembered Miss Apworth's eyes bright with angry tears behind her gold-rimmed spectacles as she told of the loss with all hands of six of those 'coffin-ships'.

Harlyn's eyes and thoughts drifted on up the river to where it curved out of sight at Trevissome and headed up towards Penryn.

In front of her, despite the early hour, the harbour and river were busy.

Quay punts with sails set to catch the morning breeze wove in and out between bigger sailing boats and ships tethered to huge mooring buoys awaiting space at the quays to discharge cargo, or take on water and supplies for an outward voyage, or even to take their turn in one of the yards for major or minor repairs.

Harlyn had seen only two steam-powered boats in her life, one was an excursion boat which had masts and sails as well, the other a steam tug which had brought a dismasted barque up to Lemon Quay the previous year.

But the Falmouth waters seemed home to quite a few steam vessels, all different sizes, puffing and chugging about their business, spewing out clouds of thick black smoke from their tall chimney stacks into the crystal clear air.

Harlyn thought them ugly, dirty things. Instead of being in harmony with the elements, they appeared to defy them, challenge them.

Through the forest of masts and over the roofs of the warehouses and workshops, Harlyn looked at the sprawl of Falmouth town, which reached from where she stood on the deck of the schooner all the way up the river as far as she could see.

Along jetties, wharves and quays jutting out into the river, sheds, warehouses, workshops and stores formed a breakwater behind which narrow three-storied houses rose tier upon tier up the hillsides along which the town had spread, their windows flashing and sparkling like jewels, reflecting the morning sun.

As her eyes wandered over the scene Harlyn was impressed, against her will, by the difference between this busy sprawling seaport and her home of Truro.

Apart from the number of ships, there were the smells, or rather the lack of one particular smell. The stench of accumulated sewage was strangely absent. Instead, as she sucked in great lungfuls of air, Harlyn smelled the sweet scent of freshly sawn timber.

Huge stacks of it were piled beside the sawyer's pit where sawdust lay in drifts like golden dunes.

Giant logs floated in a vast timber pond over to her left. There was a smell of tar from new rigging and a freshly blackened hull on her right. Oil from tanned brown sails mingled with the smell of seaweed, salt and mud exposed by the ebbing tide.

There was noise too. The rough burr of men's voices, the shriek of gulls overhead. The sounds of sawing, hammering and the scream of straining blocks, the rhythmic, harmonious clink of mallets on caulking irons.

Harlyn remembered her father telling her when she was a child and they visited one of the yards at Sunny Corner, that each mallet head had a differently shaped notch cut in it. This produced a musical note as it struck the caulking iron which wedged the rope fibres called oakum, between the ship's planks, which when covered with pitch, formed a watertight seal.

The sound of her name being called brought Harlyn back to the present with a start. She spun round heart pounding and lips parted in fear.

Jared Carlyon swung his lithe figure up the gangplank.

'Kindly fetch the bag up from below,' he ordered coolly.

Harlyn's chin came up as anger rose hot inside her. She was about to make a furious retort then she noticed two men following Jared onto the ship.

They were better dressed than the shipwrights she could see about the yard. Both cast speculative glances at her as they approached.

She switched her gaze back to Jared. His face was a mask revealing nothing, but his eyes held a strange glint, a combination of challenge, warning and amusement. He had warned her to keep her wits about her. Could this be one of the reasons why?

'Quickly, girl, I don't have all day,' his irritation was plain.

Praying she had read the situation correctly, Harlyn bobbed a quick curtsey and murmured, 'Sir,' then scuttled to the companionway hatch and down the stairs.

She paused for a moment listening intently, and heard the younger of the two men ask Jared if she needed help with the bag.

Jared's reply was a dismissive snort. 'Certainly not, any maid taking up employment in my household is physically fit and has been properly trained. She's perfectly capable of carrying a bag.'

His tone conveyed with absolute clarity her station in life, and his opinion of the man's effrontery in mistaking her for someone worthy of consideration.

Relieved that she had interpreted the situation correctly, Harlyn could not help wondering if Jared Carlyon's contemptuous tone applied to her in reality as well as this make-believe situation.

Even if it did, why should she care? and why did it hurt?

Holding tightly onto the protective blanket, the bag bumping against her legs, Harlyn followed the men through the yard. She kept her eyes lowered and tried to hide her blushes at the ribald comments her passage excited among the working men.

Jared discussed with the two men, whom Harlyn gathered to be Charles Carne, the yard owner and his son, the repairs he wanted made to *Karis*. After what seemed like hours, but was in fact about twenty minutes, they reached the gate.

The men all shook hands and the Carnes turned back into the yard.

Jared walked through the open gateway out on to the road. The driver of a cab waiting a few yards away flicked the reins urging his horse forward.

'Captain Carlyon?'

Jared nodded briefly.

'Mr Laity said I was to wait, sir.'

Jared nodded again. As the cab drew level and the driver reined in his horse Jared turned to Harlyn, took his bag from her and placing one hand on the door handle raised a quizzical eyebrow.

'Well, you are now in Falmouth, what next, Miss Tremayne?'

8

Harlyn pulled the blanket tightly about her. 'I shall go to my Aunt Becky,' she said simply.

'And where, pray, does your Aunt Becky live?' Jared drawled, but there was nothing languid about his piercing yellow eyes.

'I have an address in the High Street,' Harlyn's mouth was dry, 'and need trouble you no further.'

Her heart thumped uncomfortably, partly in apprehension of what lay ahead of her in this strange town, and partly from the mixed emotions roused by this tall man with the ironic twist to his mouth and a heart of ice. Harlyn wanted to get away from him, yet she owed him so much.

She raised her eyes to his. Her voice softened momentarily.

'I am greatly in your debt, Captain Carlyon, I—'

'Then honour your debt, miss. Permit me to see you safely into your aunt's care.'

'But — but you have business to attend to, many demands on your time, you said so yourself,' Harlyn stammered.

'Miss Tremayne,' he leaned forward slightly holding her captive with his penetrating stare, 'you dropped into my busy, well-ordered life with all the disruption of a stone splashing into a glassy pool, and your ripples are still spreading. It would give me the greatest possible satisfaction to deliver you to your aunt.'

Harlyn was lost for words. Now she was actually in Falmouth her thoughts were strangely confused. Like most girls of her age and background she was not accustomed to being in the streets unaccompanied.

She had not yet reached the centre of this alien town but already she sensed the difference between it and her home of Truro.

Even the air here was charged with energy. The tang of salt on the brisk sea breeze was invigorating and there was an atmosphere of restlessness and bustle. Harlyn found it a little frightening.

Yet Jared's mocking politeness, which made no effort to disguise his wish to be rid of her, was more than she could bear.

Her chin came up in the proud, appealing, defiant manner Jared recognised.

'I could not impose further on your kindness, Captain,' she said coldly, 'except to ask, where is the High Street?'

'At the other end of town,' was his bland reply, 'and today being Thursday, is Market Day. I fear for you may find the streets even at—' he took out his watch and glanced at it, '—7.30 somewhat crowded and busy.'

Harlyn inclined her head. 'Then I must not detain you, sir.' Her emerald eyes held his for an instant. 'You have my heartfelt thanks.'

With that she turned away, crossed the road, and began to walk quickly towards the town centre.

There was nothing to be afraid of, she told herself firmly. She had only to walk through the main street and find Aunt Becky's house. In her torn grubby dress, with the blanket about her shoulders, she would be indistinguishable among the poorer working people going about their business. Harlyn was unaware that her proud carriage and wide-eyed, fine-boned face set her apart like a swan among crows.

She heard horses' hooves behind her and moved to the edge of the road as she passed Arwenack Manor and the elegant, obviously new houses of Grove Place.

A cab drew alongside her and Jared Carlyon leaned out of the window.

'Miss Tremayne, you may walk if you so wish. I have no desire to impose my company upon you. I shall simply follow you to ensure your safe arrival at your aunt's house.'

Harlyn spun round. 'You can't do that,' she protested.

'Oh, but I can,' came the cool rejoinder. 'You forestalled me delivering you safely back to your parents when I caught you trespassing on my ship in Truro. I will not have the same thing happen twice.'

His slight smile was belied by the steel in his voice which told Harlyn that argument was useless.

It would be too mortifying to walk through the streets of Falmouth with a horse and cab containing this infuriating man at her heels.

Her colour high and indignation in every line of her body, Harlyn climbed into the cab and Jared shut the door behind her.

The driver leaned down. 'Where to, sir?'

Jared raised an eyebrow at Harlyn.

'Fifty-one High Street,' she said clearly, uttering the words which encompassed all hope for her.

Jared repeated the address to the driver, who looked puzzled.

'Got the right number 'ave 'ee, sir?'

Jared nodded impatiently, 'Get on, man.'

The cabbie shrugged, and with a lurch and a clatter of wheels and hooves, they were on their way.

Harlyn's cheeks burned with a mixture of anger and awareness as the movement of the cab jolted her against his lean body on the shiny leather seat. 'It seems, Captain, that my obligation to you grows by the minute.'

'Your obligation, such as it is,' he drawled, glancing sideways at her, and seeming quite undisturbed by their proximity in the confined space, 'will be totally discharged once I see you beyond your aunt's front door. Then we may resume our separate lives as though none of this had occurred.'

His words, delivered in tones of cool disdain stung Harlyn like a slap. Withdrawing as far as possible, she stared away from him out of the window as they passed the mock Regency columns of the Custom House and continued along Arwenack Street.

The offices of the ship agents and insurance brokers were as yet unopened and the chandlers and provision merchants still had their blinds down, but the hammers of the iron-smiths at Blamey's clanged loudly on the anvils, and the brick makers in John Roberts' yard were already busy at their moulds.

The cab rounded the bend in front of the Church of King Charles the Martyr, passed the King's Head Hotel and entered Church Street.

Already there were more people moving purposefully about. Women in long, dark skirts of serge, homespun or calico, partly covered by aprons, had thick shawls tied over their high-necked blouses against the cool of the autumn morning and the brisk breeze.

There were fishwives, with huge baskets on their arms, washer-women and cleaners. Many had children at their skirts.

Pale, skinny children in patched hand-me-downs, with large flat caps, and old-young faces.

Here and there, in a shop doorway or an ope leading to a court behind the main thoroughfare, lay a drunk, a sodden heap of ragged humanity, sleeping off the previous night's excesses.

The doors of inns and kiddley-winks, hotels and beerhouses stood open as boys wielded brooms, sweeping out yesterday's debris. Skivvies mopped the flagged floors before scattering fresh, sweet-smelling sawdust to soak up the inevitable spillages.

Fires were being kindled and meat and fowl placed on the spits. Bakers were doing fine trade, their trays already half-empty as housewives and servants of the gentry hurried home with hot crusty loaves straight from the huge ovens at the back of the small shops.

The wailing note of a horn, the thunder of hooves and jingle of harness close by made Harlyn jump.

'What's that?'

'The mail coach leaving the Royal Hotel just ahead,' Jared replied. He pulled out his watch and frowned. 'It's late this morning. It usually goes at seven.'

When their cab did not immediately move on, Jared leaned out of the window. 'What's the delay?'

The cabbie leaned down. 'Coach 'orse broke a leg, sir. They 'ad to shoot 'un. The knackers are shiftin' 'un now the mail 'ave gone. We'll be upalong d'rectly.'

Harlyn waited for Jared to relay the driver's explanation which she had not properly heard. When he said nothing, curiosity overcame her and she leaned forward to look out. Jared restrained her with a light touch on her arm.

'A dead horse is not for a lady's eyes.'

Harlyn glanced at him quickly but there was no trace of mockery in his expression. She settled back against the padded leather and the cab moved forward.

Harlyn felt Jared's eyes upon her. He seemed to be debating something within himself.

Harlyn watched the activity in the street, shy under his frowning scrutiny. When at last he spoke, his words claimed her total and immediate attention.

'Miss Tremayne — were I to offer to accompany you back to your parents—'

The colour drained from Harlyn's cheeks and her stomach gave a sickening lurch. Swivelling on the seat she gripped his arms with both hands.

'Please, I can't go back. I beg you, don't send me back,' she implored. 'Stop the cab, let me out.'

She spun round and with feverish hands began to claw at the handle. 'I'll go away. I never asked you to feel responsible for me. Please just forget me, forget you ever saw me.'

He seized her shoulders in a grip of steel and pulled her round to face him.

'What's the matter? Why have you run away? What have you done?' His brows met in angry puzzlement.

'You don't understand,' Harlyn cried in anguish. Her voice sank to a whisper. 'You could never understand.'

His calm voice penetrated the maelstrom of Harlyn's emotions. 'I cannot understand unless you tell me.'

'I — I — can tell you only this,' she whispered, her eyes brimming with tears as she looked up at him. 'I have done no wrong. You do believe that, don't you?'

He studied her intently then slowly nodded. 'Yes I believe you, though under the circumstances, God knows why.' He took his hands from her shoulders. Released from his grip, Harlyn's body sagged and her head fell forward.

'Despite what you have seen, what you may think,' Harlyn murmured, 'as the eldest of three daughters I was brought up to respect my parents and obey them in all things.'

A crystal tear trickled down her pale cheek. 'I was taught duty and responsibility, and that the family name and honour were of paramount importance.' Her lips trembled and she fought to steady them, clasping her hands so tightly that the knuckles gleamed white and her nails pierced the flesh.

'I believed it, truly I believed it all, but then—' She could not go on. How could she possibly tell him of her parents' betrayal of her, of the terrible choice she was being forced to make? How could she reveal her shame that her beloved father could use her so, could sell her to Sir Henry Trevellyan in exchange for clearance of all his debts and enough money to launch her sisters into society. To disclose such perfidy would be a betrayal in itself.

The thought of the baronet sent a shudder of fear and revulsion through Harlyn, she closed her eyes for an instant.

'Captain Carlyon,' her voice was taut and husky, 'I swear it is better that my family — and others — believe me dead.'

'Come now, Miss Tremayne,' Jared's voice held a note of condescension, though his eyes were alert and wary, 'are you not perhaps being slightly melodramatic?'

Harlyn stared at him poised to reply, then shook her head hopelessly. 'If you did but know,' she whispered.

'Could it be,' he hazarded, 'that you run from marriage?' His guess was based on what Laity had said on the journey downriver. Harlyn's reaction, however, shook him.

She blanched and her eyes widened in apprehension. 'What — What do you know of that? Who told you? Are you a spy for him? One of his puppets?' Her disgust was pronounced.

'Miss Tremayne,' Jared interrupted, holding up one hand to stem her flow of fear-filled suspicion, 'I have no idea what you are talking about. You are obviously of marriageable age. I wondered if, being a lady of sensitivity' — the irony was unmistakeable — 'that you flee from the idea or the reality, of marriage — of men.'

Harlyn's eyes flamed. How this man confused her. 'I am no milksop prone to the vapours, Captain—' She broke off as the cab stopped and the driver leaned down.

'Fifty-one, High Street, sir.' Harlyn bit her lip and her hands flew to her face.

Jared raised an eyebrow. 'Let us see if Aunt Becky is at home.' Stepping out of the cab, he offered his hand to Harlyn as she emerged on to the narrow pavement.

She stared at what remained of the house, then turned wild-eyed to Jared, whose face was bleak and stony.

'There must be some mistake. We've come to the wrong place,' Harlyn cried, refusing to believe her eyes. 'It must be the wrong place.'

Here and there amid the blackened rubble thin weeds poked through, new life mocking the devastation.

Jared turned to the cab-driver who watched them, idly chewing a hay-stalk.

'Are you sure this is the right address?'

The cabbie shrugged. ''Tis the one you gived me, Sir. I did wonder, mind—'

'All right, thank you,' Jared interrupted him coldly. 'When did this happen?'

''Bout three year ago, sir. Some terrible fire 'twas. Near thirty 'ouses burnt. I dunno 'ow many people—'

Jared turned to Harlyn who stared in stunned horror at the charred ruins. 'What game are you playing now, miss?' he grated.

'Game—' Harlyn whispered.

'You knew nothing of this?' His disbelief was plain.

Harlyn didn't answer. Her face was ashen and she was trembling.

'Miss Tremayne,' Jared Carlyon's voice was harsh and impatient, 'when did you last have any communication with your aunt?'

Harlyn turned her head slowly. 'Some time ago,' she whispered through dry lips. 'Several years.'

'So you have not heard from her within the last three years?'

Harlyn shook her head briefly. 'No.'

'You didn't know about the fire?'

Harlyn stared at him blankly. 'No, of course not. How could I?'

'Surely even Truro has newspapers.'

She did not respond to his sarcasm. 'I never saw it,' she whispered, staring once more at the rubble, horror stark on her face. 'I never knew.'

Jared turned to the cabbie again. 'What became of the survivors?'

The man shrugged. 'I live upalong,' he jerked his head sideways, 'so I aren't sure for certain, but I b'lieve some went to relations, some went away to other towns where they 'ad family. Some places 'ave bin rebuilt. You kin see down there,' he pointed, 'others went to the Union.'

That word stirred a response in Harlyn. 'The workhouse?' Aunt Becky would never have gone to the Union. She'd had a job since Uncle Arthur's accident, and even if he − she would have found work, I know she would.' Harlyn swallowed convulsively.

'That's what she's done, she's found work somewhere in the town.'

Aunt Becky couldn't be dead. She couldn't be. Surely the family would have been informed if − no, Aunt Becky was alive, Harlyn was sure of it. But how to find her? Where should she start looking, and how long would it take?

'I'm so tired,' Harlyn murmured vaguely, 'so very, very tired.' She swayed and staggered slightly.

Jared's arm shot out and caught her around the waist.

'I'm all right,' she muttered, 'must go now — find Aunt Becky.'

Jared heaved a sigh, swept her up in his arms as though she were weightless and placed her in the cab. He climbed in after her.

'It seems I have no choice but to take you home with me. You need to rest.' His eyes raked her critically. 'You also need a bath and some fresh clothes.' He ran a weary hand over his stubby chin. 'We both do.'

Harlyn gave no sign of having heard. Her head was bent like a broken flower. She huddled silently in a corner as Jared gave the driver his own address. The cab moved off and Jared watched the slender form almost buried in the coarse grey blanket.

'Oh, Harlyn Tremayne,' the words were barely audible, 'when will I be free of you?'

As he watched, a tear fell onto the rough dark wool. It hung on the fibre and shimmered, catching the light like a diamond with the slight movement of her uneven breathing. Another fell and trickled down to become lost in a fold, leaving no trace.

Jared was assailed by a feeling normally alien to him, uncertainty. He was moved to offer her comfort, but her silent weeping, obvious desolation, combined to create an unbridgeable distance between them.

On their silent journey through the streets of Falmouth it was he this time who resisted his awareness of her, though the topaz eyes and rock-hard features denied his inner confusion.

Jared paid off the cab, picked up his bag and pushed open the gate.

He paused with one foot on the flagged path and looked over his shoulder at Harlyn. She stood still and silent by the roadside. The blanket had slipped awry and her braided hair encircling her bent head revealed the livid bruises, now turning purple and green on her neck and throat.

Despite the sunshine which kept breaking through the swiftly moving clouds, there on top of the hill above the bay and harbour, the breeze was strong and had a raw edge to it.

A tremor shook Harlyn and her teeth chattered, though she appeared not to notice.

His impatient words were never uttered. In a couple of steps he was beside her, his hand at her elbow, guiding her up the path to the porch and the front door.

As he put his hand out to open it, the door swung inwards.

'My dear life, Mr Jared, what 'ave'ee brung 'ome now?'

'You forget yourself, Elsie,' Jared replied, but the reproof was mild. 'I've no time for explanations, nor are any due. Light the boiler in the bathroom, put warming pans in the bed in the front spare room and then make us some tea, will you?'

'Yes, Mr Jared.' Elsie's boot-button eyes burned with curiosity and disapproval pursued her lips.

Her crisply starched white apron, over a grey homespun skirt and cotton blouse, rustled with indignation as she limped down the hall and up the wide staircase.

'Is there a fire in the morning room?' Jared called after her.

'Of course, Mr Jared.' The offended reply was followed by the bang of a vigorously closed door.

Harlyn was guided into the welcoming warmth of a richly furnished room. Jared placed her gently in a large armchair beside a crackling log fire.

'Miss Tremayne?'

Harlyn slowly raised her head. Her face felt hot, the skin tight, but she met his eyes squarely and saw relief in them.

'You are recovered?'

Harlyn nodded. 'Yes. Thank you. What are you going to do?' she asked apprehensively.

Jared ran his hands through his thick, fair hair and stretched and yawned.

Harlyn was not used to such informal behaviour. His casual action, which startled her into awareness of his powerful masculinity, brought a touch of colour to her pale cheeks.

'I'm going to have a hot bath and a couple of hours' sleep. Then I have other business,' he declared.

'No, I meant—' her voice fell, '—about me.'

'My housekeeper is preparing a room for you. You too need a bath and some proper sleep — and that dress attended to,' he gestured carelessly.

Colour flooded Harlyn's face and her hand fluttered to her breast. 'Yes,' she said desperately, 'but what—'

The door opened and Elsie limped in with a laden silver tray which she placed with exaggerated care on the low oak and rose-wood inlaid table near Harlyn.

'Thank you,' Harlyn murmured gratefully with a tentative smile.

Elsie glanced at the young woman, her dubiousness evident. As she straightened up she caught sight of the weals and bruises on Harlyn's throat and neck. Her mouth dropped open.

'My dear life, whatever 'appened to 'ee, my bird?'

Harlyn's hands flew protectively to her throat. Her fingers touched the tiny barbed hooks securing her torn bodice and she looked uncertainly at Jared.

'Miss Tremayne met with an accident,' he answered for her. 'Fortunately it was not as serious as at first feared, but she has suffered a severe shock.'

'You poor soul,' Elsie clucked, her sympathy genuine, but her curiosity undiminished. 'But 'ow didn' 'ee go 'ome?'

Harlyn swallowed nervously, but before she could speak Jared broke in smoothly.

'Miss Tremayne is in Falmouth to visit a relative who, it appears, lost her home in the High Street fire.'

'Oh?' Harlyn saw Elsie's interest quicken, ''oo might that be, then?'

Jared frowned, but Harlyn forestalled him.

'Becky Collins,' she said quickly to Elsie. 'She's my aunt, my mother's sister. She married Arthur Collins, a miner from Twelveheads. He worked at Great Retallack until his accident. I believe — he lost a leg.'

'Tha's right,' Elsie's head bobbed vigorously up and down. 'I used to know she.'

'You did?' Harlyn could hardly believe her ears.

''Es, after 'e couldn' work no more, Becky took a job at the King's Arms on Market Strand.'

Harlyn felt lightheaded with joy. She flashed a delighted smile at Jared, then fastened her eyes on Elsie, hungry for more information totally unaware of the transformation happiness had wrought upon her face, and equally unaware of the devastating effect that transformation was having on Jared.

'Does she still work there?' Harlyn could not hide her excitement. It was going to be all right after all.

Elsie shook her head. 'No. After the fire she went a bit mazed.

'Er mind wandered like, you know. Well t'wadn surprising, losing 'er man like that.'

Harlyn's smile faded as she realised what Elsie had said.

'You mean − Uncle Arthur died − in the fire?'

Elsie looked surprised. 'Didn' 'ee know?'

Harlyn shook her head. 'No,' she murmured, 'we never heard. Aunt Becky never wrote.'

'Well, t'was some terrible tragedy. 'E couldn' move see, and the fire took 'old so quick nobody could git in to git 'un out.'

'Oh no,' Harlyn's horrified whisper prompted Jared to interrupt brusquely.

'Pour the tea, Elsie, then get about your business.'

Elsie glanced at her employer, interpreting his icy glare as a warning not to upset Harlyn further. She poured milk from the silver jug into delicate bone-china cups.

'Like I said, she went off 'er 'ead fer a bit o' while − not enough to be put away, mind,' Elsie added hurriedly, glancing at Jared once more. She poured the steaming tea through a silver strainer then handed a cup to Harlyn, who watched her anxiously as if to draw the words from her.

'Where did she go? Did she manage to save anything at all?' Harlyn shook her head briefly as Elsie offered her the sugar.

'Not a thing,' Elsie said. 'All she 'ad was what she stood in and that wadn much. Friends took 'er fer a while. Popular Becky was, no side to 'er, though we all knowed she wadn' really like we.' Elsie screwed up her face, 'better class like, you know. Broke 'er 'eart not 'aving no children,' Elsie mused.

Elsie watched Harlyn speculatively with folded arms as the girl sipped the hot tea.

'I never knowed she 'ad other fam'ly. She never said nothing 'bout 'er background, and I aren't one to pry.'

'But where is she now?' Harlyn beseeched.

'Elsie, go and fetch fresh towels for Miss Tremayne, and see that anything else she might need is available.' Jared's tone was pleasant, but held an undeniable ring of command.

Elsie clearly recognised it. 'Right away, Mr Jared,' she muttered, and scurried out.

Jared stood on the opposite side of the fireplace, his elbow resting on the high mantelpiece. He watched Harlyn as she carefully replaced her cup and saucer on the table.

'I can hazard a guess at what is going through your mind,' Jared observed.

'Indeed, Captain?' Harlyn looked up at him warily.

'Indeed, miss.' He leaned forward slightly. 'It's no good. You must see that. I cannot allow you to tramp the streets in search of your aunt who, for all you know, may have been dead for years,' he finished bluntly.

'You have no right to stop me,' Harlyn responded hotly.

Jared's face darkened and his eyes gleamed dangerously. 'Miss Tremayne, for good or ill, you are in my house, and therefore under my protection. In such circumstances I most certainly can stop you.'

'But Elsie — your housekeeper said—'

'Elsie occupies a peculiarly privileged position in this house,' Jared interrupted drily, 'which on occasions results in her saying more than is wise.'

'Wise for whom?' Harlyn retaliated. 'Surely I have a right to know what has become of my relative?'

'It makes no difference now,' Jared stated flatly. 'You heard what Elsie said, your aunt is not quite — herself, if in fact she is still alive.'

'She is, I know it,' Harlyn burst out.

'That is an hysterical remark based purely on emotion, certainly not on fact,' Jared retorted.

'And of course emotion carries no sway with you,' Harlyn felt warm colour flood her face.

'Not when to heed it might result in my being charged with harbouring a fugitive,' he said deliberately, his brows low over his amber eyes.

'Your concern is only for yourself,' Harlyn accused him.

Jared's eyebrow lifted and the sardonic twist of his mouth was very much in evidence. 'Miss Tremayne, my business depends upon my good name. If I show no concern for it, then who will?'

Harlyn was saved from having to answer by the arrival of Elsie who tapped on the door and walked in without awaiting a reply.

'Bath's ready for 'ee, my bird,' she said to Harlyn. 'You come along wi' me.'

Harlyn stood up. She was stiff and sore, and her head throbbed. A tiny flicker of stubborn pride tilted her chin and she met Jared's ironic gaze. 'By your leave, Captain Carlyon?'

she said, her regal tone mocking the politeness of the request to withdraw.

'By all means, Miss Tremayne,' he replied courteously, amusement briefly lighting his eyes.

Harlyn followed Elsie up the stairs and along the passage.

The room they entered was lined with pale blue glazed bricks from floor level to shoulder height. The walls were plastered and painted pale blue from tiles to ceiling. A huge mirror with a white porcelain frame hung on one wall. On another there was a row of pegs and three porcelain shelves on which stood an array of toiletries. Two brushes, a comb, a shaving mug, soap and a cut-throat razor.

Harlyn's eyes slid quickly away from the intimate reminders of the man whose house this was. Her attention was caught by the bath. It took up the whole of one wall.

A massive tub of what looked like white marble was set in a mahogany frame. At one end stood a small stove with pipes leading into the wooden case of the bath. This obviously heated the water and also warmed the room.

At the other end of the bath, suspended by a copper pipe which rose about four feet from the flat wooden endpiece, was a bell-shaped copper bowl which was full of holes.

'What's that?' Harlyn asked wide-eyed.

Elsie followed her apprehensive gaze. 'That's a shower bath my 'andsome. Abn 'ee never seen one o' they before?'

Harlyn shook her head. 'We have hip baths in our rooms at home. What does it do?'

Elsie flicked on the taps and worked the pump handle and a warm spray of water rained into the half-full tub.

Harlyn smiled in delight.

'Come on, now,' Elsie urged, 'take they clothes off and git in that water afore it do get cold.'

Harlyn was so used to Amy attending her in her bath at home that she did not hesitate to begin undressing.

But when she pulled off her shift and turned to step into the inviting water, she saw Elsie's eyes widen then narrow at the sight of the bruises and scratches which marred her creamy skin.

Suspicion sat like a dark cloud on Elsie's face. 'What kind of accident was that you was in?'

Harlyn drew her knees up to her breasts in the hot water and turned her head away.

'I was — attacked,' she said in a small trembling voice. The memory of the dreadful hours spent in the dark, stinking fo'c'sle flooded over her and she began to shake.

After watching her for a moment, Elsie patted Harlyn's shoulders. 'Come on, now. Don'ee fret, my bird. 'Tis over now.' She sighed. 'There's good men and there's beasts and sometimes 'tis 'ard to tell one from n'other jest to look at 'em. You've a good soak now. You'll feel better fer that.' She pointed. 'There's soap in the dish and towels on the rail when you do feel like getting out. I put one o' my clean nightgowns on the peg for 'ee. 'T will be too big but that don't make no mind.'

'Thank you, Elsie,' Harlyn swallowed tears of gratitude and fatigue. 'You've been very kind.'

The older woman waved the thanks aside. ''Tidn nothing.' She picked up the bundle of discarded clothing, wincing as she straightened up.

'Oh, I forgot, the fishhooks,' Harlyn gasped.

'No, 'twadn they, I seen they. 'Tis me leg,' Elsie's face was screwed up in pain. 'I got an ulcer on me leg and it do pain me something awful sometimes.'

'You've seen a physician?'

Elsie raised her eyes and her free hand to the ceiling. 'Don'ee talk to me 'bout doctors. They tried leeches, they spread some filthy muck over the place to burn 'un out.' Her face crumpled suddenly. 'It be worse now.'

'Will you let me suggest a balm?' Harlyn offered shyly.

Elsie shook her head impatiently, her scepticism obvious.

Harlyn tried to convince her. 'I do know something of the uses of herbs in healing. The person who taught me is a dear and close friend.'

Tears pricked Harlyn's eyelids as she thought of Amy and the hours spent in the huge kitchen preparing the draughts and ointments in which Amy had implicit faith.

'She was taught by her mother and grandmother,' Harlyn explained, 'and they have healed all manner of ills.'

'Well, I dunno,' Elsie was plainly doubtful.

'What have you to lose?' Harlyn asked gently.

Elsie pondered for a moment, her lips pursed. ''Tis an awful sight,' she said finally, reluctant Harlyn guessed, to reveal the wound.

'And it has a bad smell?'

Elsie nodded.

'Do you have nettles and vervain in the garden?' Harlyn asked.

Elsie nodded again, doubt still puckering her forehead.

'Gather a panful of each and place them in boiling water.' Harlyn instructed. 'The nettle infusion is for drinking, to cleanse the blood of the poisons from the ulcer. You must bathe the ulcer with the vervain infusion, then make a poultice of the wet leaves and bind it onto the ulcer with a cotton bandage. You must remember to change the poultice every day,' Harlyn stressed.

'That's all?' Elsie was surprised.

'Yes,' Harlyn smiled.

'How long will it take to git better?'

'That depends on how deep the ulcer is, Elsie. But vervain is a very special healing herb. It is said to have grown on Calvary and been used to staunch the wounds of our Lord.'

'You don't say, is that right?' Elsie's small, dark eyes opened wide in amazement. 'Well,' she drew herself up, 'if 'twas good enough for 'ee, 'tis surely good enough fer me. Now you git down in that there bath and 'ave a good soak.' She bustled lopsidedly to the door. Just before she closed it behind her she popped her head around.

'Some strange maid you are but 'tis a kind 'eart you got.' She closed the door and Harlyn listened to her uneven progress along the passage and down the stairs.

Elsie's brief and unexpected compliment was itself balm to Harlyn's bruised and battered emotions. She lay back in the water and its warmth eased her aching, weary body.

But there was no easing the despairing pain in her heart. All that she had endured in the past twenty-four hours, the risks she had taken, the terrible fear she had known, the brutal assault she had suffered, they had all been to no avail. There was no escape. Just as there had never really been a choice.

Her wild idea that she might be mistress of her own destiny was ridiculous, laughable. Except that she couldn't laugh. The deep lacerating pain of betrayal and her futile sense of outrage cut her to her soul.

Now, with Aunt Becky's house burnt to the ground, Jared Carlyon would ensure she returned to her parents.

Harlyn realised that by his code he had no choice. Once she was home again her parents would marry her to Sir Henry Trevellyan.

With that strange detachment which comes from mental and physical exhaustion, Harlyn realised that to her father's way of thinking, *he* had no choice. The good of the whole family depended upon the sacrifice of one member.

Staring blindly into space Harlyn soaped herself all over, then stood under the shower and rinsed off the silky lather.

Stepping out of the bath, she wrapped one soft towel around her and dried herself with the other. After pulling Elsie's crisp white cotton nightgown over her head, Harlyn unbraided her hair and brushed it till her arms ached.

Then she turned at last and wiping a small clear patch on the steamed mirror she stared at her reflection.

The high collar buttoned up to the pie-crust frill hid the bruises on her neck and throat, and the garment's voluminous folds and long full sleeves with their frilled cuffs covered her from chin to ankles.

Her ebony hair which rippled in waves over her shoulders in stark contrast to the white cotton gave her a childlike appearance. Apart from the scratches on her cheek which were already healing and a slight discolouration high on the left side of her face where Pascoe had hit her, there was no visible evidence of her ordeal.

Until she met her own eyes. Then she was betrayed. It was not the purple smudges beneath them. Those, Harlyn knew, should fade with time and rest. But where, before yesterday, her eyes had shone with the clarity of security and innocence, they now held dark shadows, reflections of the scars branded on her soul.

Harlyn buried her face in her hands and like a curtain, her hair swung forward to hide her wretchedness.

There was a tap on the door and Elsie walked in. 'All right, my bird? Feel better now, do 'ee? I got they 'erbs on the stove and I washed yer clothes.'

She didn't remark on Harlyn's withdrawn silence, but leading the way out of the bathroom and along the passage she prattled on, "Tis a good dryin' day so I'll 'ave they ironed afore 'ee do wake.'

She patted a door. 'The wha's' name's in there, if'n you want to go,' then she opened another door further down.

The room was airy and full of sunshine with a lightness which even the heavy dark furniture and ornate brass bedstead with its maroon quilted bedspread could not diminish.

Elsie flicked back the covers and pulled out a copper warming pan. 'In you get, my bird,' she ordered. Harlyn obeyed and Elsie turned the crisp sheet down over the blankets and tucked Harlyn in as she would a baby.

Elsie drew the curtains across the window, shutting out the bright September day and plunging the room into soft twilight.

'I'll bring 'ee a drink when 'ee do wake. Sleep tight, my bird.' She carried the warming pan out, closing the door quietly behind her.

Harlyn turned onto her side and buried her face in the cool pillows. Something inside her broke, and scalding tears, like her heart's own blood, welled up from the depths of her being and squeezed through her tightly shut eyelids.

The force of her sobs shook the bed until, overcome by exhaustion, she lapsed into deep sleep.

Outside, the sun shone and gulls wheeled, screeching on the autumn breeze.

When Harlyn woke her head felt as though it were stuffed with clouds. She wondered for a moment where she was, then remembered and immediately tried to put a brake on her tumbling thoughts.

She slipped out of bed and splashed cold water from the jug on the dressing table onto her face. It refreshed her and cleared her head.

Harlyn pulled back the curtains and looked out across the roof tops to the panorama of the harbour and the Carrick Roads and in the distance the Roseland peninsula.

She deduced it to be mid-afternoon from the shadows cast by the trees on the avenue outside. The sun had moved around to the other side of the house and her window was now in shade.

Deliberately keeping all thoughts at bay, Harlyn revelled in the view. The ships in the sparkling blue waters of the harbour looked like toys. There was a gentle knock on the door.

'Come in, I'm awake,' Harlyn called, her voice still husky from the bruising in her throat. She did not turn round. The door opened and there was a pause.

'It's very beautiful, Elsie,' Harlyn sighed softly.

'It is indeed.' Jared Carlyon's deep voice was quite serious as he gazed at the slender curving silhouette of Harlyn's body against the window.

Harlyn spun round, her hair flying wild, a crimson tide of shock and embarrassment flooding her face.

'I thought — I thought—' she stammered.

'Obviously,' Jared interrupted, his eyes gleaming strangely in the afternoon light. A note of amusement crept into his voice. 'And I thought to find you still abed, your modesty protected by the covers.'

'Oh,' Harlyn gave a muffled squeak and dived between the sheets, pulling the coverlet up to her chin. She looked up at him, flushed, shy, angry and perplexed.

'Is it then a custom in this town to burst in upon a lady guest while she is yet abed?' Harlyn blinked.

'Sadly for me the situation has not previously arisen. But were I mayor I think I would ensure that it were not merely custom, but compulsory.'

The mocking tilt of his brows and the quirk at the corner of his mouth belied the seriousness of his tone. Yet there was something else in his face, something she could not identify but which nevertheless made her heart beat a little faster.

'Besides,' his tawny eyes held hers, 'you invited me.'

'I did not, I thought you were—' Her anger evaporated. 'Please excuse me,' she stammered, 'I spoke in haste. It is I who have imposed.'

Her head fell back on the pillow and she stared blindly at the ceiling. 'I am aware you did not choose my company, and that in truth I am no welcome guest in your house.'

Jared leaned back against the door and folded his arms. His head, as he contemplated her, was tipped slightly to one side.

'I think, Miss Tremayne,' he said consideringly, 'that the sooner you are out of my house, the greater will my peace of mind.' He levered himself away from the door and came to stand by the bed. 'My reason for this visit was to give you time to collect yourself. As soon as you are dressed and have eaten, I shall accompany you to the coach.'

Harlyn sat bolt upright and seized his hand in both of hers. 'I beg you, don't do this to me. Don't send me back to Truro.'

He did not try to loosen her grip, but instead sat down on the edge of the bed.

'You know I have no choice,' he said gently, 'you must surely understand that?'

Stiff with tension, Harlyn stared accusingly at him, then her shoulders drooped.

'If you return me to my parents, they intend to marry me to Sir Henry Trevellyan.'

Jared recalled his conversation with Laity aboard *Karis*.

'Against your will?' he asked quietly.

Harlyn nodded. 'Very much against my will.'

'Then why? If they know your feelings in the matter, why are they insisting upon the marriage?'

'It is expedient,' Harlyn replied bitterly. 'I was too ashamed to tell you earlier. But now,' hopelessness filled her voice, 'now my pride is of no importance. We are all in our own way, prisoners.' She looked up at him. 'My father is facing ruin. That will not surprise you, you intimated as much when you and Mr Laity were talking in the cabin before I − before you—' Harlyn faltered then took a deep breath.

'Sir Henry has undertaken to pay all my father's debts and launch my two sisters into society, which is my mother's dearest wish. You see, she knows nothing of my father's financial problems.'

Jared's eyebrows drew together in a frown and he appeared deep in thought.

'Do you know him well?'

'I do not know him at all. I have met him only once,' Harlyn replied quietly, 'but there is something about him which repulses and terrifies me.' A shudder ran through her, moving her shoulders under the cotton nightgown.

'You may think me a foolish maid, you said as much in the cab, but it is not marriage I dread. Had it been to a man I loved—' Her voice dropped shyly and she lowered her eyes, feeling warmth colour her cheeks.

Their proximity as they sat facing one another on the bed, and the desire of each to make the other understand, was weaving its own spell.

Harlyn was vividly aware of the light pressure of his fingers on the backs of hers as she clutched his hand. '—Then I would have welcomed marriage,' she raised her eyes suddenly and met his, her voice a mere whisper, her cheeks rosy, '—and all its joys.'

Something moved deep in Jared's tawny eyes, and his jaw tightened. Harlyn's heart fluttered oddly and she was aware of a strange weakness in the pit of her stomach.

'There are rumours,' she went on, struggling to keep her voice calm and level, 'that Sir Henry is — is not as other men are, and that to compensate for his — disability, he finds fulfilment by other — unnatural means. His first wife died in a lunatic asylum.'

Her calm deserted her and her voice broke. She flung herself into Jared's arms, instinctively seeking his strength and comfort. 'I am so frightened,' she sobbed, clinging fiercely to him, her body trembling uncontrollably.

Slowly, almost reluctantly, Jared folded his arms around her, comforting her like a child, smoothing her hair with gentle fingers. Harlyn buried her face in his neck. The texture of his skin was warm against her lips. She breathed in the masculine scent of him, tinged with the fragrance of the soap she also had used.

His hand, cupping the back of her head, was still, and his other arm tightened convulsively around her.

Harlyn still trembled, but now the tremors which rippled through her were of a different nature. She could feel the rhythmic thump of his heartbeat against her breast and his breathing quickened.

Driven by forces over which she had no control, Harlyn moved her mouth softly, tentatively against his neck. She closed her eyes, shutting out everything but the man who held her, the pressure of his body against hers, the encircling band of his arm, the gentle strength of his hand holding her head, his warmth, the smell of him.

Curious, Harlyn slid the tip of her tongue between her parted lips and lightly touched the freshly shaved skin of his jaw.

With a sharp intake of breath Jared turned his head, his mouth came down on hers in a touch so gentle yet so vibrant she nearly fainted.

Harlyn sensed the tension building in him, but she felt no fear. A hollow ache, a yearning so sweet it was almost painful, but no fear.

Jared made a soft low sound deep in his throat. He pressed Harlyn to him, his hand on her back burning through the thin cotton nightgown. His lips moved on hers, at first gentle searching, then with a strength and passion that was almost savage in its intensity. Harlyn felt like a leaf caught in the violent cross currents of a storm.

Then, with an abruptness that left her gasping, Jared tore his fingers in her hair, wrenched her head back.

'Girl, what do you think you are doing?' His voice was low and harsh.

Harlyn's dark lashes parted to reveal her brilliant emerald eyes. Her voice was husky with pain and tears.

'Please — I did not intend — I did not mean — I have told you what is planned for me. If there is no escape — I beg you, don't send me back today.' Her voice was barely audible, 'Let me stay with you — like this, please, oh please let me stay.'

Jared's face was incredulous, he leaned back and stared at her. 'Do you know what you are saying?'

Harlyn met his gaze, her eyes huge in her pale face. She nodded.

Jared gripped her shoulders and held her away from him. 'Have you no modesty, no shame, to suggest such a thing?'

'Shame?' Harlyn laughed wildly, her voice breaking on a sob. 'I am betrayed by my family, sold to pay my father's debts, condemned to a living hell, and you speak of shame?' She swallowed her tears. 'Of what am I guilty? I pray you tell me. Is it that I spoke openly of what I felt? Is such honesty something to be ashamed of?' There was no defiance in her voice, only bewilderment and unhappiness.

As Jared studied her, his expression was stern but his eyes held something akin to wonder.

'Am I ugly to you?' Harlyn asked, her forehead puckering suddenly. Her hands flew to her throat. 'Is it because of what happened on the boat? I thought — I thought you felt as I did, but — was I wrong? Do I repel you?'

'No, No, it has nothing to do with what happened on the boat, I did — I was—' Jared admitted, 'but—' he sighed in exasperation. 'Good God, Miss Tremayne, I'm not in the habit of discussing such matters, let alone with a woman.'

'I have shocked you, I'm sorry,' Harlyn murmured. 'Truly I didn't mean to. But I don't understand why,' her voice quavered, 'if you felt — were moved — why do you turn away from me?'

Jared got up abruptly from the bed, and walked to the

window, running his hands through his hair. He shrugged helplessly, staring out towards the harbour.

'God knows. I don't understand myself — yes, I do.' He turned and faced her. 'I shall be brutally frank with you. When I discovered you on board my ship I assumed you to be a whore, or at least a woman of easy virtue. The possibility has lingered in my mind — until a few moments ago. Now I know you are not.'

Harlyn was bewildered. 'Am I undesirable then?' she asked in small voice. 'It is true I have no experience in these matters, but I would learn, you could teach—'

'Stop it, stop it at once,' Jared roared, confounded. Amazement and anger vied with one another causing his eyes to flame. 'How can you say such things.'

'I would say them to no one but you,' Harlyn replied hotly. 'Don't you understand?' she entreated. 'I am condemned to a life without love, without children, a travesty of marriage. I do not expect or ask that you should change that.'

Scrambling out of bed she ran to where he stood by the window and grasping his hands in hers she pressed them to her breast.

'All I ask, all I beg is that you allow me one beautiful memory to cling to, one precious hour to sustain me in the darkness that lies ahead. I promise I shall never trouble you again.'

Jared looked down into her pleading eyes, his face grave. Harlyn could feel the tension emanating from him. He freed one of his hands from its soft prison and touched her lips and cheek with gentle fingers.

'If I were to do what you ask,' he said hoarsely, 'you would trouble me for the rest of my life.'

He disengaged himself gently but firmly. 'Elsie is preparing food for you. She will bring your clothes in a moment.'

His voice was returning to normal and as he strode to the door, his face had assumed once again its mask of cool disdain.

'I shall return you to your family, Miss Tremayne, honour and duty leave me no choice. However,' he added, 'it may be possible to discover a means of circumventing this proposed marriage which does not involve bargaining with your virginity.' He walked out closing the door behind him.

Harlyn's face was on fire, her mind in turmoil. Before she could begin to sort her thoughts into any coherent order, there was another knock on the door.

'What—? Who is it?' Harlyn asked breathlessly. She couldn't face him again, not so soon, not until she had restored some calm to her confused and turbulent emotions.

''Tis Elsie, my bird.' The door opened and Elsie peered round it. 'I brung yer clothes. All washed and ironed they are, and I mended that there rip in yer bodice. If'n you ask me that was some lucky escape you'ad,' she added meaningfully.

'Yes, it was.' Harlyn bit her lip. With a swift movement she pulled the nightgown over her head and turned to Elsie, revealing the full extent of the vicious bruising, scratches and bites she had suffered at Pascoe's rapacious hands.

'Tell me truly, Elsie,' Harlyn said tightly, 'am I deformed? Am I ugly?'

Elsie's eyebrows rose to her hairline in surprise. Her small piercing eyes flitted over Harlyn's body appraisingly, then met once more the girl's fear-filled gaze.

''Course not, my 'andsome,' Elsie scoffed. 'You be marked, sure 'nough, but that wint last long. You're some pretty maid, an' tha's a fact.' She gave a determined nod, adding more weight to her opinion.

Harlyn's shoulders sagged in relief.

'Wha's matter, my bird? Afraid you'll lose yer young man, are 'ee?' Elsie asked shrewdly as she helped Harlyn dress.

Harlyn's voice wavered and her lips quivered momentarily. 'I have no young man, Elsie, nor will I ever.'

Elsie was sceptical. 'Aw, c'mon now, lovely maid like you, you'll be a bride afore yer next birthday—'

'Stop it, Elsie,' Harlyn cried, burying her face in her hands.

'What ails 'ee, girl?' Elsie was alarmed.

'I'm sorry. I'm sorry,' Harlyn choked. 'Elsie, if you know, for pity's sake tell me − where is my Aunt Becky now? What has become of her?'

Elsie's face closed up. 'I aren't s'posed to say nothin' 'bout she. Mr Jared was some cross wi' me.'

'I swear I won't ever breathe a word to a living soul,' Harlyn promised, 'least of all to Jared Carlyon,' she added with such vehemence that Elsie was convinced.

'Well, I do owe 'ee sommat fer me leg.' Harlyn could see she was torn between divided loyalties.

'Please, Elsie,' Harlyn beseeched.

'Well,' Elsie whispered conspiratorially, 'I 'eard she've gone to one of the beer 'ouses down Quay Street. I aren't sure mind, 'twas only 'earsay. In any case I tell'ee 'tidn no fit place fer you. You've 'ad one close call—' she warned.

Harlyn planted an impulsive kiss on Elsie's cheek. 'Bless you, Elsie,' she said gratefully, 'you may have saved my life.'

'I dunno,' Elsie was dubious. 'If'n you go down there you'd better be some careful, and jest you remember your promise, else my life wint be worth much. Now sit down and I'll do yer 'air.'

Harlyn did as she was told, her mind working feverishly. So busy was she with her own thoughts that she almost missed Elsie's next words as the older woman picked up the brush from the dressing table and began brushing Harlyn's dark mane.

'Since Mr Jared's mother went back to 'er family in Denmark after 'is father died, I 'abn 'ad no lady to look after,' she sighed wistfully. 'Mr Jared's no trouble, and any'ow 'e's away at sea quite a bit o' the time, but 't 'edn the same. Still,' her voice rose hopefully, 'if 'e do wed Camilla St Aubyn, and she do come 'ere to live—'

Harlyn spun round, sending the brush flying from Elsie's hand.

'What did you say?' she whispered, her face pale as death.

'I said Mr Jared's mother went back to Denmark. She was some lovely woman. 'E do take after she in 'is colouring. 'Igh born she was too, 'ad connections with the Danish royalty, I b'lieve—'

'No, no, not that. I mean about — did you say Jar — Captain Carlyon is to be married?' Harlyn could scarcely get the words out.

'My tongue will, 'ang me, so 't will.' Elsie put her hand to the side of her face and grimaced. 'Now don' you go saying nothing, 'cos 'tedn settled yet. But 'e do see 'er regular. Well, 'e do see 'er father but she's always there too, and she do write 'un letters, perfumed they are, and I do know 'e dined at the Red Lion wi' they last night, 'cos 'e told me afore 'e went up Truro.'

Elsie retrieved the brush and resumed her task. 'Time 'e was wed,' she said sagely. 'A man like 'd do need a wife. She's some pretty maid, Miss Camilla, and she'll bring a good dowry. Got skin like buttermilk, she'ave—'

Elsie chattered on, enjoying the rare opportunity for a little gossip, her capable hands separating Harlyn's raven tresses, brushing them to a rich gloss.

Harlyn sat frozen on the upholstered stool, deaf to Elsie's voice, unaware of the sweeping strokes of the ivory-backed brush.

Why hadn't she *thought*? She should have realised he would be married or betrothed. Why had it not occurred to her? What had possessed her to imagine that Jared Carlyon might have been interested in her, or sympathetic to her problems?

How she must have embarrassed him, or maybe he was quietly laughing at her. After all he was about to marry the richest girl in the county.

The St Aubyns were one of the oldest and noblest families in Cornwall. They had position and wealth and Camilla was their only child. None of the other branches of the family had been so successful in maintaining their position and enlarging their fortunes by judicious investment as Richard St Aubyn. Harlyn had heard her father speak of him, usually in tones of tired envy.

Harlyn had a vivid mental picture of Jared Carlyon's face. Tawny eyes gleaming beneath hooded lids, his face set in his habitual supercilious mask, his lip curled in half-ironic, half-amused contempt.

Small wonder he had rejected her. What a poor gift she had offered compared to the prize he was about to secure. How it must have amused him. Why had he not told her? Had she known he was promised she would never have said − never have asked—

Harlyn wanted to die she was so embarrassed, so mortified. Could he not have spared her such humiliation? How she hated him. She would never be able to face him again, never.

She turned to Elsie, cutting short the older woman's catalogue of Camilla's endless good qualities.

'Is Captain Carlyon downstairs?' she asked hoarsely, her throat painfully tight.

Elsie shook her head. 'No, my bird. 'E've gone down Fox's, the ship agents, then 'e've got to see Cap'n 'enderson. 'Tis 'e what look after Mr Jared's business when 'e's away, then 'e's going to the Bank. But don' 'ee fret, 'e'll be back in plenty time to take you to the coach. 'E said you was to 'ave sommat t'eat first.'

Harlyn stood up, slender, proud and defiant.

'I'm not going on the coach, Elsie. I'm going to find my Aunt Becky.'

Elsie's face puckered in worried creases. 'You can't do that, my bird. 'E said I wadn' to let 'ee out of the 'ouse. 'E said you might 'ave some wild idea 'bout stayin' in Falmouth. Lissen 'ere to me,' she urged, 'you go 'ome where you do b'long. Tidn good fer a young girl to be on the streets alone. Look what 'appened to 'ee already.'

Harlyn sat down again, and looked at Elsie through the mirror.

'Pin up my hair, please,' she commanded gently. 'It is time for you to change the poultice on your leg and while you are doing that, I shall collect vegetables from the garden for you.'

Harlyn's gaze steady and utterly determined, defeated Elsie who nodded once. Her nimble fingers twisted Harlyn's heavy hair into a coil low on her neck and secured it with pins from a painted glass bowl with a domed lid on the dressing table. She stood back.

''Tis done,' she said and both understood the significance of her words. 'Wind's cold. You take that old cloak o' mine be'ind the kitchen door,' Elsie said abruptly. 'There's bread and meat and saffron cake on the tray. If some was gone well, I wouldn' know.'

'God bless you, Elsie,' Harlyn whispered and whirled round, running lightly out of the room and down the stairs.

From the upstairs window Elsie watched the slender figure hurry down the path. The russet dress was almost totally hidden by the long brown cloak.

At the gate the girl turned and looked briefly towards the window where Elsie stood, then she pulled the hood close about her head and was gone.

'Some strange maid,' Elsie sighed, shaking her head.

9

Harlyn walked swiftly along the pavement edging the tree-lined road. Her chin was high and there was purpose in her step. She had slept well and her youth and abundant health had restored her, physically at least. Her emotional condition was something else. After the debacle with Jared, and Elsie's revelation of his expected betrothal, Harlyn's emotions were in utter confusion. She had suffered so many shocks, so much heartache, that she was incapable of knowing what she felt.

A strange calm descended upon her. A protective screen held all deep thought and feeling at bay, and her mind was functioning on a purely surface level.

Her clothes, newly washed and ironed, were crisp and clean against her skin and smelled of fresh air. Though old, Elsie's cloak, made of good quality wool gaberdine, was cut full enough to hang in folds from Harlyn's slender shoulders, and long enough to reach almost to her ankles.

It not only protected Harlyn from the strong breeze blowing in off the sea, but also provided an all enveloping disguise, and a sense of security.

In her left hand she clasped a linen napkin containing two cuts of rare roast beef, some fresh crusty bread, a slice of saffron cake and an apple, all hastily snatched from the tray on the kitchen table.

As she walked Harlyn examined the houses on the opposite side of the road. They were large and imposing, guarded by high stone walls, over which the red, orange and gold leaves of virginia creeper spilled, like a fiery waterfall. The wind ruffled the leaves and in the dappled sunlight they danced like flames.

The biggest house stood at a curve in the road. According to the name plate at the entrance to the drive this was Grove Hill, home of Robert Were Fox.

Harlyn recognised the name. She had heard her father speak

often of the Quaker family whose interest encompassed shipping, mining, fishing and commerce.

Harlyn heard voices and she slowed her step and peeped through the small gateway beside the drive entrance.

Four people, two men and two women stood talking on the broad sweep of the drive before it curved round to the front entrance of the south-facing house.

Harlyn guessed the women to be in their forties. One, she appeared to be the elder, wore a crinolined dress of plain grey silk with a narrow white collar. Her hair was drawn back into a neat but severe chignon and was covered by a white cotton bonnet.

The only colour in her ensemble was the embroidery on a cashmere shawl with silken fringes which was draped across her shoulders.

The younger woman wore a flounced dress of fawn tussore silk, covered by a dark green hip-length coat with a tasselled hood. On her head she wore a straw bonnet. Both men wore frock coats and top hats.

The snatches of conversation which reached Harlyn, borne on the breeze, increased her interest even more. The lady in grey was addressing the older of the two men. His black coat, black and grey striped trousers and black stove-pipe hat were complemented by a silver-headed cane, which from his upright stance and easy manner he carried as an affectation not an aid.

'I gather the experiments at the Docks were successful, gentlemen?'

'Indeed yes, Ma'am. I am pleased to be able to tell you that Mr Nobel's nitro-glycerine fully justified our claims concerning its immense power.'

'You see, Ma'am,' the younger man, dressed identically to his older companion, but in cheviot grey and minus the cane, broke in eagerly, 'the simultaneous action not only shattered four times as much rock as ordinary powder would have, but threw it completely out of the hole.'

The lady in grey inclined her head. 'And what of Mr Prentice's gun cotton?'

The two men exchanged a brief glance.

'Regrettably, the demonstration was not all it might have been,' the older man sighed. 'You see, for a significant result the charge should fit the hole exactly, unfortunately it did not.'

'Oh?' The inflection in the lady's voice prompted the younger man to further explanation.

'Even the slightest degree of looseness can inhibit the power of the blast, and it appears that the charges brought down for the experiment were one inch diameter, while the holes drilled to receive them were one and a half inches.'

The older man tutted, 'Such carelessness.'

The lady frowned. 'One wonders how such a discrepancy could occur, especially on such an important occasion. Mr Prentice's gun cotton has been used for mining purposes for some time I believe. This disappointing public demonstration cannot have enhanced its reputation.'

The man in black spread his hands. 'A challenge is always healthy, Ma'am, where a monopoly exists. We intend to provide that challenge.'

'With nitro-glycerine?'

The older man nodded.

'What type of detonator do you intend to use at the Exhibition?' The lady asked. 'Obviously an ordinary fuse and powder will not be suitable, and I naturally assume you will be using a far smaller quantity of the oil, won't you?'

The two men exchanged another glance and the younger took up the explanation in respectful tones.

'Well, Ma'am, regarding the detonator, either an electric filament will heat and fire a measured charge of gunpowder held in a small case suspended in the nitro-glycerine, or we might use a wire heated by electricity to a very high temperature as it passes through the oil. We might possibly even try a percussion cap lit by a safety fuse.'

The lady nodded consideringly. 'And you are quite satisfied that the Exhibition experiment will be safe? You understand that as founders of the Polytechnic Society, our responsibility to our members and to the general public is a heavy one.'

Both men were anxious to reassure her.

'Miss Fox, you have my word that Mr Nobel has developed his theories after most careful and considered experimentation of his own, based on that done by Senor Sobrero,' the older man stated with convincing sincerity. 'As his agent I am bound to adhere to his standards, and if possible even improve upon them.'

'Naturally, Ma'am,' the younger man put in, 'while every

possible safety factor is taken into account, time is of great importance. The mine owners desperately need an explosive of the greatest possible blasting power, and they are showing a growing interest in our nitro-glycerine. But there's no doubt that Prentice's gun cotton appeals to the more traditional elements in the industry, though after yesterday's fiasco—' He shrugged dismissively.

The older man glared at his young associate then his expression swiftly altered to a deprecating smile.

'We have no intention of involving ourselves in a race, Miss Fox,' he assured her, 'such an idea is totally disasteful, especially to men of science like ourselves.'

'I am not unaware of the financial considerations involved,' the lady in grey said pointedly. 'The prestige gained by winning the Society's silver medal could also influence certain attitudes, but I must stress that safety is of paramount importance.'

'But of course, Miss Fox,' the older man agreed sincerely. 'Shall we have the honour and pleasure of your company, and that of your esteemed father at the Exhibition tomorrow?'

The lady in grey shook her head. 'I'm afraid not. My father is working on a paper for the Royal Society and cannot be disturbed, and I am expected at Penjerrick this evening. But I shall await your reports with great interest. Good day, gentlemen. Come, Caroline.' She inclined her head graciously then turned away down the drive accompanied by her companion, who had watched the exchange in silence but with obvious interest.

The two men bowed and raised their hats then started towards the gate.

Harlyn was about to walk on when she noticed that the buttons on her shoe had come undone and she bent down to refasten them.

So concerned with their conversation were the men as they came out of the gateway that neither noticed the crouching girl.

'What grade of oil have you got for tomorrow?' the older man demanded.

'It's as pure as I could get in the time you've allowed me,' the other replied defensively.

'Just make certain you check for grit or air bubbles before you start. If hot spots develop when the electric charge goes through—' The man's voice faded out of Harlyn's earshot as they both walked down the steep hill.

What would happen if hot spots developed, Harlyn wondered. What were hot spots anyway? But a more immediate problem presented itself. Where was Quay Street, the place Elsie had said she would find Aunt Becky?

Realising it must be near the water, Harlyn followed the two men a little way down the hill.

Suddenly it occurred to her that this could possibly be the route by which Jared would return to his house. She had not escaped to risk capture again so soon.

Quickly she turned off down a side street on her right. Ahead of her was a broad avenue with trees down the centre and on both sides. Her steps slowed. That didn't seem to be the right way. Then on her left she noticed a narrow lane. It appeared to run parallel to the hill she had just left. That impression was reinforced by the salt-laden breeze, carrying the sounds of the town and the boat yards that funnelled up the lane.

Harlyn hurried to the bottom and looking about her, recognised on her left the Custom House on the opposite side of the street.

Hunger pangs reminded her that she had had no food since Mrs Laity's pasty on board *Karis* early that morning. She had been in Falmouth about twelve hours. How much longer it seemed.

As she turned towards the Custom House, just in front of her, jutting out onto the pavement, Harlyn saw steps leading to the white-columned porch of a three-storied red brick building. A sign-board announced this to be the premises of G. C. Fox & Co., Ship Agents.

Harlyn's heart gave a lurch. Jared might be in there. He might come out at any moment.

Bunching up her skirts, Harlyn ran across the road, almost under the wheels of a loaded cart, whose driver waved a fist at her, mouthing curses as his horse shied.

She turned down the steep slope and found herself on the Town quay. Now off the main thoroughfare she felt safer and her heartbeat gradually returned to normal.

The tide was high and the fishing boats and punts of varying shapes and sizes, each difference the trademark of the man who had built it, rubbed fenders all along the quayside. Seagulls shrieked and squabbled over bits of fish and edible refuse in the water. Fishermen worked on their boats, stowing nets, sorting gear.

Harlyn walked past the office and printing works of the *Falmouth and Penryn Weekly Times*. Glancing behind her she caught sight of the heavy iron doors of the Bonded Stores with their massive locks and painted insignia. Further up the quay she saw the square squat chimney of the King's pipe, where contraband tobacco was burned.

She walked out to the end of the quay. It was quiet there. The few fishermen still aboard their boats took no notice of her. Harlyn sat down on an iron mooring bollard and unfolding the napkin, began to eat. She gazed up the river towards the lowering sun. Gulls wheeled overhead, the bolder ones alighting nearby and stalking up and down hopeful of receiving scraps.

But Harlyn was hungry, her appetite sharpened even further by the fresh salt air and the uncertainty of when she would eat again. The gulls waited in vain.

When she had finished Harlyn gave a small sigh of satisfaction. Tossing her apple core to the gulls and provoking a squealing skirmish of beaks and wings, Harlyn shook the napkin free of crumbs.

She spread it over her knees and gently smoothed the linen square, noticing for the first time the fine embroidery which traced the letter C in curled script across one corner.

Was there no escape from that man? She could banish him from her mind, there was so much she had to think of, so much to plan.

She hated him, his contemptuous superiority, his tilted sardonic brow, those piercing amber eyes. He was so confident, so self-assured, so completely in control. And yet, there had been moments — moments when she'd glimpsed another side, a gentle, tender, compassionate side. She did not, could not, hate that part of him. He had saved her from Pascoe, he had sheltered her in his house.

Her mind cried stop. She must not think about him, he was the past, an incident, over, finished. She must look to the future. But what future?

Swallowing the tightness in her throat, Harlyn stood up to shake out her dress and adjust the cloak about her. As the sun went down, the wind took on a keen, cold edge and Harlyn was glad of its heavy folds.

The napkin was still clutched in her hand and Harlyn

wondered what to do with it. For an instant she thought of throwing it away, but somehow she couldn't.

Then an idea struck her. Spreading it flat, Harlyn folded it in half cornerwise, and pushing back her hood, she placed the triangular piece of linen over her head, tying the ends beneath the coiled hair on her neck. Then she pulled the hood up again. It would afford her another small piece of disguise, hiding her hair as well as keeping it tidy.

Now to find Aunt Becky. But first she had to find Quay Street. She thought of asking, but that would be admitting she was a stranger, and someone, if questioned, might remember.

Harlyn was under no illusion. She knew Sir Henry Trevellyan would make at least some attempt to find her, to save face and extract revenge for the humiliation her flight might have caused him. She had to make his search as difficult as possible.

She was on the Town quay, so Quay Street could not be far. She walked back up the steep slope, glancing quickly at Fox's offices before pulling the cloak around her bending her head and scuttling quickly past the Custom House.

She came to another junction. Looking up at her left Harlyn saw a roughly paved and cobbled street with a gutter running down the middle. The houses, three, sometimes four stories high, were squashed together on either side of the narrow street. Poles with washing flapping on them stuck out from the upper walls at angles.

Harlyn saw a name plate, discoloured and almost hidden on the wall of the first house. It read Quay Hill.

She must be close. Searching the walls of the buildings on her right, at last Harlyn found what she sought. Almost hidden by a notice proclaiming the facilities offered by the Dolphin Hotel, outside which she now stood, was a small sign which said Quay Street.

The narrow road dropped steeply and seemed darkened by the buildings which rose tall on both sides, the upper floors jutting out over the doorways and covered alleys leading off to left and right.

Harlyn wondered why Elsie had stressed the danger of this place. It didn't appear any different to many of the smaller streets in Truro, although there did seem to be quite a lot of men and very few women entering and leaving the various doorways.

A group of men came out of the side entrance of the hotel behind Harlyn. They were laughing and joking and had obviously just dined.

One stumbled as they turned to go down into the streets on which Harlyn's attention was focussed, affording his friends much amusement and provoking ribald remarks, many of which Harlyn did not understand. But those she did brought a flush of embarrassment to her cheeks.

Three more men came out of a doorway a few steps below street level, about halfway down. They noticed Harlyn standing hesitantly on the corner and one hailed her. Harlyn did not recognise the language he spoke, but when encouraged by his friends, he shouted again and made an obscene gesture, Harlyn suddenly realised the nature of the place she was in, and the reason for Elsie's warnings.

The knowledge flooded her face with crimson colour and her heart with cold fear, as vivid memories of the incident with Pascoe sprang into her mind.

Her shoulder was stabbed by a sharp finger and Harlyn spun round, wide-eyed and nervous.

'Wha' d' you want 'ere? This edn your patch. G'wan, get off out of it.'

The speaker was a girl of about her own age or possibly younger, but with a garishly painted face, hair hennaed to brilliant orange and eyes as old as time.

'I'm − I'm looking for someone,' Harlyn stammered, startled by the belligerence in the girl's attitude.

The girl gave a barking laugh. 'Well, I aren't 'ere fer me 'ealth.'

'No, you don't understand,' Harlyn tried to explain, 'it's my aunt, she works in one of the hotels, but I don't know which one.'

'Pull t'other one, 'e's got bells on,' the girl scoffed in patent disbelief. 'You get on out of it, find yer own place. Move up the town somewhere, but you git away from 'ere, else the girls and me'll make you sorry.'

The threatening scowl on the girl's face told Harlyn she was perfectly capable of carrying out her promise. But while it unnerved Harlyn, making her heart beat faster and her hands tremble so that she hid them quickly beneath the cloak, Harlyn stood her ground.

'I'm no threat to you,' she said quietly. 'I've come to find my aunt, nothing more.'

'Well, you'd better start lookin' then,' the girl snapped peevishly, and pulling the frilled neckline of her grubby white blouse even lower, she hitched her scarlet shawl trimmed with ragged black lace higher up her shoulders and pushed past Harlyn, sauntering down the street towards the three foreign sailors who hooted and whistled their appreciation.

As she reached them the girl looked over her shoulder, a spiteful grin twisting her mouth. She whispered something to the men who looked at Harlyn and sniggered before returning their attention and their groping hands to the giggling girl.

Harlyn bit her lip, fighting down the fear and disgust that rose in her throat, threatening to choke her.

Don't think, she commanded herself desperately, concentrate on finding Aunt Becky, ignore everything else.

She would start here, in the hotel outside which she now stood. It was possible they might know where Aunt Becky worked. If they did she would not have to venture any further down this shocking, frightening street.

The hotel proprietor, aloof and disdainful, informed her that no such person worked on his premises which adhered to the very highest standards of cleanliness and moral rectitude.

With rosy patches on her cheeks from the anger that burned within her at this slight upon her aunt's character, Harlyn nevertheless thanked the man politely and walked out of the hotel.

She tried the Commercial Hotel, the Pilot Boat Hotel and the Navy hotel, all with similar results. Each one took her further down the street and each denial sapped a little more of her courage and will-power.

Try as she might to quash them, doubt and panic began to rise. Perhaps Elsie had made a mistake, maybe Aunt Becky wasn't here at all, but somewhere else in the town, and if she didn't find her, what was she going to do? It was almost dark. She had no money, no food and nowhere to go. What was she to do?

Harlyn closed her eyes, fighting tears of fearfulness and despondency, and leaned against the rough stonewall beneath the steps of the hotel she had just left.

'What we got 'ere then?' A rasping voice slurred in her ear.

Harlyn's eyes flew open. She hadn't noticed the dark mouth of the alleyway in the shadow of the wall. Rigid with fright, her heart racing madly, she opened her mouth to scream but no sound came.

The man grabbed Harlyn by the shoulder, trying to turn her round. His touch freed Harlyn from her paralysing terror and she shook off his hand with a violent movement, and whirled round to face him.

He was shorter than her, of stocky build, with a thatch of greasy, spiky hair sprouting from under a dirty cap. He rocked unsteadily and his face was screwed up with the effort of focussing his eyes on her.

'Don't touch me,' Harlyn hissed, trembling from head to foot. 'Don't come near me.'

'Aw, c'mon,' the man swayed, blearily reaching for her. 'Don't be like that. I kin pay, I got money – 'ere, look—' he fumbled at his pockets.

Harlyn gave a shuddering gasp and pushed him away with all her strength.

He staggered, tripped and crashed backwards onto the cobbles, rolling into a heap against the wall on the other side of the alleyway.

'Hey, what's going on?' Harlyn darted a glance over her shoulder. Two men who had just come out of one of the hotels further up, were walking down the street towards her.

Choking back a sob Harlyn bunched up her skirts and plunged into the alleyway. It was dark and wet and foul-smelling.

Halfway along light spilled out as a door leading into the alley suddenly opened. The smell of frying onions met Harlyn's nostrils and a panful of dirty water missed her by inches.

Harlyn threw herself at the door as it began to close. 'Please, please help me,' she gasped.

'Wha'd 'ee want?' A red-faced woman, her apron streaked with grease, and sleeves pushed up to her elbows, eyed Harlyn with suspicion poised to slam the door in her face at the first sign of trouble.

'I'm looking for someone, my Aunt Becky,' Harlyn panted. 'She works as cook in one of the beer houses down here, but I don't know which one. I've got to find her, it's terribly important. Oh please don't shut the door, please,' Harlyn begged, her breath coming in ragged sobs.

The woman hesitated a moment, then pulled back the door, jerking her head sideways.

'You'd better come in. I don't b'long 'ere. I'm jest 'elping out while me sister's bad. Sid, 'e's my brother-in-law, 'e might know. 'E's in the taproom. You'd better ask 'e.'

She led the way through the low ceilinged kitchen, past a heavy wooden table laden with plates and dishes, several loaves of bread and a huge chunk of roast mutton that had obviously just come off the spit. A large iron frying pan, full of onions, spluttered on the range, the powerful aroma making Harlyn's mouth water.

A narrow passageway separated the kitchen from the tap-room. The woman indicated a doorway leading off the passage. A fog of tobacco smoke, beer fumes, heat and male voices billowed out of the opening.

'You wait there,' the woman directed. ''E's jest serving, when 'e come back, you can ask 'un.' She disappeared back into the kitchen.

Behind the rumble of conversation and guffaws of laughter, Harlyn heard voices singing. She crept forward and peeped round the doorway.

The crowded room with its low, beamed ceiling was lit by oil lamps. They stood on the tables and hung from the beams. From her quick, cautious glance Harlyn was surprised to see that there did not appear to be one woman in the place.

More and more voices were joining in the singing. The song was a slow, powerful ballad of the sea. The chorus, sung in harmony, died away, and a clear tenor voice took up the verse.

The talking died away as more men gave their attention to the soaring notes that filled the hot, crowded room with effort-less purity.

Harlyn peeped round the edge of the door, curious to see the owner of such a beautiful voice.

He stood on a stool in the corner of the room, along from the hearth where small flames licked around two large, half-consumed logs on a thick pile of ash. His back was to Harlyn, but as he sang he gradually turned, opening his arms to encompass his audience.

The chorus swelled once more. Beer was forgotten, pipes abandoned as every man added his voice to the emotion-filled blend of sound.

The man on the stool swayed out of Harlyn's line of vision, behind one of the oil lamps hooked to the ceiling beam. Then he moved forward again and as the song reached its climax hewas facing Harlyn, his arms wide, his eyes closed, head thrown back until the last notes died away.

In the momentary hush his head came forward, the carroty mop of hair flopping over one eye.

'Tom Grenville,' Harlyn whispered in stunned disbelief. She was even more shattered when, a moment later, a big, burly sailor with tears streaming down his face, wrapped his arms around Tom's hips, burying his face in the young man's belly, until pulled away by an obviously disgruntled friend.

Far from being furious, Tom smiled and patted the sailor's face in a gentle, curiously feminine gesture, before leaping off the stool, accompanied by whooping shouts and coarse yells, into the arms of another man who kissed him full on the mouth.

Harlyn was transfixed. So taken aback was she by Tom's behaviour, she didn't notice the landlord come up behind her.

'This idn no place fer you, girl. Wastin' yer time 'ere, you are.'

Harlyn jumped and looked round quickly.

'I'm sorry, I didn't mean to intrude,' she apologised quickly, 'but your sister-in-law said − I'm looking for someone, you see − the singer, I know him. Please, would you ask him if he could spare a moment to talk to me?' Harlyn smiled tentatively at the man, whose impatient expression cracked into a malicious grin.

'Wait 'ere,' he ordered, and pushed through the crowd, shouting at the top of his lungs.

'Mr Grenville, Mr Grenville, *sir*, there's a young lady outside wishes to speak with you.'

There was a salacious leer in his tone and something else which Harlyn did not comprehend. The room erupted. Cat-calls, derisive yells, blasphemous curses rained from all sides.

Harlyn was stunned by the volume of noise and bewildered as to its cause.

Above it Tom's voice rang out, clear and confident. 'A young lady, to see me? But I know no young ladies, landlord.' There was a ripple of laughter. 'I am careful of the company I keep,' he concluded archly, and his words provoked further laughter and comment.

'Well, she knows you, and she's waiting,' the landlord insisted.

Tom heaved an exaggerated sigh. 'Then I'd best see what the jade wants and be rid of her, that I may turn my attention to more — pressing matters.' He finished the sentence on a rising note, resulting in another gale of laughter, and followed the landlord to the passage doorway.

The landlord stood back his red-rimmed eyes bright with malice and curiosity, as Tom stepped through the doorway, his expression one of ostentatious boredom.

'Hallo, Tom,' Harlyn said uncertainly. She hardly recognised this languid stranger as the exuberant boy she had once known.

The colour left Tom Grenville's face so suddenly that his freckles stood out like spots of gold paint on white paper.

'Harlyn!' The word came out as a soft explosion. Recovering immediately he turned to the hovering grinning landlord.

'That will be all. Get back to your work.' The order was issued in a voice betraying generations of aristocratic arrogance, and brooked no argument.

The landlord slunk back into the taproom, his face a sullen mask, his eyes darting malevolently from one to the other.

'Tom, what is this place? It's so — strange. What are you doing here?' Harlyn shivered.

'Never mind that,' he snapped. 'What are *you* doing here?'

'It's a long story, Tom.' Another roar of laughter and jumble of shouts billowed through the doorway. 'Please can we go out-side?' Harlyn begged. 'I don't like it here.'

'Yes, yes of course,' Tom muttered and ushered her down the passage through the heavy wooden door which opened onto the street further down from the alley.

'What in God's name are you doing in this part of town?' he demanded angrily. 'What are you doing in Falmouth for that matter?'

'I ran away from home,' Harlyn blurted. 'I'm looking for my aunt, my mother's sister Rebecca Collins, she's known as Becky. I've found out that she works round here somewhere and I've got to find her, Tom. It's terribly important, she's the only one who can help me—' The words tripped over one another in a breathless rush.

Tom pulled Harlyn round to face him. His face was incredulous. 'What d'you mean, you've run away from home? Harlyn, you can't have.' He seemed lost for words. 'Girls of your background simply can't do things like that and expect to remain in society. Why, for heaven's sake?'

'Oh Tom,' Harlyn's voice broke, 'I can't tell you the whole story now, I've got to find Aunt Becky. But I'm supposed to be marrying Sir Henry Trevellyan, and I can't – I can't.'

'Sir Henry Trev—?' Tom interrupted. 'Oh I see,' his voice became suddenly thoughtful. 'Does he know you've run away?'

'I don't know. I pray he doesn't,' Harlyn murmured fervently, 'but no doubt he will find out soon and will send men to search for me.' She clutched his arm with both hands.

'Tom, you are obviously no stranger here. I beg you, if you know where Aunt Becky is, please take me there, or at least tell me.'

Tom Grenville stared at the pleading girl. 'Why should I?' he asked conversationally.

'Why?' Harlyn's eyes widened in shocked surprise. 'I thought we were friends, Tom.'

He gave a short, bitter laugh. 'Friends, you say? As far as your family was concerned, I was not worthy of your friendship.'

'Tom, I never said any such thing. You know it was not my wish that you stopped calling,' Harlyn was wounded.

'And how was I to know that?' Tom shot back. 'Since we never spoke again after your father informed me that both my name and my prospects were inadequate and my continued presence might discourage more suitable callers.'

'Tom, I never knew,' Harlyn was stricken. 'My mother simply told me that you would not be visiting any more. I could not argue, for while I enjoyed your company, I – we – neither of us, I think, was ready for marriage.' Harlyn bent her head.

'Your father, though he never knew it, changed my life,' Tom said in a strange voice. 'In the weeks after our last meeting I moved to new circles, met new people, did things that looking back—' he broke off. 'Oh yes,' he said bitterly, 'there is much for which I am indebted to your family, Harlyn.'

'Then you will help me?' she asked uncertainly.

'Yes, I'll take you to your aunt,' he said. 'It's but a few yards away, through the ope onto the North quay.'

'Thank you, Tom. Thank you with all my heart,' Harlyn said with a surge of gratitude and relief. 'I confess what little courage I had left has deserted me. I do not know how I would have gone on, had I not recognised you,' Harlyn shivered. 'Tom, what—?'

'How did you get here from Truro,' Tom interrupted quickly, forestalling possible questions concerning his present life.

'I stowed away — on a schooner,' Harlyn confided hesitantly.

'You did what?' Tom cried in shocked surprise. 'Were you not discovered?'

'Yes, I was,' Harlyn replied in a small voice. 'But the captain was mindful of his own reputation and so did not call the police. It was very frightening, Tom, I—'

'The captain,' Tom interrupted her again, 'what was his name?' His question seemed casual, but there was a discordant tension in him that disturbed Harlyn. Besides, she had her own very private reasons for not wanting anyone to know of her meeting with Jared Carlyon.

'I — I don't know,' she lied, 'he did not tell me.'

'The boat then,' he persisted. 'What was her name and where was she from?'

'I don't know,' Harlyn cried. 'I was upset. I did not think of such things. Tom, why do you question me like this? What does it matter, who or how?'

'Forgive me, Harlyn.' Tom replied smoothly. 'My patron has instilled into me that information of any kind is a valuable commodity. 'Tis a lesson I find hard to forget.'

'Your patron?' Harlyn was curious. 'Who is that, Tom?'

'I cannot tell you,' he said with regret. 'The nature of my commissions for him is secret, and I am sworn to protect his identity.'

Harlyn was glad she had kept silent. Tom had changed. It wasn't just his manner and appearance, there was an element in his character which was unrecognisable to her.

'Tom,' she began hesitantly, 'I must trust you, there is no one else I can ask to help—, please, I beg you, do not tell—'

'Must?' Tom said archly. 'Is that the word to use to a friend?' 'Come, let us find your aunt. For my own peace of mind I want to see you safely into her care.'

A pang pierced Harlyn at his words, almost the same words Jared Carlyon had used. Jared — his name was a lonely cry in the darkness that filled her heart.

'Harlyn?' Tom guided her forward. 'Are you all right?'

'Yes, yes, I'm quite all right,' she said quickly and they entered another alley, dark and smelly like the first. But this one was not empty.

Harlyn was aware of at least two couples entwined in furtive, writhing embrace. Their panting moans echoed loudly, shame-fully, in her head, and her cheeks burned like fire as she realised what the sounds signified. Tom was silent as they hurried out onto the quay.

A few yards along he turned and pushed open a door which opened into a passage, similar to the one they had recently left.

The door into the main room was open and shrieks of shrill, female laughter mingled with the rumble of men's voices and the clatter of glasses and tankards on table tops.

The sour, earthy smell of beer and wet sawdust caught in Harlyn's throat, as in her haste she pulled free of Tom's supporting arm and rushed forward.

She stopped at the second door, hesitated, then knocked twice and pressed down the latch.

The door swung inwards to reveal a small, stooped figure bending to lift a bucket of water to the stone sink.

'No customers allowed in here,' came the weary instruction. 'Go on, get back to the taproom.' She didn't even turn around.

'Mrs Collins? Mrs Becky Collins?' Harlyn's voice was a tremu-lous blend of hope and fear.

'Who wants her?' The woman emptied the bucket into the sink and replaced it on the floor with a clang before looking round.

'It is her, it's my Aunt Becky,' Harlyn whispered quickly to Tom, who was behind her.

The hair, which Harlyn remembered as rich chestnut, was now streaked with white, and scraped back into an untidy knot from which wisps and strands had escaped and hung untidily over her forehead and down her neck.

'Aunt Becky, I'm Harlyn, your sister Harriet's eldest daughter, do you remember me?' Harlyn was deeply affected at the sight of this thin, careworn woman who had once been plump, pretty and full of vitality.

'Harriet? We haven't spoken in ten years. She's no sister to me.' The full eyes glistened with a sudden flash of anger. 'If you've come with a message from her, you can go back and tell her, I have no sister. My Arthur was all the family I needed, he was everything to me.' The defiance faded. 'Everything,' she repeated softly.

'Aunt Becky, look at me,' Harlyn begged. 'You do remember me, don't you? There were three of us, your nieces, me, Rosella and the little one, Veryan. She was only five when you married

Uncle Arthur. I'm Harlyn. You do remember, don't you?' she
entreated desperately.

The faded blue eyes wavered over Harlyn and were about to
drift away, when a frown appeared between them, and a spark
of recognition flared.

'Harlyn?' Becky's face screwed up with the effort of reconcil-
ing the child she had once known with the young woman who
stood before her.

'What do you want?' There was caution rather than welcome
in her tone.

'I'd like to stay with you for a while if you'll let me.'

'What for?'

Harlyn searched for words to convey her need for refuge without putting her aunt into the position of feeling duty-bound to
return her to her parents.

'There are problems at home. A situation which involves me.
My father can see only one solution, one which I find totally
unacceptable, so I have come away for a while, to try and think
things out.'

'Run away, more like,' Becky said shrewdly. 'You always were
a wilful child, as I remember.'

'Please let me stay,' Harlyn pleaded. 'I've nowhere else to go.'

'You should have thought of that before you flew the nest,'
Becky retorted sharply. 'Besides, I don't know where I'm going
to put you. I've got a room in the attic, but it's very small.'

'I won't take up much room, I promise, Aunt Becky, and I'll
work. I'll do anything, cook, scrub, wash, anything, if you'll
only let me stay,' Harlyn implored.

'Well, I could surely use another pair of hands, and that's a
fact. There's more than I can cope with. But I'll have to speak to
Mrs Eddy. She's the widow woman who owns the place. You
wait here.'

Harlyn turned to Tom Grenville, her eyes dancing. 'It's going
to be all right, Tom, I feel it in my heart. I know I'll have to
work hard, but I shan't mind that. I'm young and strong.' Her
face fell. 'Poor Aunt Becky, she looks so tired, but with me here
to help she might be able to get a little more rest.'

'No doubt you'll be a great help,' Tom agreed. 'It appears you
are safely settled, so I'll bid you goodnight, Harlyn.' He studied
her closely for several seconds. 'Life leads us a tortuous, twisting
dance, Harlyn. I wonder if my path would have been different

had I married you?' He appeared to be talking more to himself than to her.

'Tom, I—' Harlyn began.

He raised his hand briefly in a strange gesture of dismissal and farewell. 'It is of no consequence now,' he said abruptly.

'Perhaps I'll see you tomorrow?' she said tentatively.' You are my one friend in this town.' She had not forgotten Elsie, but nor could she have any contact with her.

'I'm sure you'll very soon find yourself surrounded by friends,' Tom replied.

'What do you mean?' Some of the things he said, though it was more the way he said them, sent a tremor of unease down Harlyn's spine, though she could not have explained why.

'This is no time for false modesty,' Tom said with a shrug. 'You are a beautiful girl. The moths will soon gather around the flame.'

'But not you, Tom.' She did not say it to tease, but rather to try and understand the change she sensed in him.

'Not me, Harlyn. Whatever there was between us is long since over, part of another life. One cannot go back. No wishes, no regrets can undo—' he broke off with a sudden shake of his head. 'Don't think too badly of me,' he said quietly.

'I don't understand, Tom. How could I think badly of you? I'm so grateful for your help.'

'Goodbye, Harlyn,' he said bleakly and turning on his heel he vanished down the passage, then Harlyn heard the outer door slam.

She did not have time to dwell on Tom's mysterious behaviour, for at that moment Aunt Becky returned, followed by a tall woman of imposing bulk, swathed in crimson taffeta. The dress had obviously been made when its owner weighed considerably less than she did now, for the seams were stretched almost to bursting point. The woman's massive bosom erupted from the scooped neckline edged with frayed grubby lace, in mounds of dead white flesh, which, like the dress, was none too clean.

Her hennaed hair was tortured into bunches of ringlets either side of her rouged cheeks, and frizzy curls formed a row across her forehead.

With eyes as dark and hard as agates she surveyed Harlyn from her head, which was still covered by the white napkin, to her toes. The carmined lips opened to reveal several rotten teeth.

'Becky says you're lookin' fer work.'

'Yes,' Harlyn answered, hurriedly adding, 'Ma'am.'

The woman folded her hands in front of her. 'What do you do?'

'Anything, Ma'am,' Harlyn said quickly. 'I can cook, clean—'

'Have you waited on table?'

'No, Ma'am.' Harlyn was torn between saying she'd be willing to learn, if it would ensure her employment, yet not wanting to work in the taproom where there was always the possibility she might be recognised.

'Well, we'll see about that later. Take yer cloak off.'

Harlyn did as she was bid.

'Now turn round.'

Again Harlyn complied, too anxious to feel resentful.

'You'll do,' Mrs Eddy said brusquely. 'You're drab, but at least you're neat. Where's yer bag?'

'I — I beg your pardon?' Harlyn had not been prepared for that.

'Yer bag, luggage.' Mrs Eddy was impatient.

Harlyn glanced quickly at her aunt for assistance, but Becky's dull eyes and glazed expression told Harlyn that she was beyond reach.

'I have none, Ma'am,' she said quietly, her cheeks flushing rosy as she met the inquisitorial stare.

'Like that, is it? Not in trouble with the law, are 'ee?'

'No, Ma'am,' Harlyn shook her head.

'Nor in the family way?' Mrs Eddy stared pointedly at Harlyn's flat midriff.

'No, Ma'am, I am not,' Harlyn said firmly, her cheeks burning.

'I run a good class place what I built up myself without no 'elp from nobody, from the rundown pig'ole Eddy left me when 'e died, God rot 'im. There's four in the 'ouse besides me,' Mrs Eddy said briskly. 'Eliza and Mary serve in the taproom and 'elp with cleaning. My boy Willie, the little layabout, is s'posed to sweep out and run errands, ef'n you can ever find 'un, bloody little skiver. Cunning as a rat, 'e is.' She sounded almost proud.

'Any'ow, if you're going to work fer me, you abide by the rules.' She ticked them off on sausage-like fingers. 'No drinking, tha's strickly fer the customers, and no whoring. Them as wants it can get it at Dolly Bray's, down the road.' She sniffed, signalling her disgust at such goings on.

'Of course we do 'ave gen'lemen in now and again what requires special attention. Liza and Mary do take care o' they,' she paused delicately, 'for certain financial rewards, of which I naturally git 'arf.' She stuck her head forward suddenly. 'So don't go thinkin' to make yer own arrangements, else you'll be out on yer ear.'

'Yes, Ma'am, − no, − I don't know what you mean. I want only a roof over my head and the chance to work.'

'Mmmm.' Mrs Eddy fixed Harlyn with a sceptical glare which became suddenly speculative. 'I'll take 'ee on a week's trial, you can share wi' Becky, seeing as she asked fer 'ee. You get yer keep and two shillings a week,' she sniffed again. 'Edn nobody can say I don't pay a fair wage.'

Harlyn had no idea what a fair wage was, but two shillings didn't seem very much to her. But she was in no position to argue. She was so relieved to have the security of somewhere to stay for the next seven days, she was quick to voice her gratitude.

'Thank you, Ma'am. I'll give you no cause for complaint.'

'Mmm.' Mrs Eddy sniffed once more. 'Well, git yerselves away to bed, and mind you're down 'ere be 5.30 in the morning.'

'Yes, Ma'am,' Harlyn murmured, and Mrs Eddy swept out, leaving a lingering odour of cheap scent and stale perspiration.

Harlyn turned to her aunt who was lost in her own far-away thoughts. 'Aunt Becky? Will you show me where I'm to go?'

Becky pulled herself together with some effort. She went to the mantelshelf above the range and took down a candle holder and lit the stub of candle.

'That won't last long,' Harlyn pointed out. 'I'll get a new one for you. Where are they kept?'

'Mrs Eddy keeps them in her room,' Becky replied dully, 'we take the old stub to her every Saturday and then we get a new one,' she explained tiredly.

Harlyn swallowed the angry words that rose to her lips. She was new here. Becky had been here some time and obviously had her reasons for accepting such petty meanness.

They trudged up two flights of steep, narrow stairs to the attic, pausing only to pick up sheets and two coarse blankets from the huge linen chest on the top landing.

Becky opened the door to her room and led the way in. The

narrow room contained a bed, a chest on which stood a basin and ewer and a tall cupboard which, Harlyn guessed, was used as a wardrobe. The room was cold and stuffy.

Harlyn went across to the window which had a piece of old torn sheet hung over a thin cord instead of curtains.

'It doesn't open,' Becky said, guessing Harlyn's intention. 'She nailed it up two winters ago. She said it was to save the heat.'

'But the heat downstairs wouldn't reach up here,' Harlyn exclaimed. Becky simply shrugged.

'Oh well, perhaps it's not so bad in the daytime when you get the warmth of the sunshine.' Harlyn tried to make the best of it.

'Don't get the sun in here at all,' Becky replied. 'It's cut off by the houses behind and the warehouses on the quay.' Without waiting for Harlyn's reaction she went on in the same dull monotone, 'There's an old horse-hair mattress in the little box room next door. You'd better get it while I shift the chest to make a bit more space.'

Half an hour later, having undressed in the dark to save the candle stub, which would not be replaced for another two days, Harlyn lay in her shift between the two rough sheets.

She mentally thanked Elsie once again for the cloak, which spread its warmth over her as a quilt.

Would her flight from his house have plunged Elsie into serious trouble with Jared Carlyon? Harlyn could only hope that the privileged position Elsie occupied was strong enough to deflect the worst of his wrath.

Would he be angry? Would he be furious at her having slipped through his fingers a second time, or might he simply be relieved to be free of her, happy to have been saved the trouble of returning her to her parents.

Perhaps he had already forgotten her existence, erased her memory from his mind as a prospective bridegroom that would be the logical thing to do.

Harlyn's innate honesty forced her to admit that Camilla St Aubyn would make him an excellent wife.

Just for an instant Harlyn relived the sweet yearning ache the searing pressure of his lips had roused in her. She tossed restlessly on the hard, motheaten mattress. The smell of mouldy dampness came up through the blanket which she had carefully placed upon the mattress before covering it with the sheet. It brought her back to the present with tears in her eyes and a sense of loss which prompted her to remember the woman on the iron cot a few feet away.

'Aunt Becky, are you awake?' Harlyn asked softly.

'Yes,' came the weary reply.

'I just wanted to say how sorry I was — about Uncle Arthur.' There was a silence. 'No need to be sorry, you never knew him.'

'No, I know that, but you miss him, and I'm sorry about that.'

'Miss him? Yes.' An odd note of bewilderment crept into Becky's voice. 'But it won't be long and I'll be with him again,' she finished with a secret satisfaction that startled Harlyn almost as much as her aunt's actual words.

'Aunt Becky, you mustn't say that.' Harlyn was horrified. 'You aren't ill, are you?'

Becky tutted impatiently. 'No, I'm not ill. Why do you think I've stayed in this dreadful place with that filthy harridan Millie Eddy?'

Harlyn turned her head towards her aunt, though she could see nothing in the darkness.

'I don't know, Aunt Becky, why have you?'

'Because I've been saving, that's why,' came the impatient reply.

'Saving?' Harlyn was nonplussed. 'For what?'

'The fare to South Africa, of course. Soon I'll have enough, then I'll be able to join Arthur,' she announced triumphantly. 'It was always our dream to go out there, to the gold mines and the sunshine. We waited and planned for so long.' Her pensive tone lightened as she explained, 'He didn't want to go without me, but he had to, you see. He made me promise that I'd join him just as soon as I could. Well, it won't be long now. Listen.' There was a scrabbling sound and then the rattle of pieces of metal in a tin box. 'It's nearly enough. Won't be long now.' The box was replaced.

Harlyn's initial dismay gave way to overwhelming compassion.

'You'll help, won't you, Harlyn You've got work and a place to stay all through me. I know it's a midden compared with what you're used to, but it's better than nothing and I have helped you, haven't I?'

An eager, childlike insistence had replaced her aunt's usual monotone and Harlyn fought back tears as she struggled to keep her voice level.

'Of course I'll help you, Aunt Becky. You've been wonderfully kind to me.'

'Yes, I have,' came the satisfied reply. 'So you'll give me sixpence for my savings tin?'

'Aunt Becky, I haven't any money at all, not till Mrs Eddy pays me.'

'That's all right, dear. You can give it to me then. Only you won't forget, will you, because Arthur's getting impatient. He needs me with him. You do understand, don't you? I wouldn't ask anyone else, I'm not looking for charity. But you are family, and I've helped you so that's different, isn't it?' She yawned and sighed. 'I shall tell Arthur about you when I see him. It's a shame you never met. He's such a fine figure of a man, straight and tall. I was the envy of many a girl when we were wed, I can tell you, and he hasn't changed, not one bit. He can still dance any other man off the floor.'

'But his leg—' Harlyn couldn't help herself. As the words left her lips, Harlyn held her breath, terrified that she had punctured the bubble of her aunt's dream. She waited in dread, wondering what form the let-down would take, raving anger or broken-hearted weeping.

'That was nothing,' came the dismissive reply, accompanied by a light laugh. 'A man like my Arthur troubled by a little thing like that? It's all better now.' She yawned again. 'I shall write to Arthur soon, so that he can start getting things ready for when I arrive. I do wish sometimes that he'd write back,' she said wistfully, 'but he never learned. He never had much schooling, and then down the mine he worked so hard he never had time. I tried to teach him in the evenings, but he couldn't get the hang of it. Anyway,' she broke into a soft girlish giggle, 'we were young and newly-wed, and we had other things to do.'

Her voice slurred and trailed off and her breathing depened as she slipped away in sleep to the arms of her young, lively, whole-limbed husband of ten years ago.

Harlyn lay on her back staring into the darkness, her own predicament forgotten. Hot tears slid slowly and silently down her face as she grieved for the broken mind and careworn body of her aunt.

10

'Come on, wake up. There'll be trouble if you're late down. She'll know, she always does.'

There was no trace of last night's girlish happiness in Becky's voice. Her dreams had flown with the darkness, leaving a tired, empty shell.

Harlyn sat up, yawning and stretching. 'Is there hot water to bathe?' she asked sleepily.

Her aunt grunted. 'Not till I clean out the grate and light the fire.'

Harlyn's eyes opened wide and she gave a convulsive shiver as Becky went on, 'There's cold water in the bucket by the sink and the privy is out the back. Now come on with you, else she'll stop your wages.'

Harlyn scrambled out of her makeshift bed and began struggling into her clothes. She pulled on her dress over her shift and petticoats while Becky twisted her thin, white-streaked hair into a bun, securing it with pins.

Becky stopped suddenly, her hand poised at the back of her head. 'You aren't wearing a corset.' Her tone was a blend of surprise and censure.

Harlyn was torn. She felt an overwhelming urge to laugh. Here they were, she and her aunt both women of gentle breeding and good background, living in squalid conditions in a Beer house in the most disreputable part of town, and yet her aunt could sound so shocked about such a trivial matter.

Yet at the same time, Becky's tone reminded Harlyn so strongly of her mother that she had to bite her lip hard against the sudden, knifing pangs of homesickness.

Harlyn tried to explain. 'I wasn't − I'd been helping in the garden − it's such a lovely feeling of freedom not being laced up in one of those things—' She faltered and fell silent.

Becky made no reply. Her interest, stirred momentarily, had faded once more and she had lapsed back into apathy.

Harlyn's cheeks were rosy as she fumbled with the last of the buttons and shook out her skirt. It was unheard of for any well-brought up young lady to discard her corset except in the privacy of her boudoir for a post-luncheon rest, or at bed-time.

Was she truly the only person to find steel and whalebone, however prettily covered, an uncomfortable, restricting nuisance?

Harlyn recalled the scenes with her mother when she had begged to be allowed not to wear one, especially while riding.

Harriet had nearly thrown a fit. 'What did I do to be plagued thus?' she had beseeched the heavens. 'Harlyn, how many times must I tell you, a corset is a necessary, no, a vital part of a lady's wardrobe. It is a garment of modesty, of protection. It gives our dresses their emphasis of line and fit and it is an aid to deportment, though no lady should require such a thing.'

'It's a cage,' Harlyn had murmured rebelliously. But faced with her mother's implacable determination, she had obeyed, except on such rare and delightful occasions as helping Nathan in the garden in the early hours of the afternoon while the remainder of the household rested.

'Oh, my hair — I haven't,' Harlyn gasped.

'No time now,' Becky said shortly. 'Just pin the braid round your head and tie that white square over it again. You look neat enough.'

They crept down the dark stairs, Harlyn heeding her aunt's warnings of dire consequences should Mrs Eddy be awakened before 7.30 a.m.

Becky unbolted the back door and pulled it open, indicating the privy next to the coal shed.

The grey light of drawn revealed a fine drizzle falling from low, unbroken cloud.

Harlyn scuttled back into the kitchen, shocked by the primitive sanitary facilities. She rinsed her face and hands in the stone sink and dried them on a piece of rough, coarse towel. Depression settled over her like a thick, stifling blanket. Adjustment to this new way of life was going to be very hard.

With a conscious effort she turned to her aunt who was raking out the dead ashes from the range.

'What can I do?'

'Can you lay a fire?' Becky's tone suggested she expected a negative reply.

'Yes, of course I can,' Harlyn answered, wanting to be helpful, remembering the debt of gratitude she owed her aunt.

Becky climbed stiffly to her feet. 'Well, you do that while I put out the ashes and get us a bite to eat.'

Harlyn stuffed paper, kindling and coal into the small fire box, but when she tried to light it, the only result was a cloud of smoke. There was not a flame to be seen.

'Aunt Becky, it won't go.' Harlyn wailed, her hands and arms streaked with soot and coal dust.

Becky looked up from the loaf she was slicing. 'Have you opened the damper?'

'The what?' Harlyn looked flustered.

'That, there,' Becky pointed with the knife, 'and take some of that coal off for a minute.'

Harlyn followed her instructions and this time the fire caught. She'd done it. The orange flames licking round the crackling, spitting wood warmed her heart like no others had ever done.

'Come on,' Becky broke in, 'we're all behind. Get your breakfast quick. There's bread, a slice of cold meat and a mug of milk.'

Harlyn pulled out a hard wooden chair across the scarred table from Becky and began to eat. Though she tried she could not prevent a picture of the dining room at Chyvallon springing into her mind; the polished walnut table, covered by a handmade lace cloth, the four ladder back and two carver chairs with their tapestried seats, silver dishes on the sideboard from which they could choose oatmeal, kippers, eggs, bacon and sausage, or, as Harlyn frequently did, take a little of everything. It was so different, so far away, it was another world.

Harlyn was finishing her milk when the door opened and two buxom young women staggered sleepily into the kitchen, both yawning noisily and rubbing sleep from their eyes.

Neither was fully dressed. Each had on a grubby robe over equally grubby shifts and under-petticoats.

The first one kicked out a chair and slumped onto it resting her elbows, which were covered by thick folds of dirty, calloused skin, on the table, she supported her head in her hands, holding it as though it might fall off. Her hair resembled a brown bird's nest.

'Any 'ot water yet, Becky?' she mumbled thickly.

'Kettle's boiled,' was Becky's brief reply.

'I would dearly love a cuppa tea. 'Liza wha'd'ee say?'

'You'll be for it if Mrs Eddy finds you've been at her tea. You know we aren't supposed to touch it,' Becky warned wearily.

'Aw, shut up, you old bessom,' Eliza sneered.

'Don't you talk to her like that,' Harlyn flared, turning round in her chair to face Mary, who only then seemed to notice her presence.

''Oo the 'ell are you?' Mary glared truculently at Harlyn from bloodshot, sleep-crusted eyes.

'She's my niece, she's come to work here,' Becky said defensively.

'Oh yeah? Doin what?' demanded the other girl. 'She idn takin' non o' my tables, that's fer sure.'

'Nor mine neither,' added Mary. ''Liza, see if Mrs 'ave left the leaves in the pot from yesterday. We might git a brew from they.' She groaned. 'My 'ead's fit to burst. Why did I 'ave that gin? It always makes me bad. I donno 'bout mother's ruin, 'twill be the ruin of me, I tell 'ee.'

With her tangled, greasy locks falling like tarred rope over her shoulders Eliza peered into the small teapot on the dresser.

'There's still some in 'ere,' she sounded doubtful.

'Well, for chrissakes pour some water on 'em and gimme a cup.' Mary groaned again.

Eliza shrugged and did as she was told. After stirring it thoroughly she poured the pale yellow liquid into two mugs and pushed one towards Mary who lifted it, with trembling hands.

'Jesus, 'tis 'ot,' she yelped. 'Tryin' to burn the roof off me mouth, are'ee?' she screamed at Eliza.

'You daft bugger, you jest seen me make it. You knowed it was 'ot,' Eliza screeched back.

'All right, all right, no need to shout,' Mary moaned; then she cocked a bleary eye at Harlyn.

'What you come 'ere for?'

'To see my aunt and to find work,' Harlyn replied carefully.

'Oh, Miss La-de-da,' Mary mocked Harlyn's clear, dialect-free speech. She lunged forward and grabbed one of Harlyn's hands. After giving it a cursory examination she dropped it with a derisive laugh.

'G'wan, maid, they 'ands never done no rough work. What are 'ee doing 'ere really?' Her eyes narrowed.

Eliza leaned menacingly over Harlyn, hands on her hips. 'Missus set you to spy on we, 'ave she?'

'Stop it, the both of you,' Becky banged the table with the handle of her knife. Two spots of rosy colour burned high on her cheeks and her eyes glittered with the greatest show of animation she had revealed since Harlyn's arrival.

'You let her be. She's no threat to you. Mrs Eddy took her on to work in the kitchen, so just leave her alone.' Becky jabbed the knife point at each of them in turn.

'All right, no need to take on like that, we was only lookin' after our interests.' Eliza backed away. 'Bloody asylum this is,' she grumbled, 'bloody mad'ouse.'

Becky ignored her, turning away to stoke the fire, her temper gone as quickly as it had flared.

Mary winked at Eliza. 'Missus said yesterday that the privy's stinkin', it 'ave got to be washed out,' she remarked innocently.

'And the spittoons and ashtrays scrubbed,' Eliza added gleefully.

''Course, we 'abn got time, not with the floor to sweep, the tables to wipe and the fire to do,' Mary said sadly.

'And there's the barrels to tap, mugs to wash and sawdust to fetch—' Eliza ticked off on her fingers. She picked up the teapot and emptied it into the sink. 'Now jest look at that,' she said in surprise.

'Missus would be some mad if we was to tell 'er you took 'er tealeaves, Becky,' Mary cooed.

'She might even throw'ee out and yer niece with 'ee. Then where'd 'ee be to? No more buttons fer the savings tin, then eh?' Eliza grinned malevolently. Mary laughed and swallowed the dregs of her tea.

'No, no,' Becky whimpered. 'I can't do any more, I've got too much already – no time—'

Harlyn leapt to her feet and patted her aunt's scrawny arm. 'It's all right, Aunt Becky,' she assured the frail, weeping woman. Then she turned on Eliza and Mary. Cold fury had drained her face of colour.

Heedless of the fact that she was no physical match for the two strapping girls, she rounded on them like a tigress protecting her cub.

'Touch my aunt, or anything belonging to her, and I swear you'll regret it.'

Something about the slim, taut figure and the soft icy tone unnerved both Eliza and Mary.

'Well, jest so long as you understand—' Mary muttered.

'Oh, I understand,' Harlyn said through tight lips.

'C'mon, Mary,' Eliza went to the door, 'we'd best git dressed. Missus'll be down soon. Yer 'ead better, is un?'

Mary stood up slowly and shook her head carefully, then moaned. 'Not much. Oooh I do feel some bad. Think she'd gi' me some laudanum do 'ee?'

'I wouldn' ask if I was you—'

The door closed behind them.

'This is no place for you,' Becky shook her head at Harlyn. 'You've got no business here.'

'Then neither have you,' Harlyn retorted gently. 'We're family, remember? If you can work here then so can I. You'll just have to be a bit patient until I get into the way of things. Now, you tell me where everything is, and I'll get started.'

Harlyn spent the next two hours breathing as little as possible and trying desperately to retain her breakfast.

She poured the last bucketful of filthy water down the yard, followed it with another of clean, then stumbled into the kitchen to slump weakly into the hard, wooden chair.

The coarse sacking Becky had helped her to tie around her waist had only partly protected her dress, which was spotted and stained. She had broken two nails and her hands were scratched and bleeding from the rough edges of the spittoons and the brick walls and stone floor of the privy.

'You all right?' Becky looked up from the dough she was kneading. Harlyn took a deep breath and nodded.

The kitchen door opened and Mrs Eddy swept in, her vast bulk swathed in a wrapper of vivid purple satin trimmed with black and lilac lace and lilac ribbon fastenings. Not one hair seemed to have moved since the previous night and her face was already heavily painted. She resembled a bloated, garish doll.

She had evidently decided to breakfast before encasing herself in the steel framed corset needed to shoe-horn her into her dresses.

As Mrs Eddy sailed into the kitchen Harlyn could not help noticing how her unfettered flesh trembled and swayed beneath the wrapper.

Mrs Eddy stopped abruptly but her bosom trembled on. She

frowned. 'What's this? Nothing to do? Sitting about? This isn't what I'm paying you for. I won't have this, oh dear no—'

Her voice and manner were reminiscent of Mrs Kelloway, an actress Harlyn had once seen at the Town Hall, when a travelling theatrical troupe had visited Truro.

Harlyn stood up quickly. 'No, you don't understand, I wasn't—'

Mrs Eddy's head reared back. 'Now don't you give me none of that, girl. I know what my eyes tell me, and they say you was sitting down instead of working.'

Over Mrs Eddy's shoulder, Harlyn caught a glimpse of Eliza and Mary peering round the doorway, stifling their giggles with hands pressed to their mouths.

Realising argument was both risky and futile, Harlyn folded her hands and bent her head, hoping she looked suitably abject. She kept her lashes lowered for her eyes sparked with anger.

Harlyn wondered momentarily why Becky did not explain, and give Mrs Eddy the true picture. Then with a flash of insight she realised that the fighting and bickering, the threats and blackmail must have been going on since Becky first went there. Harlyn guessed her aunt was utterly weary of it all, the stress, the bitchiness, Mrs Eddy's whims and moods. It was no wonder that, faced with such wrangling every day on top of her own grief and loneliness, Becky had withdrawn into her own shadowy world of memories.

'Really, Becky, if you expect me to show charity to your relation, you'd better make she's worthy of it.'

Charity? Harlyn clenched her hands together tightly. This was not charity, it was slavery.

Mrs Eddy sniffed and waddled across to the dresser. She picked up the teapot a suspicious frown furrowed her thickly powdered forehead.

She shook the teapot then removed the lid and peered in. She swung round, all pretension to genteel refinement erased by the crimson rage swelling her face until her small eyes almost disappeared and she looked about to burst.

'Which thievin' wart 'as 'ad me tea?' she screeched. 'I could'a got another brew outa they leaves. You scurvy maggots, the lot of 'ee. I'll find out, jest see if I don't, and when I do—'

Knowing that Eliza and Mary would put the blame on herself or her aunt, Harlyn, thinking on her feet, forestalled them.

'It was I, Ma'am,' she said with as much surprised innocence as she could muster.

There was a simultaneous intake of breath from Eliza, Mary and Becky. The silence that followed Harlyn's admission bore down on them all like a weight.

Mrs Eddy was once more in control of herself. She turned slowly and majestically, like a tatty galleon, to stare at Harlyn.

'You?' The single word contained such a wealth of furious incredulity that the observers let out their breath in a concerted sigh.

'Why, yes, Ma'am,' Harlyn replied, her eyes wide with surprise, 'I assumed that a lady of such qualities as those you possess would naturally insist upon a freshly made drink, so I threw the old leaves away.'

Mrs Eddy's mouth had fallen open during Harlyn's apologetic speech. She shut it again with a snap. She had not sensed the irony in Harlyn's description of her, and the conflict between being flattered and anger at what she considered to be waste, showed itself in the working of her face.

Noting Mrs Eddy's hesitation Harlyn clutched at a straw and plunged on, 'In my previous place, Ma'am, the lady of the house never touched tea in the mornings. She found a herbal infusion much more soothing to her delicate nerves.'

'What place was that, then?' Mrs Eddy demanded cunningly.

Harlyn ignored the question. "Tis all the rage among the gentry, Ma'am,' she said.

'Is it really?' Mrs Eddy's interest was immediate and obvious.

'In my ignorance I assumed that you too — please forgive me, Ma'am,' Harlyn shrugged helplessly. 'I have made a stupid mistake.'

Harlyn caught Becky's eye and quickly bent her head. Her aunt was gazing at her with an expression of mingled amazement and dismay.

'No, no,' Mrs Eddy interrupted quickly. She fixed Harlyn with a piercing, suspicious stare. But Harlyn was totally committed to her role, and met the small porcine eyes without flinching.

Mrs Eddy heaved a sigh that caused her massive body to quiver like a jelly. 'Look at me,' she demanded, 'jest look at me. Strong and 'ealthy I look, don' I? Well, 'tis all a lie. Nerves, see. I do suffer something awful with my nerves.'

She placed a pudgy hand with dirty nails upon her billowing bosom and sighed again. 'Nobody do know the pain I do suffer, the worry of this place — why I do 'ardly sleep of a night—'

A muffled snort came from behind the door. 'You can 'ear she snorin' down Market Strand,' one of the girls whispered loudly.

'There's 'nough laudanum and brandy goes down 'er throat of a night to knock out 'alf the town,' the other one added.

'Git your fat asses out to that taproom, you idle 'ussies,' roared Mrs Eddy. A burst of giggling was followed by the scuffle and thump of running feet.

Mrs Eddy raised the back of her hand to her forehead in a gesture so studied that Harlyn was tempted to smile. Obviously Mrs Kelloway and her company had visited Falmouth too. But Harlyn stifled the impulse almost as it occurred, all too aware of the suspicious cunning that lurked at the back of Mrs Eddy's small dark eyes, ready to pounce should Harlyn betray the slightest hint of her contempt for the grotesque woman facing her.

'This 'ere herbal stuff—' Mrs Eddy scratched at a mark on the table top, 'cost much, do it?'

'No, Ma'am,' Harlyn shook her head. 'For a penny or two I used to buy several different herbs and mix a blend that was exclusive to my m — mistress.' She amended hastily, but Mrs Eddy had not noticed the slip. An expression of smug satisfaction was spreading across her choleric face.

'Exclusive,' she repeated, savouring the word. 'That mean that nobody else abn got none like it, don' it?'

It took Harlyn a few seconds to work out Mrs Eddy's convoluted grammar, then she shook her head readily. 'You would be the only person with that blend of those particular herbs mixed in special amounts just for your particular needs,' she answered.

'That'd be one in the snitch fer Dolly Bray,' cackled Mrs Eddy, then she turned decisively to Harlyn.

'Becky 'abn finished the baking, so you'll do the shopping. She'll give 'ee the list after I checked 'un, and I'll give 'ee the money. There's some places I do 'ave credit and some places I don' ask. There's a shop what sells 'erbs and such up Market Strand. You git what you need to make me up a special brew fer me nerves.' She wagged a finger at Harlyn. 'And don't think to cheat me an' spend too much else it'll come out yer wages.'

'No, Ma'am,' Harlyn promised, wondering if she would, in fact, ever get any wages. She had been there not twelve hours and had already been threatened with two fines.

Half an hour later she was walking back through the alley into Quay Street, armed with shopping basket, list and a grimy leather purse, and strict instructions to hurry back to complete the rest of her chores.

Harlyn put the latter out of her mind, glad to be outside in the fresh air despite the heavy drizzle.

With her cloak warm around her, the hood protecting her head, Harlyn walked up the steep cobbles to the junction with Arwenack Street. She had first to go to the offices of the *Falmouth and Penryn Weekly Times* to buy a copy of the previous week's issue. This, according to Mrs Eddy contained a description of the latest fashion in dinner dresses. Dolly Bray had been so impressed that she had already chosen material and was having one made, a fact which infuriated Mrs Eddy.

The newspaper office was in the commercial buildings on the Town Quay. Once again Harlyn had to pass the offices of G. C. Fox & Co., the ship agents Jared Carlyon dealt with.

Harlyn's heart beat a little faster as she hurried past the bay windows which seemed to follow her like eyes. Forget him, forget him. The words beat a tattoo in time with her swiftly moving feet.

She was passing on her return journey, head bent, paper safely folded in the basket, when she collided with someone coming out of the Telegraph Office.

She looked up quickly, eyes huge, mouth dry, to see the freckled face of Tom Grenville.

Harlyn smiled with relief. 'Hallo, Tom, I hoped I'd see you again.'

To her surprise and dismay, he ignored her completely. Stepping past her he walked swiftly down the street towards the town centre, his face closed and blank.

'Tom?'

Harlyn took a step forward. But he was far ahead, walking so fast he was almost running. Within moments he was lost among the other people on the pavement.

Harlyn was bewildered. What had happened? What was wrong? Last night he had recognised her with no difficulty. He had helped her. Through him she had found Aunt Becky.

This morning it was as if they were total strangers. No, it was more than that, for Tom's manners had always been impeccable. He would have apologised to a stranger, but he had not opened his mouth to her.

Heavy-hearted, feeling something was wrong, but having not the faintest idea what it could be, Harlyn walked on through the town. She had thought Tom her friend. Though he had obviously been embittered by her parents' dismissal of him, she was sure he could have realised that was not of her doing. Friends were something she desperately needed in this strange bewildering town, and to lose the second one she had found made her very sad, and strangely uneasy.

The clock on the church tower showed 8.30 a.m. and the streets were getting busy. Tradesmen were opening their shops and businesses for the day. Early shoppers mingled with fish packers and shipwrights on their way to work at the yards and docks along the Bar.

Horses and carts clopped up and down the streets, delivering wood to the timber merchants, casks of ale from the brewery to the inns and beer houses, and taking sacks of provisions from the chandlers to the quay for transport out to ships in the harbour.

Harlyn passed the shop of Moss Jacob, silversmith and jeweller, and paused for a moment to examine the selection of rings, brooches and necklaces displayed in glittering splendour on velvet lined trays.

She entered the bakery shop next door and purchased a quarter of tiny iced biscuits, the second item on Mrs Eddy's list. As she continued down Church Street, Harlyn's eye was caught by the imposing building which had tall pillars like sentinels on either side of the three upper windows.

A sign over the entrance proclaimed it to be the Royal Cornwall Polytechnic Society. Harlyn wondered what that meant. Then she recalled the conversation she had overheard the previous afternoon between the people on the drive at Grove Hill.

She remembered it had had something to do with experiments and an exhibition. But her thoughts were distracted as her eyes lighted upon the china shop, whose window featured a large collection of Bohemian, French and Dresden vases, a special interest of her mother's.

By the time she had reached the ironmonger's to collect two

kitchen knives left for sharpening, her curiosity concerning the Exhibition was forgotten.

Pushing open the door of the herbalist's tiny shop, Harlyn experienced a tingle of pleasure at the sight of the rows of shelves packed with jars. They contained roots of marshmallow and valerian, dried chamomile flowers and rose petals, oil of juniper, juice of male fern, loosestrife, hyssop and ivy; seeds of rosehips, hibiscus and caraway. Bunches of fresh parsley, a specific against kidney disease and rheumatism; and peri-winkle, for cramp and boils, stood in shallow dishes next to an apothecary's scale.

Harlyn could have happily spent several hours examining the infinite variety of herbal and homoeopathic preparations, many of which were new to her, but she dared not linger.

Sorely tempted to select herbs which would give Mrs Eddy a thorough purging, Harlyn resisted, knowing that to do so would expose her, and both she and Aunt Becky would be thrown out onto the street.

So what if we were, Harlyn thought defiantly, I'm sure I could find more congenial work. Maybe the herbalist would employ me, I do have some knowledge of the subject. But what of Aunt Becky? She would not find other employment so easily, other-wise surely she would have done so, and escaped from that awful place.

Harlyn sighed. She had no right to jeopardise her aunt's position. A better idea occurred.

'May I have an ounce of chamomile heads, an ounce each of rosehips and hibiscus and a piece of valerian root please?'

Harlyn knew that this was the best month for harvesting the fresh rhizome, the bitter, brownish-yellow underground part of the stem which was the part actually used and from which the true root extended.

She asked the herbalist to divide each quantity in half and wrap it separately. The man complied and Harlyn handed him the money, placing four of the packets in the basket, and keep-ing the other four in her hand to secrete in the sleeve of her dress once outside.

She had chosen herbs most suitable for treating her aunt's nervous exhaustion. If Mrs Eddy's 'nerves' were also soothed, so much the better.

Harlyn did not feel the slightest twinge of conscience at using

Mrs Eddy's money for her aunt's benefit. From what she had observed and experienced in her short stay, Becky's life in that house was anything but a happy one.

Harlyn walked up Market Street and into Church Street on her way back to the beer house.

The wind had freshened and was funnelling down the street in gusts, driving the drizzle into her face.

Sheltered by umbrellas, or huddled inside coats and cloaks, people hurried about their business.

Harlyn noticed several men and women gathered outside the entrance to the Polytechnic Hall. A furious argument was in progress. The younger of the two men from the drive at Grove Hill was shouting at two workmen, each of whom was carrying a large wooden crate.

'We made it perfectly clear yesterday,' he raged, 'the extra explosives were to remain at the docks. I already have the purified oil here.'

'I dunno nothing 'bout that,' the nearest of the carriers grunted. 'We was told to bring they crates, so we brung 'em.'

'But you can't put them in the building,' the young man repeated. 'There's no proper storage for them.'

'Well, we aren't taking 'em back. We wasn' paid fer no return journey,' the second man retorted sullenly, and slammed the crate down on the stone step.

The young man flinched and visibly paled. 'For God's sake, be careful,' he hissed. 'Don't you realise what you're dealing with?'

A small crowd had gathered by this time and more people hesitated on the fringes as the first carrier raised his voice.

'Look, mister,' he leaned forward, a surly frown darkening his face, very aware of the audience, 'we got other work to do, there's other stuff to be moved and we can't bugger about 'ere all day, now do you want these 'ere crates inside, or shall us leave 'em on the step?'

'Are you deaf, or something?' the young man shouted, red-faced and flustered by the attention the argument was attracting. 'Haven't I just told you—'

He got no further. The second man stepped forward and slammed his crate down on top of the first.

The thunderous roar and shockwave knocked Harlyn backwards but she was not even aware of falling.

Glass from the shop windows, hurled at bullet speed by the

blast, pierced clothing, flesh and bone. Chunks of masonry crashed and shattered on the street.

A terrified horse reared and bolted, its driver falling to be crushed beneath the wheels as the frenzied animal careered down the street, dragging the heavy cart at breakneck speed, its load of fruit and vegetables scattering in all directions.

Faces, white with shock, peered from windows and doorways.

Bodies lay, powdered with dust and broken glass, in sprawled confusion on the wet ground. Blood pulsed or seeped from life-sapping wounds to flow into the gutter, paling from crimson to pink as it mingled with the rain.

Harlyn staggered to her feet and stood swaying, clutching the empty frame of the shop window for support.

Something warm and sticky was trickling down her face. Raising a trembling hand she touched a long gash high on her temple. She gazed at her hand with strange detachment. It was as though the blood which ran in a scarlet stream down her fingers and palm did not belong to her at all.

After the first thunderclap of the explosion there had been total silence, but now the shrieks and moans of the wounded began to penetrate Harlyn's consciousness.

Still clinging to the window frame, she straightened up and carefully moved her arms and legs. Everything functioned. Apart from the cut on her temple she had miraculously escaped injury. A brief faintness washed over her and her knees buckled, but she fought it off with several deep breaths.

In the shop window to which Harlyn clung, a cream cashmere shawl embroidered in a paisley pattern with fine silk lay in a shredded heap, covered with dust and glass splinters. Scarcely aware of what she was doing, Harlyn reached in the pulled it from the display stand. Shaking off the debris she wiped the blood from her face, and pressed the soft fabric to the wound on her head.

All round her the noise was getting louder, women were screaming, children sobbing and men shouted. As she gazed numb with shock at the site of the explosion she could see huge dark cracks crazing the front of the building. The heavy black doors were splintered to matchwood and hung lop-sidedly on their iron hinges.

Directly opposite, not only glass but complete window frames had been blown out of the walls, leaving jagged stumps of wood like rotten teeth in gaping mouths.

A dull roaring sound reached Harlyn's ears. Smaller explosions followed by a splintering crash were occurring with increasing rapidity.

The cry went up: 'Fire!'

'It's the dispensary.' A thin, balding, white-faced man in black apron and sleeve protectors lurched out of the printers and pointed. 'Gas,' he shouted hoarsely. 'The gas pipes have broken. There's jars of spirit and vats of pure alcohol in there, and if the fire reaches the wine store next door—' He didn't go on.

From the Savings Bank on the other side of the Polytechnic staggered a rotund little man in what had once been a smart business suit of dark jacket and grey striped trousers. It was now smeared and streaked with plaster dust and blood from tiny cuts all over his hands and face.

In his arms were clutched a bundle of ledgers and cash boxes. He stared wildly up and down the street. 'The money's safe,' he panted and stumbled off up the street, stepping over the bodies that littered the road and pavement in inert bundles.

'I've saved the money — responsibility you see — lifetime — duty to—'

'What about Miss Clemmow?' the printer shouted, starting across the road.

The little man hesitated. 'She's dead, I think,' he giggled, 'but I saved the money.' His face contorted and he burst into tears, and began another stumbling run up the street to the steps of the Cornish Bank on the corner.

The printer's shout and the little man's reaction acted as a signal, releasing the onlookers from their paralysis of shock as the printer disappeared inside the Savings Bank in search of Miss Clemmow, shouts went up on all sides.

'Get the fire engine!'

'Somebody call the police.'

'Is there anyone still inside?'

A large, ruddy-faced man with a shock of white hair and mutton-chop whiskers appeared in the doorway of the wine and spirits shop, and bellowed for silence.

Gradually the noise subsided.

'You all know me,' he shouted, 'I'm William Carne, the Mayor of this town, elected by you, the people of Falmouth—'

'For chrissake, this edn the time for a bloody speech,' an

agonised female voice shrieked from the throng, 'there's folk dyin' 'ere and mebbe still people inside the Poly.'

'I know that,' Carne thundered, 'that's why we've got to organise ourselves properly, else even more will be hurt. Now listen to me,' he pleaded holding his hands high, scanning the gathering crowd for faces he recognised.

'Joe Chegwin, Sam Behenna and Dickie Hodge, you get up to the Market and bring the engines. Get some others to help. The key to the engine house is at Miss Downing's next door. If you can't make her hear, there's one at the Police Station.' The three men took off at a run, pushing their way through. 'Let's get a bucket chain started, as many of you as can find a basin, bucket, saucepan, anything that'll hold water. The tide's on the ebb so you'll be in the mud, Upton Slip's nearest way—'

'No's not,' someone argued, 'the ope 'cross the road 'ere is quickest.'

'No 'tedn' 'tis fenced off at the bottom,' someone else put in.

'For God's sake,' Carne roared, 'move yourselves, get down Upton, we know for sure that's open.'

The people behind Harlyn began diving into shops and houses, grabbing any receptacle capable of holding more than a pint of water. They began to form a straggly line.

Carne didn't wait. 'You women do what you can for the wounded. Sam Dibell, you find the rector and get the church opened up, we'll take the dead there. Spread the word so that folk'll know where to look if someone's missing.'

'Where shall us take the wounded?' a voice shouted.

He turned round to two well-dressed, but dusty and dishevelled men a few feet from Harlyn.

'That you, Harry Bassett? and Saul Teague? You two get down to the subscription rooms and make sure they're open. We'll take the worst of the wounded there. Percy Tonkin, you go and find Mr Vigurs the Physician, and you Bert, fetch Mr Williams, we'd best have the surgeon present. God willing they'll both be at home. And tell them the dispensary's burning,' he shouted after them, 'tell them to bring what medical stuff they've got at home.'

He passed a hand over his eyes, as if to get a grip on his racing thoughts.

The crackling roar behind him drew the attention of the rest of the crowd.

'You, you and you,' he pointed at three brawny men with bulging muscles, wearing the leather aprons of foundry workers, 'soak some blankets and wrap them round you and see what you can save from the dispensary. Just grab what you can, but don't risk yourselves.'

Willing hands passed over cloaks, lengths of canvas and old blankets, while yet others doused scarves and kerchiefs to tie over the men's noses and mouths.

Water was beginning to pass along the chain of volunteers which was growing by the minute as word spread through the town and people rushed to the scene.

'Where's the caretaker? Anybody know if the back doors are unlocked?' Carne shouted.

A muffled roar and the crash of falling masonry inside the building made the crowd flinch and stir restlessly.

'Someone get round the back to Porhan Lane and see if you can get in. Look, I can't ask anyone to go in there,' Carne shouted above the din, 'but I'm going in myself, will anyone come with me?'

He looked out over the faces in front of him. 'There's the Public Library, the Masonic Room, the Art Gallery and the Exhibition Hall inside that building.' His voice cracked with the strain. 'There could be people trapped in any of those places.'

A tall, fair-haired figure pushed his way forward to stand beside Carne.

'Somebody give me a blanket,' demanded Jared Carlyon.

Carne shot him a grateful glance as more men began to step forward, preparing themselves to brave the thick smoke that billowed from the glassless window and doorway.

Harlyn found herself moving as if in a dream. She ripped off her cloak and pushed it at two women who had full buckets in their hands.

'Quickly,' she gasped, 'soak this.' They emptied the buckets over the cloak and Harlyn squeezed the thick material into a bundle to wet it right through, then she rushed forward and thrust it wordlessly into Jared's arms.

His face mirrored his shock at seeing her and it turned to horror as he caught sight of the blood caked wound on the side of her head. Their eyes locked for a brief moment, then he turned and plunged ᵗhrough the smoke-filled doorway, as crackling flames began to lick at the empty windows on either side, piercing the smoke pall with an eerie orange flow.

With a shattering crash more chunks of masonry fell from the front of the building.

'Keep back,' Carne yelled, 'keep well clear.' Then he too vanished into the smoke.

Three men moved forward, dragging a piece of sail canvas and began collecting the remains of the men who had been at the centre of the blast.

''Ere maid, gimme a 'and.' One of the fishwives tugged Harlyn's arm, and as she looked round, indicated a well-dressed woman sprawled face down on the wet, muddy ground.

'I b'lieve she'm still breathing.'

Harlyn didn't want to move. She wanted to remain close to the burning building and watch for Jared's tall figure. But she could not ignore the desperate plight of the wounded.

Praying fervently that Jared would be safe, she crouched beside the still figure and gently turned her over. The woman moaned softly and Harlyn bit her lips to prevent herself crying out at the sight of the pool of blood beneath the woman's body. The front of her dress was soaked and the material had been sliced open diagonally from shoulder to waist.

'Good job she were well covered, else she'd 'ave bin dead be now,' the fishwoman grunted as they carefully lifted the woman between them and began their awkward stumbling journey to the Subscription Rooms.

As they reached the doorway the men Carne had sent for the fire engines rounded the corner, dragging the unwieldy appliances behind them helped by several other men pushing from behind.

The bucket chain had established a steady rhythm with every conceivable vessel being employed in the fight against the fire which had taken hold in the building on either side of the Polytechnic Hall.

After settling the woman as comfortably as possible, Harlyn and her companion left her to the care of the other women who were clearing the rooms and tearing sheets and towels for bandages, and went back to the carnage wreaked by the explosion.

Now the street was crowded with people, firefighters, gasmen trying to turn off the supply and assess the damage, people moving dead and wounded and shop keepers trying to clear the debris from their premises and sweep up the glass and masonry.

There were old folk and children frantically searching for relations they thought might have been in the area when the explosion occurred. Three constables and a sergeant were trying to stem the tide of others who had come, like vultures, to stand and watch. Lips parted, eyes avidly bright they hovered and stared, choking the routes for those attempting to move the dead, they broke through the bucket chain and hindered the rescuers.

Mostly they were ignored as those with reason for being there got on with their business, but now and again an anguished cry would rend the rain-filled, smoke-laden air, 'Wha'd'ee starin' at? Abn 'ee got nothin' better to do? Git away, fer Chrissake, git away!'

Harlyn lost count of the number of men, women and children she and her sturdy companion moved.

Once a cheer went up, but Harlyn, staggering away from the scene burdened with the lolling dead-weight of a horribly injured man whose legs had been crushed by falling stonework, could not stop or even look back.

Once she thought she recognised a man they were about to lift. He must have been coming out of the Polytechnic building just as the explosion occurred, for he had been hurled across the street and through the doorway of the shop opposite.

Enough remained of his black frock coat and grey and black striped trousers to tug a thread in Harlyn's memory. But as they tried to straighten his crumpled limbs he gave a peculiar gargle and his eyes glazed over.

'One for the church,' the fishwoman said grimly and leaving him where he lay, she pulled Harlyn away to a moaning bundle huddled against the wall.

Harlyn gently pulled aside the blood-stained coat to reveal a lad of about ten. He was clutching his stomach with both arms and raised a tear-streaked face, white as chalk beneath the smeared blood and grime.

'Want me ma,' he whispered, his lips blue and scarcely moving.

'We'll find your mother,' Harlyn tried to comfort him, her own throat choked and her eyes blurred with tears.

'Come on, John 'Enry.' The fishwoman heaved him up in her

arms, and Harlyn flinched at his thin scream of agony. 'Yer gran's down the road with th'others. She've cut 'er legs but she'll be all right. She bin some worried 'bout you.'

'An' me ma?' the boy whispered eagerly, his wan little face lighting up. 'We was all together, is me ma there too?'

'No boy,' the fishwoman replied gruffly. 'Yer Ma's dead.'

The boy said nothing. He closed his eyes as if unbearably tired, and seemed to age before Harlyn's eyes.

As her strength faded and her senses shrank from the sickening sights, Harlyn staggered on, unthinking, unseeing, moving automatically, obeying the orders of the woman who toiled beside her.

Then suddenly it was over. All the dead and wounded had been removed from the street, the fires were under control and the worst of the debris had been cleared away. Countless buckets of water together with the ceaseless, wind-blown rain had washed the blood from the street and pavement and on the surface at least, the life of the town returned once more to normal.

Someone thrust a mug of mulled ale into Harlyn's hand. She stared at it for a few moments, then unable to help herself she began to shake as peal after peal of laughter rang from her lips.

A sharp smack across her face choked off the hysteria and she looked up through a haze of tears into the kindly eyes of a grey-haired man with side-whiskers and a moustache.

'Come along now, you're simply tired and overwrought.' His voice was firm and gentle. 'Drink up the ale and get along home. Do you live nearby?' Harlyn nodded dumbly. 'Do you want someone to go with you?' She shook her head.

'Drink up then,' he urged and she did as she was told, feeling some of her strength return as the hot, spiced and sweetened liquid warmed her.

'You helped bring in the wounded didn't you?'

She nodded again, draining the mug.

'Now go home, get out of those wet clothes and have some hot food and a rest.'

'Excuse me,' Harlyn said diffidently, 'but who are you?'

Momentarily taken aback, the man gave a small smile. 'John Vigurs. I'm the physician.'

'Can you tell me please,' Harlyn begged hurriedly, 'the men who went into the Poly — Poly — to see if there was anyone inside?'

'Only three bodies were found,' the physician assured her, 'all in the entrance hall. Far less than we expected.'

'Yes, but the men who went in, Mr Carne and — and Mr Carlyon—' she swallowed convulsively, 'are they all right?'

Vigurs nodded. 'Yes, they're both fine, suffering a little from the effects of the smoke, but otherwise they're unharmed.' He frowned, 'Who—?'

Harlyn gave him a glowing smile. Jared was safe. Unexpected tears of relief sprang to her eyes. She blinked them back.

'Thank you,' she breathed, 'thank you so much.' Pushing the mug into his hand she turned away.

'Just a minute, young woman.'

The physician's peremptory tone froze Harlyn to the spot.

'Is this your basket?' He held it out to her. 'It was found in the street and brought to the Subscription Rooms.'

Harlyn nodded and took it from him. 'Thank you,' she murmured and walking as quickly as her weary legs would carry her, she started up the street towards the beer house.

11

White-faced, soaked to the skin and haunted by the carnage she had witnessed, Harlyn stumbled into the kitchen. Becky stood at the scarred table, placing slices of hot roast meat between hunks of bread and piling the sandwiches on to a thick blue and white platter.

'I thought you'd gone,' she said in a small voice, not looking up. 'I heard about the fire, we all did, but Missis wouldn't let me out. You were away so long, I thought — I thought you were — gone.' Her voice trembled.

Harlyn dropped the basket on the table and sank into a chair. She closed her eyes.

'Arthur did, you see. He went, like that, after the fire. Never told me. But you've come back.' Becky sounded puzzled. 'Why didn't Arthur come back?'

Bone-weary, Harlyn tried to think of something to say, but before she could open her mouth, Becky shook her head in agitation.

'What a fool I am, I keep forgetting, he went to Africa. Of course he did.' Her tone became conversational and for the first time she glanced up at Harlyn. Her face had lost its wary, defensive frown and wore a slight smile. 'He's waiting for me to join him, did I tell you?'

Harlyn looked into her aunt's eyes. They were quite blank.

As Harlyn covered her face with her hands, the passage door burst open and Mrs Eddy stormed into the kitchen.

Seeing Harlyn she stopped short and placed her hands on her massive hips, now tightly girded beneath the crimson taffeta. She thrust her head forward, enveloping Harlyn in a cloud of foetid breath.

'And where the 'ell 'ave you bin?'

Startled, Harlyn looked up. 'The explosion,' she began, 'people were hurt, killed—'

'Fergittin' sommat, aren't 'ee?' Mrs Eddy interrupted.

Harlyn's mind refused to function. 'What—? I don't—'

'On yer feet when you talk to me, missy. I got me s'picions 'bout you, but I'll 'ave none o' yer airs and graces 'ere.'

Harlyn pushed herself to her feet. 'Beg pardon, Ma'am,' she murmured.

'Why was you so long?' Mrs Eddy demanded.

'I was trying to tell you, Ma'am. I had to help move the wounded.'

'Whad yer mean? 'Ad to 'elp? I'm the one payin' you,' Mrs Eddy stabbed her gargantuan bosom with such force that her grimy finger almost disappeared into the quivering flesh.

'But, Mrs Eddy—' Harlyn cried, shocked.

'No 'buts'. They other two 'ussies skived off and abn come back yet and I got some crowd out there. Now you git yerself cleaned up and come and 'elp.'

'But, Mrs Eddy, Ma'am—' Harlyn began again.

'No "buts", I said,' roared Mrs Eddy, 'you jest do what you're told.' She stormed out, slamming the door behind her, only to reappear a second later.

'Git my 'erbs, did'ee?'

'Yes, Ma'am,' Harlyn nodded wearily.

'You get they ready afore you come out, my nerves is in some terrible state, and 'urry up!' Mrs Eddy bawled as she departed.

Harlyn took the heavy kettle from the top of the range and poured the contents into the sink. She added cold water from the bucket, refilled the kettle and returned it to the stove.

'Aunt Becky, please have you an old skirt and blouse I can borrow?'

Becky nodded and went out of the kitchen. Harlyn heard her on the creaking stairs. By the time her aunt returned, Harlyn had stripped off her dirty, blood-splattered dress and was bathing the cut on her temple, careful not to disturb the scab that was already forming.

Harlyn washed her face and arms then dried them on the rough towel. She quickly pulled on the black serge skirt and high-necked blouse Becky had brought down. Both were old and darned, but they were clean and even smelled faintly of lavender. The blouse was too big and the skirt too short but Harlyn scarcely noticed.

She smoothed back her hair, tucking stray tendrils into the braid pinned around her head. She looked at the initialled linen square, now wet and creased, then hung it on the brass rail in front of the range to dry.

The piece of cloth had acquired a strange significance for Harlyn. Since she had tied it over her hair on the quay after leaving Jared Carlyon's house, it was almost as if it had become an amulet, protecting her in some strange way.

First she had met Tom Grenville who had brought her to Aunt Becky. Then, despite being so close to the explosion, she had escaped with only a slight injury. Harlyn was reluctant to leave the linen square on the rail. What superstitious nonsense, she admonished herself, it would be completely ridiculous to wrap a soaking wet cloth around her head. She'd probably catch a chill.

Harlyn turned to her aunt. 'Listen,' she said softly, urgently, 'these herbs are really for you, I chose them for you, and you must keep them somewhere safe.'

As she talked Harlyn mixed the contents of the eight slim packets into two separate piles, varying the amounts of the different herbs in each pile. 'Can you get me a small basin?'

While Becky fetched one, Harlyn scraped the mixed dried herbs into two twists of paper. She handed one to her aunt.

'Take one teaspoonful in half a cup of boiling water, three times a day,' Harlyn directed, pressing the package into Becky's work-scarred hand.

Becky studied her niece cautiously, then stuffed the packet inside the neck of her blouse.

Harlyn poured some warm water into the basin and washed the valerian root thoroughly. She shook off the excess water then emptied the basin and refilled it with cold water.

Becky watched warily as Harlyn scored the surface with a fork then dropped the root into the bowl of cold water.

'That must soak for twelve hours to soften, then I'll grate it. It tastes horrible on its own,' she warned, 'but if I mix it with the chamomile and rosehips, equal amounts of each, in boiling water, it's not so bad.' Harlyn stood the bowl on the dresser and dried her hands.

'What does it do, this stuff? What's it for?' Becky asked suspiciously.

'It soothes the heart, Aunt Becky, and calms the nerves. It will help you to sleep peacefully, to rest, that's all.'

'Soothes the heart,' Becky repeated softly, her eyes distant.

'I'll try to prepare yours at the same time as I do Mrs Eddy's,' Harlyn spoke quickly and quietly, 'but if I can't or she's around, you must remember to—'

Heavy footsteps thumped in the passage and the door opened. Mrs Eddy poked her head into the kitchen.

'You ready yet, maid?'

'Yes, Ma'am,' Harlyn replied.

After scrutinizing her briefly, but thoroughly, Mrs Eddy jerked her head sideways, causing her ringlets to jiggle madly, as she indicated that Harlyn should precede her out of the kitchen.

As they crossed the passage into the taproom, Mrs Eddy grated in Harlyn's ear, 'You be nice to the customers, mind. They pays good money and they expect a bit o' friendliness.'

Harlyn felt a flutter of fear in the pit of her stomach. What was she supposed to do? How should she behave? What would the men expect of her?

She hesitated in the doorway. The full roar of male voices raised in talk and laughter and the thick pungent smell of tobacco smoke and stale sweat hit her like a blow.

For an instant Harlyn knew blind panic, then a forceful shove from Mrs Eddy catapulted her into the noisy crowd.

Harlyn dodged behind the wooden counter and at once the thirsty men began hammering on the bar top.

'Two pints o' mild.'

'Three halves of bitter and two o' stout.'

'Two cider and two pale.'

The orders, a foreign language to Harlyn's ears, rained down on her thick and fast.

Mrs Eddy showed Harlyn which keg was which. But after serving four customers, taking the money and passing orders for food through to Becky, as well as keeping up a lewd and lively banter with the men at the bar, she sent Harlyn to wait at the tables.

Harlyn struggled not to spill the frothing tankards as she edged her way through the crush to the booths and tables edging the room. Her cheeks burned scarlet and she kept her eyes lowered to hide the tears of mortification as men leered, jostled and pinched, whispering things which she barely understood but which she knew instinctively were shameful and degrading.

As she returned to the counter with four empty tankards gripped in her aching hands, Mrs Eddy leaned across and without lessening her black-toothed smile even a fraction, hissed, 'Be friendly, I said. You look like you jest crawled out the cemetery.'

Harlyn raised anguished eyes, 'I can't,' she cried hoarsely.'

'You'll do as you're bid, maid,' Mrs Eddy replied dangerously, 'else you'll get no pay. Now, smile.'

With no choice but to obey, Harlyn swallowed her humiliation and summoning all her resources set her face in a stiff smile that was so strained her cheek muscles jumped and twitched.

Strangely, this had the effect of rebuffing the advances of all but the most inebriated customers, and they were so uncoordinated in their movements that Harlyn could usually avoid their unsteady pawing.

She was carrying a tray of full glasses to a corner table when a tall, burly man entered the taproom. Harlyn had her back to the door and so did not see him. Even had she done so, his face would have meant nothing to her.

The man pushed his way through to Mrs Eddy and spoke to her. Her eyes narrowed and her face took on a foxy expression. She asked him a question. Without replying, the man took a gold sovereign from his pocket and tossed it onto the wet, beer-stained counter.

Mrs Eddy's eyes lit up and she grabbed greedily for the coin. As she was about to grasp it, the man slammed his hand down on top of hers crushing it, fingers bent, against the wood.

Mrs Eddy's face contorted but her screech was lost in the general hubbub. The man spoke once more and she pointed, her face twisted in pain. He followed her finger and said a few more words. Mrs Eddy nodded. He released her hand then turned and shouldered his way out, leaving Mrs Eddy clutching the sovereign while she rubbed her bruised fingers.

Harlyn squeezed her way back to the bar. She tried to dissociate herself completely from her body, which was bumped and jostled from all sides. She was so tired she almost dropped the tray loaded with empty glasses as she reached the counter.

'Watch out, you clumsy lummox,' Mrs Eddy screeched at her. 'You'll 'ave to buck yer ideas up, my girl. You seen Mary or 'Liza?'

Dumbly, Harlyn shook her head.

'Bloody skivin' 'ussies. They'd better 'ave done some business, else I'll 'ave their 'ides when they git in.' She paused then in a markedly different tone she said, 'Leave they glasses. Git out in the alley and call Willie, 'e abn 'ad no tea yet. 'E might be playing down the north quay.'

Harlyn was so thankful to escape from the taproom, if only for a few moments, she did not notice the curious expression on Mrs Eddy's face.

She hurried down the passage to the back door, shivering as the chill evening air struck through her thin blouse. The drizzle had stopped, but the flags and cobbles were slick and wet and heavy grey clouds hung low in the dusk.

'Willie,' Harlyn called. She had not yet seen the boy, so had no idea what he looked like.

'Willie, your mother wants you,' she called again. Still no reply. There was nothing for it, she would have to go through the alley into Quay Street.

Harlyn had taken two steps into the gloom when a dreadful foreboding clutched her heart and dried her mouth. She had half-turned, poised to run back to the dubious safety of the Beer house, when a brawny arm encircled her body, pinning her arms to her sides.

As she opened her mouth to scream a cotton pad was clamped

over her nose and mouth. She knew a moment's terror, a sickly-sweet smell, then blackness.

As Harlyn returned to consciousness she was aware of a jolting movement. Her head pounded in an agonising, rhythmic thump, and her stomach churned uneasily.

She raised her hands to her aching head and her fingers touched the partly healed cut on her temple. Taking several deep, shuddering breaths in an effort to calm her heaving stomach, Harlyn opened her eyes. Careful not to move her head, she looked about her.

The movement and sound of hooves and harness told her she was in a carriage. But it was pitch dark, she could see nothing at all. For one terrible moment she wondered if she had gone blind.

Harlyn put her hand out to touch the window, but instead of cold smooth glass she touched stiff cloth. The blinds were down.

The realisation dawned. She was not alone. Instant recollection of the fo'c'sle on board *Karis*, and what had happened there, constricted Harlyn's throat with icy terror. She held her breath.

'So, you have awakened at last.'

Harlyn did not immediately recognise the high-pitched, oddly sexless voice. She said nothing.

'I expect you have a headache, an unpleasant side-effect of chloroform, I'm afraid. Here, drink this.'

As the last word was uttered, the blinds on the opposite side of the carriage snapped up. Leaning towards her, proffering a silver flask which gleamed in the twilight, his small pale eyes glittering with amusement, was Sir Henry Trevellyan.

Harlyn gasped, then a barely audible moan escaped her. She was trapped. A helpless fly in this cruel spider's web. But how? No — who? Who had betrayed her.

Harlyn's thoughts raced. Not Aunt Becky, Harlyn had told her nothing. Not Elsie, she had known nothing either, nor had Mrs Eddy. Only one person had known the whole story. One man to whom she had given her trust, who at the same time, unknowing, had taken her heart. A man who had spurned her timorous offer of love, who considered her an irritation, a nuisance, Jared Carlyon.

Harlyn recoiled from the thought. He had said he would help. Though he had wanted to return her to her parents, that had been for her safety and for her parents' peace of mind. He had promised to try and find some way of extricating her from the arrangement and she had believed him.

But now doubts crowded in, too strong to resist. Why should he care what happened to her? He was about to announce his betrothal to one of the prettiest, wealthiest young women in the county.

He had told her plainly that her unexpected and unwanted appearance in his life had caused him a great deal of inconvenience. So it was only to be expected that he would try to rid himself of her.

But to have done this, to have informed Sir Henry of her whereabouts after she had bared her innermost secret fears and hopes, her very soul, to him. Surely he could not have done such a dreadful thing. Yet what other explanation was there?

A pain such as Harlyn had never known pierced her heart. The heart which Jared Carlyon had stirred from girlish sleep and fired with the emotions of a woman.

'Why so silent, my dear?' enquired Travellyan. 'Is it perhaps fatigue? Now what have you been up to since leaving your home so thoughtlessly, four long days ago?' He shook his head, dolefully. 'My beautiful bird of paradise has become such a drab little wren,' he tutted.

'You require a period of rest and quiet to restore your beauty and your spirits. I will personally ensure that nothing and no one disturbs you.' He paused and leaned forward slightly, his eyes glittering in the semi-darkness.

'I myself will visit you, of course. A prospective bridegroom must avail himself of every opportunity to discover his bride's little secrets, her character, her personality, her likes and dislikes.' He reclined against the buttoned leather, surveying her with a hooded, snake-like gaze.

'Oh yes, my dear,' he continued softly, 'we will have plenty of time to talk. You will tell me all about your visit to Falmouth and the kind of people who helped you. After all, such kindness must be rewarded, don't you agree?'

He unscrewed the top of the flask, poured a measure into it and tilted it against his mouth, never taking his unblinking gaze from Harlyn. He held out the flask to her. She turned her head away. The pungent odour of brandy was sharp in the confined air of the coach.

Screwing the cap back on, Trevellyan returned the flask to his pocket.

'Harlyn, my dear,' his voice brimmed with calm reason, 'while modesty and reticence are most becoming attributes, they can be carried to excess.' The syrup-sweetness in his falsetto voice suddenly revealed a barbed edge.

'Talk to me.'

Harlyn turned her face towards him. Physical and emotional exhaustion battled with fear and loathing, and won.

'I have nothing to say,' she replied, her voice flat and lifeless.

'No, no, that will not do, I cannot accept that,' he smiled at her, the cold, deadly smile of a shark. 'You have lots to tell me. But I can wait − for a little while.' He sat very straight on the leather seat. 'I have decided that our happiness must be postponed no longer. The marriage will take place in two weeks.'

So soon! Despite the chill of the autumn evening, Harlyn felt perspiration break out all over her body. Her heart gave a thud which took her breath away. Her throat and mouth were suddenly dry and she felt sick and faint.

'A week on Saturday will be ideal. The ceremony will take place at my house, in the great hall, with a grand ball to follow so that I may show off my beautiful, so desirable bride. The cream of Cornish society will attend, and no expense will be spared.' His smile grew cynical. 'Even my enemies will fight for an invitation to what will, without doubt, be the social event of the year.'

Harlyn felt Trevellyan's eyes upon her, probing, watching her closely, avidly.

Harlyn made a valiant attempt to keep her voice level, free of the numbing horror that threatened to choke her.

'My parents − the preparations—' she stammered. There had to be some way of putting it off. While the ceremony had not yet taken place, there was still a chance, a hope that somehow—

'Your parents are almost as anxious as I that nothing should stand in the way of our nuptial bliss,' Trevellyan said silkily. 'They are quite content to leave all the arrangements to me. I am expert at organising anything that will afford me pleasure, and marriage to you, my dear Harlyn, will afford me the utmost satisfaction,' the baronet purred, his round face a moon-like blob in the gloom.

Harlyn recoiled, pressing herself tightly into the farthest

corner from him, choking back the sickness of terror and revulsion that threatened to suffocate her.

Suddenly the coach veered off the road, slowing then stopping. The door was opened and the man who had seized her in the alley stood framed against the light spilling from the doors and windows of the inn.

"Coach and 'orses', Sir,' Trevellyan's coachman announced, his eyes flickering expressionlessly over Harlyn.

'Thank you, Jenkins.' The baronet was positively jovial, which, though she did not know why, unnerved Harlyn more than the anger she had expected.

'Don't allow her out of your sight, Jenkins,' Trevellyan said conversationally to his henchman. Then he stepped lightly down onto the flagged yard and turning, offered his small, pudgy hand to Harlyn, who had no choice but to place her hand in his damp grasp.

The light struck Harlyn's face and the baronet's eyes grew diamond hard. 'Well now,' he breathed, 'what's this? Scratches on your cheek, a fading bruise, and what of this cut on your temple? What misfortune has befallen you on your foolish excursion?'

Harlyn stared straight ahead. 'There was an explosion in the street. The blast knocked me to the ground and I was cut by flying glass.'

'Ah yes.' The faintest hint of relief was audible in Trevellyan's voice. 'It was caused by nitroglycerine, so I'm told.' Harlyn was jolted by the accuracy and speed with which he had received his information. Trevellyan's voice dripped scorn, 'The clumsy fools, the stuff's unstable. Conducting experiments with it is one thing, though it appears they're not even capable of that. But replacing the blast-man after every charge used in the mines is going to prove somewhat expensive,' he spat. 'Careless idiots.'

His utter indifference to the loss of life and devastating damage chilled Harlyn to the marrow. With her hand still imprisoned in his, they entered the inn.

They passed the noisy, crowded public dining room and as they arrived at the inner hall, a strikingly beautiful woman with bronze coloured hair piled in a mass of curls high on her head came forward to meet them.

Her crinolined gown was exquisitely cut, and the flounced applegreen silk shimmered as she walked. Coral earrings set in gold and shaped like teardrops hung from her dainty lobes, and a magnificent coral pendant necklace lay between her breasts.

Harlyn was aware of being instantly appraised by slate-grey eyes which slid from her to Sir Henry. Despite the woman's wide smile, a challenging light sharpened her gaze.

'Henry, how nice to see you again.' The throaty contralto combined welcome with respect, but Harlyn did not miss the deliberate lack of formality or title in her address. 'We thought you had forgotten us.'

'Cora, my dear,' Trevellyan strutted forward, maintaining his grip on Harlyn's hand, the width of his smile matching that of his greeter. 'It is a great pleasure to be here after so long an absence.'

'Dorinda,' she corrected, her smile stiffening, 'my name is Dorinda. You surely cannot have forgotten,' she chided.

Trevellyan smote his chest with his free hand. 'But of course, Dorinda. Such a pretty name. An eminently suitable choice. Your taste does you credit, my dear. However, you will not forget who picked you out of the gutter and nurtured such talents as you possess, will you, Dorinda?' His tone was light and friendly. 'What pretty baubles, and such a becoming dress. What I created I can as easily destroy.' He smiled but his voice held a cold and unmistakable note of menace.

Dorinda's smile did not waver, but Harlyn saw her throat work and her cheeks flush.

'My house is your house,' she murmured with great self-effacement. 'Will you be staying overnight, Sir? May I offer you my private suite for your comfort?'

'How kind,' Trevellyan cooed, 'but we return to Truro tonight. We have broken our journey only to sup and rest.'

Dorinda nodded. Her nostrils flared and her brows lifted delicately as her glance slid once more to Harlyn, observing the ill-fitting worn-out clothes, the absence of any coat or cloak, and the half-healed cuts and scratches.

Harlyn felt a prickle of anger at the woman's thinly-veiled contempt.

'Dorinda,' Trevellyan said smoothly, 'you have the honour of meeting my fiancée, Miss Harlyn Tremayne of Truro. Harlyn my dear, Dorinda is an old — friend of mine.'

Though Harlyn merely inclined her head, the blonde woman was forced by Trevellyan's mode of introduction to acknowledge Harlyn's status, she dropped an impeccable curtsey.

'May I offer my best wishes for your future happiness,' she said expressionlessly to Harlyn, 'and my congratulations to you, Sir Henry.' She addressed the baronet with the merest hint of a smile touching the corners of her mouth.

'You may, Dorinda, you may.' Trevellyan said coolly. A glance passed between the two and Harlyn was aware of undercurrents, positions challenged and defined, an exchange without words.

'We shall eat privately, Dorinda,' Trevellyan stated.

Dorinda smiled, but unmistakable agitation was evident in her clasped hands rubbing uneasily against one another.

'As I was unaware of your intended visit this evening, Sir Henry, I have allowed two other couples, Mr Bonython and his wife and Reverend Rouse and Mr Pendray to use the private dining room,' she said quickly, with an apologetic shrug.

Trevellyan turned his pale cold eyes upon her. 'That is most – irritating, Dorinda, but no doubt you will persuade them to vacate the room before we sit.'

Dorinda was obviously torn. 'Sir, they are regular customers, people of some standing—'

Trevellyan's brows rose in studied amazement, 'Do you mean to imply that I am not?'

'No, no, of course not,' Dorinda babbled. 'I only wished to point out—'

'Then kindly see that they have gone within fifteen minutes,' Trevellyan snapped. 'I shall enjoy a glass of sherry in your sitting room while I wait. Ah, one more thing, Dorinda. Due to circumstances which need not concern you, Miss Tremayne has no suitable dress in which to dine. I know I can rely upon you to supply everything for her comfort, you have such an eye for detail, and as I recall, a very extensive wardrobe.' The cold smile which stretched his fleshy lips did not soften the command.

Harlyn saw the brief flash of rage in Dorinda's grey eyes. Could this woman possibly be an ally?

'Your memory does you credit, sir,' Dorinda murmured, her eyes lowered. She turned to Harlyn. 'If you will follow me, Miss Tremayne.'

Trevellyan turned away and opened a door marked 'private'. As Harlyn and Dorinda reached the wide staircase, Dorinda excused herself and went to speak in a low voice to a uniformed waiter. The man's face registered shock, but Dorinda cut short his protest with an abrupt movement. She spoke a few more terse sentences and the waiter nodded several times and scurried away.

Dorinda led the way up the richly carpeted staircase to the first floor. Her stiffly held head and rigidly straight back proclaiming her fury more eloquently than words.

She stopped at the third door, and withdrawing a key from the ruffles at her bosom inserted it in the lock.

Opening the door, she stood aside to let Harlyn enter, then followed and was about to close the door when the burly figure of the coachman who had silently followed them, stepped over the threshold.

Dorinda tried to stop him. 'Get out, you great ox, she's safe enough with me.'

Jenkins brushed her aside. There was no malice in his action. There was no emotion of any kind.

'He said stay. I stay,' Jenkins replied expressionlessly.

'But you can't,' Harlyn cried, shock and embarrassment shattering her self-imposed vow of silence, she spread her arms, encompassing the pale mahogany dressing table, dotted with lace doilies on which stood fluted jars and elegant bottles and other articles of feminine toilet, the two mahogany wardrobes, the chaise longue with its gold emboidered damask upholstery, the rose velvet button-back boudoir chair and the large lace and velvet covered bed.

'This is a boudoir, Sir Henry didn't mean—' she broke off as Jenkins turned his heavy eyes on her.

'He meant. I stay,' he repeated with finality. He folded his hands in front of him and placed himself in front of the door with his feet slightly apart. He looked quite relaxed and totally immoveable.

Dorinda shrugged and glided across the thick, soft carpet to tug on an embroidered bell-rope beside the sumptuous bed.

'You may remove your outer garments behind the screen,' she waved a graceful hand at the japanned panels, the centres of which were painted with vividly coloured but delicately executed oriental leaves and flowers on a glossy black background.

There was a knock on the door. Jenkins opened it. A uniformed maid stood blank-faced on the other side.

'Bring hot water and fresh towels,' Dorinda ordered and as

Jenkins closed the door and resumed his position, she opened the nearest wardrobe.

It was crammed with dresses of every imaginable colour and material. Dorinda riffled through them, casting an appraising eye along the rail, then lifted out three and laid them across the bed.

The maid returned with a large ewer and two fluffy, white towels which she took behind the screen. Harlyn heard the water being poured into a basin. The maid scurried out again.

Dorinda gestured crossly at Harlyn who, gathering her courage, as she passed Dorinda whispered, 'Please, help me get away.'

Dorinda looked at her quickly, surprise wrinkling the smooth perfection of her forehead. She laughed, a harsh bitter sound.

'Still testing me, is he? After all these years?'

'No, you don't understand,' Harlyn whispered desperately. 'I—'

'You are Sir Henry Trevellyan's fiancée,' Dorinda stated with a cold smile. 'That is what he said, so that is what I believe. He wants me to clothe you suitably for an intimate supper.'

The veneer cracked and for an instant her rage and resentment were clear and ugly. Even her carefully modulated voice reverted to its Cornish origins, 'My clothes, my gowns, that I've worked my arse off for,' she broke off, took a deep breath and continued in her normal throaty contralto.

'I have known Sir Henry Trevellyan for a long time and over the years I have learned one thing above all others, when he wants, whatever he wants, you comply, because if you don't you may as well slit your throat in a dark alley, a fate not unknown among those who have crossed him.' She stared coldly at Harlyn.

'I have no intention of suffering the slightest discomfort on your behalf. Now get your clothes off or I'll call Jenkins to do it for you.'

Harlyn stepped behind the screen and with her back to Dorinda who followed her, she unbuttoned the high-necked blouse and took it off, then stepped out of her aunt's old black skirt.

As she turned to the basin Dorinda grabbed her shoulder and spun her round. 'Well, well, a lady is it? Come on, missy, who are you fooling? No lady would set foot outside her own bedroom unless she was properly dressed. Where's your corset?' Her eyes lighted upon Harlyn's neck and throat and like lightning her hand flashed out, caught the neck of Harlyn's shift and with one swift, savage tug ripped it from shoulder to hem.

A smile of wry amusement twisted Dorinda's beautiful face and she threw back her head and laughed.

'Plucked your cherry already, has he? And he's still going to marry you? You must be something special,' she said with acid archness.

'No, you really don't understand,' Harlyn stuttered, clutching the remnants of her shift about her.

Dorinda stared at the trembling girl with a puzzled expression.

'You mean it wasn't Sir Henry?' She pointed at the purple and green bruises on Harlyn's throat and breast.

Harlyn shook her head, shuddering violently. Her face crumpled in despair.

Dorinda stared at Harlyn then a smile of ferocious glee broke like a wave over her face. 'He doesn't even know,' she whispered triumphantly. She leaned forward. 'He doesn't, does he? He thinks you're still virgin.'

'But I am,' Harlyn cried, crimson with shame and embarrassment.

'Don't tell me, tell him,' Dorinda laughed in delight. 'See if he believes you.'

Harlyn closed her eyes. What was the use of explaining? Anyway, how could she explain without naming names. Nothing she said was going to make any difference, Dorinda had made that clear. Wretched and weary, Harlyn turned to the basin, concentrating her whole mind on the act of bathing.

Dorinda went to her dressing-table drawer and returned with a clean shift of finest cambric and a whalebone corset covered with lace and spotted with tiny pink rosebuds.

As Harlyn put them on, it occurred to her that this was the second time in twenty-four hours she had dressed in someone else's clothes, and that did not include Elsie's cloak.

What did it matter? she thought hopelessly. She was not her own person any longer, she had no rights, no say in what was to become of her.

'Come along, hurry up, there is still much to do,' Dorinda snapped. Harlyn followed her to the dressing-table, still clutching the towel, her cheeks flaming as she passed Jenkins standing like a monument in front of the door.

Dorinda pushed Harlyn down onto the stool and flicked the towel out of her grasp.

'It's a little late for modesty, don't you think?' she said tartly.

With nimble fingers Dorinda unbraided Harlyn's hair and began to brush it with such force that Harlyn's head was jerked backwards at every stroke.

Harlyn gritted her teeth and made no sound.

'That I should be acting lady's maid to Trevellyan's whore,' Dorinda muttered fiercely. 'I'll get even with him for this.'

Harlyn swung round and gripped Dorinda's hand, stopping the brush in mid-stroke. 'Then help me get away,' she whispered fervently. 'Just let me escape, what sweeter revenge could there be?'

'You stupid little fool,' Dorinda retorted. 'Do you think I'd live to see morning if I did as you ask? What do you think Jenkins is here for? He can have you and welcome. My chance will come.' She snatched her hand free and flung down the brush. Leaning forward over Harlyn's shoulder she picked up a comb and removed the lid from a green glass bowl of hair pins.

'But it will be when I'm ready,' she whispered fiercely in Harlyn's ear, 'and on my terms. I am very patient and I have a long memory.'

She stepped back behind Harlyn and making a centre parting drew most of the ebony tresses together with the comb, arranging them in heavy waves, then she curled the ends into a full chignon high at the back of Harlyn's head, securing it with pins. The hair she had left loose Dorinda curled into two heavy love locks and pinned them to fall over Harlyn's shoulder.

That Dorinda stepped back to admire her handiwork in the mirror. Harlyn too stared at the pale, haunted reflection and realised Dorinda's cunning. For instead of disguising the ugly blotches on her creamy skin, the twisted curls emphasised them, pointing like accusing fingers.

'Now the dress.'

Harlyn stood while Dorinda fastened a crinoline puff around her waist, the steel hoops covered in ruched satin to protect the material of the gown.

Dorinda turned to the bed, folding her arms she tapped her

fingers as she frowned over the three magnificent dresses spread across the coverlet.

'With that hair you could wear any colour,' Dorinda murmured almost in accusation.

Harlyn waited in silence. Dorinda would have her own reasons for whatever choice she made, and Harlyn knew she was merely an instrument of Dorinda's resentment.

'The gold brocade? No,' Dorinda pushed it aside, 'too insipid for such a special occasion. Now, what about the wine silk?' She picked it up and held it near Harlyn. 'No. Too dramatic, not at all the required effect.'

Part of Harlyn wondered what the required effect was, but the rest was too wretched to care.

'Now this, this is perfect,' Dorinda murmured, smiling. 'Ice-blue velvet. Such a demure colour for someone newly betrothed, so chaste.'

The dress was slipped over Harlyn's head. She stared into the mirror while Dorinda fastened the hooks at the back then straightened the matching lace ruffles which formed tiny cap sleeves and edged the decolletage.

In complete contrast to its delicate purity of colour, the cut of the neckline was more blatantly revealing, more deliberately provocative than any gown Harlyn had ever seen. Her breasts pushed up by the tightly laced corset, were scarcely covered.

A crimson tide of shame flooded over Harlyn. Her eyes burned with hot tears as she shut them tightly to escape her own reflection.

After adjusting the curls over Harlyn's shoulder, Dorinda opened another drawer in the dressing-table and from a tray containing dozens of ribbons, artificial flowers and hair ornaments, she selected two matching combs decorated with blue organdie and ostrich tips. She placed one just above the love locks, the other at the side of the chignon, then stood back to examine the total effect.

Harlyn opened her eyes and saw for herself Dorinda's evil genius. In contrast to the subtle shade of the gown, her exposed breasts, bearing the plum and purple bruises, were the vivid brand of a harlot.

The malice in Dorinda's satisfied smile was so pronounced that Harlyn could not contain herself.

'Why?' She spun round to face Dorinda, her eyes green as

stormy seas in her deathly pale face. 'Why? I have done you no harm.'

Dorinda laughed, an ugly, tearing sound. 'You?' she scoffed. 'What do I care for you? You are of no consequence. But he'll not make a fool of me again. Now let us see what he thinks of his little virgin bride.'

She seemed to recollect herself and her manner calmed quickly, becoming self-contained and aloof. But her eyes glittered with anticipation. 'If you are ready, Miss Tremayne – the door, Jenkins.'

The coachman opened the door and stood aside. Dorinda swept through and Harlyn, feeling the first stirrings of dread, slowly followed with Jenkins close behind her.

Dorinda led the way down the stairs and through the hall. She hesitated for an instant in the doorway, glancing at the waiter who stood outside, moving from one foot to the other. The waiter nodded briefly and Dorinda glided in to where Trevellyan sat at the far end of a large oak refectory table. A decanter of sherry and a half-empty glass stood in front of him.

'Forgive our tardiness, Sir Henry,' Dorinda simpered, 'but I'm sure you'll agree the wait was worthwhile.' Dorinda's eyes were bright with spite as she stepped aside leaving Harlyn face to face with her captor. But some strange quirk in the arrangement of the gas lamps left Harlyn partly in shadow.

Trevellyan had not moved when they entered the room, but now he pushed back his chair and stood up.

Harlyn's senses were so finely tuned that despite her trepidation she noticed the perspiration beading his forehead and the hectic flush on his moon-like face, making it look more bloated and fleshy than ever.

He extended his hand to Harlyn. She rested her fingers as lightly as a breath on his palm, but his own fingers closed over hers like the slimy wet tentacles of an octopus.

Impelled by some force stronger than herself Harlyn raised her eyes to his. Trevellyan pulled her forward, raising her hand to his fleshy wet lips. The voracious lust that swelled in his eyes was so overpowering that Harlyn felt the icy sweat of fear and loathing break out on her body.

He pulled her towards him, into the light. His gaze flickered greedily downwards and stopped, transfixed by the mutilated flesh which rose and fell unevenly with Harlyn's ragged breathing. His fingers tightened convulsively.

The heat in his pale eyes was suddenly doused and his gaze was as cold and hard as splintered ice. A violent tremor shook him. So rabid was the fury that distorted his face, that Harlyn thought she would faint. She waited, her nerves stretched to breaking point, for the explosion.

Trevellyan's glance flicked sideways at Dorinda, who stared boldly back, an insolent, mocking smile curving her mouth.

Trevellyan instantly regained control of himself. 'I knew I could rely on you, Dorinda,' he said softly, with a shark-like smile. 'A delightful colour and such a stylish coiffure.'

He reached out and with a pudgy finger that trembled very slightly lifted one of the curls that rested on the swell of Harlyn's breast.

'Lovelocks, how apt,' he murmured, allowing the curl to fall back into place, his finger hovering over it, while Harlyn stood rigid her skin crawling as she fought the urge to scream.

Trevellyan released Harlyn's hand and pulled out the chair to the right of his own. 'Sit down, my dear,' he commanded in a silky voice that sent shivers down her spine.

As Harlyn moved, her legs gave way. She grasped the table for support and sat down quickly, clinging desperately to the remnants of her composure. Trevellyan resumed his own seat, pulling it closer to Harlyn's. He leaned towards her and Harlyn steeled herself not to flinch away.

'I hope the experiences of the past few days have not robbed you of your appetite, my dear,' he piped. 'I confess the thrill of the chase always adds an edge to mine.' His tongue darted out to moisten lips already slick.

'The menu, Dorinda.' He held out an imperious hand.

The beautiful blonde, her face clouded with disappointment, stiffened. 'I shall summon the waiter, sir. He will attend to your wishes.' She turned to the door.

'No, Dorinda.' Trevellyan's tone froze her in mid-stride. 'It would please me far more to have you wait upon us.' He smiled, enjoying the effect of his words, visible in the conflicting emotions chasing each other across her face.

'It is important that you please me, isn't it, Dorinda?'

The flame of rebellion flickered and died as the elegant

beauty retreated from confrontation. She bowed her head. 'Anything you say, Sir Henry,' she said demurely.

'That's right, Dorinda, anything I say.' He turned to Harlyn. 'Now my dear, what would you like to eat?'

Trevellyan's high-pitched voice rasped across Harlyn's nerves like a blunt saw. She was not deceived by his apparent disregard of the bruises. His eyes had revealed all too clearly their impact upon him.

Sitting rigidly upright, her hands clasped tightly in her lap and the sick fear of apprehension churning inside her, Harlyn spoke through parched lips, 'I am not hungry, thank you.'

'No?' Trevellyan seemed surprised. 'So capricious, a lady's appetite. I'll wager you haven't eaten since luncheon.' He sighed. 'I see I shall have to tempt you.' He turned to Dorinda.

'Bring a baked red mullet with cream and sherry sauce and a fillet of Dover sole with lemon. To follow I want two fillets of beef with tomatoes, carrots and buttered broad beans, and also a dish of chicken breasts in port wine with mushrooms and parsley.' He snapped his fingers. 'The wine list, Dorinda.'

Her lips compressed in a thin line, she handed him the leather folder. 'I will order your food, sir.' She smiled stiffly.

'Don't keep us waiting too long, will you,' Trevellyan said curtly. Dorinda inclined her head and glided out.

Trevellyan leaned towards Harlyn. 'Now my dear, we are alone.' His sibilant murmur poured over her like treacle. 'A man and his fiancée, a young woman who has caused him much concern.' He paused, and lifting his right hand, with one pudgy finger he traced tiny circles on Harlyn's neck, slowly working his way down to her shoulder.

Harlyn's nerve almost broke. She scarcely dared breathe. Panic fluttered dark wings in her head, and her nails bit into the flesh of her palms.

'You have been sullied, Harlyn,' he crooned, his finger caressing her shoulder lightly, ceaselessly. 'A man has laid hands on you, you are damaged, defiled—' a tremor had crept into his voice. 'Look at me, Harlyn. Look into my eyes, tell me, Harlyn, tell me who it was and I'll crush him like the insect he is. Look at me, Harlyn, tell me—'

Unable to resist the compelling, hypnotic drone, Harlyn turned her head. Trevellyan's eyes bored into hers like needles.

'What happened? Tell me what happened. Who was he? His name, Harlyn tell me his name.'

Somewhere in the shifting swirling clouds that filled her mind, a warning sounded. No names, she must not give names. Trevellyan would never know on whose ship she escaped to Falmouth, not from her lips, not if he threatened her with death itself.

'I — I was attacked,' she whispered. 'A drunken seaman—'

'Where?' he hissed. 'On a ship? Whose ship?'

Harlyn shook her head wildly, groping for words. 'In a side road, near the quay. There was a fight — lots of people — I ran away.'

Trevellyan's fingers bit into her shoulder. 'You ran away?'

Harlyn gasped in pain. 'Yes, yes.'

'Then he did not deflower you? You are still virgin?'

Harlyn nodded, clenching her teeth against the throbbing agony where his fingers dug into her bruised flesh.

His grip tightened and it took all Harlyn's will-power not to cry out.

'If you have lied to me—'

'I have not lied,' she gasped, then blurted desperately, 'but if you doubt me, then do not wed me.'

Trevellyan released her shoulder and began stroking her neck once more. He laughed softly.

'I shall wed you, Harlyn Tremayne, do not doubt it. You stir a fever in my blood I have not known for many years.' He laughed again. 'De Sade considered himself a master, but I doubt even he attained the heights to which you inspire me, my dear.'

There was something unutterably evil in his pale, glittering eyes.

The door opened and Dorinda entered followed by the waiter pushing a trolley on which rattled several covered serving dishes.

Trevellyan tapped the wine list. 'Really, Dorinda, this is most disappointing. You don't have a Hock or a Moselle worthy of the name. A Chablis would have been ideal.' He touched the tip of his fingers together in an oddly feminine gesture. 'That fresh, fruity bouquet and light body with a hint of crispness would have complemented the fish.' His round face assumed an annoyed frown. 'There isn't even one listed.' He sighed crossly. 'I suppose I shall have to make do with the Graves.'

Dorinda signalled the waiter who hurried away to fetch the

wine, then she set warmed plates in front of Trevellyan and Harlyn.

'I want all the dishes placed upon the table, Dorinda,' he demanded. Surprise raised her eyebrows momentarily, then without comment she complied.

The baronet glanced up at her. 'Standards are slipping, Dorinda. Have you grown bored with inn-keeping? Do you crave the more — unconventional satisfactions of your former occupation?'

Dorinda's head snapped up, a small frown of anxiety knitting her brows. She stared at him warily, but his apparent good humour reassured her and a slow, languorous smile curved her mouth.

'Fortunately, Sir, I am able to pursue both with equal facility. But while I apologise for the limited choice in my cellar, I must point out that few of my clientele have your discerning palate.'

She rested her hand lightly on his sleeve. 'However, if you will excuse me for one moment, I think I can redeem myself.'

'Let us hope so,' Trevellyan warned coolly, 'you have tested my patience and my goodwill enough this evening.'

'I assure you, sir, you will not be disappointed.' Dorinda hurried away.

Trevellyan lifted the lids from all the dishes and sniffed appreciatively. At first, the sight of all the hot food revolted Harlyn.

Trevellyan lifted the fillet of sole onto Harlyn's plate and the mullet with its rich sauce onto his own, pushing the dishes aside.

'Come now,' he cajoled, 'you must eat.'

Harlyn looked at her plate. The sole had been lightly and expertly cooked. The fine white flesh was moist and succulent with just a hint of melted butter, sprinkled with fresh parsley and twists of lemon. Despite the tension that knotted her stomach, Harlyn's mouth watered. Save for the mulled ale she had drunk after assisting with the wounded, she had had nothing since breakfast fifteen hours ago.

Yet to eat with this man, to swallow the food he chose for her, would be to accept his tyranny, admit his dominance. She would starve first.

'Thank you,' her voice quavered imperceptibly, 'but I am not hungry.'

'Dear Harlyn, sweet child,' he crooned with a knowing smile, 'your voice says one thing, but your body another. Your eyes betray you, Harlyn. They are a mirror of your thoughts, and I can read, Harlyn. There is nothing you can hide from me.'

His soft, lisping voice, so patient, so confident, slithered into Harlyn's fear-numbed brain.

He picked up his fork and broke off a piece of the red mullet on his own plate. Dipping it in the creamy sauce he lifted it to his mouth. As his lips closed over the morsel and he slowly chewed, he closed his eyes in ecstasy.

'Mmm, delicious.' He broke off another piece, this time passing the loaded fork under Harlyn's nose.

Her nostrils widened at the aromatic scent, and in spite of herself she swallowed reflexively.

Trevellyan placed the fork in his own mouth once more, making small mewing sounds of enjoyment. Again and again he repeated the action, bringing the fork closer and closer to Harlyn's lips, taking first from her plate, then from his own.

Harlyn's body craved nourishment and her stomach ached for the food so temptingly offered, and so tantalisingly close.

Harlyn almost sobbed with relief as Dorinda re-entered the dining room, bearing a bottle hastily wrapped in a clean white napkin. With great care she placed the bottle in front of Trevellyan.

He flung his fork down noistily onto his plate. 'I did not wish to be interrupted.' There was cold fury in his voice. 'This had better be worthwhile.'

'I think you will find it so,' Dorinda purred confidently.

Trevellyan's small fat hands peeled back the napkin with all the delicacy of a woman and his wet-lipped mouth, glistening with fat from the food he was devouring, formed a perfect O.

'Le Montrachet,' he breathed. 'Queen of the white Burgundies.' He glanced at Dorinda. 'To the best of my knowledge there is only one cellar in the county which contains this vintage.'

Dorinda tilted her head with a coquettish smile, 'A token of appreciation from a young gentleman of rather unusual tastes. I was able to provide him with a perfect playmate.' She shrugged her elegant shoulders. 'I like to make people happy.'

Trevellyan caressed the bottle lovingly. 'That can sometimes be dangerous, Dorinda.'

She arched her fine brows and laughed lightly, 'All life is a hazard is it not, Sir Henry?'

The waiter stepped forward to open the bottle.

'Don't touch it,' Trevellyan snapped. 'This is a wine of aristocratic distinction. It must be handled with delicacy and care, no, with love.'

The baronet eased the cork from the bottle and passed it beneath his nose, his eyes were half-closed as he inhaled deeply.

He held a long-stemmed glass up to the light, eyeing it critically. 'Give me that,' he snapped and snatched the waiter's napkin from his arm. He polished a blemish from the surface of the glass, then flung the crumpled napkin into the waiter's face. The man retired in confusion to the doorway.

Picking up the bottle, Trevellyan poured a small measure of the wine into his glass. He swirled it around, sniffed it, then took a mouthful, holding it on his tongue for several seconds before swallowing.

'Superlative,' he sighed. He placed his glass upon the table and filled it three-quarters full, then poured the same amount into two more glasses.

'Tell me, Dorinda, does the father know of his son's — proclivities?'

Dorinda shook her head. 'I think not, sir. When I last spoke with him, he rambled on as usual about finding his son a suitable wife, and continuing the family name, though even he admits there is little but debts and a good cellar to go with it.'

'A useful piece of information,' he handed one glass to Dorinda and placed the other in front of Harlyn, pushing the plates aside, then picked up his own.

'We will drink a toast,' he announced.

'I've no head for wine, sir,' Harlyn murmured, almost reeling from nervous exhaustion.

'Nonsense,' Trevellyan brushed her protest aside. 'This is a wine without equal. There is none more suitable for celebrating our betrothal. One sip, and your flagging appetite will be restored and you will enjoy the delicious food I have chosen for you.' There was more than a hint of menace in his jocular tone. He went on smoothly, 'There is nothing I have desired that I have not possessed, sooner or later.'

Harlyn could feel his eyes upon her like probing fingers. The pale almost colourless liquid held just a hint of amber.

'And those things most difficult to acquire have usually afforded me the greatest satisfaction.'

As she stared at the wine, Harlyn's mind played a trick on her, and she saw faintly, becoming more and more distinct, two eyes, amber-gold beneath straight fair brows. A tawny gaze, aloof and sardonic, changing; becoming quizzical, intrigued; softening, reaching into her very soul to kindle a flame of tender yearning that not time, nor distance, nor the anguish of betrayal, nor even death, would extinguish.

'I propose a toast to — pleasure.' There was a moment's silence. Then Dorinda laughed, a soft, knowing chuckle. She raised her glass, exchanging glances with Trevellyan over the rim.

'To pleasure,' she echoed, excitement dancing in her eyes.

They both turned to Harlyn, holding out their glasses. She sat frozen, a statue in ice-blue velvet.

Suddenly she reached out and touched her glass. The liquid shimmered, the image dissolved. Its magic was lost to her, like the man. All that was left was the wine. Fear, utter despair, and the wine.

Harlyn gripped the glass with both hands and raised it to her mouth. She tilted her head back and the smooth potent wine burned its way down her throat like acid. She drank until the glass was empty, then flinging it from her to shatter against the panelled wall, she snatched Dorinda's glass from her and before the bemused woman could stop her, she drained that too.

Harlyn replaced Dorinda's glass on the table with a crack that echoed like a pistol shot.

She lifted her head and the room swirled about her. Reality ebbed and flowed. Trevellyan's shrill rage was but the cry of a seagull as the world spun.

Blackness approached like a gaping mouth. Harlyn was drawn towards it. 'Lost,' she murmured, and enfolded oblivion.

12

Harlyn opened her eyes. She looked uncomprehendingly around. She was in her own bed, in her own room at Chyvallon. She was home, and safe — *safe?*

She sat up and hugged her knees, resting her chin upon them. Apart from a slight headache, a tightness at the base of her skull and a feeling like a weight over her eyes, she was strangely empty.

Surely there should have been some pleasure and relief at being home again, safe from the perils and dangers into which she had stumbled since fleeing from the house — when — only four days ago?

It seemed so much longer. So much had happened to her. There was little left of the girl she had been, but who was she now?

The door opened quietly and Amy's rosy, weatherbeaten face peered round it.

'Amy,' Harlyn held out her hands.

Amy closed the door quickly and hurried over to the bed. She seized Harlyn's hands in hers, squeezing them, her face wreathed in smiles.

'My dear life, Miss 'arlyn, you didn' 'alf give we some scare! Wha'd'ee want to run off like that for?' Amy scolded.

Harlyn didn't reply and Amy's eyes slid away uncomfortably.

'Any'ow,' she said quickly, 'thank God you're 'ome safe agin.'

'How are my parents?' Harlyn asked.

Amy dropped her glance once more. She released Harlyn's hands and fidgeted with her apron, smoothing non-existent creases, pulling at a loose thread on the seam.

'Your father — I don't s'pose I should say nothing really, but 'e bin drinking some 'eavy, and 'e wint eat much. I tried to tell 'un 'e's makin' 'isself bad and 't wouldn' do no good, but 'e wint listen to no one.' She shrugged helplessly.

'Yer mother couldn' do nothing wid'n neither and she've bin in some state, I tell 'ee. She've worn 'erself to a shadow keeping up a good face, pretending ev'rything was fine and you was jest in the bed with a summer cold.'

Amy threw up her hands. 'Then Rosella and Veryan come 'ome from your aunt's and they'ad to be told sommat. They near drove us all mad, you know what jackdaws they two are. What with yer mother in tears one minute and in a temper the next, well—'

Amy looked at Harlyn and shook her head sympathetically. 'Wha'd'ee run away for, maid? Didn' do 'ee no good, did'un?'

Harlyn clasped her knees again and shook her hair back over her shoulders. She gazed out of the window at wind-torn clouds scudding across the early morning sky.

'I was kissed, Amy,' she confided softly, remembering. 'For the first time in my life I was kissed as a woman, by a man who made me feel — strange, wonderful, frightening things.'

'Hush your mouth, maid,' Amy looked nervously at the door. 'I do know well enough 'tidn Sir 'enry you be talking about.'

Harlyn glanced at her.

'Did you put me to bed last night, Amy?'

Amy nodded. 'Yer mother and me between us, after Sir 'enry bring 'ee 'ome in 'is coach. Spittin' mad 'e was. Where'd'ee git that dress? I never seen the like of it. 'E took un away wid'n. Your mother near fainted when she seen they marks on you.' Amy's voice dropped to an awed whisper. 'Sir 'enry never did that to 'ee, did 'un?'

Harlyn shuddered violently. 'No. That happened — on the way to Falmouth. Oh Amy,' Harlyn clutched the older woman's arm, 'I thought I was going to die—'

''Oo was this other man then?' Amy frowned in confusion. 'Surely 'twadn 'e—?'

'No, it wasn't,' Harlyn said quickly, 'he saved me. Oh Amy, he was such a strange person, cold and unfeeling one moment and so gentle and tender the next. He made me feel like a naughty child, then seconds later, like a desirable woman.'

'Now you stop that,' Amy placed her fingers on Harlyn's lips. 'There's nothing but grief can come of even thinking on it. 'Tis finished, whatever it was. You're betrothed to Trevellyan. Put all else out o' yer 'ead. Yer mother'll be in to see 'ee d'rectly. The doctor's coming later this morning and Sir 'enry after that.'

'The doctor? What for? I'm not ill.' Harlyn was puzzled.

'Sir 'enry insisted, said you was to be examined, to make sure—' Amy didn't finish.

Harlyn's cheeks flamed. She caught Amy's hand. 'You know the kind of man Sir Henry is, don't you, Amy?'

The older woman compressed her lips and her eyes slid away from Harlyn's penetrating gaze. She nodded.

'You know that I am nothing more to him than a possession, an object to be used to satisfy his depraved appetites?'

Amy nodded again, reluctantly.

'The man who rescued me,' Harlyn swallowed, 'I offered myself to him, Amy. Not because he had saved me, it was more, much more than that. It was as though I had been waiting for him all my life, but I had not known it. Oh Amy, he unlocked a secret place deep within me, and released feelings I had never before even dreamed of.'

'My gawd,' Amy whispered, eyes wide with shock, ''e never—?'

'No, he didn't.' Harlyn tried to smile but her lips trembled and the smile dissolved. Her emerald eyes filled like two limpid pools, and heavy tears spilled over her lashes and slid forlornly down her face.

'He did not share my feelings. He rejected me, Amy. Then he told Sir Henry where to find me.' Harlyn closed her eyes. 'Amy, it hurts so.'

The older woman's eyes brimmed in sympathy, 'My poor little bird.' She pulled Harlyn against her comfortable bosom and stroked the long, luxuriant hair.

''Tis better 'e didn', my 'andsome. B'lieve me, 'tis better this way. Sir 'enry would 'ave made 'ee pay some terrible price. The grief you feel now idn nothing to what it would've bin. 'Sides,' she attempted a watery smile, 'what you never 'ad, you can't miss.'

Footsteps sounded in the passage and the door opened. Amy sprang to her feet, surreptitiously wiping her eyes on the corner of her apron.

Harriet Tremayne swept into the room in a flowing peignoir of apricot taffeta with a shawl collar and full sleeves gathered at the wrists, her hair covered by a matching bonnet. Her face was set in a severe frown.

'That will be all,' she said coldly to Amy, who bobbed a curtsey and hastened out.

'It's a little late for tears, Harlyn,' Harriet sniffed aggrievedly, 'though I suppose we should be grateful for some small recognition of all the trouble you have caused us.' She turned on her daughter. 'What on earth possessed you, Harlyn? Running away like that, you have no thought for anyone but yourself, your father always spoilt you. If you had the faintest idea of what I've been through in these past few days—' She broke off and buried her nose in a fine cambric handkerchief.

'Well,' she raised her head and squared her shoulders, 'the strain has taken years off my life, my nerves are in shreds. As for your father—' Harriet closed her eyes and shrugged, expressing a blend of anger and accusation, 'he is completely overwrought. Your behaviour has so shocked him, Harlyn. Such ingratitude, such selfishness, we are both utterly ashamed of you. Sir Henry would have been quite justified in washing his hands of you. It is only due to my pleading on your behalf that he has not.'

Harlyn's face was alabaster white. She had harboured a wild dream that somehow she would reach her mother's heart, convince her to think again, to withdraw her consent to the marriage.

But Harriet's feelings on the matter were crystal clear, and Harlyn's last slender hopes were crushed.

'Now,' her mother said briskly, 'I will send Amy up with water, you will bathe and prepare yourself for the Doctor's visit.' She wagged a finger at Harlyn. 'You don't know how lucky you are, my girl, Sir Henry is such a caring man. No detail concerning your welfare escapes his attention.'

Lines of worry appeared on her face and she made a vague gesture.

'You have obviously been involved in some − mishap. But I expect the doctor to find you − intact, Harlyn.' She twisted the handkerchief between her fingers, patches of vivid colour burned high on her cheekbones.

'God knows what would become of us all if you were to incur Sir Henry's displeasure again.'

Harlyn spoke for the first time since her mother had entered the room. 'Don't worry, Mother,' she said quietly, 'you have nothing to fear.'

Harriet wrung her hands. 'To think that a daughter of ours should have risked such disgrace. It is Sir Henry's own doctor who is coming, you know. He would not permit our own physician − I mean, had it been necessary, we might have been able to persuade Dr Lander − if I had explained the situation − the importance—'

Harlyn could bear no more. 'Stop it, Mother,' she cried. 'I

told you, there is nothing to fear. It doesn't matter which doctor examines me, or how many. Sir Henry can send a dozen. The goods are undamaged, the seal is unbroken!'

The patches on Harriet's cheeks burned brightly. 'Calm yourself, Harlyn. I will not tolerate such — vulgarity, kindly remember your manners. After you have bathed, your sisters, naturally, will wish to see you. Discretion, Harlyn, please remember that. I do not wish their heads filled with ridiculous nonsense.'

'What did you tell them, Mother?' Harlyn was curious.

'Merely that you were overwhelmed by the honour and generosity of Sir Henry's proposal and had gone away quietly for a few days to compose yourself and reflect upon the great changes the future held for you.' Harriet's fingers continued to twist and shred the cambric handkerchief. 'The girls were sworn to secrecy, and our friends informed that you were confined to bed with a slight fever.'

'I saw Aunt Becky,' Harlyn said quietly.

Harriet blanched and her mouth sagged open. She recovered immediately. 'I know no one of that name,' she stated flatly, and turned to the door.

'Mama,' the anguished cry tore itself from the depths of Harlyn's heart.

Harriet faltered for an instant, then her back stiffened and she swept out, closing the door firmly behind her.

*

Displaying the shrewd judgement which made her business the success it was, Hetty Knowles turned her whole workshop over to Harlyn's trousseau. Ladies, high-born or low, requiring one item or several, were tactfully, apologetically but firmly refused, while for ten days the dressmakers and seamstresses worked day and night.

Mrs Knowles knew that news of the commission would spread like wildfire and the closed doors of her emporium would act as a magnet to every fashion-conscious lady in the borough. She would be in a position to be much more selective in future. Her prestige would soar and so would her charges. Hetty Knowles smiled contentedly.

Assuring the baronet that his generous allowance for Harlyn's new wardrobe would be wisely spent, Harriet totally immersed herself in the preparations.

Designs were selected, materials chosen and patterns made. Morning dresses, afternoon dresses, dinner dresses, ball gowns, short coats, long coats and a richly beautiful mantle of emerald green velvet, edged with gold braid, trimmed with ermine and lined with white satin, which would cover Harlyn's bridal gown.

There were shifts and petticoats of lawn and cambric, pantalettes and underskirts of linen and jaconet, nightgowns of finest white cotton, and negligees of organdie, cashmere, satin and lace.

At least twice and often three times a day Harlyn was required to try on various partially completed garments.

The dressmakers were supervised by Hetty herself. She in turn was watched by a hypercritical Harriet Tremayne, who lost no opportunity to remind Hetty of the honour of being dressmaker to the future Lady Trevellyan.

While Hetty sewed, Alice too was busy. Hats, bonnets and nightcaps sprang into existence under her nimble fingers, as well as frothy creations of feathers and ribbons, of lace and velvet and satin to complement a dinner gown or ball dress.

The bridal gown, an exquisite drift of white silk over white satin, embroidered with seed pearls, had its basis in a French design chosen by Sir Henry, who went himself to Hetty's workrooms to ensure that the very finest materials and most experienced dressmakers were employed upon it.

Harlyn sat, stood, turned, tried on and took off enclosed in a capsule of silence.

She ate what was placed in front of her. She drank the elixirs and bathed in the infusions her mother instructed Amy to prepare. She had no need of either.

Without any assistance her face assumed the translucent pallor of fine porcelain and her eyes, once clear, sparkling emerald, now with the opacity of a bottomless lake, grew huge in her finely drawn face. Her skin lost its golden glow and despite Amy's rosemary rinses and one hundred strokes of the brush night and morning, the luxuriant tumble of ebony hair had not its usual glossy sheen.

Sir Henry Trevellyan called every day. Harriet would find a different excuse to leave the baronet and her eldest daughter alone for at least part of the visit.

He would sit in the leather armchair, his plump body stiffly upright, his short legs barely reaching the carpet, and he would question Harlyn.

Always the same questions. Always the same sibilant lisp, patient, cajoling. How had she travelled from Truro to Falmouth? Who had helped her? Who had she seen there?

Harlyn refused to answer, utterly determined not to betray those who had helped her, Jared Carlyon, Elsie, Tom Grenville and Aunt Becky.

Her refusal to speak of the episode was her symbol of defiance over the baronet's control of her life and her destiny.

But the incessant questioning was beginning to fray her nerves, and she sensed that Trevellyan knew it. The gloating voluptuousness that swelled in his pale eyes as his soft voice slithered like a poisonous snake into her brain, brought Harlyn out in a cold sweat.

A battle of wills raged between them. Harlyn tried desperately to hide her panic. Summoning all her will-power she fought to control her mounting dread. But her stubborn pride seemed to excite Trevellyan further.

Within a few days, just the sound of the doorbell would cause Harlyn to shake like an aspen leaf.

She was never alone. If she was not with her mother undergoing fittings, her two sisters were constantly beside her, plying her with questions and incessant chatter.

She was forbidden to go riding or to help in the garden, on her mother's orders. Neither was a fitting occupation for the bride of a baronet. Even the kitchen and Amy's companionship were denied her.

Between Sir Henry's visits Harlyn grew visibly paler and more withdrawn, but her brave spirit, like a captured wild animal, sought desperately, frantically, for some means of escape.

There was none.

*

Jared Carlyon settled himself in the comfortable chair in the smoking room of the Red Lion, nodding his thanks as the waiter placed a glass of madeira on the table in front of him.

He had come deliberately early. There were still twenty minutes before he was due to meet Richard St Aubyn. But he needed some time to think.

The past week had been an exceptionally busy one. Captain Henderson had wanted discussions concerning tenders for *Seaspray*'s cargo from the Mediterranean. Jared had been down to see Charlie Carne once more to get a more definite idea of when *Karis*, now *Seawitch*, would be ready for Lloyd's inspection and relaunching.

He had also begun preliminary investigations into the possibility of exploring a new market with her, but the related paperwork and correspondence were frustratingly time-consuming.

There had been a message from Captain Lukies aboard *Seabird* saying that while loading in St John's harbour, the schooner had sustained damage from another boat dragging its anchors in a freak storm. Repairs were being made and it was hoped they would get away before either the cargo was spoilt or the winter storms set in.

There had been agents to see, and accounts to check and a new set of sails to be ordered for *Seawind* on her return from the West Indies.

On top of all that he had been inflicted with a stubborn, self-willed, hauntingly beautiful runaway, who had resisted all efforts to return her to her home and safety.

Now, in fact in a matter of minutes, he was faced with accepting or rejecting an offer which would have a profound effect on his whole future, both business and personal.

Jared toyed with his wine. His own confusion and hesitancy annoyed him. He had not achieved his present status by being indecisive. He knew himself to be an astute businessman, which was obviously why St Aubyn had selected him as a good prospect in terms of investment.

He had forged his own path, made his own way without fear or favour in a highly competitive occupation. He enjoyed the cut and thrust of the brokers' market and the bargaining for contracts as much as the feel of a canting deck beneath his feet and the crack of sail canvas on a fast passage. This was his life, the reality he knew.

St Aubyn's proposition was an incredible stroke of luck. It meant that long-term plans could be brought forward and implemented at once.

The expanding economy offered new markets, and trading opportunities were opening up all over the world, promising prestigious contracts and excellent profits, and the necessary capital was almost within his grasp.

This was what he had worked towards and planned for since he had struck out on his own after the death of his father.

The condescension and ridicule he had faced as a young man of twenty from established merchants and skippers had served only to temper him to a perfect balance of ruthlessness and flexibility. He had resisted the trap of tendering low to grab every contract, knowing that in the long-term a reputation for speed and reliability would compensate for higher charges. It was a decision he had never regretted.

His mother, though devastated by the loss of her husband, had remained in her adopted country, guiding her only son, helping him gain the confidence he needed, not only to take his father's place as owner-skipper of *Seawind*, but to fulfil his father's contracts and to seek more, ploughing back the profits into a second then a third boat.

Once she had seen the seeds sown by Jared's father and herself begin to bear fruit, realising he no longer needed her, with quiet dignity she had withdrawn from his life and returned to her family home in Denmark.

His mother would approve of Camilla St Aubyn, of that Jared was sure. She had an impeccable pedigree, social position, wealth, beauty, and when she put her mind to it, considerable charm. She was intelligent and though a little spoilt, was that to be wondered at, the only daughter of adoring parents with the money to indulge her every whim?

Jared did not doubt his ability to handle Camilla or to make her happy. He was fond of her and it seemed she cared for him. She would slot into his busy, ordered life with a minimum of disruption. Camilla had scant interest in his business affairs and would no doubt devote her spare time to charitable works and social entertainments. Such pastimes bored him to death and so he would be free to devote his energies to ensuring that St Aubyn's investment secured the greatest possible return.

A black-haired, green-eyed ghost flitted through his mind. Visions of Harlyn Tremayne's mobile face, its fluid expressions of anger, bewilderment, shock and fear, tumbling over one another.

'I'm so frightened,' she had cried. She whom he had seen to be brave, impulsive and strong. Her lips, dewy-fresh and innocent had touched his and burned their brand on his heart. Her slender, trembling body had clung to his in a paroxysm of dread, but that contact had unleashed a tide of passion in which it would have been so very easy to drown.

All the barriers he had erected over the years, rejecting involvement, denying emotional chains and bonds, had melted like snow in summer sunshine, and he knew as surely as he breathed that no other woman would ever stir him as she did.

Jared thrust the thought from him, rejecting it, ridiculing it. It was nothing but silly, romantic nonsense. He did not want such involvement. The thought appalled him. He had no time for fanciful dreams.

The upheaval of his thoughts surprised and unsettled him. He could still see her pale, drawn face, streaked with blood from the wound on her head. Her green eyes had held his as she had pushed the saturated cloak into his arms. What had he read in those emerald pools? What had she tried wordlessly to tell him.

Jared shook his head impatiently. He was behaving like some besotted schoolboy. Harlyn Tremayne had no place in his life. She had been merely an incident, an inconvenient episode. Besides, she was betrothed to someone else, a baronet, no less. She was not his problem.

He had tried to do the right thing and return her safely to her family, but on both occasions she had eluded him. Why should he concern himself with such a headstrong, impulsive, infuriating young woman?

Why was he such a blind, self-righteous, pompous fool? his inner voice asked quietly.

Jared refused to listen. She had run away again. He had no idea where she was. Even if he had the inclination to look for her, he simply didn't have the time. There was absolutely nothing more he could do; short of marrying her himself.

The thought appeared without warning and the treachery of his own mind shook him.

Marriage to her would be no contract of convenience, no comfortable partnership, each keeping to their own sphere of responsibility and interest.

Marriage to Harlyn Tremayne would be a collision, a fusion, a volcanic blending of minds and bodies, impossible to tell where one ended and the other began. It would mean soul-searing ecstasy and total commitment.

The idea of such involvement with another human being was completely alien to Jared. He was a solitary person. All his life he had walked alone. It appalled and fascinated, repelled and enticed him.

Though a battle waged within, his face retained its habitual mask of cool disdain. The cynical creases on either side of his mouth deepended fractionally as head and heart warred.

Richard St Aubyn entered the smoking room and approached Jared, his hand extended in greeting.

Jared, his mind made up, unfolded his length from the chair and greeted his host. 'Good evening, Sir. A fine evening for a sacrifice.'

St Aubyn repressed a smile. He recognised Jared's allusion to the reception he anticipated as the only Falmouth man among the worthies of Truro.

'Test of mettle, my boy,' St Aubyn returned blithely. 'A business record is one thing, behaviour under fire something else.'

'Am I to take it then that you prefer to witness the sport before placing your bet?' Jared asked lightly.

St Aubyn eyed him seriously. 'My offer was made some days ago, and still stands. It was you who required time to consider,' he rebuked.

'Then, sir, my hand on it.' Jared gripped St Aubyn's bony fingers and in that instant felt a sharp stab of regret which he resolutely ignored.

'I accept with gratitude. Rest assured that you will have no cause for regret.'

St Aubyn pumped Jared's hand and a warm smile lit his thin aristocratic face. 'Come, we've to be at the quay at Sunny Corner by 6.30. Call a cab and we'll talk on the way, I want to hear your immediate plans concerning the business.' St Aubyn laid a restraining hand on Jared's arm.

'I make only one stipulation. Our agreement is to remain strictly secret until you and my daughter are betrothed.' He waved a dismissive hand. 'The opinions of others are of no importance to me, and if it is assumed you are a fortune hunter I could not care less, we both know that is not the case.'

His face darkened in warning. 'But I will not have Camilla regarded with pity, or as part of a bargain. My investment is to be seen as part of her dowry.'

'I understand, sir,' Jared was again touched by the deep love St Aubyn had for his daughter.

Part of a bargain, the words echoed hollowly, stirring unease in him.

'I am to be sold to pay my father's debts,' Harlyn Tremayne had cried, cringing in revulsion and fear from the prospect of marriage to Sir Henry Trevellyan.

He, Jared Carlyon, had just agreed, on a promised investment of £50,000 into his shipping business, to marry a girl he did not love. Was he treading the same path as Trevellyan?

Jared shook off his doubts with angry impatience. The girl must have bewitched him. The whole matter was getting out of proportion. His was a legitimate business arrangement, harming no one and benefiting many. He must put the whole ridiculous episode out of his mind and concentrate on the future.

As they jolted along, passing the warehouses and timber yards that edged the foreshore, Jared focussed his attention on outlining his ideas to St Aubyn.

'First, I want to buy into Charlie Carne's yard on the Bar at Falmouth. The schooner I bought at the auction is being refitted there. A cash investment would enable him to increase the work-force, buy new equipment and so lower the turnaround time for ships under repair, giving priority to mine.' Jared ticked the items off on his fingers.

'I'd also get a new schooner on the stocks. The Carnes have a family tradition of boat building that goes back five generations. What they don't know about schooners isn't worth knowing.'

St Aubyn nodded, content to listen as the words poured from Jared.

'The wars in Peru, Paraguay and Brazil are making the export of South American cotton a very unreliable and hazardous affair. My plan is to establish a trading agreement with the North African ports. British influence in Egypt is growing and Egyptian cotton is reputedly the finest in the world. This is the time to move in and secure contracts to export that cotton to England.'

'That seems a reasonable start,' St Aubyn gave a dry smile. 'There is no doubt that once your mind is made up, you are a man of action.'

Jared accepted the compliment and its pointed undertones without comment.

The cab juddered to a halt and the two men alighted. As host for the evening St Aubyn insisted upon paying the driver, then they walked down to the quay where the pleasure steamer *Louisa* floated amid the jetsam on the rising tide. A huge blue silken flag, with the borough coat of arms on a white circle in the centre, rippled from her mast in the early evening breeze.

St Aubyn was greeted with great deference by the Mayor, minus his regalia on this occasion, and several other corporation dignitaries, who Jared learned later, were also members of the Improvements Commission, a body of men of substance whose responsibilities included the purchase and maintenance of fire fighting equipment, and also cleansing, paving and lighting the town.

As St Aubyn introduced him Jared watched with wry, inward amusement the wide, obsequious smiles fade, replaced by suspicion, uncertainty and open dislike the moment Falmouth was mentioned.

Sir Henry Trevellyan was one of the last to arrive. As the rest of the party of thirty were already seated, and the baronet was lost among the crowd of heads, Jared, curious in spite of himself, had no opportunity to observe or overhear him.

Louisa chugged away from the quay, spewing out clouds of thick, black smoke from her stack into the mellow September evening. Waiters circulated among the passengers with trays of sherry and madeira.

St Aubyn was drawn into conversation with the men on his right, who appeared from what little Jared could catch to be trying to interest him in various development schemes for the town.

The instant Jared was observed listening, voices were lowered, and heads turned aside. So, leaning with his back against a bulkhead, Jared closed his eyes and allowed the snatches of conversation eddying around him to float past as the steamer ploughed through the dirty, stippled water to King Harry Passage.

'Of course Cornish elm is better value for a quarter boat than English elm. It's stronger, cuts cleaner to narrow scantling and lasts twice as long, but the Cornish is two and six a foot, while English is only tenpence a foot and grows three times as fast—'

'There's no two ways about it, costs will rise now slavery's been abolished. As if we didn't have enough problems trying to make a profit—'

'There's another revival meeting at Gwennap Pit this Sunday, I don't know who's preaching.'

'When you think about it, there's precious little difference, if you discount these emotional displays which I personally find somewhat distasteful, between this Methodism and the Anglican church.'

'I can remember Norwegian Fir being rafted up from barques moored along here by King Harry. Beautiful wood, sixty feet long and twenty inch section—'

'Saw it in the *West Briton*, the Peruvian ports expect to be blockaded any day, and you can be sure that will hit the guano exports landing at Restronguet.'

'Sherman's got into Georgia—'

'Four hundred and fifty in the workhouse at St Clement's now—'

'Go on, South Caradon and the rest of them only got going when the western mine's production started falling. Penstruthal and Great Wheal Busy had been supplying the African market after the Swedish ores pinched out. A good part of Tresavean's output went to the West Indies for copper bottoms and plates for the sugar industry and rum distilling.'

'The soup kitchens are charging a penny a quart—'

'The two small fire engines will have to go up for sale. We've got no choice, there's complaints coming in on all sides. We'll use the money to get a bigger one.'

'There's typhus over in Mitchell Hill again.'

'—That's all very well, but if we levy higher rates to pay for these schemes, we're the ones who have to pay the most—'

'There's sewage draining into the wells in Tippet's Back, but they're still drinking the water.'

'—Throwing good money after bad. Let the charities take care of it, that's what they're there for.'

Jared listened and learned as the boat reached Tarra Point off Mylor and turned towards Messack Point on St Just, steaming down the invisible line which separated the Port of Truro from Falmouth waters.

The waiters darted about replenishing glasses. Then St Aubyn was called upon as guest of honour to propose the customary toast.

Anticipation lit every face and glances slid from the aristocrat to Jared as St Aubyn stood, slightly unsteady on the moving deck, and raised his glass.

'The toast is—' all glasses were raised, '—the Prince and Princess of Wales, in honour of whose visit to Cornwall the water bounds are being beaten this day.' St Aubyn had neatly side-stepped the issue of having to publicly proclaim his loyalty to either of the two towns.

After a moment's surprised silence, the toast was repeated and glasses emptied. It was not until the party disembarked at Tregothnan boathouse, their venue for dinner, that swords were drawn in earnest.

The large room above the actual boathouse had been taste-fully decorated with bunting and flowers by Pearce's hotel who were also supplying the food.

The party sat at three large trestle tables which were covered with snowy cloths and set with silver cutlery and fine glass.

Strains of martial music drifted in through the open win-dows, played by the Band of the Second Cornwall Yeomanry Cavalry, who sat in their boat moored off shore.

As waiters brought in the first course of lobster served with a sauce of garlic, mushrooms, lemon juice and cream, garnished with parsley and slices of fresh lemon, the man at the end of Jared's table leaned forward.

'Carlyon, you say? Any relation of the banker?'

St Aubyn performed the introduction. 'This is Mr Thomas Daniell. His family are partners in the Pencalenick Tin Smelt-ing Company together with—' he indicated two other men at the table, 'Mr Jonas Michell and Mr Percy Teague.'

Jared nodded at all three. 'I am honoured to make your acquaintance, gentlemen.' He returned his gaze to the man who had spoken.

'Only very distantly, sir. Though I do believe an ancestor of my father's was one of the originators of the present banking system.'

'Eh, how's that?' Daniell frowned.

'He was a smelter, sir, like yourself, and like others of his time he advanced money on the strength of the black tin brought to his house.'

'Ah, yes, yes,' Daniell nodded briskly. 'Is this German or

French?' he demanded of the waiter at his elbow about to pour white wine into his glass.

'German, sir. A hock made from Riesling grapes,' the waiter murmured, and pulling back the napkin, revealed the distinctive brick-red sloping shouldered bottle.

'All right, all right,' Daniell gestured for the man to continue, 'those Froggies make a decent red wine, but the white—' he grimaced in disgust, 'no body, far too thin,' he grumbled.

'How is business, Mr Teague?' St Aubyn enquired.

'In a bad way, your lordship,' Teague replied gloomily. 'There's less ore coming into the works every week. We'll be laying men off again very soon.'

'It's not that the ore isn't there,' Michell said angrily, 'though I admit the lodes in some mines are pinching out, it's the expense involved in getting it out. Not to mention the problems they're having with the blasting charges. Obviously all this has to be reflected in our prices, especially those of us who have interest in the mines as well. We are fast reaching the point where we simply can't compete with foreign ore.'

'Mines in Australia and Tasmania are working surface and stream tin and producing vast quantities of ore at a fraction of our costs,' Teague added.

'Do you feel this is purely a local problem,' St Aubyn asked, 'or is the mining industry throughout Cornwall in as bad a state?'

'As Lord St Aubyn has already withdrawn his holdings in three mines which are about to close, it would appear he has already decided it is,' Sir Henry Trevellyan, occupying the remaining chair at that end of the table, said waspishly.

'You are exceedingly well informed, sir,' St Aubyn acknowledged blandly. 'Perhaps your information did not include the fact that the lodes had pinched out in all three. But I would welcome your advice on what course to take in the present circumstances.' St Aubyn's impeccable manners veiled the sharp irony of his remark.

'Diversification is the only answer if you wish to survive,' Trevellyan replied, 'and I have every intention of not only surviving, but of maintaining my profit margins.' The high, fluting voice of the baronet, seated on Jared's left, was totally confident.

'With respect, sir,' Michell was controlling his anger with some difficulty, 'few of us have the funds available to diversify, having reinvested our profits in the belief that the slump is only temporary.'

'Then no doubt you will lose the lot,' Trevellyan said coldly.

'It has been noted that your mines have the worst record of accidents in the area, Sir Henry,' Teague's face was puce, and his politeness to the baronet an obvious effort. 'Has that influenced your decision to pull out of mining?'

'Certainly not,' Trevellyan snapped. 'Such accusations, and I don't acknowledge their truth, are totally irrelevant. I am a businessman, I invest capital in going concerns; when they cease to return what I consider sufficient profit, I withdraw my capital. The human element is of no interest to me whatsoever.' He took a sip of wine.

'Only a fool or a blind man could have failed to read the signs. This is no temporary lull. The mines in Cornwall are dying, and aside from owners who won't accept facts, the fault lies with the miners themselves.'

'How so?' Jared was curious. This was the first time he had spoken to the baronet, and he had to admit to instant dislike of the man. His gut reaction had been reinforced by the baronet's complete disregard for the people he employed.

Jared's initial impression gained at the auction, of tightly contained pressure at a dangerously high level was even stronger now he was physically close to Trevellyan.

The baronet's high colour and bloated appearance made him appear ready to burst out of his skin. There was a vibrating tension in the rigid uprightness of his posture, and his strangely colourless eyes glittered as though with fever.

'Greed,' Trevellyan said succinctly, putting a forkful of lobster dripping with rich sauce into his mouth.

'Greed? That's ridiculous!' Michell exploded. 'The miners earn every penny of their wages. They work under appalling conditions. The heat on the lower levels is suffocating and there's constant danger of rockfalls and flooding. Before the man engine was installed to take them from the surface to the working levels and bring them up again, those men had to climb hundreds of feet by ladder at the beginning and end of every shift. Dozens have been killed or terribly injured falling off the ladders from sheer exhaustion.'

'Your compassion does you credit,' the sarcasm in Trevellyan's tone belied his words, 'and no doubt it will bankrupt you.

Every occupation has its hazards,' he said, unmoved by the shock on Michell's face. 'If they aren't prepared to take the risks they shouldn't be there. Anyway,' he went on, brushing aside Michell's protest before it could be voiced, 'the emigration figures to mines in South Africa, Australia and Mexico appear to be rising daily as the rats desert the sinking ship.'

'That still leaves the unskilled men,' Teague pointed out. 'With no work for them, their families are starving.'

'That is their problem,' Trevellyan shrugged.

'But men are coming into the town from outlying districts and vagrancy is becoming a real problem.'

'It's groups now, not just individuals who are getting involved in disturbances and fights,' Daniell put in. 'Things are becoming very serious.' Teague's face mirrored his deep concern.

'What about law enforcement?' Jared asked.

'The police are badly undermanned,' Teague answered. 'There are only two constables on night watch and one as street-keeper during the day. They can't possibly cope with this kind of situation.'

'Could not more be employed?' St Aubyn enquired. 'That would seem the most sensible course.'

'Indeed, sir, you are right, but we just don't seem to get the right sort of men applying for the job,' Teague answered.

'And those that are acceptable are soon frightened off,' Michell put in. 'We had one chap, excellent fellow, highest character reference, resigned after two days.' He shrugged helplessly.

'Assuming then that the mining industry is going into a permanent decline, what alternative commercial prospects are there for Truro?' St Aubyn demanded.

'Maritime trade,' Trevellyan answered briskly. 'I have a large interest in the Truro Mercantile Shipping Company and I am quite sure that if it wasn't for that precocious little town at the mouth of the river—' his eyes slid to Jared and back to St Aubyn, '—skimming off the cream, Truro would have a thriving commercial traffic in shipping.'

'That is most unlikely, Sir Henry,' Jared retorted coldly. 'For a start, though the town of Falmouth covers only twenty-six acres as opposed to Truro's fifty-one, we have a population of almost six thousand compared with your three and a half.

Figures which in my opinion speak for themselves. Secondly,' he continued, totally disregarding the baronet's ill-concealed fury at this open contradiction, 'Truro's loss of trade to Falmouth is due not to any specific efforts on Falmouth's part, but to this town's appalling mismanagement of its own affairs.'

There was complete silence around the tables, arranged in an open square as the attention of each man had been caught by or drawn to the discussion taking place at the top table.

The only sound was the clatter of crockery and cutlery as the waiters deftly cleared the fish course and brought in for each table a roast crown of mutton surrounded by roast potatoes and flanked with dishes of peas and carrots, accompanied by bowls of redcurrant jelly and onion sauce.

After an initial glance at the impressive joints, all attention was once again focussed on Jared Carlyon. There were one or two cries of 'Shame' and mutters of disgruntlement and disapproval.

'I did not seek this confrontation, gentlemen,' Jared pointed out calmly, as the waiters carved and distributed the meat on heated plates and the wine waiter silently, almost unnoticed substituted claret for the hock.

'Pray enlighten us, Captain Carlyon,' St Aubyn gestured with a bony hand, a gleam of amusement lighting his cool grey eyes. 'Doubtless you have some facts with which to back such an — inflammatory statement?'

'Naturally, sir,' Jared addressed St Aubyn, but his voice deliberately pitched to carry to the listening men. 'It is not my habit to enter any discussion without being fully aware of the issues involved.'

'Well, do hurry up and expound this preposterous theory of yours,' piped Trevellyan with a supercilious sigh, his eyes as sharp as broken glass in his red, puffy face.

'This is not theory, this is fact,' Jared stated boldly. 'The condition of the river, your trade link to the sea, is an utter disgrace. You, the Mayor, the burgesses, members of the council, the corporation and the Improvements Commission—' Jared looked around at them all, and his derision was naked and unmistakable, 'you cannot *all* be unaware of the silting up that has been taking place for years, due to the mud and slime washings from the mines and to this town's own remarkable system of sewage disposal.'

Mutters rippled round the room while the food cooled on the tables.

'Then there is the clutter of wharves, quays, timber pounds and warehouses along the foreshore, constricting the river still further. I know of several plans that have been put forward for dredging the river over many years, and they have all been rejected. On a variety of reasons have been given, but they all boil down to one thing — money. Or, rather, your reluctance to spend it.'

Jared leaned forward. 'As the river has choked up and big ships can no longer use it, naturally trade has migrated to ports they can reach, Devoran and Falmouth. Yet still you have done nothing.' Jared's impatience was scathing.

'The closest you ever came was when the Borough Council wanted to apply for a Parliamentary Bill to fund the purchase from the Duchy of the foreshore between the town and Sunny Corner. The plan was to deepen the channel between Malpaso and the town quay. But even then you couldn't agree.

'Lord Falmouth, on whose property we now sit, along with Lord Vivian, Sir William Lemon and one hundred and eighty-nine residents of note, opposed the Bill. Why? Because the expense was not justified by the amount of trade now coming into Truro by river.'

Jared's gaze was cold and disdainful as he surveyed the room.

'The Bill failed, gentlemen, and the reason it failed was spelled out. The corporation had already incurred massive debts and had not used the revenue from anchorages and other shipping dues to maintain and improve Truro's facilities as a port.' A contemptuous smile touched Jared's lips.

'You have fouled your own doorstep for too long, gentlemen. Now the mess has choked you.'

Jared leaned forward and helped himself to roast potatoes. Others also began to take a belated interest in the food and soon the shocked silence was broken by the sound of knives and forks being wielded and the rumble of earnest conversation as discussions and counter-arguments sprang up all around the room.

'Assuming that what you say is, er, true,' Daniell said uncomfortably, 'and I must say that I don't consider the situation to be quite as simple as you make out, I am still convinced that Falmouth will never supersede Truro as a business centre. We have a long established reputation in banking and related concerns.'

'Indeed, Mr Daniell,' Jared readily agreed, 'a reputation highly esteemed.'

Trevellyan pursed his lips over a forkful of mutton topped with redcurrant jelly. 'I hear the coastguard ship *St George* is to be removed from Falmouth,' he observed. 'A serious financial loss, I would imagine,' as he chewed, his small eyes challenged Jared, 'not to mention the blow to the port's prestige. Still, let us rejoice that a replacement is soon to drop anchor in Mylor Pool.'

Trevellyan put down his fork and raised his glass. The rich ruby wine glowed in the evening light.

'The town of Falmouth and her surrounding waters will henceforth be under the protection of HMS *Ganges*, the naval training ship for boys!'

Trevellyan tilted his glass at Jared in mocking salute and drank deeply. A roar of malicious laughter echoed round the room as few lost the opportunity of revenge on the unwelcome outsider.

Jared caught St Aubyn's eye. A brief, grim smile touched his mouth. He made no reply. General conversation bubbled around them.

The meat dishes were removed and replaced by a selection of deserts. A huge bowl of stuffed peaches, baked in wine and sugar was accompanied by small dishes of whipped cream. A large lemon meringue pie stood beside a platter of caramelled oranges and a honey fruit pudding. The cheese board was within easy reach for those who preferred savoury to sweet.

Percy Teague spooned cream on to his peaches and bit into one with relish. He looked up enquiringly at Jared.

'Were you at sea in that gale we had earlier this week, Captain Carlyon? I've not known one like it so early in the season before. There were chimney pots flying all over.'

'As a matter of fact I was on the Truro river that night,' Jared replied thoughtlessly. 'We lost the topmast and some rigging.'

Trevellyan's head snapped up. 'On the river?' There was a sudden intensity in his stare. 'What caused the damage to your boat?' he asked, but even as he spoke Jared could see he was preoccupied.

'Insufficient room to manoeuvre and frayed lines, we couldn't get the topsails down.'

'That must have been a most unpleasant experience,' Michell commiserated, his spoon poised over a slice of lemon meringue.

'It sounds more like poor maintenance, the very sin of which Captain Carlyon accuses us,' Trevellyan taunted.

'You are right, sir. It was due to poor maintenance, but the fault was not mine. I had bought the schooner at auction only hours before and was taking her back to Falmouth for refit.'

Trevellyan paled, then hectic colour flooded his face.

'You,' he whispered, and his small pale eyes burned. 'You bought Tremayne's schooner – then—'

Jared was suddenly aware of the dangerous ground he was on.

'That is correct,' he said coolly.

'Speaking of Tremayne, Sir Henry,' St Aubyn broke in, 'allow us to drink a toast to your future happiness, for I believe you are to wed his eldest daughter.'

The baronet's bloated features struggled with suspicious rage directed at Jared, and arranged themselves into a stiff smile.

'How gracious of your lordship. Indeed I am the most fortunate of men. To have found such a jewel after the unfortunate demise of my dear late wife, was indeed a blessing, and then to have my proposal so willingly accepted—' the baronet, warming to this theme, made a deprecating gesture.

'Gentlemen, you see before you a man renewed, rejuvenated, a man receiving the gift of youth,' he smiled, shark-like, 'while retaining the knowledge and enlightenment of a man of – experience.'

This remark prompted a certain amount of muffled comment and coarse laughter.

Trevellyan turned to Jared. 'I believe you have met my fiancée?' His tone was light, but jealousy and suspicion burned with white-hot intensity in his gaze.

Jared made a rapid decision. To protect Harlyn Tremayne's reputation he had no choice but to deny all knowledge of her. He felt a quick stab of anger. Though he'd washed his hands of her, she was still causing him trouble.

'You are mistaken, sir,' he said levelly. 'I have not been introduced to the lady.'

Trevellyan impatiently brushed aside Jared's attempt to fence with words. He was like a hound that had scented its quarry.

'Come now, Captain Carlyon, the acquaintanceship of such a

beautiful woman is surely not to be denied?' Trevellyan protested roguishly, his eyes boring like a gimlet into Jared's.

'I fear you confuse me with someone else, sir,' Jared replied. 'For I am certain that had I met your fiancée, it would have been an experience not easily forgotten.'

Trevellyan's expression did not alter, but his eyes revealed a molten fury that flared, then was instantly controlled.

'You will have cause to remember,' the baronet hissed softly, so that only Jared caught the words. Then he raised his voice to its normal level.

'Well then, Captain, so that you may fully appreciate my good fortune, I insist that you attend the wedding as my personal guest.'

Though he hid it well, Jared was taken completely by surprise.

She had willingly accepted his proposal, that's what Trevellyan had claimed. But the bedraggled, shivering girl hiding in the cabin, and that same girl desperate to find refuge with a long lost relative in Falmouth, and her sobbing pleas as she had clung to him gave the lie to Trevellyan's boast.

Was she then back with her parents, Jared wondered. Had she returned willingly, even after twice eluding him in his attempts to ensure just that? Or had Trevellyan discovered her whereabouts and retrieved her himself? But if so, how? Who would have told him where she was? Who beside himself even knew?

'I thank you for the invitation, but I fear I shall be at sea,' Jared excused himself quickly.

Trevellyan pounced. 'When do you sail?' he demanded.

'In just over a week,' Jared replied calmly, sure that he would be far from Cornish shores on the day of Harlyn Tremayne's marriage to the baronet. 'I have a new overseas contract and it will be *Seawitch*'s first voyage following her refit.'

Trevellyan's smile was slow and deadly. 'How fortunate then that the wedding takes place this Saturday. You will be able to attend after all, Captain Carlyon. My invitation will reach you by morning.'

Jared could only nod. Why did Trevellyan want him there? Why should the thought of seeing Harlyn Tremayne again disturb him so?

The remainder of the evening passed Jared by in a kaleidoscope of wine and talk and laughter.

As the cab took them back to the Red Lion, each busy with his own thoughts, St Aubyn broke the silence.

'Why don't you come with my wife and Camilla and myself?'

'I beg your pardon, sir?' Jared was jolted out of his confused introspection.

'To the wedding. Trevellyan is sending our invitations to Poldice. I shall be there by midday.' St Aubyn gave a wry grin, 'Doubtless I'll be met by two females clamouring that they don't have a thing to wear.'

Jared's responding smile was barely discernible. 'Thank you Sir, that is most kind.' He tried to inject some enthusiasm into his voice.

'Not at all, my boy,' St Aubyn murmured complacently. 'After all, what better opportunity or more suitable occasion for Camilla to receive your proposal.'

13

Sir Henry Trevellyan crooked his little finger as he lifted the tea-cup to his lips and sipped delicately. He replaced the cup on the saucer.

'So,' he said softly, 'it was Captain Jared Carlyon who so thoughtfully transported you to Falmouth, causing me such inconvenience.'

Harlyn's bowed head snapped up. No vestige of colour remained in her face. 'I did not say so,' she whispered.

'No, my dear,' Trevellyan's smile was both smug and malicious. 'He did. Not in so many words of course, but we both know it was he. So let us drop this ridiculous charade.' His tone grew sharp and menacing. 'I begin to wonder why you go to such lengths to protect a total stranger.'

Trevellyan sipped his tea. 'Whatever reasons Richard St Aubyn had for bringing Carlyon to the dinner, I'll see that he regrets them.' He looked up at Harlyn, his eyes as cold and hard as pebbles.

'I intend to destroy that young man. He had the gall to contradict me, the effrontery to accuse us, the commissioners, of mismanaging the town's affairs.'

The baronet's wrath overcame him and his face was livid as he recalled the incident. 'I don't give a damn about this town, but nobody criticises me, or questions my competence in business matters, nobody,' he repeated vehemently.

'He did that?' Harlyn was stunned. 'I don't understand—'

Trevellyan appeared not to hear. 'That skipjack will be down in the gutter where he belongs before I've finished with him.' He looked up, fixing Harlyn with a piercing stare, 'And you, my dear, will help me put him there.'

Harlyn flinched. 'I? How?' she gasped.

'You will swear out a charge of kidnapping against him.'

'No,' Harlyn blurted defiantly. 'He did not kidnap me, he did not even know I was on board the boat when it sailed. Besides,' she could not hide her bitter anguish, 'he made sure you found me again. Surely such a generous act merits reward rather than punishment.'

It was Trevellyan's turn to look puzzled, then his face cleared.

'Why, Harlyn, my dear, I do believe you are cross with him. Wouldn't you enjoy a little revenge?'

'I have no feelings whatever for Captain Carlyon,' Harlyn replied quietly, forcing herself to voice the lie, 'so revenge is of no interest to me. But I will not give false evidence against him.'

'My dear Harlyn,' Trevellyan studied her closely, 'you profess your lack of interest with a shade too much force.'

Harlyn felt warm colour rise in her cheeks. She looked down quickly, willing herself to remain calm, to reveal nothing of the battle raging within her over her fear of what Trevellyan might do, and her confused feelings for Jared himself.

'I see no point in this discussion,' Harlyn tried to keep her voice expressionless.

'Then it will hardly interest you to know that it was not Captain Carlyon who informed me of your whereabouts,' Trevellyan gloated.

Harlyn felt the shock like a slap. 'Not Jar — Then who?' she whispered.

Trevellyan cackled with laughter, shaking his head. 'My dear child, you are transparent. No, it was not Jared Carlyon, though I thought for a while it might be amusing to allow you to believe it was. But now I find it more amusing that you know it was not he who betrayed your confidence. Who was it?' he piped, 'a little bird — a sweet singing little bird.'

Trevellyan watched her avidly, drinking in her every expression as bewilderment, dismay and finally shocked realisation fled across her fine-boned face.

'Tom?' she murmured in horrified disbelief. 'Tom Grenville — but I thought—'

'And you were blaming Captain Carlyon for something he hadn't done,' Trevellyan chided, but at the back of his pale eyes, Harlyn could see cold fury and implacable hatred for the man who had helped her.

Oh Jared, her heart wept, forgive me for doubting you.

'It is of no consequence,' she murmured through dry lips.

'Oh, but it is,' Trevellyan insisted. 'I intend to convince Captain Carlyon, who swears he has never met you, that in fact he has.'

Harlyn's head was reeling. Jared had denied meeting her? Then he must have denied her presence on board his ship. So it was she who had revealed the truth and incriminated the man she had sworn to protect. Trevellyan's fiendish cunning had gained him the knowledge he sought. He would use that knowledge to destroy both her and Jared, of that she had no doubt, and there was no way she could warn the man she loved.

Trevellyan's eyes had not left her face, and excitement danced in them at the tumult she was trying so valiantly to disguise.

'What do you mean?' she cried.

He leaned forward and picked up the cup once more. 'At my personal invitation Captain Jared Carlyon is attending our wedding. Whatever your true feelings for him or his for you,' Trevellyan hissed, 'he must stand by and watch in silence while you and I are bound together for life,' he finished triumphantly.

As he sipped, his little finger curved outwards, like a question mark.

*

The sinking sun was a glowing fiery ball in a sky shot with apricot and rose. Filmy swathes of cloud streaked the western sky, their edges tipped with gold, as the coaches of the Cornish gentry began to turn in through the tall iron gates of Sir Henry Trevellyan's mansion on the outskirts of Truro.

The great hall at the side of the house was ablaze with light as the massive chandeliers spilled their brilliance through the tall windows, as if competing with the radiant sunset.

The scent of carnations, roses, freesias and lilies, banked in alcoves and arranged in glorious displays on pedestals and in baskets around the hall, drifted out into the mellow September evening together with the strains of lilting melodies played by the Truro Philharmonic Society's orchestra, seated on a stage at the opposite end of the hall from the white-pillared entrance.

In the dining room close by a sumptuous buffet was spread. Crystal glass, crested silver and finest linen were a fitting background to the dishes of Russian caviar resting on beds of crushed ice, and cold salmon dressed with cucumber slices, radish roses, and piped with savoury butter. There were whole baked hams, glazed with honey and brown sugar and studded with cloves; surrounded by skinned peaches and crisp green salad; a huge quarter of beef, roasted to succulent perfection was flanked by dishes of fresh and cooked vegetables of every colour and description, and accompanied by sauces and dressings of infinite variety.

Syllabubs flavoured with liqueur brandy, sherry trifles, chocolate gateaux, apple and blackberry pies, raspberry tarts, and rich confections of meringue and cream awaited the guests, together with a hundred bottles of vintage champagne set in a mountain of ice decorated with flowers.

The butler gave last minute instructions to the staff and warned those not on duty in the dining room to remain below stairs and out of sight.

One of the kitchenmaids who had been in the baronet's employ only a few weeks begged to be allowed to assist at the reception. The butler at first refused, but he was short of staff and her earnest desire to be part of the great occasion touched him.

Being a kindly man beneath his stern exterior, he allowed that she might carry the lady guests' cloaks and mantles to the room set aside for the purpose upstairs. He was quite surprised by the gleeful satisfaction with which his concession was met.

Sir Henry Trevellyan descended the curved staircase with short, precise steps, his back ramrod straight beneath the black, waisted, tailless coat. The fluted frills of his immaculately white dress-shirt and tie were in startling contrast to his swollen, florid complexion.

He strutted through the dining room, followed at a respectful distance by his butler who breathed a silent sigh of relief when the baronet passed into the ballroom without a single comment.

Trevellyan's eyes darted about, missing nothing, and he allowed himself a small smile of satisfaction as he walked to the entrance where the waiting footman was opening the door to the first guests.

Outside in the fading light, men were moving. They came from all directions. Men in ragged clothes, with torn and rotten boots. Men with hunger gnawing their bellies and rage firing their hearts. They came from villages and hamlets and from the town itself, across fields, through woods, over rough, rock-strewn hills, and down gorse and heather-lined valleys. For a week the word had been spreading, a murmur here, a whisper there, the day, the time and the place.

The trickle grew into a river and the river became a torrent as the men from silent, empty mines converged on the home of the man they held responsible, and hated above all others.

The muffled tramp of feet was the only sound until a voice, high with suspicion, broke the silence.

'What you doing 'ere, Joseph? I thought you was agin this.'

The man called Joseph raised red-rimmed eyes and in a voice cracked with grief and anger he shouted for all to hear, 'Our youngest died last night, choked on a bit o' dried bread. 'Twas all we 'ad to give 'er. She were but a twelvemonth.'

Another voice called, 'We're sleeping on straw. I can't feed my family, let alone buy bedding.'

More joined in. 'Flour is thirty-six shilling a sack now, even more if you want to buy a bit at a time. 'Ow can we pay they prices ifn we got no work?'

'Trevellyan kept the prices 'igh. 'E don't care if we starve, nor our little ones.'

''Twas 'e that shut Rosugga—'

'—and Pentreath,' someone added.

'But not 'til 'e'd killed my Pa and two brothers when 'e refused to lengthen the safety fuses,' an unkempt youth cried bitterly as he limped along, supported by a friend.

'That trading company of 'is controls the food prices.'

'While 'e wines and dines the bloody gentry, we can't even buy bread.'

"E've took our jobs, what do the bastard want now, our lives?"

A roar of anger went up from the restless crowd and they swept onward.

*

Harriet Tremayne was in her younger daughters' bedroom. She fussed with her gown, shaking out the skirt, checking that the collar lay just so, as she fretted over last-minute details.

'Rosella, Veryan, have you your posies?'

'Yes, Mama,' the two girls chorused, waving aloft the small bouquets of rosebuds and freesias bound in satin ribbon.

'And clean handkerchiefs?'

'Yes, Mama.' Exasperation mingled with excitement as they prinked and preened in front of the long mirror, edging one another aside.

Both wore identical dresses of flounced, rose-pink tulle over satin petticoats. Rosella's brown hair and Veryan's blonde was twisted into dozens of tiny ringlets falling over each ear, and both had headdresses of pink satin ribbon decorated with tiny pink rosebuds.

Harriet herself was resplendent in magenta velvet with a pelerine of white lace over the bodice. Her hair was dressed in a chignon of three rows of curls, one on top of the other, with more curls falling behind each ear from the hair looped back at the sides from a centre parting. She too wore a headdress of satin ribbon and lace, to match her gown.

Amy poked her head around the door. 'Coach is 'ere, Ma'am,' she announced.

'Oh my goodness,' Harriet pressed a hand to her bosom. 'Come along, girls. Amy, where's the master? Now have I seen to everything? Is Harlyn ready? I must make sure—' She swirled out and along the passage, leaving Amy to shepherd the two excited girls down to the waiting coach. Their plaintive squeals echoed up the stairs.

'Rosella, mind my skirt, you'll crush it—'

'Veryan, don't wave your posy about, the flowers will get bruised—'

Harlyn, standing by her window, barely heard their chatter.

looked out onto the garden. The long shadows and softening light told her of the sunset she could not see.

As the sky changed from crimson and gold to turquoise and pearl, Harlyn thought how appropriate it was that her wedding should take place in the evening. The end of this day would see the end of life as she had known it. What would tomorrow's sunrise bring? Perhaps it would be better if she did not—

'Ah, there you are,' Harriet burst in, a preoccupied frown drawing her brows together. 'Now, let me look at you.'

Harlyn turned from the window to face her mother. Her dress, a froth of white tulle and lace over white satin, fitted her perfectly. Her hair was drawn back, fastened high on the back of her head and fell in a loosely braided cascade to just below her shoulders, a French hairstyle chosen like every other item of her apparel, by Sir Henry Trevellyan.

Her veil of fine guipure lace was held in place by a coronet of white satin ribbon, orange blossom and pearls.

Harriet's gaze swept over her daughter from head to toe. Her face crumpled suddenly and she searched her sleeve for her handkerchief, pressing the wisp of lace and cambric to her nose.

'All the effort, all the problems, it's all been worth it. You look so beautiful, Harlyn.' Dabbing her eyes, she peered more closely. 'But you really are terribly pale. Still,' she stuffed the handkerchief out of sight up her sleeve, 'that's hardly surprising. This is the greatest day of your life.'

Harriet adjusted a fold in Harlyn's veil, and fractionally altered the position of the coronet.

'Now just remember who you are, and what's at stake, and let us have no nonsense. If you should happen to feel a little faint, and it could happen, what with all the excitement and the sense of occasion, a few slow, deep breaths will soon put you right.' Harriet stepped back.

'Now I must go, the coach is waiting. It is so kind of Sir Henry to send his own carriage for you. But then, as I've said all along, and I still don't think you appreciate, Harlyn, nothing is too much trouble for him as far as you're concerned.'

Harriet took a pace forward and pressed her face against the cold, pale cheek of her eldest daughter.

'Don't let us down, Harlyn,' Harriet warned, and hurried out, calling for her husband.

'William, William? Where are you? Harlyn is ready and Sir

Henry's carriage will be here at any moment. William, I must go.'

Harlyn heard a door slam. 'Goodbye, Mother,' she whispered.

Amy bustled in. 'C'mon my bird, 'tis time you was gone.' Her round, kindly face fell. ''Ere, you'm shakin' like a leaf. You'd best 'ave a drop o' chamomile afore you go, 't will calm 'ee down a bit.'

They walked down the stairs, Harlyn gripping Amy's arm as if her life depended upon it.

William Tremayne stood in the hall, swaying very slightly. His face was flushed and his eyes blood-shot. He looked at his hands, at the floor and over Amy's shoulder. He could not meet his daughter's gaze.

Even now Harlyn was aware of a pang of compassion for the wreckage of her once proud and respected father.

'Oh my Gawd,' Amy muttered, 'be all right, will'e, Master?' She was plainly doubtful.

William Tremayne squared his shoulders and took a deep breath.

'This is my daughter's wedding day,' he enunciated carefully. 'Today at least, I shall not shame or disgrace her.' His brimming eyes at last met Harlyn's in mute appeal.

Careless of her dress, Harlyn flung herself into her father's arms.

'God pity us both, Pa,' she cried, crystal tears spilling over her dark lashes.

The knocker crashed down making all three jump. Amy opened the door. Harlyn looked over her father's shoulder and her stomach contracted painfully as she recognised the liveried coachman standing on the step.

'Are you ready, miss?' Jenkins touched his cap. 'Sir Henry is waiting.'

Harlyn turned from her father and put her arms around the woman she had known as nurse, servant, friend and confidante since babyhood.

'Take care, Amy,' she whispered, unable to trust her voice. 'And thank you, for everything.'

Amy's hands flew to her mouth, 'The chamomile, my bird—'

'Too late, Amy.' Harlyn attempted a tremulous smile. 'Much too late.' She placed her hand on her father's arm and picking up her bouquet from the hallstand, she walked slowly and steadily out into the fading light.

The coach, with the baronet's crest on each door, pulled away. Amy stuffed her apron into her mouth to muffle her sobs and stumbled blindly back into the house.

As Harlyn and her father began the journey to Trevellyan's mansion Lord and Lady St Aubyn's carriage turned into the courtyard and liveried footmen ran to hold the horses and open the carriage door.

Richard St Aubyn, his bony features rendered even more aristocratic by his formal attire, descended onto the paved courtyard and turned to assist his wife, who managed her voluminous gown of lilac brocade with the ease born of long practice.

Next came Jared Carlyon, tension visible in the set of his jaw and the deep creases on either side of his mouth. The last to step out was Camilla St Aubyn, glowing with happiness and excitement in peach silk.

They were met on the steps of the wide, colonnaded porch by an effusive Trevellyan, who came swaggering out, like a puffed-up bantam, to meet them.

'So glad you could come, especially you, Captain Carlyon,' he lisped, a mocking light in his eyes.

Jared was deeply uneasy. He tried to shrug off the dark foreboding that had settled over him like a cloud. Maybe there was going to be a change in the weather. Maybe as a man of the sea he felt out of place amongst those whose lives were bound up with the land. Maybe it was simply an awareness of being an outsider among Truro society, though in honesty, on that point, he could not have cared less.

Jared looked about him keeping one ear alert to enable him to respond to Camilla's witty observations, made behind a deftly manipulated fan, concerning the other guests.

He noticed several of the men who had been present at the boathouse dinner. Some, Teague and Daniell amongst them, acknowledged him with a brief smile or a curt nod, others turned deliberately and ostentatiously away.

Jared's eyebrows lifted in amused contempt. What in God's name was he doing here anyway? Trevellyan was almost a stranger, and after meeting him Jared wanted no dealings of any kind with the baronet, business or personal.

As for his bride – Jared's thoughts were all tumult and confusion. He had spent only a few hours in her company, hours which had been, to say the least, stressful.

But when he had held her in his arms it was as if she belonged there, as if he had known her always. Yet she was still a mystery, an enigma, a challenge to every concept of order in his life.

A self-mocking smile curved his mouth. Perhaps it was simply that he had too long denied himself female company, and if that were the case, then instead of contemplating another man's bride, he should concentrate on his own.

Still, the fact that he was here at all discomfited him. Had he been a free agent he would have refused the invitation. He doubted his presence would be welcomed by Harlyn Tremayne.

But now, because of their agreement, he was obliged to consider St Aubyn's wishes. Camilla had wanted him as her escort and there was no denying St Aubyn's point that this gathering provided an excellent opportunity for himself and Camilla to be seen together in public preparatory to announcing their betrothal.

Jared's tall figure, wide-shouldered and slim-hipped in his formal black coat and grey trousers appeared relaxed as he moved with the St Aubyns among the other guests, smiling indulgently at Camilla's whispered asides, acknowledging introductions, responding politely to questions concerning his health, his business and the state of the economy.

But while tinkling laughter and rumbling conversation eddied around him, Jared was aware of a tightening of his muscles, and while part of him fought the lassitude of boredom, his eyes, topaz-hard in the refracted light, were those of a prowling tiger, wary, restless, searching.

In the gathering dusk the angry mob was drawing closer. The sound of their tramping feet was a sullen, rhythmic pounding on the dirt road.

Inside the ballroom the trilling laughter and carefree chatter of the ladies in their elegant gowns and sparkling jewels, like brilliant butterflies in a tropical garden, blended with the music and the deeper tones of the men. The swelling volume of noise insulated the privileged company from any warning sound that might have carried on the still evening air.

Jenkins cracked the whip over the backs of the matched pair of bay horses drawing the carriage. Anxious not to be late, knowing Trevellyan would hold him responsible regardless of the reason for any delay, Jenkins urged the horses on.

Trees grew on either side of the rutted track where it curved round through a shallow valley between two small hills, and down to the gates of the mansion. Jenkins did not see the men spread right across the track, their backs to him, until he was almost upon them.

At the sound of the thundering hooves the men at the back of the column turned. Crude, flaming torches revealed their ugly mood, stamped like a brand on their faces.

That the men meant trouble Jenkins had no doubt, should he slow up and risk getting caught in the middle of the angry rabble? For angry they certainly were. He could feel their rage and hatred as surely as he could hear their shouts.

Anger turned to shock and then to panic as they realised the driver was not slowing down. Shoving and shouting they pushed one another in a frantic effort to reach the banks at the side of the track.

Jenkins thought of his passengers. Trevellyan wanted that girl. If something should happen to her — Jenkins didn't bother to complete the thought. He knew well enough that if anything happened to her he was a dead man.

Bringing the lash down viciously across the backs of the bays, he gave a blood-curdling yell. The horses, maddened with pain and fright, leapt forward, eyes rolling, ears laid flat, hurtling straight for the scrambling men.

Harlyn heard Jenkins yell and clutched her father's arm as the carriage surged forward, swaying wildly.

'What's happening, Pa?' she cried fearfully.

William Tremayne was jerked out of the semi-stupor into which he had sunk, and shot upright. 'What? What?'

Harlyn looked out of the window and as the carriage plunged through the human barrier she saw the gaping mouths and terror-stricken eyes of men slipping and falling to be crushed beneath the iron-rimmed wheels.

Above the tortured screams and hoarse cries, Harlyn heard someone yell, 'That's Trevellyan's coach, the murderin' bastard.' And the howl that greeted those words made her blood run cold.

The carriage lurched and shuddered as it smashed its way through the mob, jolting over the bodies of those not quick or agile enough to get out of the way. Then it was free and hurtling at full gallop towards the iron gates, followed by running men, the remains of the shattered mob, now totally out of control and screaming vengeance.

The orchestra ended their melody and struck a chord. A large, heavily-built man of about sixty, with luxuriant white hair worn fashionably long and curling about his ears, resplendent in vestments of white and gold, entered from a side door and with a beaming smile creasing his flushed face walked majestically to the small dais in front of the orchestra.

At his appearance a gradual hush fell over the assembly, then as another chord was played, they withdrew to either side of the ballroom, the ladies taking their seats on the blue and gold brocaded chairs with the gentlemen standing behind them. A wide passage was left in the centre down which, with an air of immense self-satisfaction strutted Sir Henry Trevellyan, leaving the entrance to join the priest.

Harriet Tremayne glanced self-importantly around, scanning the company from her exalted position to the left of, and just below the orchestra. Rosella and Veryan waited just inside the entrance, ready to fall in behind Harlyn when she stepped through the door on her father's arm.

In the quiet, the sound of the approaching carriage grew clear. Certain people frowned. Such a noisy and obviously hasty arrival hardly befitted the solemnity of the occasion. Others masked a smile. This bride certainly did not intend to be late.

Jared stiffened, every nerve quivering, all his senses signalling danger.

As the terrified horses galloped through the gateway, Jenkins misjudged the distance and the hub of the right hand back wheel caught on the edge of the heavy iron gate, wrenching the carriage off balance. The strain on the harness was too great, the traces on one side snapped, and the carriage slewed sideways.

The howling mob hurled themselves upon it like a pack of ravening wolves. As the carriage was dragged to a halt, the two bays, lathered in sweat, flanks heaving as they plunged and kicked, were cut free and bolted down the courtyard.

The carriages of the guests had been parked in neat rows by grooms and drivers outside the stables, and the horses had had their harness loosened and nose-bags put on.

The sudden appearance of the two fear-crazed bays careering down the yard caused immediate panic among the coach horses, who reared and bucked, sending the coaches crashing into one another, terrifying the startled animals still further.

Shouts went up as grooms, drivers and footmen stumbled out of the servants' quarters where supper had been prepared for them.

Meanwhile the burly figure of Jenkins was dragged from his seat, still shouting and laying about him with the whip, until he disappeared under a hail of blows and kicks.

Harlyn was bruised and shaken from the buffeting she had received. 'What is it, Pa? What's happening? What do they want?' she cried, clutching her father's coat.

William Tremayne clung to the seat. His face was ashen, his eyes started out of his head and the cold sweat of fear trickled down his face. He kept wiping it away with a trembling hand.

'I don't know. It's all a terrible mistake. It must be,' he moaned.

The door was wrenched open and hands reached in to seize them. Harlyn screamed as a torch was thrust close to her face.

'All right, Trevellyan, get out.'

'Come on, you murdering bastard, let's see your face.'

'He's not here,' William Tremayne's voice cracked as he tried to shout above the noise.

'This is 'is coach, idn it?' the man with the torch demanded.

'Yes,' Tremayne nodded quickly, sweat dripping from his putty-coloured skin. 'He sent it for us. He's not here, see for yourselves, there's just my daughter and me, I swear.'

More faces peered round the door and through the windows jostling for position.

'That's Tremayne and 'is girl,' someone shouted. 'She's to wed that bastard tonight.'

'Not now she idn,' another voice bellowed. 'Sir 'Enry Trevellyan won't need no bride, not when we finished with 'un.'

'Then she'll be sport fer we,' someone bawled excitedly, 'an' 'er bridegroom can watch.' A cheer went up and eager hands reached into the carriage.

'Father,' Harlyn shrieked, 'don't let them − For God's sake, stop them—'

William Tremayne flung himself forward in a crazy, terrified, courageous effort to protect his daughter from the ragged, frenzied men.

'Get away,' he panted, flailing his arms, fear and anger almost robbing him of the power of speech. 'Leave her alone.

Whatever Trevellyan has done, she's no part of it. Stop it, get back, you've no quarrel with her. Stop—'

Ducking his head to avoid most of Tremayne's ineffectual blows, the front man thrust himself into the coach and seized Harlyn's arm. A second man followed. She gave a piercing shriek. Her father flung himself at the first man who smashed a fist into his face.

As William Tremayne collapsed onto the seat the second man brought a lump of wood down on his head with a sickening thud, and blood sprayed in a mist of crimson droplets onto Harlyn's white gown.

'Pa,' she screamed, gazing in disbelief at the still, crumpled figure. She crouched beside him, cradling his face in her hand. 'Pa?'

She stared up at the men. 'You've killed him, you've killed my father. You filthy murderers,' she sobbed wildly, lashing out with her free hand she raked her captor's cheek with her nails and kicked out violently with both feet. But her crinoline and the folds of her mantle hampered her movements.

The man shook her so hard her teeth rattled. 'Do you know 'ow many dead and dying' is back there on the track? And 'ow many men 'ave died in the mines, '*is* mines? And 'ow many little children will starve this winter? 'Tidn we that's the murderers, 'tis Trevellyan and 'is kind,' he spat.

'But I'm not—' Harlyn began.

'Come on, get she outta there,' voices clamoured, drowning Harlyn's plea to be heard.

'Get back, the lot of 'e,' the first man roared. 'We're takin' 'er inside first. I wanna see Trevellyan's face when we burn 'is 'ouse and share 'is bride afore we kill the swine.'

The whoops and cheers deafened Harlyn as she was dragged, kicking and fighting from the coach, and hustled towards the house.

Inside the ballroom whispers and mutters buzzed uneasily on the air. People turned to look at one another, moving restlessly.

Elbowing the priest aside, Trevellyan mounted the dais and raised his arms.

'Ladies and Gentlemen, do please calm yourselves,' he admonished in his fluting lisp. 'It appears there is a slight disturbance outside. It sounds as though one of the horses has got loose. I shall attend to the matter at once and you may rest assured that whoever is responsible for this inconvenience will be severely punished. Now, for the few moments this will take,' he turned to the orchestra, 'a little music—?'

The conductor nodded rapidly, turned to the musicians and whispered. They rustled their music sheets to the correct page, then as the conductor raised his baton, they launched into a popular waltz.

Trevellyan nodded and smiled to left and right, reassuring placating, apologising, while his small eyes blazed with white-hot fury at the disruption as he marched down the centre of the ballroom.

He was half-way to the double glass doors when they crashed open, kicked back with such force that the glass shattered, tinkling to the floor in a sparkling cascade.

A woman screamed and the mob poured in like a tide, surging along the walls behind the shocked assembly, while the leader dragged Harlyn through the door and into the ballroom.

Her dress was splattered with her father's blood but though her veil and coronet had been torn off, her emerald velvet mantle still hung from her shoulders, held in place by satin ribbons. Her face was streaked with tears and she sobbed with pain and rage as she struggled vainly to escape the miner's iron grip.

'Where are you, Trevellyan? You thievin', murderin' bastard,' the miner roared.

The gathering erupted in a confusion of screams and shouts and a flurry of gowns and dress suits as the ladies and gentlemen scrambled to find a way out. The baronet was swallowed up in the mêlée.

Harriet Tremayne stood below the orchestra, waving her arms and shrieking at the top of her voice. 'No, stop, come back, all of you. You can't leave now, come back at once—'

She was knocked aside and pushed to the floor by the orchestra as they scrambled from the stage, kicking over their chairs, and rushed out through the dining room.

St Aubyn, his thin face taut with concern, had his arm around his wife, attempting to guide her through the uproar to a side door. He shouted over his shoulder to Jared. 'Take care of Camilla. If we should get separated, we'll hold the carriage for you outside the main gates.'

Jared was staring as though hypnotised at the desperately struggling figure in white.

'For God's sake, Carlyon,' steely anger underlay St Aubyn's anxiety, 'get my daughter out of here.'

'Sir, I'm sorry.' Though genuine remorse filled Jared's voice, his face was set and determined. 'I can't come with you.'

St Aubyn spun round, visibly shocked. 'What are you talking about, man? Come on now, we must get the ladies out of here. Remember,' he warned pointedly, 'we have an arrangement—'

Jared was unbending. 'Sir, I'm truly sorry — I should have realised — I can't possibly — our contract is cancelled.' He turned to the golden-haired girl whose cornflower eyes, filled with startled bewilderment, gazed worriedly up at him.

'Jared, what is this? What's the matter? What are you talking about—?'

'Forgive me, Camilla,' Jared said quietly, interrupting her flood of questions, 'but I—' he squeezed her shoulder. 'Go with your parents, quickly.'

'But, Jared—' Camilla wailed.

'Go on now, hurry,' he commanded, and tearing himself free of her clinging hands he turned away, pushing through the shouting, jostling crowd, searching for the only person who mattered.

Near the toppled seats of the orchestra he saw a woman in magenta velvet and white lace hammering her fists on the floor and screaming with hysterical rage while two young girls in identical rose-pink dresses alternately clung, sobbing, to each other, and tried to comfort the raving woman, frightened as much by her behaviour as what was happening around them.

A man Jared recognised as Percy Teague pushed through the milling crowd and with some difficulty got the woman onto her feet. Then with the help of the two girls, they joined those making for the side exit.

The frenzied mob were rampaging through the house, smashing, burning and looting.

As the guests streamed from every possible exit and carriages thundered through the gates and along the track, the acrid smell of smoke was sharp on the cool night air and hungry flames cast an orange glow into the dusk.

The mob had discovered the champagne and the wine cellar and now alcohol added fuel to the flames of their frenzied lust for revenge.

Jared kicked and elbowed his way to where Harlyn was, the centre of an ugly confrontation between two groups of miners quarrelling over what they should do with her.

The sound of breaking glass was all around as empty bottles were smashed against the walls and fireplaces, and flung through windows.

As Jared reached the knot of men surrounding Harlyn, he seized a bottle from one drunken lout on the fringe, pushing him aside with a mighty shove.

Using the bottle as a club, Jared laid about him totally oblivious of the kicks and blows raining in on him as he fought like a man possessed.

Crying, pleading for someone to help her, pleas which were ignored or lost in the uproar, Harlyn searched frantically around. She caught sight of Jared's tall figure plunging towards her, his face a harsh, cruel mask as he lashed out, scattering the men in all directions, and her heart gave a great leap.

One man turned to fight, drawing a knife. Jared brought the bottle down onto his shoulder with such force that the man's collar bone snapped like a twig and the knife went spinning across the floor as the man clutched his shoulder with a howl of agony.

The force of Jared's blow smashed the bottle, leaving a razor-sharp, jagged edge from which the remaining men, inflamed though they were with anger and alcohol, shied away.

Jared seized Harlyn around the waist, snatching her free of the men who held her, keeping them at bay with the jagged glass.

'This is my woman,' he snarled, his tiger eyes glowing and deadly.

With all his attention on the men, Jared did not notice Harlyn's startled glance. Her eyes were wide with awed amazement and a dawning joy she scarcely dared believe.

'You have no quarrel with her,' he went on, 'nor with me. Trevellyan is the man you came to find. Get back and let us through.'

The men muttered amongst themselves. Then as a couple, drunk and furious at seeing a prize snatched from their grasp lunged forward, and Jared raised the bottle in warning, a cry went up from the far end of the ballroom.

'Trevellyan's on the balcony.'

The men surged out into the courtyard, yelling and shouting, dragging their reluctant companions with them.

Jared glanced down at the trembling girl in his arms as she swallowed her sobs.

'Are you all right?' he asked brusquely.

She nodded. 'They killed my father — in the coach — they—'

'Not now,' Jared cut her off, his deep voice gentle but firm. 'We've got to get out of here before Trevellyan sets his men to find you, or realises you've gone.'

'My mother and my sisters,' Harlyn cried, struggling against him. 'They are here somewhere, they have no one to protect them—'

'They are safe,' Jared reassured her. 'Percy Teague is taking them home.'

Harlyn stared up at him suspiciously. 'You are sure? You would not lie to me?'

'I swear it,' Jared said impatiently, then added in a calmer, quieter voice, 'I would never lie to you. Now come *on*.' He half-ran, half-carried her out through the shattered glass doors and round to the stable yard.

A scene of utter confusion met their eyes. Grooms and drivers struggled to control restive horses as coaches and carriages bumped and scraped in their efforts to get quickly away.

Skirting the edge of the crush, Jared dragged Harlyn into the stable building.

'Can you ride?' he demanded. She nodded. He quickly saddled and bridled a snorting chestnut hunter, then thrust the reins into Harlyn's hands. 'Hold him steady.'

The only other horse in the stalls was a coal black mare whose shiny coat was slick with nervous sweat. As Jared approached, the mare bared her teeth and rolled her eyes.

Fuming with impatience Jared tried to drag the mare's head down to fit the bridle. The animal whinneyed in fear and snapped at him.

Suddenly Harlyn was beside him, she took the bridle from his grasp. She blew softly into the fractious animal's nostrils, then began crooning to it as she rubbed the velvety muzzle with gentle, knowing hands. Within moments the mare was calm enough for Harlyn to slip the bridle over its head. Jared tightened the girth on the saddle.

'You'll have to ride astride. Will you be able to manage the mare?' he asked.

Harlyn nodded. 'I hate riding side-saddle.' She patted the mare's neck, still crooning softly.

'I might have guessed,' Jared smiled for the first time that day, and as their eyes met in the dim lantern-light Harlyn's heart gave another uneven thud.

Jared lifted her into the saddle. 'Follow me, and keep close,' he ordered, mounting the chestnut gelding.

They slipped out of the yard unnoticed in the milling crowd of angry men and shocked and weeping women searching for their coaches.

Keeping close to the boundary wall, seeking the protection of its shadow as they passed in front of the house, they saw the whole west wing was on fire. Flames leapt into the sapphire sky, lighting the scene with an incandescent glow. There was a tearing crash, and like an exploding firework, a shower of sparks flew skyward.

'Jared,' Harlyn called, horrified yet unable to tear her eyes away, 'look.'

He followed her pointing finger. On the balcony which stretched almost the full length of the centre block of the house, stood Trevellyan.

His arms were spread wide and he was haranguing the seething mob in the courtyard below.

The noise of the angry crowd prevented Harlyn hearing what he was saying. Then she noticed on one side of the balcony, a crouched figure, dressed in the black dress and white cap and apron of a housemaid, creeping towards the baronet.

Some sixth sense seemed to warn Trevellyan she was there. He spun round and his eyes were drawn at once to the long gleaming blade of the carving knife.

She held it in front of her, handle low, the cutting edge of the blade pointing upwards and rock steady.

The volume of noise from the angry rabble dropped as they too noticed the crouching girl.

'Get down, get away from here, you stupid wench, don't you think I've got enough to cope with?' The baronet blustered, his eyes darting from the girl's face, a twisted mask of hatred, to the knife, and back again. 'Who are you anyway?'

'My name don't mean nothin' to you,' she hissed, edging forward.

'Then if you won't tell me who you are, tell me what you want. But for goodness sake put that knife down. This is ridiculous. If it's money you're after, you can see I'm somewhat busy just now—'

Trevellyan's teeth were bared in the rictus of a smile as his monstrous ego refused to acknowledge the danger of his situation.

'Don't want yer money,' the girl hissed.

'Then in God's name, what do you want?' Trevellyan shrilled impatiently, and the girl crept closer.

'I want fer you to die,' the girl howled, 'to die on the end of a knife, like my sister Jessie died.'

'I don't know your sister, I don't know what you're talking about,' Trevellyan babbled, the beginnings of fear audible in his piping voice. 'Keep away, don't come any closer.' His reedy lisp carried clearly out over the watching crowd, now almost silent.

'You knowed 'er,' the girl screeched, edging along the face of the building and forcing Trevellyan to move out towards the low, carved stone pillars topped by a stone coping that edged the balcony.

'My sister Jessie didn' 'ave no 'usband, no man to keep 'er, but she did 'ave two little babies.' The girl inched forward, her back to the window through which Trevellyan had come out onto the balcony.

'What has this to do with me? I know nothing of it, nothing I tell you,' the baronet protested shrilly, leaning away from the gleaming blade.

'She loved they kids, Jessie did, but 'ow could she buy food and clothes fer they an' 'erself when she couldn' get no work? Where else could she go but on the streets? Tha's right, mister bloody 'igh and mighty, Jessie was a whore,' the girl spat. Her eyes glittered in the dancing light of the flames and she crouched lower.

'Then you come along, lookin' fer someone to play with. Jessie was warned. She was told you was dangerous, but she 'adn' got no food, nor a lump o' coal fer the stove in that flea-pit of a basement room, and 'er babies was sick wi' fever.'

Suddenly the girl's voice changed and the hand holding the knife shot forward. 'Remember now, do 'ee? You cut her up, you dirty swine,' the girl's strident, shrieking accusation carried over the crowd, her hand darted forward again and a concerted gasp went up from those watching.

'It was an accident,' Trevellyan squealed, waving his hands to keep the girl away as he stumbled backwards.

'She bled to death an' it took a long time,' the girl howled, despairingly, and the rumble that ran through the crowd echoed her bitter grief.

'It was an accident, I swear,' Trevellyan repeated hoarsely, naked terror showing in his pale eyes. 'Slip — just a little slip — I never meant—'

The girl gave a choking cry and lunged forward, the knife rising in the slashing arc which was intended to disembowel Trevellyan.

He leapt backwards and the stone coping caught him behind the knees. Trevellyan lost his balance and toppled. His arms flailed wildly, clutching at air and with a piercing scream he fell over the balcony and landed with a bone-shattering thud on the paved terrace thirty feet below.

There was a moment's utter silence then as the sprawled, broken figure stirred and twitched, a roar went up from the watching crowd and they surged forward.

'Come on, quickly,' Jared ordered curtly over his shoulder, urging his horse forward. 'Keep close, we'll have to leave the track, there might be more coming,' he called and kicked the chestnut into a gallop.

Once through the gate he turned off and headed up over the rolling grassy hill. Over fields, through woods, up hills, down valleys, jumping hedges and ditches, the pounding hooves drummed like thunder as Harlyn's black mare matched Jared's chestnut hunter stride for stride.

Harlyn's mantle billowed about her and the fine gauzy stuff of her gown was snagged and torn on twigs and branches in their headlong flight. Her hair had come loose from its stylish coiffure and streamed over her shoulders in a tumbling ebony mane.

It seemed to Harlyn that they had been riding for hours and she felt her strength ebbing as reaction, combined with relief at her escape and dawning uncertainty about her future, overcame her.

She fought to control the spirited mare who now had the bit between her teeth and showed no signs of tiring.

Jared seemed to sense her exhaustion for he reined in the chestnut, grabbing the mare's bridle, and pulled both horses to a halt on a grassy knoll topped by a stand of beech trees.

He dismounted quickly and came to Harlyn's side. Placing his hands on her waist he lifted her down from the sweating mare. The two horses lowered their heads and began to crop the grass.

Harlyn's legs were like jelly and but for Jared's firm grip she would have fallen.

Suddenly, Harlyn was intensely aware of the silent man holding her. During the past few hours there had been no time to think, but now—

Harlyn tried to convince herself that her pounding heart and the strange hollow feeling in the pit of her stomach were due to the shocks of the evening and the physical effort of their hard ride.

The sky had darkened from sapphire to indigo and in its velvety depths stars twinkled like diamonds. A harvest moon, fat and yellow, was rising above the tree-covered hills. The only sounds were the hoot of an owl, the whisper of the soft night wind in the trees, the creak of leather and the contented chomping of the horses.

Harlyn looked up at him and in the moonlight his amber eyes gleamed as they stared down into hers. His eyebrow was tilted in that familiar half-sardonic, half-questioning expression. There was no trace of a smile on his lips.

Totally vulnerable, stripped of all her defences by the harrowing experiences of the past week, Harlyn waited.

'Harlyn Tremayne,' his voice was a deep, caressing murmur, that sent a tremor right through her, 'I once wondered when I would be free of you.'

Harlyn's heart turned over. She held her breath, all emotion suspended as she gazed wide-eyed into his stern face. Had he rescued her only to reject her once more? She would as soon die—

'Now I know,' he said quietly. 'The answer is never.' His arm tightened around her waist holding her close while his other hand stroked back the tendrils of hair that tumbled about her face.

Unable to hold them back, the words wrenched themselves from Harlyn's lips, words that could shatter the indescribable joy she had just glimpsed. 'But — I thought — what about Camilla?'

He held her away from him. 'What do you know of Camilla?' he asked in surprise.

Harlyn's lashes veiled her eyes as she bent her head. 'Elsie said—'

'Elsie,' Jared exploded looking heavenwards. 'Elsie has been trying for years to marry me off. Camilla was the latest favourite.'

'Then Elsie was wrong?' Harlyn asked shyly. 'There was nothing?'

'Not entirely,' Jared admitted. 'There was a possibility, for a very short time, that I might have married Camilla—'

Jared saw Harlyn's head droop a little lower. A tender smile softened the harsh planes of his face. 'There was no love match,' he said gently. 'It was something between her father and I, which she wanted, but which I—' he shrugged, 'once I had met you—' his voice hardened, 'Harlyn, look at me.'

Harlyn's eyes were brilliant in the pale moonlight.

'You are my woman,' he whispered fiercely. 'My one and only love.' But when his mouth came down on hers, his kiss was so warm, and tender, so gentle and achingly sweet that tears scalded Harlyn's eyes.

She touched his face with incredulous fingers, then ran her hands through his tousled hair. His arms tightened about her, moulding her against his lean hard body.

When at last he released her mouth from its glorious captivity, Harlyn was breathless.

'Where—? What—?' she began.

'We ride to Falmouth tonight,' he stated. 'You will stay in my house until you are fully rested. No doubt Elsie will be happy to see you,' he said drily. 'It seems you made quite an impression on her.'

Harlyn felt her cheeks warm as Jared took his arm from her waist. He kissed her fingers, then collected the mare's reins. He lifted Harlyn into the saddle, then mounted the chestnut. 'Then we will leave Cornwall for a while.' He gently heeled the chestnut forward, the mare followed.

'Where will we go?' Harlyn asked, hardly caring. If he said the end of the earth she would be content to follow.

'You remember where we met?' he asked.

Harlyn blushed crimson. 'Yes,' she murmured.

'The schooner's refit is almost complete, and I've renamed her,' Jared said. 'She'll soon be ready to sail.'

Side by side on horseback, beneath a star-spangled sky, the tall man and the ebony-haired girl moved over the brow of the hill and began the slow descent towards the Falmouth road.

'What have you named her, Jared?' Harlyn asked.

'*Seawitch*,' came the reply. 'She was named for you. This time next week she'll be carrying us towards the coast of North Africa, to Egypt.'

There was a silence.

'Jared,' said a small, uncertain voice. 'We can't — I mean — Isn't there something you've forgotten?'

'No,' came the laconic reply.

'Jared,' in an agony of embarrassment, 'we aren't married.'

'How like a woman, always fussing over details.'

'Jared, I—'

His deep, throaty chuckle cut across her words, and grew into exultant laughter.

'Oh,' Harlyn spluttered faintly. 'You — you — Falmouth man, you,' then she began to giggle and the sound of their laughter blended, and floated behind them on the cool night air.